Markham felt a cool breeze rush past, and after a moment heard a clanging sound coming from another part of the cellar. He cracked open his eyes and quickly scanned his body. He was tied up, but not down to anything; he could roll over onto his back if he wished. Yes, he had to be in the Impaler's cellar—the cement walls, the trickling sound of the blood and water running down the floor drain.

Footsteps approaching again and Markham shut his eyes—another cool breeze and the sense of movement behind him. His mind spun furiously; he was starting to panic, felt as if any second he would open his eyes and try to bolt—when all of a sudden he felt the Impaler's arms slipping underneath his torso.

Markham's muscles tensed. He thought surely the Impaler had to have felt them tense, too—but a moment later he was being lifted off the workbench.

I'm to be next, he thought. *Whatever the Impaler did to the others before he skewered them he intends to do to me . . .*

Books by Gregory Funaro

THE SCULPTOR

THE IMPALER

Published by Kensington Publishing Corporation

THE
IMPALER

GREGORY
FUNARO

PINNACLE BOOKS
KENSINGTON PUBLISHING CORP.
www.kensingtonbooks.com

PINNACLE BOOKS are published by

Kensington Publishing Corp.
119 West 40th Street
New York, NY 10018

All Kensington titles, imprints, and distributed lines are available at special quantity discounts for bulk purchases for sales promotions, premiums, fund-raising, educational, or institutional use.
Special book excerpts or customized printings can also be created to fit specific needs. For details, write or phone the office of the Kensington special sales manager: Kensington Publishing Corp., 119 West 40th Street, New York, NY 10018, attn: Special Sales Department; phone 1-800-221-2647.

This book is a work of fiction. Names, characters, businesses, organizations, places, events, and incidents either are the product of the author's imagination or are used fictitiously. Any resemblance to actual persons, living or dead, events, or locales is entirely coincidental.

PINNACLE BOOKS and the Pinnacle logo are Reg. U.S. Pat. & TM Off.

ISBN-13: 978-0-7860-2213-7
ISBN-10: 0-7860-2213-2

First printing: February 2011

10 9 8 7 6 5 4 3 2 1

Printed in the United States of America

For John Scognamiglio and Michael Combs

O mighty lord! O exalted god of battle!
Thou art brilliant in the bright heavens!
Let me proclaim thy greatness!
Let me bow in humility before thee!
                    —Ancient Babylonian prayer

Prologue

Criminal defense attorney Randall Donovan had really stepped in it this time—was in the shit way over his head and sinking fast. The man in the ski mask would not answer, would not even *listen* to him.

"I'm begging you!" Donovan screamed. "This hasn't gone so far that there's no turning back. I don't know who you are—who your people are—but your beef isn't with me. I swear, whatever they're paying you, I'll double it!"

Nothing. Only the flashing strobe light above his head; only the deafening pump of eighties music and occasionally what sounded like power tools coming from the next room. He recognized the tune from way-back-when in law school—*Depeche Mode or New Order or some other shit band like that*—but he couldn't remember the name of the song or the band that sang the cover; didn't even know there *was* a cover until he met the man in the ski mask. For the man in the ski mask had been cranking the two versions back to back for days, and now Randall Donovan knew all the lyrics by heart.

"How could you think I'd let you get away?
When I came out of the darkness and told you who
you are."

He was in the man's cellar, naked and strapped to a chair. Of that much he was sure. The room was cold, the chair soft and cushiony like a dentist's chair. Indeed, when he first woke up, Donovan thought for a moment that he *was* at the dentist's—his senses dull, his vision cloudy as the steady pulse of the strobe light brought him slowly back to consciousness. Then the smell hit him. Two smells, really. A bitter, chemically smell—close, in his nostrils—and another underneath it: something foul, like rotting garbage.

But now, days later, even though Randall Donovan's senses were sharp, he could smell nothing but the vague odor of his own feces. His arms and legs were tied down, and there was a strap across his waist. And then there was the pain, the dull, heavy pain in the back of his head that throbbed like the drumbeat surrounding him. Despite the chilly temperature he was sweating badly, and the lines of strange symbols that the man had drawn all over his body were now all runny and drippy-looking.

"I thought I heard you calling. You thought you heard
me speak.
Tell me how could you think I'd let you get away?"

"I understand," Donovan called out. "I get it. You think I've wronged you in some way. But I swear to you, on my kids, I don't know what I did. Let's talk this out! I'll give you whatever you want!"

"There were many who came before me, but now I've
come at last,

From the past into the future, I'm standing at your door."

Donovan let out a cry of frustration and struggled against the straps. He could move only his head, but the sharp pain at the base of his skull made him stop immediately. He didn't remember the man in the ski mask hitting him at home in his driveway. Never even saw him coming. But when he awoke to the music and the strobe light some time later, the man in the ski mask gave him two Tylenols and a glass of water. They did nothing.

That had been days ago now. How many days? He could not be sure. The man had given him Gatorade and some oatmeal to eat. He'd also adjusted the chair a few times so the cushion dropped out from underneath the lawyer's buttocks. "Move your bowels," was all he said, and placed a bucket underneath. Donovan tried pleading with him each time, but the man ignored him. And so Donovan moved his bowels. He'd also pissed himself many times, but the man in the ski mask didn't seem too concerned about that.

"I thought I heard you calling. You thought you heard me speak.
Tell me how could you think I'd let you get away?"

The spoken part was next—*"Your body is the doorway,"* the lead singer said—and then came the brief drum break. An opening, Donovan had learned.
"Please listen to me!" he shouted.
But then the chorus kicked in and Donovan was silent.

"How could you think I'd let you get away?
Tell me how could you think I'd let you get away?"

He had long ago given up calling for help; he knew that his only chance was to reason with the man in the ski mask. *But how? Who was this guy?* He couldn't be one of Galotti's boys. No, he'd gotten that greaseball guinea a sweet deal; got him back in the Witness Protection Program despite the stupid fuck's narcotics rap. And he certainly couldn't be a friend of the Colombian. Yeah, the Colombian's buddies hacked up their enemies with machetes and fed them their own testicles. But the eighties music? The hieroglyphics all over his body? It didn't add up. No, even though he hadn't gotten the Colombian off, he'd prevented his family from being deported—and the motherfucker loved him for it!

> *"Look for my light in the nighttime; I'll look for your dark in the day.*
> *Let me stand inside your doorway and tell you who you are."*

Donovan heard the sound of hammering coming from the next room, and all at once he felt the panic beginning to overwhelm him again—felt his chest tighten and his breathing quicken.

> *"You thought you heard me calling. You thought you heard me speak.*
> *But tell me how could you think I'd let you get away?"*

The spoken part was coming up again—*"Your body is the doorway"*—and Donovan was about to call out, when a voice in his head said, *It's pointless. Just count the papers and time your breathing to the counts.*

Yes, that had helped calm him before. How many times before? He wasn't sure.

"One . . . two . . . three . . ." he began, inhaling slowly between each number as the chorus asked over and over: *"How could you think? How could you think?"*

The walls were completely covered with newspaper and magazine clippings of various shapes and sizes—some with headlines and grainy photographs; others just shadowy scraps of paper. There were also some large numbers tacked to the wall directly ahead of him—*9:3* on one side of the door, *3:1* on the other. Donovan could see the numbers clearly. They had been all but burned onto his retinas. But during his days in the chair, he'd also discovered that he could read some of the articles if he focused long enough and blinked in time with the strobe—stuff about the war in Iraq; an archaeological find outside Baghdad; something about astrology and meteor showers. Sometimes the clippings rustled in the breeze from the open door—from the darkened hallway where yellow light often flashed—and Donovan sensed movement.

> *"How could you think? How could you think?*
> *Tell me how could you think I'd let you get away . . ."*

The chorus began to fade, the hammering stopped, and the songs transitioned again for what had to be *the millionth fucking time!*—the distorted synthesizer, the popitty-pop-pop of the electric drums threatening once more to drive him insane. Donovan lifted his head, wincing from the pain, and for a split second thought he saw light, a passing shadow outside the doorway.

"I know you're there!" he shouted. The song's intro was the quietest part; the best time, he'd learned, to call for the man in the ski mask. "Think about my kids, goddammit! They're eight and six. Zach and Amber are their names. The best kids in the world. Zach plays baseball and Amber takes dancing lessons. We got her a tutu last Christmas. Jesus Christ, don't do this to them!"

Like the Depeche Mode or New Order or whatever-the-fuck song it was, Randall Donovan had played this tune many times, but he hadn't seen the man in the ski mask since about twenty versions of the song ago.

"Will you know him when he comes for you?" the man in the ski mask had asked.

"I already told you, yes," Donovan whined. "You want me to say it, okay, yes, I understand my mission. The equation, the nine and the three as written in the stars—I get it! How many more fucking times can I say it, you son of a bitch?"

The man in the ski mask simply left him after that. Yes, that last time had to have been almost two hours ago now. And Donovan was running out of ideas. Sure, he'd already tried the tough-guy routine; tried the taunting and the name-calling and even thought for a moment about doing it all again. But then the hard-driving guitar of the cover version kicked in and he was silent—his throat dry, his voice hoarse, almost gone.

He closed his eyes and gave in to the music; had learned that it was better just to take it, to just let it pass through him rather than to try to block it out. He had slept little during his days in the chair, but he *had* slept. He would try again—would close his eyes and just focus on his breaths. And he was doing quite well—had succeeded in steadying his breathing by about the halfway point in the song—when suddenly the dentist's chair tipped backwards.

Donovan let out a cry of surprise and opened his eyes, but the flash of the strobe blinded him momentarily.

Then he felt the seat cushion drop—felt it peel away from his sticky buttocks.

Donovan fought the pain at the base of his skull and raised his head just in time to catch the man in the ski mask tightening the straps around his legs, which were now raised and spread apart at right angles from his torso—just like his wife's had been when she gave birth to Zach and Amber!

"What the fuck are you doing?" Donovan shrieked.

An icy chill hit his body, his muscles flash-frozen in terror. The man in the ski mask had stopped, stood gazing down at Donovan from between his legs. He now wore gloves and a sleeveless white robe cinched at the waist with a thick leather belt. Around his massive biceps were matching leather armbands, and the robe was open in a V that partially exposed his tattooed chest. Donovan couldn't make out the tattoo, and was about to try reasoning with him again, when something else caught his eye.

The man's white robe was spattered with blood.

Jesus Christ! Donovan thought. *Whatever he's about to do he's done before!*

The man in the ski mask disappeared through the darkened doorway.

"Please don't do this!" Donovan called after him—crying, his mind racing. "Please, God, seriously, I'll give you whatever you want. I'll give you all my account numbers right now. My Bank of America PIN is the birthdays of my kids: five-two-three, six-two-eight. Zach is May twenty-third and Amber is June twenty-eighth. It's the same for my credit cards, my ING account, Franklin Templeton and Vanguard and my—they're all on the uptick! And we have a house out near Asheville, too. Zach and Amber, they—oh my God, my—*listen!* Can you hear me? You've got some big money coming if you play this right. I swear I'll help you link all the accounts. Tell me how you want to do it. Blindfold me and take me to the bank. No! Just get me out of here and we can get on the computer and I'll dump everything off to you! Set up an offshore account in a phony name. I know how to do all that. I'm not fucking with you. I mean it. I won't even look at your—"

FACE!

In the pulse of the strobe the man returned—this time, without his ski mask.

Donovan gasped in horror.

The man's face!—no, not a face, but a terrifying, gaping mouth with fangs as long as fingers. And his eyes—floating fierce with yellow fire as they flashed down at him like lasers between his legs. Donovan's mind began to crack, began to scream that this couldn't be happening.

"But I didn't *do* anything!" he cried, the tears beginning to flow.

Then he saw the long wooden stake in the man's right hand.

Donovan shrieked—struggled against his bonds and tried to move his hips—but the man only leveled the stake and ran him through.

The pain was excruciating, incomprehensible in its brutality, but Donovan was silent, his breath ripped from his lungs as the stake tore him apart inside.

"Tell me how could you think I'd let you get away?"

Mercifully, in the *flash-flash-flash* of the strobe, Randall Donovan went insane—watched his own death through the eyes of a madman before the stake finally burst from his neck and drained his life onto the floor.

PART I
ENTERING

Chapter 1

As always, Michelle sits gazing up at him from the bed—her eyes, the crystal of her wineglass sparkling in the candlelight.

"To us," she toasts. "You, me, and baby make three."

Strawberry Quik, *he thinks.* She always drinks strawberry Quik.

"What's a good name for a strawberry?" she asks.

"I won't let it happen," he replies. "Not this time."

But the voice comes anyway—out of sight, from behind. Just like it always does.

"How 'bout Elmer?" cackles the man in the closet. "Elmer Stokes is a good name for a strawberry."

He tries to turn around, tries to cock his hands back à la Spiderman and shoot the webs from his wrists like he did the last time, but his muscles are slow and rubbery today, and the hulking, square-headed figure of Elmer Stokes glides right past him.

Pop-pop goes the gun—a silly pop that reminds him of bubble wrap—and then the blood begins to pour from his wife's head.

Elmer Stokes laughs and disappears into the kitchen.

"You got anything to eat, Agent Dipshit?" he calls out of sight. "I got the munchies from smoking your wife!"

But he does not follow—knows from experience that it is better to stay with Michelle, to spend what little time he has left with her. He rushes to her side, takes her in his arms, and tries to plug up the bullet holes with the bouquet of pink tulips that had only moments ago been her glass of strawberry Quik.

It's cold, *he thinks.* Her blood is always so cold.

"Cold like a shower to wake you up," his wife spits through bloody lips.

And with a start Sam Markham opened his eyes—his lungs clawing at the darkness as the wave of despair washed over him. He swallowed hard, gritted his teeth, and pushed the pressure in his sinuses down to his stomach. And after a moment he felt his breathing level off, felt his heart rate slow and his face relax.

He rolled over and stared at the big orange numbers beside his bed—*5:11 . . . 5:12 . . . 5:13*—and when his mind had settled, he reached for the nightstand and checked the date on his BlackBerry.

Wednesday, April 5th, he said to himself. *Almost two weeks since the last one.*

He closed his eyes and made a mental note of it.

Later, just after dawn, he sat at the kitchen table watching the ducks dawdle around the pond. He crunched his Wheaties methodically, in time with the waddle of a fat one that was poking around in the reeds. He had many years ago given up analyzing the dream itself; stopped trying to understand exactly why sometimes he saved Michelle and sometimes he didn't.

True, for a long time he hadn't dreamed of her at all. Started up again only after that nonsense in Tampa. No need to ask why. No need to worry. No, just as he had learned to do in another lifetime, if he absolutely *had* to dream of his dead wife, he preferred instead to control and catalog his feelings afterwards. Like a scientist.

Pensive, he said to himself as the fat duck plopped into the pond and paddled away. *Buoyant? No. Treading water.*

He gulped down the last of his milk and dropped the bowl in the sink; walked aimlessly from the kitchen and felt pleased for some reason with how spongy his running shoes felt on the hardwood floors of his new town house. He ended up in the living room, the boxes from Tampa and his ten years with the Bureau stacked before him like crowded gravestones. The move, the promotion to supervisory special agent at Quantico had been quick and painless, no attachments, no regrets—just the way he liked it.

Of course, his people would welcome him, would try to bond with him in subtle ways like inviting him to the occasional poker night or asking him to join their fantasy football league. And when he refused, like he always did, he knew what they would say about their new boss: at first, that he was arrogant and aloof, perhaps snobbish and condescending; then later, that he was simply reserved and private. But he also knew that, in time, his people would grow to respect him—would grow to admire his work ethic and eventually accept his desire for distance.

And for Sam Markham that was enough.

He scanned the boxes and quickly settled on one labeled MISC BEDROOM. If the Bureau was good at anything it was packing, he thought, admiring the organization and care with which they moved him from Tampa.

That's because you're a "special" special agent, a voice said his head. *Not standard protocol for everybody. Just another carrot they dangled to get you back here.*

Markham sliced open the MISC BEDROOM box with his

house key, unwrapped some newspaper, and found what he was looking for: a long, wooden plaque with neatly engraved letters that read:

LASCIATE OGNE SPERANZA, VOI CH'ENTRATE

"Abandon all hope, ye who enter here," Markham whispered.

Dante's *Inferno*, Canto III, line 9. The warning posted over the gates of Hell. A student in his English class had made it for him in wood shop as a joke, and Markham had enthusiastically hung it above his classroom door. That had been over twelve years ago—on another planet, it seemed—and all at once he felt ashamed when he realized he could no longer remember the name of the student who made it for him.

As always, his first order of business was to hang the plaque above his bedroom door. There had been some women over the years who'd asked him about it; others who'd not even noticed it. He knew there'd be more of each variety here, but he also knew he wouldn't reveal the plaque's true meaning any sooner than he would reveal anything meaningful about himself.

When the plaque was straight and secure, he zipped up his hooded sweatshirt and began stretching his hamstrings. It was going to be a bit chilly, he could tell. That was good. He would shoot for six miles today—would follow the road out of the complex and up to the park just as the real estate lady had shown him on Monday.

Markham had just finished knotting his house key into the drawstring of his track pants, when suddenly a knock on his front door startled him. He glanced at his watch.

7:20? Who the hell could that be?

Peering through the peephole, he recognized the man in the gray overcoat immediately: Alan Gates, chief of Behavioral Analysis Unit 2 at Quantico.

His boss.

Markham opened the door.

"What's wrong?" he asked.

"They found another body in Raleigh," Gates said. "Male, spiked like the others, but forensics came across something interesting. It's ours now."

Markham was silent for a moment, then nodded and let him inside.

Chapter 2

"How much do you know about the Rodriguez and Guerrera murders?" Gates asked. The unit chief sat across from Markham at the kitchen table, sipping a cup of instant coffee and gazing out at the ducks.

"Not much," Markham said. "Only what came across the Tampa wire back in February for the Gang Unit. MS-13, they seemed to think it was. The brutality of it, the victims being from the gang's territory. Only reason they brought it to my attention was because of how they were killed. Morbid curiosity more than official business."

"*Mara Salvatrucha,*" Gates said. "Salvadorans, Guatemalans, and Hondurans mostly. Raleigh's been having trouble with them these last couple of years, but the local homicide and gang units want to keep the media out of it. Don't want to give them any more recognition than they're already getting. That's one of the reasons why the details of the lawyer's murder were kept out of the papers—why the media has yet to make the connection to Rodriguez and Guerrera."

"And Homicide has been able to keep the details of the Hispanics' murders quiet, too?"

"For the most part. They were lucky a policeman found Rodriguez and Guerrera. Drove by the cemetery on an anonymous tip and discovered them in the adjoining field. Cemetery is in Clayton, country town about fifteen minutes south of Raleigh. Papers said the victims were found together, shot and stabbed and, I quote, 'put on display.' Guerrera also had some tattoos common among the *pandilleros*."

"Sounds similar to what's being going on in South America," Markham said. "The drug cartels cutting off people's heads and skewering them on pikes, bodies propped up on stakes with warning signs around their necks."

"Still, not a real public interest piece," Gates said. "Low-income, Hispanic immigrants from the projects. Story received barely a byline and quickly died down. Wasn't so easy with the lawyer. He was found by a groundskeeper who needed a little convincing to keep his mouth shut. But he'll talk eventually. They always do."

"And you're saying this lawyer—I'm sorry, what's his name again?"

"Donovan. Randall Donovan."

"Donovan. They found him displayed exactly like Rodriguez and Guerrera?"

"For the most part, yes. Impaled with a wooden stake through the rectum, exit wound here at the base of the neck, just under the collarbone. Only difference, the Hispanics' heads were tied to their stakes across their faces. Donovan's head was tied to his stake at his neck. He was found in a baseball field; Rodriguez and Guerrera outside the cemetery walls. Willow Brook is the cemetery's name."

"May I see Donovan's file?"

Gates slid the file across the table and Markham opened it. The first page was an eight-by-ten photograph of the crime scene: Randall Donovan's naked, lifeless body skewered about a foot off the ground. His eyes were open, his neck lashed to the stake with a thin black cord—but his neck appeared to be broken, his head arched unnaturally backwards, giving him the appearance that he was screaming up at the sky. Donovan's killer had also left on the lawyer's glasses. Markham made a mental note of it, quickly studied the series of close-ups, and then turned to the victim profile.

"Criminal defense attorney," Markham said, reading, flipping. "Forty-five years old, married, father of two. Runs with some loveable characters, I see. This was the guy who got that mobster off last year? Raymond Galotti, Junior, am I right?"

"Yes."

"He also represented Ernesto Morales on the trafficking and obstruction-of-justice rap. I read about that in the papers. The Bureau's evidence was overwhelming, but Donovan got him a nice plea deal. Will do only a few years."

"Donovan saved the Colombian's family from being deported, too."

"I didn't know the Colombians were using MS-13 on the interstate level. Didn't think the gang was organized or dependable enough for that kind of thing."

"They're not. An operation like Morales's, the distribution from Miami all the way to DC, would be too high-maintenance for MS-13. Still a lot of territorial infighting, and the Colombians don't trust them. Keep all the big-money stuff close to the vest."

"But a hit like Donovan is right up their alley, don't you think?"

"Maybe," said Gates. "But the Colombian connection to MS-13 in Raleigh is all but nonexistent. They're actually in competition with them, at least on the lower-level stuff. Rise of the new Honduran drug lords and that kind of thing."

"But what does this have to do with BAU? This isn't our fight."

Gates turned from the window and loosened his tie. *Q&A*

is over, Markham thought. Yes, any second now his boss would adjust his glasses, would push the silver wire up on his nose and then gently straighten the arms. It was Alan Gates's "tell," Markham discovered many years ago—his signal that he was getting down to business. He used to do the same thing in his lectures at the Academy. Back then, the naïve trainee secretly wished to play the unit chief in poker; wanted to see if the old man would tip his hand as he so often did in class. However, over the years, Markham began to suspect that Gates was fully aware of his tell, and would probably sucker the shirt off his back.

And sure enough, when his boss began fiddling with his specs, Markham suddenly felt anxious. As if Gates had just put him in for all his chips.

"Rodriguez and Guerrera," Gates began, "were both shot in the head. Close range, same nine-millimeter handgun."

"Ballistics report?"

"Originally from Homicide, but turned up nothing. The state medical examiner reported that the Hispanics had been dead before they were skewered. Donovan, however, was not."

"You mean he was impaled alive?"

"Yes. They found his body early Sunday morning; had deep ligature marks around his wrists, his ankles, and across his waist as if he'd been strapped down. However, the state medical examiner found nothing near his mouth or on his face to indicate he'd been gagged. Killer wasn't worried about anyone hearing him scream. He'd been dead for almost four days before he turned up in center field."

Markham was silent.

"Homicide still doesn't know where Rodriguez and Guerrera were shot. Rodriguez was reported missing by his parents the day after he disappeared, but no one said anything about Guerrera until the authorities found him. Prints turned up a match in IAFIS. Both lived in the Fox Run apartment complex in the southeast part of town."

"And their bodies? Discovered in the same general area as Donovan's?"

"No. The two crime scenes are in rural areas on opposite sides of Raleigh, neither site near Fox Run. Rodriguez and Guerrera had both been dead for about forty-eight hours and appear to have been shot at roughly the same time. MS-13 activity has picked up recently in the Fox Run area, but it looks as if Rodriguez was not associated with the gang or any of its enemies. Guerrera, on the other hand, is known to have been a member of a low-level gang back in Mexico. Can't tie him to anything here. Problem is, we can't tie Rodriguez and Guerrera to each other, either."

"I'm sure Raleigh has their informants. What's the word on the street?"

"Nothing. No chatter at all about any gang connections."

"What about Donovan?"

"Only thing we know for sure is that he was taken from outside his home in Cary, next town over from Raleigh. Happened late Saturday night, a week and a day before he turned up dead. He'd just returned from a fund-raiser downtown. Wife and kids asleep. No blood, no sign of a struggle, keys to his fancy Peugeot found in the driveway. ME said the back of his head showed blunt-force trauma. Killer used chloroform on him, too."

"You said killer. How do you know there was only one?"

"There's a wall of hedges separating Donovan's property from his neighbor's. Forensics found a set of fresh footprints in the surrounding mulch. Same tread, only one set, size twelve. Matched a group of partials from the baseball field. Forensics is working on tracking down the shoe model."

"And where the Hispanics were found?"

"Again one set, same tread partial. Looks like our boy uses a posthole digger. Kicks up a lot of dirt, doesn't seem too concerned about covering his tracks."

"May I see the file on Rodriguez and Guerrera?"

Gates slid it across the table.

Jose Rodriguez, age seventeen, born in Honduras; Alex Guerrera, age twenty-seven, originally from Mexico. Rodriguez: legal, clean, high-school senior. Guerrera: illegal, back and forth across the border at least twice, and a bit of a record—gang activity in Mexico, petty theft, misdemeanor drug possession in the States. Nothing hardcore, however, and appeared to have gone straight; had a wife and three kids back in Mexico, worked as a dishwasher at a restaurant in downtown Raleigh, and sent the money home every month.

Markham removed a photo of the victims: naked, side by side, impaled like Donovan, heads fastened to their stakes with the same thin black cord. However, unlike Donovan, the cord was tied tightly across their cheeks, causing their vacant, open eyes to stare straight ahead and giving their faces a strange, squished expression that reminded Markham of Sylvester Stallone getting his face slow-motion punched in *Rocky*.

"Other than his record," Gates said, "Guerrera is a bit of a mystery. Hadn't been in Raleigh very long; was living with a cousin and two other men, illegals, all of them sending their pay back to families in Mexico, all ruled out as suspects. Guerrera's cousin is still there, but the other two men have taken off. Raleigh PD has turned it over to ICE."

"Looks like the Rodriguez kid was a straight arrow," Markham said, reading. "Good grades in school, planned on attending community college for computers, it says."

"He also had a part-time job at Best Buy and told the family he worked Wednesday and Saturday nights at a Mexican restaurant downtown. Raleigh PD followed up, found that the restaurant job was bogus. No record of him anywhere. Left open the possibility of the drug connection. Checked the kid's cell phone bill and saw a number of calls from prepaid, untraceable calling cards. All that's pretty standard for the drug dealers nowadays, but they couldn't prove anything. Regardless, looks like whatever the kid was into on Saturday nights got him killed."

"What about the kid's brother?" Markham asked. "Says here Rodriguez has a sister, eleven, and a brother, fifteen. About the time the gangs usually start recruiting, isn't it?"

"Nothing there. Family, the kids are devastated; parents moved them out of Fox Run to live in another apartment complex in North Raleigh. All dead ends since the beginning of March. Of course, Raleigh's abandoned the MS-13 theory now that it's been turned over to us, but who knows what will happen if the media gets wind of the similarities between the crime scenes."

"What about the possible link between Donovan and the Hispanics exclusive of outside entities?"

"That's being explored, yes, but nothing so far."

Markham scanned through the Donovan file again.

"You'll find what you're looking for at the end," Gates said.

The FBI forensics report. Alan Gates knew him well; knew that his former student would look next for the real reason why his boss had decided to pay him this early-morning visit—the answer to Markham's *"Why me?"*

"The field office in Charlotte's got a good team," Markham said at last, reading. "And I've heard of Andy Schaap—used to be one of the best forensic specialists around until the restructuring went down and he took the supervisory position in Charlotte. State medical examiner's got a decent setup, where Schaap's been working so far. ME's preliminary report shows no physical evidence. No semen or saliva, no trace DNA; nothing left by the killer except—is this right? *Comet* residue?"

"Yes. Looks like our boy scrubbed the lawyer clean. Sound like a hit to you?"

"And the others? State ME find anything on them?"

"No Comet residue, no. Killer just shot and impaled them, but it looks like he did scrub them clean. ME found traces of water in their ear canals."

"Covering his tracks?"

"Maybe."

"But a bit too cliché, too simple if we're speaking metaphorically of dirty drug dealers and a dirty lawyer—the Comet, the cleaning. You wouldn't be here if you thought it was that easy a read, would you?"

"No, I wouldn't. The killer wasn't concerned about using Comet on Rodriguez and Guerrera. Might not have been important until Donovan; might have done something different to him that needed attending to."

"Developing his MO, you think? Evolving?"

"I think so, yes."

"The bodies—were they facing in the same direction?"

"Good question, but no. Rodriguez and Guerrera faced due east; Donovan, his body turned west, his head tilted back at almost a ninety-degree angle. The killer attaches a crossbar at groin level so the bodies won't slide."

"Then he's a planner. It's about more than just the violence of the impalement. The aesthetic is important, too. The display."

"And the head tilted backwards?" asked Gates. "The glasses, the eyes open?"

"Textbook. The victim is supposed to see something and understand. However, the victims' sight lines, the directions are different. Rodriguez and Guerrera, the cord across their faces, their eyes looking almost due east; Donovan's body to the west, the cord around his neck, his head arched back looking up at the sky."

"Right."

"Our boy drops them off at night; has to have a van or a large truck. Might be a moon freak. Do the disappearance dates correspond with the new moon?"

"No, different visuals on the nights the victims were last seen. However, on the nights they were found, there was a crescent moon. Could be a textbook lunar pattern; seen it many times before. Most recently, in that long-haul-trucker case—"

"The crescent moon," Markham said suddenly. "Isn't that the symbol for Islam? A star inside a crescent moon?"

"That's right."

"Could he possibly be imitating Vlad the Impaler? The Romanian prince who was the inspiration for Bram Stoker's *Dracula*?"

"I'm glad to see you're still up on your history," Gates said, smiling. "And that was my first thought even before I made the crescent-moon connection. After all, before Stoker immortalized him in *Dracula,* the historical Vlad was known as one of the great defenders against the spread of Islam during the Middle Ages. Definitely the cruelest, as his moniker would imply."

"And the victims?" Markham asked. "Any Islamic connection?"

"None that we can see so far, but we're looking into it."

Markham was silent, thinking.

"Then again," Gates said, "we could be totally off base. Everything happening toward the end of the month could indicate something with calendars, but why the displays in February and April and not March? Might all be just a coincidence."

"You wouldn't be here if you thought that."

Gates shrugged and smiled, his eyebrows arching like a pair of thick, white caterpillars. Markham flipped again through the Donovan file, the forensics report.

"This light scratch that the ME notes," Markham said. "The one he picked up near Donovan's right armpit that looks like an arrowhead. Is that it?"

"Is that what?"

"The reason you're here. The reason you're convinced this guy is a wannabe Vlad and not just some cartel hit man with a flair for the dramatic."

"Why *you*, you mean?"

"Yes. Why me? Why do you want to pull me off my new assignment at Quantico and fly me off to Raleigh when you've got good people in Charlotte? After all, that's what you're getting at, isn't it?"

Gates rose from the table and dumped the remainder of his coffee into the sink, rinsed the cup out, and placed it on the counter upside down on a paper towel. The silence, the intended dramatic effect was beneath him, Markham thought, and suddenly he felt himself getting irritated.

Gates walked back to the window and looked out over the pond; but much to Markham's surprise, he did not adjust his glasses.

"You've been in ten years now, Sam," he said finally. "Only reason I didn't ask you back after five is because I knew you'd be happier in the field. Agents are banging down our door to get reassigned to BAU, but it never occurred to you to put yourself in for a promotion back home, did it?'

"I thought about it."

"That's a load of crap. Your biggest fear is becoming a bureaucrat, a pencil pusher like me. You need your boots on the ground; would rather take orders and get things done than give them and lose touch with why you signed up with us in the first place. And that's your problem. You're too obsessed with your work; you've let it define who you are to the exclusion of everything else. It's why I played the personal favor card with you, but that's not why you agreed. No, only reason you took me up on my offer is because you know deep down you'll be more of an asset here."

Markham said nothing.

"We were lucky to have you in Tampa with Briggs. I think because you were already assigned there, you don't believe we couldn't have nabbed him without you."

"I got lucky in Tampa."

"Maybe," said Gates. "But you didn't get lucky in my class. Your paper, your application of that physics principle to behavioral science—what was it called again?"

"The superposition principle. Says that the net response at a given place and time caused by two or more stimuli is the sum of the responses that would have been caused by each stimulus individually."

"Of course," Gates said, arching his eyebrows again.

"It's most often applied to wave theory," Markham added. "Or in the case of my paper, to almost-plane waves converging diagonally in a body of water. More of a metaphor, really, if one were to apply it to both the predictability and unpredictability of human behavior in a linear system such as—"

"Over my head," Gates said, waving him to stop. "I just remember it had something to do with the wakes of two ducks swimming side by side. How their waves would intersect and come out on the other side of each other unbroken. First time a trainee ever dumped something like that on my desk. Physics. And to think you were an English teacher before you joined us. History minor in college, too, from what I remember. Qualified under the Diversified Critical Skill. That kind of thing just doesn't happen anymore."

Markham shrugged. "You give me too much credit. I don't quite understand the physics of it all, either. Was only a metaphor for gut instinct, that briefest of moments when the waves from the hunter and the hunted are one. It can't be measured scientifically. At least I don't think it can."

"I still don't get it. Only that what you're saying makes perfect sense to me. It's the same thing with Jackson Briggs in Tampa. I'm still not sure how you caught him. I just know that you did."

"And the reason you're here?" Markham asked. "That thin, oddly shaped little scratch near Donovan's armpit?"

"That's not the reason the Bureau initially got involved. Because of Donovan's profile, because of his involvement with the FBI's case against Ernesto Morales, when we got wind of Donovan's murder, Charlotte sent Schaap to Raleigh."

Gates reached into the inside pocket of his overcoat and handed Markham the first of two glossy photographs. Yes, Markham thought, Gates had been waiting to show him his aces all along.

"This first picture," said Gates, "is a close-up of Donovan's chest under normal light. You'll notice the scratch on the right pectoral near the armpit is almost imperceptible in the photograph. Schaap bought into the dirty-lawyer idea at first, and thought the bleach from the Comet might yield some clues under the Wood's lamp. He never expected to find this."

Gates handed Markham the second photograph. It was a close-up of Donovan's torso on the autopsy table. Under the ultraviolet light, Donovan's skin looked bluish-purple. The writing was a faint, glowing pink: a series of neat lines running across his chest in what looked to Markham like hieroglyphics from a pharaoh's tomb.

He felt his stomach tighten, his tongue go dry.

"According to Schaap," Gates said, "the killer could've used a charred stick or something. Whatever he used, it was just a little too sharp when he started."

"And even though the ash would've rinsed off much more

easily than ink," Markham said, studying the picture, "the stick and the properties of the ash could still damage the epidermis enough to react with the Comet and also remain invisible to the naked eye. Did they find any other chemical residue?"

"Other than the chloroform in Donovan's nostrils, no. But Schaap has two running theories regarding the writing: the first, that the killer wrote on Donovan for some reason having nothing to do with the final display; the second, that the killer intentionally used the Comet to produce the effect you see before you."

"That would mean he's not trying to cover his tracks."

"Well, not if you approach it from the angle that the writing was meant to be discovered by someone with a UV lamp."

"And Rodriguez and Guerrera?" Markham asked. "State ME use UV on them?"

"No, not standard unless the murder is sexual in nature. Guerrera's body was sent back to his family in Mexico, but we fast-tracked a court order for exhumation of Rodriguez. Family's been notified, taking place as we speak. Kid'll be shipped with Donovan to Quantico later today."

"A possible message then," Markham mumbled to himself. "But to whom?"

"The official autopsy report on Donovan won't be issued for a while. But given the crossover on the case, until we can get a gag order, Schaap and the ME are going to delay submitting anything about the writing. His funeral has also been delayed while his body undergoes further analysis in our labs here."

"And the writing?" Markham asked. "You've already sent the information to our language specialists?"

"Yes," said Gates. "Report came back late last night. A single phrase written over and over in six ancient scripts: Aramaic, Hebrew, Arabic, Babylonian Cuneiform, Egyptian, and Greek."

"Nothing in Romanian?"

"No."

"What does it mean?"

Gates motioned with his finger for Markham to turn over the photograph. He obliged, and felt his stomach go cold when he saw his boss's handwriting on the back. It read simply:

I have returned

Chapter 3

Now he was the General.

Seated at the computer in his white robes, the General scrolled his mouse to the top of the Web page and hit the print button. An article from the *Raleigh Sun* about the murder of Randall Donovan—details still sketchy, appeared to be some kind of drug hit, investigation ongoing. Just as he expected. Everything part of the equation.

The General rose from his chair, tore off a piece of Scotch Tape from the roll on the workbench, and retrieved the article from the printer. The cellar felt cold to him this morning—colder than usual—and as he sauntered out of the workroom, he thought he could feel his nipples grow hard.

"I thought I heard you calling. You thought you heard me speak.
Tell me how could you think I'd let you get away?"

The music in the background was much softer than it had been for Randall Donovan. "Dark in the Day" was the song— a Clone Six remake of the 1985 version by the one-hit wonder High Risk. The General had been only five years old when the original came out, but still he remembered it from the days before his mother died. There had been messages back then, too—keys to his understanding of the equation— but back then, through the ears of a child, the General had simply been too stupid to understand.

Now, however, the General understood the equation perfectly. The others were capable of understanding, too, but they needed to be reeducated, needed to hear the song over and over—old and new, old and new—to finally understand like he did.

> "There were many who came before me, but now I've
> ' come at last,
> From the past into the future, I'm standing at your
> door."

The General entered the adjoining room—the reeducation chamber, he called it—and taped the article to the wall. He stood back and admired how it looked among the others— thousands of messages he'd printed from his computer or copied on the machine during his day-life.

All parts of the equation.

The General breathed deeply. The dentist's chair and the floor were clean now, and the room smelled refreshingly of Pine-Sol.

> "I thought I heard you calling. You thought you heard
> me speak.
> Tell me how could you think, I'd let you get away?"

"Your body is the doorway," the General said along with the Clone Six lead singer. And then the chorus kicked in.

The cover version was slightly different from the original, but the message was the same—always the same, always

part of the equation. Just as it had been long before his
mother died.

The General often thought about his mother, but never
about his father. He knew him only from a yearbook photo
that his mother sometimes showed him before bedtime. "All
right," she'd say. "You can kiss your father good night." The
General could no longer remember what his father looked
liked; only blurry rows of black squares that smelled in his
mind like perfume and old paper. His mother kept the yearbook hidden underneath a loose floorboard in her bedroom,
and made the boy promise never to tell his grandfather she
had it. And the boy kept his promise.

For even as a boy, the General *always* kept his promises.

Smiling, the General walked from the reeducation chamber, down the darkened hallway, and entered into the last of
the cellar's three rooms: the Throne Room.

The General dropped to his knees and bowed his head.

The Throne Room was the smallest but most sacred room
in the house. It had once served as his grandmother's pick-
ling closet, but was now empty except for a large wooden
throne at the far end. The General had constructed the throne
himself out of pine—it had to be light enough to carry, that
was part of the equation, too—and the softness of the wood
made it easier for him to carve the intricate designs that
adorned the arms and legs and back. He also painted the
throne gold and illuminated it with a single spotlight hung
from above. The General had stolen the spotlight during his
day-life, but unlike the belt sander and other tools he'd taken
from his place of employment, his boss never missed it.

"I shall return, my Prince," the General whispered, but
the figure on the throne did not respond. That was all right.
The General hadn't expected the Prince to respond. Not
today. Not for a few days, perhaps, or at least until the General fulfilled the next part of the equation.

9:3 or 3:1 was the proper ratio, the equation that held the key to the formula.

The Prince understood the equation. And although he was demanding, he also understood that his General had worked hard to keep the formula in balance—knew that it was time for him to rest. After all, the Prince was a general, too. The supreme general, a general spelled G-E-N-E-R-A-L in big capital letters—the most fearful of them all, in fact. "The Raging Prince," his soldiers used to call him on the battlefield; sometimes, "the Furious One."

The General rose to his feet, bowed perfunctorily, and turned off the spotlight. He climbed the cellar stairs in the dark, emerged into the kitchen, and locked the door behind him. He was hungry, but would wait until lunchtime. He had learned to resist temptation; needed to stick to his diet and keep his muscles lean. No more cheeseburgers. General's orders. That had been the hardest sacrifice of them all. He really missed the cheeseburgers.

Then again, war was all about sacrifice, wasn't it? At the very least, war was not meant to be easy. Even for the greatest generals. Nonetheless, the General felt confident in his mission. He'd been preparing for it for two years now; could see the results of his hard work in the sinews of his muscular physique; could feel his growing strength in the ease with which he lifted the heavy loads during his day-life.

And the Prince had rewarded him for all his hard work, had promoted him to second in command. A general, too. A warrior-priest who served only the Prince.

Then again, the General was born to serve. And hadn't the Prince been grooming him for this mission nearly all his life?

The General made his way quickly from the kitchen, through the hallway, and up the stairs to his bedroom. He was going to be late today, and would have to work doubly hard to keep up the appearance of his day-life. But that was all right; the Prince would allow him a respite before the big push toward May. Yes, now that he had laid the groundwork for the Prince's return, everything would come together much more rapidly in the weeks to come.

Everything would have to if the equation was correct.

And the General was sure the equation was correct.

Chapter 4

"The appeal from Stokes's mother was denied," Gates said. He stood with Markham on the tarmac, at the bottom of the mobile stairs unit that led up to the FBI plane. "Connecticut Supreme Court struck down her request to postpone his execution. Found that Stokes was entirely competent to drop the appeals process on his own behalf. The execution will proceed as planned a week from Saturday. He wants to die, Sam."

Markham said nothing.

"I've already made the arrangements for you to be there," Gates said, handing him a brown cardboard envelope. "There's a copy of his last letter in there on top of the Donovan file. Your in-laws faxed it to the Tampa Office by mistake."

Markham looked down at the elastic-banded packet. It felt heavy. Cold. Like a stone tablet.

"I'm sorry about the timing," Gates said. "But if there's anything I can do, you know where to reach me."

"Thank you," Markham said, and boarded the plane.

* * *

Alone in the cabin, Markham stared down at the brown cardboard envelope. The loud drone of the plane's turbo-props set him on edge. He made a quick body scan—cataloged his breathing and the tension in his forearms and toes. Suddenly, the plane throttled forward, and Markham told his body to melt into his seat. He felt himself relax immediately, and by the time the plane began its ascent, he decided he was in a better frame of mind to analyze the situation objectively.

The date for Stokes's execution had been set for almost two months: a vague point of light on the horizon to which Markham neither looked forward nor dreaded as it drew closer. He'd always planned on being present in support of Michelle's family, but personally had no desire to see Elmer Stokes ever again. He'd seen enough death in his ten years with the Bureau to know that no closure would come of it.

At least not for him. At least not *that* way.

Before he killed Michelle Markham, Elmer Stokes had been known up and down the East Coast as a charming singer of traditional sea shanty songs. He'd been performing for the summer at Mystic Seaport when he spotted the pretty, twenty-six-year-old "scientist lady" and her friends taking water samples from the harbor. In his confession, Stokes told police that he followed them back to the aquarium, where he waited for Michelle in his car. He said he'd only wanted to "get a feel for her" and see where she lived. However, later that evening, when he spied Michelle leaving the aquarium alone, the man who called himself the "Smiling Shanty Man" could not resist taking her right then and there.

Stokes told police that he wore a ski mask—said he "pulled a pistol on the bitch" and tried to push her in his car. But Michelle Markham fought back—kicked him in the balls and bit him hard on the forearm. She also tore off his ski mask, and Stokes said it was then he panicked—said he "shot the bitch twice in the coconut" with his .38 Special and fled. Two days later another performer at the seaport spotted the bite marks on his arm and called the police. They found the ski mask and the .38 in Stokes's car. He confessed to everything, and the authorities eventually tied him to nine rapes in four states going back over a decade.

The fact that his wife had been the Smiling Shanty Man's only murder was of little consolation to Sam Markham, who discovered her lying dead in the Mystic Aquarium parking lot after she failed to return home that evening—his happy two-year marriage, his idyllic life in the sleepy little town of Mystic all shattered in the blink of an eye. It took him a year to pass through the wake of his wife's death, the waves of which brought him straight to the shores of the Federal Bureau of Investigation.

Gates was right, Markham thought as the plane leveled off. *The superposition principle.* It was how he caught Jackson Briggs, the man the press called the "Sarasota Strangler." And so Markham knew the only justice for Elmer Stokes lay in the superposition principle, too. After all, there was no way a Neanderthal like Stokes could ever comprehend the totality of his crimes unless he experienced what his victims experienced. And just like Michelle, the bastard would come out on the other side with two bullets in his head, courtesy of Sam Markham himself.

Markham often fantasized about killing Elmer Stokes. Usually, he substituted himself for Jackson Briggs and Stokes for the Sarasota Strangler's victims. What Briggs did to his little old ladies would be perfect for Elmer Stokes, and Markham himself wouldn't even have to touch the filthy son of a bitch when all was said and done. That Markham so enjoyed these fantasies of playing Jackson Briggs was what bothered him the most—a mixture of elation and shame as he stared down in his mind at the Smiling Shanty Man's violated corpse. Briggs didn't finish off his little old ladies with bullets, but in order for the superposition principle to work—

But of course, none of that could ever happen.

Markham gazed out the window into the gray-white fog, the wispy patches of green and brown breaking through the low-lying clouds like memories sent up from the world below. He thought about Michelle's parents, who in the eleven years since their daughter's murder had enrolled themselves in Connecticut's restorative justice program. Markham knew they had met with Stokes via a mediator at least twice, but had corresponded with him many times. He understood his in-laws' need for closure, but never understood why they always forwarded the Neanderthal's letters to him.

Even worse, he never understood why he always read them.

He opened the brown cardboard envelope and removed the files. On top was the letter from Stokes, along with a printout from CNN.com about the pending execution—only Connecticut's second after nearly forty-five years of rehabilitative bliss. Markham crumpled the news article into a ball and tossed it on the empty seat across the aisle. But as always he read the letter.

Dear Mr. and Mrs. Keefe. This letter here is going to be the last one I send most likely I think. It is going to be the shortest one to I think because all I have to say is I just want to thank you for meeting with me all them times, and that I am sorry again for what I done to your daughter. I deserve to die for doing that to her, and may be for what I did to them other ladys to. I hope you knowing that I want to die because I deserve to makes all of you feel better. I know I am not going to heaven, but if I was I would apolagise to your

*daughter up there because I know that is where she is
living now. Yours truly, Elmer Stokes.*

Markham traced his finger over the Neanderthal's words—
the childlike print, the poor grammar, the refusal to call Michelle by her name.

*The name Stokes is one letter in the alphabet away from
Stoker,* a voice whispered in his mind. *What are the chances
of that? Is there a connection here, Sammy boy? Is something in the collective consciousness bringing you and Vlad
the Impaler together?*

Markham crumpled Stokes's letter into a ball and tossed
it onto the seat with the discarded CNN article. Then he
opened the Donovan file.

Gates had placed the UV close-up of Randall Donovan's
torso on top of some preliminary research, including a brief
biography of Vlad the Third, Prince of Wallachia—more
commonly known as Vlad Tepes, Vlad the Impaler, or Vlad
Dracula.

Thought these might be of interest to you, Gates had
scrawled along the margin of the first page.

Vlad the Impaler, Markham read, scanning quickly.
*Prince of Wallachia, the area known today as Romania. The
Romanian surname of Draculea means "Son of Dracul."
Vlad's father's title was Vlad Dracul the Second, or Vlad the
Dragon. His son, Vlad the Third, earned the moniker Tepes
after his death. Tepes is the Romanian for "Impaler"—derived from his preferred method of executing his enemies.
Vlad Dracula was born in 1431, and had three separate
reigns from 1448 to 1476. A member of the Order of the
Dragon, he was a fervent and violent defender of Wallachia
against the expansion of the Ottoman Empire. Known today
for his exceptionally cruel punishments and as the inspiration for Bram Stoker's* Dracula.

"The Ottoman Empire," Markham whispered. "Modern-day Turkey. The Ottoman Turks conquered in the name of Islam and adopted Arabic as their official language. Is that what you're getting at, Alan?"

Yes, replied the unit chief in Markham's mind. *Look on the next page.*

Markham obliged and quickly read through some background on the Ottoman Turkish language—the heavy Arabic borrowings, the Persian phonological mutations, the three major social variants. It all meant nothing to him, didn't register in his gut as important, and he flipped to the next page—information on the symbol for Islam.

☪

"Interesting," Markham said, reading. "It wasn't until the Ottoman Turks conquered Constantinople in 1453 that they officially adopted the crescent moon and star as their symbol. Around the same time Vlad began his reign."

Another connection to the crescent moon, Gates said in his mind.

Markham read on—discovered that many Muslims today reject the crescent moon and star as a pagan symbol, especially in the Middle East, where the Islamic faith traditionally has had no symbol.

"I have returned," Markham whispered.

To defend against Islam? Which would mean then that the Arabic and the other Middle Eastern scripts are a message to the Muslim community. But why Rodriguez and Guerrera? Why Donovan? What's the Islamic connection there, and why didn't you write anything in Romanian, Vlad?

Markham flipped to the next page.

Impalement has been an institutionalized method of torture and execution for thousands of years, dating as far back as the tenth century BCE in the ancient Mesopotamian civilizations of Assyria and Babylonia. Throughout history, however, the fundamentals of impalement have remained the same.

The practice involves a person being pierced with a long stake—most often through the rectum, sides, or mouth—and can be modified to prolong or quicken death. To prolong death, an incision is made between the genitalia and the rectum, and a stake with a blunt end is inserted, then manipulated through the thorax to avoid damage to the internal organs. Hence, the victim suffers excruciating pain for an extended period of time as he slowly bleeds to death internally. For a quicker death, a sharp pointed stake is inserted into the rectum or vagina with the intention of piercing the internal organs.

In both cases, it is desirable for the stake to emerge from the body between the clavicle and the sternum, upon which the stake is most often set under the mandible to prevent the body from sliding. Typically, the stake is then hoisted vertically and inserted into the ground. Thus suspended, the impaled person dies an agonizing death that can take anywhere from a few seconds to three days. Sometimes the stake is installed upright after partial impalement, whereupon the combination of gravity and the victim's own struggles completes the process.

Markham closed his eyes—felt his stomach knot and his buttocks tighten when he thought about what Randall Donovan must have suffered.

"But what were they supposed to look at, Vlad?" Markham asked out loud. "The little crossbar so the body won't slide; the heads tied to their stakes. The whole setup could be more about what they are supposed to see rather than what we are."

But the angles of sight, Alan Gates replied in his mind. *The different directions, they wouldn't be looking at the crescent moon.*

There's the rub.

Markham read on.

Throughout history, impalement has been used as a quick and efficient method of execution during wartime, as shown in the accompanying Neo-Assyrian reliefs depicting the impalement of Judeans. The ancient Greek historian Herodotus wrote of the Persian king Darius the Great's impalement of thousands of Babylonians. The ancient Romans not only impaled their enemies but also their own soldiers in extreme cases of cowardice and treachery.

Used throughout Europe and Asia during the Middle Ages (and in some regions, like Ottoman Turkey, well into the nineteenth century) perhaps the most infamous instance of institutionalized impalement is that associated with the reign of Vlad the Third (Vlad Dracula), Prince of Wallachia, who came to be known as Vlad the Impaler. Some historians estimate that, during his lifetime, Vlad the Third impaled not only thousands of his country's enemies (mostly Ottoman Turks) but also hundreds of his own people, including rival members of the Wallachian aristocracy, unmarried girls who lost their virginity, thieves (some of them children), adulterous wives, and homosexuals.

Maybe it's not just about the Muslims then, Markham thought. *Maybe Vlad is once again expanding his repertoire among his own people. The lawyer could be seen as a thief. Dirty, dishonest. Also the possibility that he defended some-one of Islamic faith—need to look into that. And Rodriguez and Guerrera? Maybe Vlad thought they were gang mem-bers. Dirty drug dealers. Washing them clean. Sending a message. A moral message.*

Markham looked at his watch and registered somewhere that he'd be arriving in Raleigh in twenty minutes. His head felt heavy, his brain swimming in a soup of data as the Vlad the Impaler tie-in became clearer.

But something was off. He could feel it.

It's that little bit about the Romanian, isn't it? Gates asked in his mind. *Why didn't Vlad leave his message in Romanian? Or at least in English. Wouldn't that make sense if Vlad was "expanding his repertoire" among his own people?*

Maybe he thought we'd get the message anyway. After all, we did, didn't we?

Gates was silent, and Markham turned back to the UV close-up of Donovan's torso—the evenly spaced, meticu-lously drawn pink letters.

"You kept him tied down for a while," he whispered. "But how'd you get him to sit so still? Was Donovan dead or un-conscious when you wrote on him?"

I have returned, a voice answered in his mind. *I have re-turned, I have returned, I have returned.*

Markham closed his eyes and sank uncomfortably into the drone of the turboprops—into the low hollow hum of not knowing where to begin.

Chapter 5

Marla Rodriguez still missed her big brother very much. It had been over two months since the police found him and that other man in the field near the cemetery. And as Marla waited with the other children to see Father Banigas, the pretty eleven-year-old wondered if Jose could see her up through the church floor.

She knew, of course, that if her brother had been in Heaven he most certainly would have been able to see her sitting there in her bright yellow sweatshirt. But Marla wasn't sure how things worked down there with the Devil; didn't think that even *he* had the power to see into God's house. And the fact that Jose might not be able to see what she was up to made her sad; for even though her parents had assured her that Jose was in Heaven, Marla Rodriguez knew for a fact that her big brother was stuck in Hell.

"No te preocupes, Jose," she whispered to the floor. "I'll take care of it for you."

Marla felt stupid that she hadn't come up with the idea herself, felt guilty and sad that it had taken her so long to fix things. Deep down she knew Jose would forgive her. True, it had probably been really hard for him to reach her dreams all the way from Hell, especially since there wasn't much room in them now with all the worries filling up her head— Papa and Mama always crying, the move to the other side of Raleigh, the new school, the new catechism class, and the new church—not to mention all the space taken up in her head from missing him! Oh yes, sometimes Marla's head felt even more crowded than the place they'd moved into; it had *way more* worries than her uncle's two-bedroom apartment had people. Nine altogether—people, not worries—well, *ten,* if you counted her cousins' cat Paco.

Marla didn't like her cousins very much, and she certainly didn't like having to sleep on the floor with her brother in the same room as Mama and Papa. But Marla had to admit that she liked living with Paco, who always slept on her pillow even though Diego was right there beside her. Marla could tell that Paco didn't like Diego very much; and even though Marla didn't like Diego very much, either, she still felt guilty for wishing sometimes that he'd gotten killed instead of Jose.

I must remember to tell Father Banigas that, too, Marla thought. *But I bet if Father Banigas ever met Diego, he wouldn't like him, either.*

Whereas everybody used to like Jose, it seemed to Marla that the only person who liked Diego was Hector, the oldest of her three cousins. Hector was thirteen, two years younger than Diego, and Marla could tell that Hector thought Diego was *el mejor* because he could freestyle faster than anyone. Her other two cousins were just little boys and too young to give a crap about Diego's flow, but even Marla had to admit that sometimes Diego's rapping was pretty cool—but that didn't change the fact that she didn't like him! No, her big brother Jose had never called her names or pinched her arm when he wanted to use the iPod the three of them had shared back in their old apartment.

However, after Jose died, as soon as her family moved into their cousins' apartment, her father bought Marla her own iPod and stuck Diego with the old one. She hadn't expected *that,* even though her father had picked up another job in addition to his one as a janitor at the Crabtree Mall. Marla had heard him and her mother arguing about the iPod late at night, but at least Papa wasn't crying anymore before he fell asleep. Marla could never tell her Papa that the iPod didn't make her stop crying, though—didn't make her like her cousins or their apartment any better, either. But at least Marla could admit that things were quieter outside now: no cars revving up and down the parking lot; no bottles clinking and gangbanging *pandilleros* yelling at each other late at night. And best of all, there were no gunshots to wake her up from her dreams of Jose.

"You can ask God for an iPod when you get to Heaven, Jose," Marla whispered to the floor, and the boy sitting next to her elbowed her.

"Silencio, chalada," he said. "You'll get us in trouble with Sister Esperanza."

Marla elbowed him back, and the boy let out a squeal that made Sister Esperanza get up from her seat across the aisle. All the children froze, but when Sister Esperanza passed by Marla without a word, it suddenly occurred to her that maybe the reason Jose was finally able to speak to her in her dreams was because it was so much quieter now at her cousins'.

That had to be it! Yes, maybe there was something good about living there, after all. For even though Marla would never be able to ride in the car Jose had been saving up for while working at Best Buy, she would much rather just be able to talk with him like they used to when he was alive.

However, once she and Father Banigas had fixed things—once her brother was in Heaven where he belonged—Jose might not have time to talk to her anymore. God might not even let him! Well, Marla thought, that was a risk she'd have to take. Yes, the most important thing right now was to get Jose out of Hell. It's what her brother wanted.

But you promised your brother you'd never tell, said a voice in Marla's head. *Are you sure it really was Jose speaking to you in your dreams? Are you sure it's okay to tell his secret even to Father Banigas?*

Yes, the girl replied. *Of course it was Jose! Only the two of us knew his secret.*

The voice in Marla's head was silent; and when another girl came out of the confessional, Sister Esperanza signaled to Marla that it was her turn.

Marla slipped out of the pew and walked quickly down the side aisle to the confessional, shut herself inside, and knelt on the padded knee rest. She made the sign of the cross and realized her heart was beating much faster than normal. She usually liked being inside the confessional—liked the dark, and how safe and clean and polished it smelled. And even though this confessional smelled just like the ones in her old church, today Marla Rodriguez didn't feel safe in there at all.

Father Banigas slid open the shutter to his compartment, the dim outline of his head visible beyond lattice screen.

"Perdóname, Padre, porque he pecado," Marla said.

"You speak English?" asked the priest.

"Sí, Padre."

"You must be new. At this church, it is important that we learn to be good Americans. The children make their confessions in English."

Marla felt her face go hot, her stomach tighten. "I'm sorry. Bless me, Father, for I have sinned. It has been three months since my last confession."

"That's all right, dear. What do you want to confess?"

"Well," she began, "I don't have much bad that I did since my last confession. Only that I sometimes wish it was my brother Diego who died instead of Jose."

"Jose?"

"Yes, Father. My oldest brother. He is who I wanted to confess for today. He told me to do it for him in some dreams I had because he didn't get a chance to do it himself before the *pandilleros* killed him. That's why he's stuck in Hell right now, but if I can confess for him, God will forgive Jose and let him into Heaven. Jose told me so."

"I see," said the priest.

"Jose told me in my dreams that if he knew he was going to die he would have confessed to Father Gomez back in our old church. But we don't go to that church anymore because Papa moved us away from our old neighborhood because of the *pandilleros*. They thought at first that it was them who killed Jose and that other man, but now the police say they don't know. But everybody says that only *la Mara Salvatrucha* would do something like that, and Papa wanted us to go live with his sister. So, last time I spoke to Jose in my dream, I asked him who killed him, and he said he didn't know, but that he also thought it was the *pandilleros*. And so I asked him if I could confess to you instead of Father Gomez, and he said yes. So now it's up to you to get Jose out of Hell."

"Why do you think Jose is in Hell?"

"Because of his secret."

"His secret?"

"Yes," the girl said tentatively. "No one but me and Jose ever knew. Jose said if Papa ever found out, he would kill him, or at least throw him out of the house. And Mama and Papa and Diego always used to say that people like Jose were going to Hell. But I don't know why that's true, because Jose was the nicest person in the whole world to me. He would bring me home CDs from Best Buy, and he promised me he was going to take me to the movies in his new car when he got it."

"What did he do that was so bad that your parents would think he was going to Hell? Was he involved with the *pandilleros*?"

"Oh no!"

"Then what?"

Marla swallowed hard, took a deep breath, and said, "May I confess Jose's secret for him now, Father Banigas?"

"But, my child, only a person who accepts Jesus Christ as his Savior and seeks forgiveness himself can be absolved in the name of our Father."

"Please, Father Banigas," Marla cried, the tears beginning to flow. "You have to help me. You have to ask God to let Jose out of Hell. *Please.* I don't want my brother to be stuck down there forever. He was the best brother I ever had."

"Ssh, my child. It's all right. I will take care of it for you, okay? I will grant a conditional absolution for Jose so he can stand before God and ask Him for forgiveness himself. Will that make you feel better?"

"*Sí! Gracias*—I mean, thank you, Father Banigas."

"Now tell me Jose's secret."

"Well," Marla began, "Papa and Mama think Jose wanted to go to college for computers, but I know that he was saving up his money so he could go for fashion design—you know, to make clothes and stuff. I only know this because it was Jose who took me to the father-and-daughter dance at school."

"I don't follow."

"Papa couldn't get out of work because this other guy had his appendix out, and we didn't have enough money to buy a dress for me. I outgrew my stuff from fourth grade. I was real sad, but then Jose said he could fix it for me. He undid the stitching on my old dress and added some material from another dress, and it really looked great. He made me promise to keep it secret, and we didn't tell Mama and Papa and

Diego—just told them that one of Jose's girlfriends from school had done it. Jose would never tell Papa, and especially not Diego, because they would think that making dresses was for *maricóns*."

"That is not a nice word, child," the priest said. "I believe you mean homosexual."

"I'm sorry, Father Banigas, but that's what Papa and Diego call them. Oh, and I already confessed lying about the dress to Father Gomez."

"I understand," said Father Banigas. "So is that Jose's secret?"

"Well," Marla hesitated, "not all of it."

"Go on then."

"Well, you see, Father Banigas, I'm confessing today for Jose because my brother *was* a mar—a homosexual."

"Why do you say that?"

"Because he told me he liked boys instead of girls—but only after I found out and asked him and promised never to tell Mama and Papa and Diego."

"How did you find this out?"

"Jose had a job after school at Best Buy in the computer section, but on Wednesday and Saturday nights he worked at this other place where he said he made more money. He never told me where—said it was a Mexican restaurant downtown. But one day I overheard him talking on the phone when he thought I was playing outside and, well, he told the person that they could pick him up after the show at Angel's and then gave them the address on West Hargett Street. I googled the words 'angels' and 'show' and 'West Hargett Street' in the library at school, and I found out that Angel's is a club in Raleigh where the homosexuals go for drag shows. I didn't know what a drag show was until I looked it up. It's a show where boys dress up as—"

"Yes, yes, yes, I know what a drag show is—but did you tell your parents?"

"Oh no! I didn't want to get Jose into trouble. But I did ask Jose about it when we were alone. And at first he was mad at me and said he didn't know what I was talking about and told me to mind my own business. But after I told him that I didn't care if he was a homosexual, that I would keep it a secret and I would still love him more than Diego no matter what, he started crying and told me everything. He told me about the drag shows, too, and made me swear on Mama's Bible that I would never tell anyone."

"But, my child, you should have told the police this after he was killed."

"I couldn't, Father Banigas. Papa and Mama would kill me if they knew I knew Jose was a homosexual and didn't tell them. And they have both been so upset with him dying, this would kill them, I just know it. Why do they or the police need to know anyway? They said they thought it was the *pandilleros*. And even though they say they don't know now, everybody still thinks it was. I can't have Papa throw his memory of Jose out of his head the way he would've thrown Jose out of the apartment if he'd known he was a homosexual."

Father Banigas heaved a heavy sigh and asked, "What else did Jose tell you?"

"Well, after he told me he liked boys, after he confessed to me about working at Angel's, he told me how much money he made there. Fifty dollars plus tips—sometimes over a hundred dollars a night! He said they let him keep his costume and his makeup at the club. Leona Bonita, he called himself, and the makeup and his wig and stuff sort of made him look like a lion, he said."

"I see," said Father Banigas.

"So that's why you have to help me, Father Banigas. Because I know if Jose had gotten the chance before he died, he'd have asked God to forgive him for being a homosexual. He told me so in my dreams. He said he was sorry. He said he didn't like being in Hell and wanted me to help him get into Heaven."

The priest was silent for a long time.

"I conditionally absolve Jose of his sins," he said finally. "In the name of the Father, the Son, and the Holy Ghost."

"Thank you!"

"Say ten Our Fathers and ten Hail Marys, and Jose will be able to ask God for forgiveness himself. Then say another five of each for wishing the death of your brother Diego."

"Thank you! Thank you, Father Banigas!"

Marla ran back to her pew, knelt down, and said her Our Fathers and Hail Marys as fast as she could. And when she was finished, the pretty eleven-year-old in the big yellow sweatshirt got up from her seat and dashed down the aisle to the side door. The children gasped, and Sister Esperanza called after her, but Marla didn't stop—didn't care if she would have to sit in the corner or write on the blackboard a hundred times.

No, as she ran outside into the courtyard, all Marla Rodriguez cared about was waving good-bye to Jose. For now that she'd fixed things, she was certain she'd be able to see his spirit flying up to Heaven.

Chapter 6

Special Agent Andy Schaap was starving. It was his own fault, goddammit. Should've snagged one of those stale donuts before he left. However, if there was one thing he'd learned from the boys at the Raleigh Resident Agency, it was that the steaks at the Dubliner Hotel were the best-kept secret in town.

But now it was getting late, and an appetizer would spoil his experience of a well-earned fourteen-ounce hunk of wet-aged rib eye. Eating. The only thing in his life other than forensics that Andrew J. Schaap had developed into an art form—especially when it came to stretching every penny of the Feds' strict voucher program. And if he'd been waiting for anybody else, well fuck it, he'd have ordered his steak half an hour ago. But he couldn't do that to Sam Markham. Sure, Andy Schaap didn't want to appear rude; but more than that, Andy Schaap didn't want to appear weak.

The forensic specialist knew all about Sam Markham and his little dance with Jackson Briggs down in Florida. He'd seen the pictures of the citation ceremony and heard the stories of how he'd taken that big motherfucker down. Schaap pegged Markham to be about his age—mid to late thirties—but whereas a ten-year marriage and a bitter divorce had left Andy Schaap with a bald spot and a nicely developed gut, Markham looked young and lean. Still, there was nothing physically remarkable about him; and certainly nothing in his background that would indicate him being able to take down a six-foot-four monster like Briggs.

He looked at his watch. *7:30.* His stomach groaned, and he answered it with a sip of warm beer. It was only his second bottle, but after he'd been nursing it for half an hour, the beer tasted stale and sour. The craving for steak, the determination to enjoy and savor the experience were perhaps a bit of subliminal suggestion, he thought, from all that business with those other kind of *stakes.*

Fucked up the way the mind works.

Schaap replayed his examination of Donovan over and over again in his mind—the glowing pink symbols scrolling across the backs of his eyeballs like an electronic stock ticker. Yeah, they were going to have a problem with this dude. Schaap could feel it. "Vlad," the boys at the Resident Agency were already calling him. "Vlad the Impaler."

Just wonderful.

Schaap sighed, swigged the last of his beer, and reminded himself not to take it personally that Markham was a half hour late. He took off his wedding ring and began bouncing it on the table. He'd been divorced for over a year now, but for some reason he still couldn't part with it—wore the thick platinum band on his right hand instead of his left, and often found himself fiddling with it when he was agitated.

Platinum. His ex had insisted on them getting his-and-hers platinum rings. It was the strongest of all the metals, she said, and symbolized the strength of their bond. Lot of fucking good it did them. She just woke up one morning and said she didn't want to be married anymore. He tried to get her to go the counseling route, but she didn't want to hear it. He wondered if she'd been two-timing him, but could never prove anything. In a way he wished she had been screwing someone else. At least then he'd know what happened. That was the hardest part. Not knowing what the fuck he did wrong, not knowing exactly what made her fall out of love with him.

True, he couldn't give a shit about her now, but it was the way she tried to screw him in the end that still bothered him—almost as if she thought he was the one who'd been fucking around on her. She got the house, the kids, a nice fat alimony check, of course, but the judge stopped her short of taking the ring back. That's why he still wore it. A big "Fuck you, bitch." He toyed for a while with getting it resized for his middle finger, but decided against it in the end. Figured his wife would get the message anyway when he picked up the kids and she saw the ring on his right hand.

Schaap had slipped the ring back on and was about to signal for another beer, when he spied Markham standing by the vacant hostess station. Schaap thought he looked shorter than in his photo: clean cut, chiseled features, his jaw more pronounced. *All-American apple pie*, he said to himself, and made a mental note to order dessert.

Schaap waved him over.

"I apologize for making you wait," Markham said. "I lost track of time. Drove out to the crime scenes, took me longer to get back than I expected. Left you a voice mail. Looks like you didn't get it. Sam Markham, by the way."

The men shook hands.

"Probably no reception in here," Schaap said. "And call me Schaap."

Markham slid into the booth across from him.

"Can I get you something to drink?" Schaap asked, signaling his waitress. "An appetizer or something?"

"A beer is fine. And no appetizer. They tell me the steaks here are the best in the city; want to make sure I savor every cent of my piece-of-shit per diem."

"I heard that," Schaap said, laughing, and ordered for the both of them. And as they exchanged small talk over a fresh round of beers, Schaap found his new partner to be quite pleasant and down to earth—much less brooding, much less "intellectual" than he had come to expect from all the water-cooler talk.

But after the waitress brought them their dinners, Markham grew quieter—hardly touched his steak, for that matter—and Schaap began to wonder if the celebrated Quantico profiler hadn't been putting on an act simply to disarm him.

"I assume the report came back on that steak," Markham asked out of nowhere.

Schaap looked up from his plate—was confused for a moment until he realized he meant *s-t-a-k-e*.

"Oh yeah," Schaap said, swallowing. "Same as the others. Long piece of pine two-by-twelve that the killer rips down and tapers to a point. Standard lumber found all over the place—Lowe's, Home Depot. Too long to turn on a wood lathe, so our boy makes them the old-fashioned way. Uses a wood plane and finishes them with a belt sander; takes his time to get the contours smooth and rounded."

"Same process for the other two as well?"

"Yeah. I expedited them to the labs at Quantico. The Firearms-Toolmarks Unit came back with their report yesterday. Typical belt sander, it looks like; standard iron-bladed wood plane with about a two-inch-wide cut. The taper, the proportions from the base of the stake to the point are the same, but the heights are different. Customizes them to fit his victims. Guerrera was only five-three, but his stake had the same angle of taper as the other victims. Cuts them so they'll go about three feet into the ground, but adjusts the height and the little crossbar according the length of the victim's torso."

"Since the Hispanics died of their gunshot wounds," Markham said, "the killer could have made their stakes after he killed them. But with Donovan, he must have made his stake while the lawyer was still alive. Donovan died differently from the others."

"From the stake itself, right."

"FTU find anything else?"

"Nope. Trace Evidence Unit came up empty, too. No fingerprints or skin tissue other than the victims'. We were hoping our boy maybe got a splinter or something, but he must've used gloves. He's pretty thorough; seems to know what he's doing."

"A woodworker then? Maybe makes a living as a contractor? Construction?"

"Maybe. I've already got things moving at the Resident Agency. Mobilizing task forces to begin covering those angles as we speak. A needle in a haystack, if you ask me."

"Anything else happen while I was out of touch today?"

"Just news from our language specialist. Said that, although Vlad wrote on Donovan's body from left to right, three of the scripts, the Aramaic, Arabic, and Hebrew, should've been written from right to left."

"You mean he wrote his words backwards?"

"Yes."

"Then he may not have known the etymology behind what he was writing."

"Right. Also might indicate that he was copying the letters from someplace. Already got a Cyber Action Team working the Internet angle. So far, they haven't come up with anything. No searches for the phrase, 'I have returned' in the languages in question. No IP addresses that look promising."

"What about local searches for Vlad and impalement and whatnot?" Markham asked.

"Oh yeah, plenty of those, but no more than usual, I expect. Of course we'll look into them, but if Vlad is as smart as I think he is, I'm willing to bet you another rib eye that he did his research the old-fashioned way at the library."

"Why?"

"The stakes, the detail and care he puts into them. Pretty thorough, if you ask me. Wouldn't make the mistake of getting caught on his home computer; would use a public one at least, but that could still pin him to a specific locale. I don't see him fucking up that way. Just my two cents, for what it's worth."

Markham was silent, lost in thought. He looked vulnerable, Schaap thought—strangely human in his puzzlement.

"I'd like us to be straight with each other," Schaap said after a moment.

Markham looked up at him from his half-eaten steak.

"I know you'll want to go most of this alone. I know from what happened in Tampa that you work best that way. I respect that. And you need to know that I don't harbor any resentment about Gates sending you into my territory. I mean it. Will give you my complete support with the understanding that I'm acting only as your NCAVC coordinator, as well as the point man for the local authorities."

"I appreciate that," Markham said.

"And I'm not going to ask you how you caught Jackson Briggs, either."

Markham narrowed his eyes at him.

"I read the report," Schaap continued. "Still have no idea how you got turned on to him. But what I'm saying is I'm not going to try to get into your head about things. You keep what you want to yourself, but you don't have to worry about me cock-blocking you if you want to bounce things off me, okay?"

"Thanks," Markham said, smiling.

"May I ask you one thing about the Briggs case, though? A minor detail?"

"Okay."

"Is it true what I read? That he came after you with a samurai sword?"

"A ninja sword, I believe it was, but yes."

"Caught you in the arm and kept slashing at you even with four bullets in him?"

"Three. The fourth was a head shot."

"He cut you bad?"

"Not too bad. Got my jacket mostly—my left shoulder. Barely even a scar there now. Not much to brag about in the locker room."

"Was he your first kill?"

"Yes."

"Feel fucked up?"

"No," Markham said simply. "Actually, it didn't."

A heavy silence—Schaap's brain spinning.

"So what about our boy here in Raleigh?" he asked finally. "Anything other than the usual logistical groundwork that you want me to take care of?"

"Yes," Markham said. "I need to get back to the crime scenes."

"Tonight?"

"I need to see them in the dark. And I could use your help—would like you to coordinate things with Cary PD. Tell them I'm going to stop by Donovan's house, and that I'll be at the baseball field around eleven or twelve. I'm going to work backwards; going to focus on Donovan tonight and Rodriguez and Guerrera tomorrow. But it's important that

I'm not bothered. Maybe you can get a detail posted for me in case the press or some nosy locals are still sniffing around."

"Trying to see what things looked like from Vlad's perspective?"

"No. Tonight I'll be trying to see things through the eyes of his victims."

Chapter 7

Doug Jennings, technical director of the Harriot University Department of Theatre and Dance, was furious—because of what happened, sure, but more so because he might have to miss his son's honor society ceremony. Stealing was one thing—but inconveniencing him? Well, that was going too far. One of these little fuckers had dicked him twice now, and *enough was enough*.

"Keep in mind," Jennings said, "George is taking valuable time out of his rehearsal so all of you, cast and crew, understand how serious this is." His voice was tight; reverberated off the theater walls and came back to him like someone else's. "Now, since it's obvious that you didn't believe me after our little talk at the beginning of the semester, George here wanted to say a few words so we're all perfectly clear about what's going to happen next."

As George Kiernan took his place at the foot of the stage, Jennings scanned the crowd. More than thirty students clumped together in the first four rows like a herd of frightened sheep. Jennings was breathing heavily; his bushy red beard damp with spittle, the perspiration beginning to pool between his flabby breasts and his big round belly. Whoever had stolen his belt sander was here tonight. He could feel it.

"Doug and his crew," Kiernan began, "busted their butts this week to get us onstage a day early, and now I have to take time out of rehearsal for this nonsense. In fact, in my twenty years as chair of the Department of Theatre and Dance, tonight is the first time I've ever had to take time out of a rehearsal for something like this, *period.*"

Kiernan set down his notepad and leaned back against the stage—the tension-filled pause, the icy stare over his wire-rimmed spectacles as only George Kiernan could pull off. Jennings had witnessed his boss chew ass many times during his eleven-year tenure at Harriot. And even though he was genuinely angry, the technical director's chest tingled with excitement.

"As you know," Kiernan continued, "this isn't the first time things have gone missing from the tool closet this year. And Doug and I are quite confident that the thief is sitting amongst you here tonight."

The students shifted uncomfortably in their seats.

"Doug and I are the only people with keys to the tool closet, and thus we've narrowed down the possible time frames in which the tools could have been stolen. That's right. The belt sander, as well as the tools that went missing earlier this semester, appear to have been stolen during *your* regularly scheduled crew hours."

Kiernan's voice was calm and deliberate, but Jennings knew the eruption was coming soon. He exchanged a knowing glance with his assistant Edmund Lambert. Lambert was a good egg, Jennings thought—the only kid in the bunch whom he still trusted. Well, Lambert was hardly a kid anymore—mid-twenties, former Army specialist, and built like a brick shithouse. It was Lambert who brought the latest theft to his attention as he was closing up after yesterday's stage scenery crew; Lambert who'd since gone to Best Buy and installed the new webcam in the scene shop; Lambert who'd offered to sniff out the thieving bastard himself and teach him a little lesson "Screaming Eagle style."

Doug Jennings felt a special kinship with his brother from the 101st Airborne. Both had done their stints out of Fort Campbell, Kentucky—Jennings in the mid-1980s; Lambert a few years ago. Finished up his bid with a tour in Iraq, saw the heaviest shit in Tal Afar, he said. Jennings kind of envied Lambert; saw him as a younger, leaner, meaner version of himself. Uncanny the way their lives paralleled each other: returning to school in their mid-twenties on the GI Bill; discovering their love of technical theatre later than most. And Doug Jennings didn't regret taking his fellow Eagle under his wing. The past year had worked out great. He would have to give Lambert more responsibility now—get a key to the tool closet made for him and all that.

"I cannot begin to express how disturbed and disappointed I am by all this," Kiernan said. "But what really burns my ass is the blatant disregard and betrayal of everything we here in the Department of Theatre and Dance stand for. And that's *trust*. Whoever has stolen the items out of the tool closet has betrayed *all* of our trust. The trust we have in each other that everybody will do their job and work together toward a purpose greater than ourselves. What I'm talking about is having each other's backs."

Kiernan's voice had grown steadily in speed and volume, his cheeks flushed, the perspiration beginning to break out like melting snow at the edges of his white receding hairline. And when he turned to retrieve his notepad from the edge of the stage, Doug Jennings knew the moment had arrived.

"But now I turn around," Kiernan said over his shoulder, "and someone sticks a knife in my back. *Again*, goddammit!"

The theater was deathly quiet, the echo of the chair's voice petering out into the stifled sobs of the female lead.

The rest of the students sat with their eyes focused on their laps. They were scared, Jennings could tell, and that made him feel better.

"Now here's what's going to happen," Kiernan said, his voice once again calm and measured. "Not only have we installed a new security camera in the scene shop, but the Greenville Police have already begun dusting for fingerprints. Harriot University is treating this as a criminal act that will be prosecuted. I will not only make sure that the thief or thieves are expelled, but have also made it my personal mission to see to it that they never work in the theatre again. *Period.*"

Kiernan paused to survey the crowd.

"However," he continued, "I'm leaving the door open for the thief or thieves to return the stolen items anonymously outside my office when no one is around. If that happens, all will be forgotten. If not, then rest assured we will find out who did this. And when we do, justice will be swift and merciless. Now get moving and get focused. We go in ten minutes."

Like a cluster of cockroaches, the students scattered from the theater in a whoosh. Jennings retrieved his boss's notepad and accompanied him up the aisle to the back of the theater.

"You think Greenville PD will find anything?" Jennings asked.

"Probably not," said Kiernan, wiping his brow. "Fucking bunch of Keystone Kops. Thing I said about the fingerprints is bullshit. Just trying to scare them."

"I know."

"'Least now we got that webcam going twenty-four seven. Nobody'll be able to get in or out of the scene shop without us recording it. Sad though that it has to come to this. Fucking times we live in."

Jennings nodded.

"Listen, Doug, I know you got that thing with your son tonight. Why don't you get going? No need for you to stick around here any longer on account of this bullshit."

"You sure?"

"We got a week before we open. And Lambert's going to be around, right?"

"Yeah. He was out sick a couple days last week—really bad, from what he says—but he busted his ass double time this past weekend. If it wasn't for him, the trap mechanism wouldn't have been finished. Wouldn't have been able to give you the stage a day early, either."

"Fine. Tell Doug Junior I said to keep cracking those books."

"Will do, George. And thanks again."

Kiernan nodded and began shuffling through his notes when Edmund Lambert emerged from the stage left vom. Jennings waved to him across the empty seats—pointed and gave him a thumbs-up to ask if everything was okay. Lambert gave a thumbs-up of his own, and with that Doug Jennings exited the theater.

The cool April air felt good on his face—chilled his pits and tickled the wetness in the cracks of his flab as he walked across the parking lot. He would not have time to shower and change into a fresh set of clothes, but that was just fine and dandy as far as he was concerned. He hated wearing a tie—that was a given—but at least now he'd have a good excuse when his wife started bitching at him in the junior high school auditorium. Good thing Lambert had been around to pick up the slack for him, too; at least now he'd get there on time.

"Yeah," Jennings muttered as he slipped into his old pickup. "I gotta get that guy a key to the tool closet."

Chapter 8

Edmund Lambert watched the final scene of *Macbeth* from the wings. He stood just far enough offstage to stay out of sightlines and still get a good view of the trap. He didn't care about the sword fight, and when it came right down to it, thought the whole climax of the play to be quite silly. He didn't understand why the director had Banquo's ghost come up from Hell, from underneath the stage to blow dust in Macbeth's eyes as he was about to kill Macduff. That wasn't in Shakespeare's original—contradicted the very nature of fate, Edmund thought.

Then again, what could the director possibly know about fate? About ghosts and killing and witches and Hell?

The clang of swords rang out as Macbeth bellowed his final words: *"Lay on, Macduff; and damned be him who first cries, 'Hold, enough!'"*

The trap had worked perfectly from day one. Edmund had designed the mechanism and built it himself: a three-stepped platform on casters that split open down the middle to reveal a stair unit that allowed the actors to disappear into the electrics shop beneath the stage. A nice effect, Edmund thought. He especially liked how, when someone died, the Witches would rise up to take the dead person's spirit down "to Hell."

Then again, he thought, getting into Hell was easy. It's getting out that's the tricky part.

Edmund also liked the design of the set very much: a two-tiered horseshoe with multiple entrances and a tall set of double doors upstage center that were intended to mimic the pattern on the oven doors at Auschwitz. However, instead of setting the play in Nazi Germany (which would've been perfect, he thought) the director had chosen to portray Macbeth's kingdom as a burned-out, post-apocalyptic fantasy world. Edmund thought this trite and juvenile—a poor man's *Road Warrior* or something—but no matter. No, as long as the trap worked smoothly, that's all he cared about.

And once the platform came apart and Banquo blew the dust in Macbeth's eyes, Edmund stepped back into the off-stage shadows feeling satisfied.

"You don't want to see him get his head cut off?" asked the girl playing Lady Macbeth.

Edmund shrugged and took his seat by the pin rail. He'd never really spoken to her—only a few words here and there over the past year—but knew her name was Cindy Smith. She was in her rehearsal clothes, but had taken it upon herself to dress like the Witches—like a spirit to represent her descent into Hell. Edmund had overheard her during crew complaining about not being able to take her bow in her queen costume, and had thought her petty and as common as her last name for bitching about such nonsense.

Then came the cheer onstage signaling Macbeth's be-heading, and Cindy whispered, "There isn't a sword in the world big enough to cut *that* guy's head off."

Edmund smiled and all at once thought better of her.

"Are you planning on going to the cast party?" she asked. "I don't know if you know, but it's after the show next Friday.

Don't remember ever seeing you at any of the other ones this year. But anyway, you should come."

"Not sure if I can," Edmund said in his thick Southern drawl. "Gotten behind on things at home because of all the work here."

"Well, I hope to see you there. I know you're a little older, but the cast parties are pretty chill—not a bunch of drunk freshmen making fools of themselves if that's what you're worried about."

Edmund nodded vaguely. A flourish was heard onstage, the signal that the newly crowned king of Scotland was about to give his final speech.

"Cindy!" hissed an assistant stage manager. "Get your ass to places!"

But Edmund knew the actress had a little more time; would only have to run down the vom stairs and into the electrics shop to get under the trap, from where she'd rise to take Macbeth's spirit into Hell. In fact, she still had to wait for the end of that stupid dance number with the Witches— something the director had inserted at the last minute so that the actor playing Macbeth would have enough time to get back onstage in *his* spirit costume. And although Edmund hadn't been around to hear it, word on the street was that Macbeth had put up even more of a stink about his bow than Cindy had.

"I gotta get moving," she said. "I'm sure I'll talk to you before then, but think about coming to the cast party next Friday, okay, Edmund?"

"Okay."

Cindy smiled and disappeared into the darkness of the vom.

A short time later, Edmund caught her eye when she stepped out of the pit to meet the spirit of her dead husband. And whereas the young actress most certainly must have thought he was watching in the wings for her, all Edmund

Lambert really cared about was that the trap was working properly.

It was just after midnight when Edmund turned his old Ford F-150 down the long dirt driveway that led to his grandfather's farmhouse. The sprawling, two-story rambler with the dilapidated front porch was set back about two hundred yards off a country road on the outskirts of Wilson, almost exactly halfway between the Harriot campus and downtown Raleigh.

Edmund's grandfather had once grown tobacco here; had taken over the family business from Edmund's great grandfather and made himself quite a killing in the sixties and seventies. And even though the tobacco fields had been barren and brown for a long time now, Edmund was glad his grandfather never caved in and sold the farm.

For now Edmund understood why.

He had lived with his grandfather all his life, but the house had only officially become his when he returned from Iraq, after his grandfather died and left him everything. That had been over two years ago now, but even then Edmund had understood that the timing was no accident.

It was just part of the equation. Everything connected.

And once he was safely past the stone pillars at the foot of his driveway Edmund Lambert was the General again.

He cut off the pickup's headlights. He liked to return home this way—the crumbling silhouettes of the old tobacco sheds passing by him like a grim honor guard as his eyes adjusted to the dark. He parked the truck by the front porch and stepped out—took a deep breath and headed for the field behind the old horse barn. There hadn't been horses in the barn for almost fifty years—only his van and his chin-up bar now.

The General wandered out to the middle of the field and

stopped—the moonlight, a wrinkled blanket of silver beneath his feet; the stars, a bag of scattered diamonds above his head. It hurt his neck to look at them tonight. He was tired, but anxious, too; felt that the crews and the building of the trap during the past few days had put him behind schedule. And then there were all the technical rehearsals coming this weekend. True, he'd called in sick a couple of days the week before—that had given him ample opportunity to take care of the lawyer—but little time to figure out who was to be next. Of course, the Prince wanted him to rest, but still . . .

Sighing, the General walked back to the house. Once inside he turned off the alarm and immediately reset it to STAY/INSTANT. He'd had the alarm installed after his grandfather's death just in case anyone should ever come snooping while he was busy in the cellar. But no one ever came snooping anymore. No relatives, no friends, no more men from Big Tobacco offering to buy the farm.

Then again, that was all part of the equation, too.

He took off his shirt in the front hall and smelled his armpits. He needed a shower, needed to wash off the residue of his day-life before got into bed. If the Prince wanted him to sleep, then he would sleep as the General

The General finished undressing in the upstairs bathroom and turned on the shower. He stared at himself for a long time in the full-length mirror until the steam billowed out from behind the curtain and made his reflection disappear. He understood the message—knew that he had watched himself become smoke, become spirit.

The General smiled and stepped into the shower.

He stood there for a long time staring down at his chest, watching with the eyes of a child as the scalding hot water reddened his flesh.

Chapter 9

Tonight had to be about Donovan and only Donovan. But as he drove away from the lawyer's house in Cary, Markham felt the beginnings of what was sure to be a splitting headache. He was tired, but knew the pressure behind his eyes was coming from his impatience to know right away how the victims were connected.

Donovan's wife and two children were staying with relatives. Schaap got him a key and squared it with the local authorities so he could have the place to himself. But after two hours of walking the property, of sorting through the family's belongings and sitting with his feet up on the desk in the lawyer's lavish home office, he'd left feeling cold and empty. Nothing had spoken to him. Nothing at all.

Of course there were a lot of people who would've liked to have seen Randall Donovan dead. But how was the lawyer connected to Rodriguez and Guerrera?

Only Vlad knew for sure.

Without the connection to the Colombian cartels tying the victims together, the killings could almost be seen as random. But Markham knew in his gut that Vlad's victims had been chosen because they met specific criteria that went beyond just fitting the bill of the historical Vlad's victims. In other words, if Vlad saw these men as criminals or moral undesirables, why did he choose these undesirables specifically?

Markham would thus have to work backwards, beginning with the victim about whom he knew the most. Randall Donovan. And other than the details of the lawyer's murder, Markham didn't know much.

He took a deep breath and concentrated on the pressure behind his eyes; envisioned it as a bright red ball and kept shooting it from his forehead until he felt the tension in his face relax. By the time he reached the crime scene about fifteen minutes later he felt much better. The baseball field was located in a more rural area of town—at the north end of a small, secluded park—and Markham arrived to find the Cary police already waiting for him.

"Thank you, Schaap," he whispered, and parked behind the patrol car. He slipped his case files into a small duffel bag and stepped out in tandem with the policeman—was about to reach for his ID, but the policeman waved him on without a word.

Markham nodded and headed down the steep embankment to the baseball field. When he reached home plate, he removed a flashlight from his bag and made his way across the pitcher's mound to the outfield. After a few seconds of searching he found the marker he'd left there earlier that afternoon: an old bike reflector placed on the exact spot where Randall Donovan had been discovered impaled. The hole had been filled in, the crime scene tape gone for a couple of days now. And to make things worse it had rained on Monday, leaving nothing to indicate that only five days ago poor Randall Donovan had played center field with a stake up his ass.

Markham rifled through his bag and removed a large

compass, charged the glow-in-the-dark coordinates with his flashlight, and then cut off the light. Turning slowly in place over the posthole, he allowed his eyes time to adjust to the dark. He settled on west, then stood for a long time gazing out over the field. The sky was clear, the moon an almost perfect half—not the same, of course, as it had been for Donovan, but he wasn't sure if its position had changed also. He had an inkling it had but would need to check that out later.

His eyes played back and forth between the moon and the jagged silhouette of trees on the horizon. He reached into his duffel bag and pulled out a bath towel he'd taken from his temporary apartment, balled it up behind his head, and lay down in the grass. Maintaining his direction west, he approximated Donovan's line of sight and stared up at the sky. The scene was breathtaking—reminded him of a Lite-Brite set he used to have as a child. He let his eyes wander back to the moon and saw that the stars were slightly washed out around its perimeter. With a crescent moon, he thought, the stars would've been clearer.

"Of course," he whispered. "Makes sense if you want to replicate the Ottoman symbol for Islam in the sky. But you can't replicate the symbol exactly; can't get the star inside the crescent. Would you accept that, Vlad?"

He scanned the sky for a long time and let his eyes wander from the crescent moon to the stars. He didn't recognize any of the constellations except the Big Dipper. That would be something he'd have to check out on the Internet, too. Maybe a constellation associated with Vlad. But how many were there? The voice in his head began taunting him with signs from the zodiac, but he quickly stifled it and allowed the stars to enfold him in their sparkly blanket of ignorance—of junior high school science projects and that astronomy class he'd always wished he'd taken at UConn.

*Donovan's glasses and the sight lines of the other vic-
tims—they couldn't have been looking at the crescent moon.*

*Well, what about the star? You need a star to complete the
symbol for Islam.*

But which one? There are thousands of them!

Markham scanned the sky and felt his brain beginning to
squirm; felt the pressure building up again behind his eyes.
He closed them and focused on his breathing, on emptying
his mind into the sounds of the night and the orangey speck-
les burned on the backs of his eyelids. His muscles began to
relax—a sinking sensation, as if he were suddenly lying on a
bed of warm sand. The day was catching up to him, and soon
his thoughts drifted to his wife, to the afternoon they drove
up to Rhode Island and the night they made love for the first
time on the beach at Bonnet Shores. Afterwards, gazing up
at the stars, Michelle pointed out the constellation Cassiopeia. Cassiopeia, she said, was one she could always find.

"A good sailor can always find his way home by the
North Star," she told him.

Markham smiled at the memory of how he tried to im-
press her with his knowledge of Greek mythology, explain-
ing that Cassiopeia was a vain queen who boasted that she
was more beautiful than the goddess Hera herself. Michelle
didn't buy it; said that anybody who'd seen *Clash of the Ti-
tans* would know that. Markham laughed, and the two of
them traded parts humming the movie's cheesy music.

Laughing. He couldn't remember the last time he'd laughed.
Not like that, anyway. Like someone else. Who was that guy
lying on the beach? And who was this guy lying here in
center field? Not the same people, but still, both of them
strangers.

Markham took a deep breath and looked for Cassiopeia.
He couldn't find her and located the North Star instead. He
closed his eyes—the sound of the waves battering the shores

of his mind. He heard Michelle ask him if he liked the name Cassie. He had said he did, and added: *"If we ever have a daughter we'll name her Cassie. Short for Cassiopeia, okay?"* Michelle agreed, and he told her he loved her. She said she loved him, too; and there under the stars they fell asleep.

Cassie, Markham said to himself. *Our daughter's name shall be Cassie.*

Then, a heavy blink, a sensation of falling forward, and Markham awoke with a start. For a moment he expected to hear the ocean—didn't know where he was or how much time had passed until he looked at his watch.

1:37 a.m.

Michelle was gone, and he was back on the baseball field. He'd been out for over an hour. So unreal. So unlike him. He needed to get back to his apartment; needed to get some sleep. By the time he got back to the Resident Agency, the FBI lab's preliminary test results on Rodriguez should be waiting for him. He was glad he didn't have to be there for that; the kid had been in the ground for almost two months.

Markham yawned and stretched, was about to gather up his things, when suddenly he stopped. The stars. They looked different somehow—the moon a bit lower on the horizon and farther to his right.

A good sailor can always find his way home by the North Star.

Markham saw that it had not changed its position, but the surrounding stars had.

Slightly.

That's because the North Star is a pole star. Polaris is its official name. Position remains constant throughout the night, while the others appear to revolve around it.

Then it hit him.

Depending on the time Vlad dropped off his victims, the

stars would have looked different. Whatever he wanted them to look at might have changed position—might have actually traveled across the sky from east to west.

Markham flicked on his flashlight and took out the Rodriguez and Guerrera file from his duffel bag. He flipped immediately to the copy of the initial police report.

The patrolman, he read, *discovered them outside the cemetery around 1:50 a.m. Was called to the scene on a report that "a gang of youths" had been observed on the premises after hours.*

That had helped boost the original MS-13 angle, but Markham wondered now if the report was even true; wondered if maybe the killer hadn't tipped off the police himself to send them on a wild-goose chase.

Markham scanned the police report again. He knew from his earlier trip to the cemetery that it closed at dusk. Most likely, to be safe, the killer would have waited until well after dark. For the sake of argument, the actual window in which Rodriguez and Guerrera were dropped off could've been anywhere between 7 p.m. and 1:30 a.m. The window for Donovan was bigger. The groundskeeper found him around 5:30 a.m.

Markham stood up, charged the numbers on his compass, and turned toward the east. He slowly arched his head from the horizon, glancing from the stars to his compass until it carried him westward into Donovan's line of sight. Whatever it was the killer wanted his victims to see could have followed this general path, and in his mind he cut a thick swath of stars with a centerline due east and west.

But how thick should he make it? There was no way now to get the exact angles of the victims' sight lines. But gazing out over the eastern horizon he suddenly realized it would be better to work from the Hispanics' point of view. Donovan was looking almost directly overhead—a wider field of vision, too many stars to choose from. But Rodriguez and

Guerrera? The angle was much shorter. Practically straight ahead.

Yes, he thought. *Whatever Rodriguez and Guerrera were supposed to look at would have had a much narrower visual field through which to pass.*

But even if you get the angles correct, how the hell are you going to find the right star? That is, if the victims were supposed to look at a star to begin with?

Markham didn't have an answer. And it was too late to go to the cemetery. The window for what the Hispanics were supposed to look at had passed. Besides, he needed to get to sleep; needed to have a clear head in the morning if he was going to be dealing with latitudes and longitudes and coordinates and who knows what else. He'd most likely have to consult with an astronomy professor, too; might be able to get on the Internet and figure out for himself what stars could have passed over the eastern horizon between—

Sleep on it, he heard Gates say, and Markham quickly gathered his things and hurried across the field, up the embankment, and into his TrailBlazer.

The drive back to his temporary government digs seemed to take forever. But only when he pulled into the parking lot did he realize that, despite the jumble of thoughts swirling in his head, the pressure behind his eyes had not returned.

Chapter 10

Cindy Smith lay in bed staring up at the ceiling. She felt tired but at the same time wound up, her mind replaying over and over again her little chat with George Kiernan.

Her performance had gone well for the most part, Kiernan said, but he still felt her *"Out, out, damned spot!"* speech was pushed. Told her to just relax, to come onstage with a fuller emotional prep and just "do her doings." Cindy understood that Kiernan wanted her to stop playing it so crazy and just try to wash the imaginary blood from her hands. But the young actress also understood why he'd pulled her aside after rehearsal instead of giving her his notes with the rest of the cast.

And that's what bothered her.

It wasn't anything George Kiernan said or did—he was just trying to help, was well aware that every other woman in the department was gunning for his lead actress to fail. Someone had even written *"egocentric bitch?"* next to Cindy's name when the cast list went up a month and a half earlier. Kiernan himself took it down and replaced it with a clean copy. Then he sent out a message via the electronic

callboard saying that kind of thing "showed a small mind
and weak character," and warned that if he ever caught a student committing such a reprehensible act again, he would
personally see to it that he or she was thrown out of the department.

Cindy pretended to shrug it all off; even wrote *"egocentric bitch?"* as her Facebook status. But the comment and
the ongoing mystery of who wrote it—as well as all the catty
whispering that she knew was going on behind her back—
still bothered her. And as she watched the bright yellow
numbers on her bedside clock roll over to 2:00, the young
actress suddenly felt lonelier than ever.

True, she had begun to feel distant from her friends toward the end of last year, when she was still a sophomore
and the plays for the following season were officially an-
nounced. Lady Macbeth was the part over which every girl
in the department was salivating, and Cindy worked her ass
off to get it. She rehearsed all of Lady Macbeth's speeches
over the summer between her morning job at the day care
center and her evening job waitressing at Chili's. She kept
rehearsing into the fall, too, and by the time auditions came
around the following spring, the seasoned junior blew away
her competition—made sure to leave no room for her class-
mates to bitch that she got the role only because "Kiernan
wanted to bang her."

Tall and thin with jet-black hair and full, round lips,
Cindy Smith thought herself an attractive woman, yes, but
nothing special really. She'd had only one boyfriend in high
school and dated him all through her freshmen year at Harriot—until she found out he was cheating on her with a
sorority girl because, as he said, "she wasn't giving him
enough attention."

Now didn't that just scream of fucking irony!

In the end, however, she was happy to break it off. She
knew deep down that they had little in common, him being a

jock and her being a "theatre dork." And although a year and a half later she was self-aware enough to see the cliché in it all, the betrayal still hurt enough for her to keep the young men in the department at arm's length—especially the ego-maniac playing Macbeth.

The prick's name was Bradley Cox, a second-year senior who wouldn't be graduating any time soon, and who only got the lead because the competition among the men was so slim. "Big Fish, Small Pond Syndrome," her mother called it.

Cindy thought Bradley Cox was a cliché just like her ex-boyfriend—the big-man-on-campus type who prided himself on banging every girl in the department. The kind of guy who had it easy in college, but whose lack of talent and over-all mediocrity would hit him hard in the real world. Would probably end up working for his father's construction firm, Cindy was willing to bet. Bradley had asked Cindy out at the beginning of the fall semester—told her she looked like Angelina Jolie and said he'd like to make her dinner at his apartment. Cindy politely declined, then did so a second time a week later at a cast party, upon which an inebriated Cox called her a "stuck-up whore" and said he wouldn't fuck her with George Kiernan's dick.

He left her alone after that, hardly said two words to her all year. However, she *did* catch him sneering at one of his buddies during the first read-through of *Macbeth,* to which Cindy had come with all her lines memorized. She got her revenge two weeks later, secretly, when Kiernan pulled her aside and said, "You know, Cindy, the title of the play is *Macbeth,* but yours is the performance people are going to remember."

She had really appreciated that, but at the same time didn't like the special treatment she always got from Kiernan.

Like her private little note session tonight.

Cindy flicked on her bedside light, and when her eyes adjusted, she tiptoed over to her desk, making sure to avoid the creaky floorboard at the corner of the bed so as not to wake her mother downstairs.

Cindy was born and raised in Greenville and still lived at home. She wasn't proud of it—living with her mother, that is—but knew that it would all pay off when she moved to New York City to pursue her acting career. She'd already saved up almost four thousand dollars in her three years of working at Chili's. She paid for school through scholarships and her work-study job in the box office and hadn't had to ask for a dime from her asshole father, either. She hadn't even *talked* to the son of a bitch since Christmas, now that she thought of it; and although the piece-of-junk Pontiac Sunfire he'd thrown her on her sixteenth birthday was about to shit the bed, she'd rather walk to school than be the first to call.

Cindy's father, an auto mechanic, ended up marrying the woman with whom he'd been cheating on Cindy's mother and bought a house out in neighboring Winterville. Still not far enough away, Cindy thought—shit, even California wouldn't be far enough away. The divorce went down when Cindy was in junior high school, when one day her mother came home from work crying and started throwing her father's things out on the front lawn. Then her father came home and smacked his wife a couple of good ones for embarrassing him in front of the neighbors. Didn't matter if he was guilty or not, he said; a good wife don't go selling out her husband no matter what he done.

Cindy saw it all, and the ensuing divorce hit her as hard as if her father had smacked her a couple of good ones, too. But like everything else, Cindy quickly learned to see the bigger picture. That was one of her "gifts," her mother always said; her maturity, her ability to rise above things. Cindy could tell that her mother was happier without the son of a bitch—had to admit that she was happier without him hanging around, too—and decided that it was best if she had as little to do with her father as possible.

Besides, he'd never shown much interest in her anyway.

Cindy turned on her computer—an old eMachine that took forever and made a weird clicking sound when it booted—and once she was on the Internet, out of habit she first checked her Facebook page. It was the usual stuff: a message from her best friend (who, unfortunately, went to State) and a couple of drunken posts along the lines of, *"Whassup, you egocentric bitch?"* from friends who had just returned from partying downtown. But only after Cindy minimized her Facebook page and saw the Google search results was she willing to admit to herself the real reason why she'd gotten out of bed.

She had googled the name "Edmund Lambert"—only a few thousand hits, most of which were links to general ancestry or genealogy pages. Nothing that Cindy could tie directly to the handsome ex-soldier who kept to himself in the scene shop.

Yeah, all the girls in the theatre department kind of had a thing for Lambert. But at the same time they were intimidated by him, and thought it strange how he didn't smile back when they batted their eyelashes and flashed their pearly whites at him. And really, only that slut Amy Pratt had made a play for him—came right out and said she'd give him a blow job in the light booth, to which Lambert replied, "No thank you, Amy." Amy told the girls about it in the dressing room the previous semester; said Lambert didn't even blush, didn't even flinch, but just looked her straight in the eye until she walked away. "Guy's weird," she said. "Looks you dead in the eye, all blank and creepy like he's looking through you. Fucking Hitchcock movie, if you ask me."

Lambert had looked at Cindy that way, too. But unlike Amy Pratt, Cindy actually liked it; liked the way he held her gaze to the point where she thought she could feel his steel-blue eyes licking the back of her retinas. Oh yeah, looks wise, Edmund Lambert was *beyond* dreamy—tall and muscular with dark brown hair and straight white teeth. But more than that, Cindy liked him because she could tell he was a thinker, could tell he had depth—the most genuine, no-bullshit guy in the department. Wouldn't even give a chick like Amy Pratt the time of day.

Cindy maximized her Facebook page and did a search there, too—came up empty, not a single Edmund Lambert on the entire site.

"*Nyet*," she said to herself in the Russian accent she was working on for her dialects class. "You don't seem like the *Fess-book* type, *Meester Lem-behrt*."

She did a search for herself on Facebook—five hundred-plus hits.

"More than five hundred of me to vuhn of you," she said in her best *La Femme Nikita* voice. "*Da*. You cannot resist me, *Meester Lem-behrt*."

Cindy opened another Web page, and after a few clicks was in the Harriot Campus Directory—did a search for Edmund Lambert and found what she was looking for.

"So, you're a Wilson boy," she said. "Makes sense. Bit of a commute—why you never come out to socialize. But now I have you right vehre I vahnt you.*"

She giggled and typed "Cindy Lambert" into the Facebook search field—again, over five hundred hits. "Five hundred to one," she said. "Yeah, I'll take those odds."

Cindy smiled and turned off her computer—was back in bed and fast asleep in five minutes without saying *"Out, out, damn spot!"* to herself even once.

PART II

APPROACHING

Chapter 11

It was Saturday night, and Hank Biehn was worried he smelled like booze. He could never smell it on himself. But then again, Hank Biehn hadn't been able to smell anything since about 1980 or so. All that snorting coke really did a number on the old factory nerves or whatever you called them; fucked with your balance, too, he thought as he walked along the side of Route 301. The dark didn't help any either—couldn't focus on nothing except random lights up ahead or the road in front of you; had to keep your head down more than when walking during the day. That's where the old factory nerves became a problem. Head down and fucked-up sense of balance. Not a good combination.

He supposed he was a bit rusty, too. Used be a pro at walking—or "drifting" as his asshole boss at the diner used to call it. "I ain't in the habit of hiring drifters," he'd said, but Hank had talked him into it. Hank Biehn had always been able to talk a good game. That'd been over two years ago now; the longest stretch he'd stayed domestic since he was paroled back in ninety-eight. Fifteen years for armed robbery after he moved from coke to the needle. Boy, that smack was a high-maintenance bitch!

But Hank Biehn had been clean since he got out, didn't even crave the methadone anymore. Besides, he'd found a new love—would *always* be married to the bottle—but he'd learned to keep her in line. Odd jobs here and there, day-laboring when you could get it was all she required. Short-order cook was a good gig, too, if you played it right. And Hank Biehn certainly thought he'd been playing this last one right, that's for sure. Stayed sober for the most part during the day and paid his rent on time.

Until he got fired.

And for what? Slapping that spic busboy in the mouth cuz he dropped them dishes on his foot? *Naw, boss, I ain't been drinking! Okay, okay, I admit I had little nip on my break— just a little one—but that fucking Chihuahua did it on purpose! Kind of talk? Whaddya mean you don't go for that kind of talk? How's a good, hardworking white man supposed to get by when them wetbacks is taking all our jobs?*

That had been the beginning of the end of his good run in Lucama, North Carolina. Same shit, different day. First you get canned; then you gotta weigh your options. And there hadn't been *any* options in shit-bowl Lucama. Small-town politics, word of mouth, bad rep now and rent due soon. Been there done that. Better to say fuck it and get outta Dodge before the money runs out and the landlady sics the sheriff on you. If he left now he'd have enough money to get by—more than he usually did when he cut bait—plus he'd be able to stretch it somewhere different until something else came along. And something would come along.

Something always did.

Besides, what was he going to do now anyway? Go back to the kind of life he had before he went in? He was fifty-two years old and didn't have them kind of reflexes no more. Being married to the bottle had seen to that; fucked with your muscles, too. But the bottle was a good girl—made you smarter, at least. Didn't make you do stupid things like he did when he was riding the needle. Boy, that smack was a high-priced whore! Was her who made him shoot that convenience store clerk in Durham—popped him one right above the left eye and killed him instantly, he saw on the news the next day. Never thought he woulda been capable of a thing like that, but, boy oh boy, the things we do for love! Luckily, they never pinned *that* one on him—stuck it on some other chump and then picked him up a year later on the armed-robbery rap in Raleigh. Yeah, Hank Biehn was smart enough to know that you only get one freebie in life, and he'd already used up his.

"Fuck it," he said, spitting into the underbrush. "Not my fault the kid didn't just give me the money."

And Hank Biehn walked on.

His plan was to make it to downtown Smithfield by Sunday morning—would check into a cheap motel and spend the rest of the day in his room drinking beer. Beer didn't stick in your pores the next day like the hard stuff, and so he'd be clean and ready to work come Monday morning. Spring was here, and they'd be hiring day laborers outside this little storefront near where Route 301 intersected with the center of town. Or at least he *hoped* they'd be hiring; he'd worked out of there before the gig in Lucama, and as far as he knew, nothing had changed in the last two years. Well, there'd be a different bunch of fucking Mexicans he'd have to work with, but as long as he kept his mouth shut and didn't smell like booze he should be fine. If they weren't hiring, well, something else would come along.

Something always did.

Back in the days when he was a professional walker, Hank Biehn learned very quickly that folks didn't like giving him a ride. Well, once he got inside and could talk his game they came around. It was just the getting-inside part that was the problem. He'd never been a looker, that's for sure. Kids used to call him "Weasel" back in the day, enough said. But that wasn't it. No, things were different now than before he went in. People nowadays were too uptight; fucked-up world, people paranoid, no one wanting to give a guy a break. Sad really, but simple as that.

And so Hank Biehn figured if he was going to have to walk, why not walk at night when it was cooler? Tomorrow was a Sunday to boot, and another thing Hank Biehn had learned since his parole was that Sundays were the worst days to try and hitch. Cops more likely to fuck with you on a Sunday, too. You'd think it'd be the opposite—people closer to God and whatnot—but for some reason that wasn't the case. Hank Biehn had never figured out why.

He shifted the duffel bag on his back and spit once more into the brush. He figured he had about four or five miles left on Route 301 before it crossed I-95, which meant at least another hour and a half of walking before he'd rest a spell with a nip by the highway. No use getting on the Interstate, though; would be around 2 a.m. at that point, and the chances of hitching a ride were slim anyway. Better if he stuck to 301 the whole way; probably another fifteen miles from there, which meant he'd make it into town for breakfast. Then he'd find a room, a case of beer (have to buy it after noon on a Sunday, fucking North Carolina!) and then a good night's sleep. Sounds like a plan.

Hank heard the car coming long before it reached him. It was quiet on 301. Only a handful of people were traveling at this hour, and all of them had passed by Hank Biehn without a second look. Fine with him. Wouldn't give them the satisfaction of sticking out his thumb for any of them anyway. Paranoid motherfuckers.

Maybe that's why, when he sensed the car slowing down behind him, he looked up from the road and stumbled a bit. Fucking old factory nerves.

"You need a ride, sir?" the driver asked. He'd rolled down the passenger side window, but Hank couldn't make out his face in the dark. Chevy van, 1970s, not a lot of light coming from the dash. "Heading down the Interstate way if you'd like a lift."

"I sure would," said Hank, approaching the door. "That's real kind of you, mister." He could see the man more clearly now—just a kid, mid-twenties and pretty built from the look of the arms on the steering wheel. Spoke with a heavy Southern drawl, too; all-American good ol' boy from the looks of it.

Hank pulled the door handle.

"Passenger door doesn't work," he said. "You gotta swing around back."

"Gotchya."

Maybe the booze had dulled his instincts over the years; maybe he'd been domesticated too long and gone all Pollyanna and shit, but Hank Biehn didn't give his good fortune a second thought as he skirted around to the rear of the van.

"It's unlocked," the kid called, and Hank opened the door. "Just leave your stuff back there and come on up front. Need a hand?"

"No, no, I got it," Hank said, hoisting his duffel bag inside. He climbed up after it, and was surprised to find the back of the van completely empty—just the grooved metal bed and the shell of the outer walls.

But what Hank Biehn didn't notice was the strong smell of Pine-Sol and the subtle yet palpable scent of rotten meat underneath.

Oh no, his old factory nerves were simply too shot to pick up on *that*.

What a good kid, Hank said to himself. *And here I am just thinking how the world's gone to shit. Weasel, your luck is changing!*

"You gotta make sure you slam that door tight," the kid said. "Latch doesn't work like it used to. Dang old-school Chevys."

"I heard that," Hank said. He was on all fours now, his back toward the driver as he pulled the door shut. It seemed to latch fine. But when he turned around again, he gasped when he discovered the driver was almost on top of him.

"What the—?"

"Your body is the doorway," the kid said.

Then he raised his gun and fired.

Chapter 12

Sam Markham stepped into his office on Monday morning feeling tired and helpless—like a dog that had been chasing its tail for days. He'd grown to despise this place—cramped, bare, with no windows and a single fluorescent light that fluttered sporadically above his head. He thought about the plaque in his bedroom back in Virginia, and was sorry he didn't bring it with him to hang over this, the gates of his own private hell.

Markham sat at his desk and turned on his computer—took a swig of coffee and replayed the last four days in his mind. It was all a blur to him, a soupy mishmash of dead ends and frustration. None of his leads had paid off—the interviews with the families, the Internet and library investigations, the connections between the victims, the ties to Islam and the lunar visuals. The forensic analysis turned out to be a wash, too—no leads on the materials, nothing new via Donovan. But worst of all, the FBI labs had come back with *nothing* on Jose Rodriguez. That's right, *no writing at all* had been found on him anywhere. Markham hadn't expected that.

Rodriguez was supposed to be reburied sometime today, and Donovan's funeral had been officially scheduled for Saturday. The same day as Elmer Stokes's execution.

His computer ready, Markham sighed and logged into Sentinel, the FBI's latest version of its case-management database. The Sentinel system had been active for less than a year, and Markham had to admit that it was better than the old Trilogy System—or "Tragedy System," as the SAs used to call it—but still he thought of it as an untrustworthy logistical pain in the ass.

Markham signed into the Sentinel file for Vlad. An agent from the National Center for the Analysis of Violent Crime (NCAVC) had finally entered the information about the killer's shoes: Merrell Stormfront Gore-Tex XCRs. Even weight distribution. Slight wear. 2004 model.

"You like to hike, Vlad?" Markham said out loud. "Or did you buy the Merrells because they're quiet on pavement?"

I have returned.

Markham signed out of Sentinel and clicked on a desktop icon he'd labeled as STARS. A Web site called Your Sky opened immediately. A physics professor at NC State had turned him on to the site, which enabled visitors to plug in coordinates, dates, and times to see what the stars looked like on any given night going back to the year 0. It had taken Markham hours of scrolling and clicking to get the hang of it; but over the last couple of days he'd become nothing short of obsessed.

"You messing with those star charts again, Captain Kirk?" Schaap said, leaning against the doorjamb. Markham nodded. "Anything new?"

"Spinning my wheels," Markham said. "Hundreds of individual stars that could've traveled across the Hispanics' field of vision during the time frame in which they were displayed. Bunch of constellations, too; never heard of most of them."

"What about the signs of the zodiac?"

"Looks like there are only four that would've passed over the eastern horizon: Taurus, Gemini, Cancer, and Leo. And that's if the Hispanics were looking directly east."

"Any connection to the historical Vlad?"

"None that I can see just yet. Most scholars agree that Vlad Tepes was born sometime in November or December of 1431, which would have made his astrological sign a Scorpio, Sagittarius, or a Capricorn."

"What about individual stars?"

"No specific stars have historically been associated with the symbol of Islam, but our astronomy consultant at NC State is working on tying one to Vlad."

Schaap was quiet, looking at the floor.

"I feel the same way," Markham said after a moment.

"What's that?"

"That I'm wasting my time. That I'm off on trying to find the star to go with the Islamic crescent; that maybe I'm off on the whole Vlad the Impaler angle, too."

"But if not Vlad, then who has returned?"

"I don't know," Markham said, turning back to his computer. "But whoever he is, I guarantee you he's laughing at us."

The day had been a waste, and later that evening, Markham found himself sitting atop the low fieldstone wall that surrounded the Willow Brook Cemetery. It was his sixth night in North Carolina, but only his third at the cemetery. He'd gotten lucky with the weather—nothing but clear skies since his arrival, which allowed him to divvy up his evenings between the two crime scenes. But as he looked toward the east, in his mind he told the stars he would not be coming back.

They answered him as they usually did—in apathetic

cricket-speak; all seeing, all knowing, and with a twinkle in their eyes that said, *"Who cares?"*

But Markham was not bothered tonight by their indifference. His mind had already shifted to Vlad the Impaler.

His return was just beginning. Rodriguez and Guerrera, Randall Donovan. There would be more to come. Markham was sure of it, was sure that Vlad would go looking for his next victim very soon if he already hadn't. So far the pattern looked as if he was into men; so far the pattern looked to be a murder every other month.

But somehow the latter didn't feel right in Markham's gut.

2006 is your comeback season, he said to himself. *So where's your calendar boy for March, Vlad? Or for January, for that matter?*

Why does it have to be a boy? a voice said in his head. *After all, you'll remember Vlad was an equal-opportunity impaler.*

There were only a handful of missing person reports around the Raleigh area for the last few months. Could one or maybe two of them be Vlad's? Schaap's team at the Resident Agency would begin looking into all that, but without bodies to go on, and without actual murder sites, they wouldn't be able to make a thorough investigation. And what was the point? Maybe none of them had to do with Vlad. Maybe Vlad only had time to get to three. Maybe there was something about the crescent moon for February and April that he was missing.

Christ, he felt desperate.

"Tell me what you know," Markham whispered.

But the stars only twinkled back with the eyes of Vlad himself.

There was no mercy them. None at all.

Chapter 13

The General unchained the drifter and let his naked body drop from the ceiling. He had been hanging upside down for almost a day and a half now—more than enough time for his veins to empty into the floor drain in the corner of the work-room.

The General had gutted the drifter and sawed off his head immediately upon his return to the farmhouse—sealed everything up in a garbage bag and buried it behind the old horse barn along with the remains of the first drifter. But the General hadn't had time to fully prepare the second drifter until now. His day-life at the university and the big push toward the opening of *Macbeth* was taking up a lot of his time. However, all that would change once *Macbeth* opened on Thursday. His role would then be complete and he'd be able to focus on the most important parts of the equation.

Then again, *Macbeth* was part of the equation, too. A template of 9:3 or 3:1, depending on how you looked at it. Just part of the formula encoded in Elizabethan doublespeak and secret messages. Shakespeare understood the equation of 3:1 back then. Three Witches, three prophecies, three spirits—lots of threes to the one general Macbeth. But whereas Shakespeare wrote his equations on paper, the Prince wrote his in the stars

3:1 or 9:3, depending on how you looked at it.

It was right there in the stars.

The workroom had an old slop sink and spigot, to which the General's grandfather had once upon a time attached a rubber hose. The General turned on the water and hosed off the remaining blood from the drifter's body. And when he was clean, he dragged him to the center of the room and patted him dry with a towel. Then the General picked up the drifter's corpse and carried it into the Throne Room.

The doorway was almost complete.

The General dressed the body in a set of white robes much like his own. He'd stolen them from the Harriot costume shop. Indeed, the Harriot theatre department had provided the General with everything he needed to accomplish his work. At first he thought he'd been drawn there because of his mother; thought he was following the path she would've taken had she lived. But soon after he landed the work-study job under Jennings, the General understood that he had been directed there by the Prince.

Yes, that was all part of the equation, too.

And when the drifter was ready, the General seated his headless body on the throne. The General had washed the robes and scrubbed down the throne itself with Pine-Sol, but the rotting stench of the first doorway still lingered. No matter. He had grown accustomed to it. After all, in order to be a general, one had to grow accustomed to the smell of death.

The General made the final touches on the drifter's position—posed his hands and draped his sleeves over the armrests—and when he was satisfied, he slid the shelf back into place. The shelf was painted gold, too, and fit seamlessly into a slot in the back of the throne. Attached to the front of the shelf was a wooden panel onto which the General had carved a pair of doors. And once in place, the entire unit fit over the drifter's torso like a pair of golden shoulder pads.

All the body needed now was its head.

That had been one of the messages he discovered in *Macbeth*—perhaps, one could argue, *the most important* of all the messages—but the General only recognized it a few months ago, after he was asked to design the trap for the set. The trap that opened into Hell.

Macbeth's message about the head was actually pretty obvious if you knew what to look for. An *armed Head* is how the First Apparition is described—which, of course, was Shakespeare's depiction of the Prince, the greatest of all warrior-generals. The armed Head is one of only three apparitions that actually *speak* to Macbeth. Thus, the General thought, it was the speaking that was most important—the High Risk/Clone Six song made that clear in the lyric, *"You thought you heard me speak."* The Witches themselves speak to Macbeth in threes, but Macbeth was too stupid to understand, so anything pertaining to the actual plot of the play was of little consequence, the General thought. There were no messages in the plot. Plot was part of the smoke screen that obscured the real messages.

Yes, the messages lay in the factor of three itself. That was the equation; that was the formula as written in the stars. 9:3 or 3:1.

The armed Head then had to be the Prince as he was now—weakened, still spirit—and thus the General would need a real head to communicate with him before his return was complete.

The Second Apparition that speaks to Macbeth is described as *a bloody child*. That one was easy, the General thought. The bloody child was the General himself—the three to the nine or the one to the three, depending on how you wanted to look at it.

And the Third Apparition? A child crowned with a tree in

his hand? That one was easy to decipher, too. That was the Prince holding the tree of life. That was the Prince resurrected.

After all, it was the words of Shakespeare's Third Apparition that convinced the General that he had read the messages correctly.

Be lion-mettled, proud, and take no care
Who chafes, who frets, or where conspirers are.

Be lion-mettled . . .

Yes, everything was clear if you understood the equation. The General had known for a long time that the body was the doorway, but once he understood that he needed a head for the Prince to speak, the only question that remained was, *"Whose head?"*

The answer came to him almost immediately.

And now, months later, as he placed the Prince's head atop the shelf and stepped back to admire the completion of the doorway, the General cracked a smile when he remembered the first time the Prince spoke to him.

But there was little time for nostalgia.

The doorway was now open again.

It was time for the Prince to speak.

But more important, it was time for the General to listen.

Chapter 14

The reason Otis Gurganus always got the big bucks wasn't because his family owned some of the best hunting grounds in North Carolina, but because he prepared long in advance. In the spring, usually five months to the day before bow season began in September. Oh yeah, the monsters—the fourteen-pointers and bigger—didn't get that way by being stupid.

Sure, you had to know your enemy; had to know the lay of the land and the habits of the deer that lived there. But for Otis Gurganus, it all came down to preseason scouting: finding out food sources and watering holes; setting up a stand in the trees just the right distance from their bedding areas; getting settled at least a couple of hours before sundown or sunup. Commonsense stuff, but a delicate operation nonetheless. He knew from experience that the biggest bucks bedded alone and came out looking for food later than the others. Yeah, nowadays, he didn't waste his time with anything less than a twelve-pointer with a twenty-eight-inch spread; always left the smaller ones for other hunters to keep the kill stats for his lodge high.

Gurganus hunted with a bow. Nowadays, he thought, the

big bucks, the *record breakers*, would only get bagged with
a bow. They weren't stupid enough to stick around or con-
gregate with other deer once they started hearing gunshots.
Gurganus was still the record holder for the biggest buck
bagged in North Carolina: a behemoth of a twenty-two-
pointer that he nailed broadside from twenty-five yards just
after his thirtieth birthday. That was almost ten years ago,
but Gurganus knew his next and biggest buck was close;
might even bag him this coming season if he was lucky.

The hunter stepped out of his pickup truck, flicked on his
night-vision goggles, and headed out into the woods. He had
been using the NVGs now for years and almost creamed his
pants two Christmases ago when his wife gave him the new-
fangled GPS calculator. Wasn't a cheap gift, either. Cost his
wife over four hundred dollars, and cost him almost a whole
week of nonstop boning her. But Gurganus never really got
the hang of the GPS calculator until the following summer,
when he started documenting deer activity and plotting it on
his son's computer. It paid off in spades for him this past season, even though he didn't bag his next record breaker.

Tonight, however, he didn't carry along his GPS calculator. No, on this, the first night of his preseason scouting, all
the hunter had with him were his NVGs and his .45-caliber
Sig Sauer. You couldn't be too careful all alone in the woods
at night; never know when you might come across something unfriendly, a rogue bear from the western part of the
state or a pack of hungry coyotes.

But Otis Gurganus didn't plan on using his gun tonight.
No, tonight was all about listening; about sitting up in last
season's stands and getting a sense of movement. He had not
been out in his woods for over three months now, but he
would not kill any deer with his bow until September. Just
like everybody else.

Yeah, Otis Gurganus always played by the rules.

The stand was only about three hundred yards into the

woods and was situated at the edge of a large clearing that the hunter knew would be peppered with spring clover. And he made good time—got there at exactly 3:30 a.m. and had set-tled himself comfortably in the tree five minutes later. He'd not heard any deer running away from him while stealing through the woods; hadn't seen them with his night vision, either. But that didn't mean they weren't around—especially the big bucks, who never gave up their positions unless they were sure they'd been spotted.

Gurganus hadn't been in his stand long when his NVGs picked up something strange. The goggles were only rated for detail to about a hundred yards, but, whatever the thing was, the hunter could tell it was closer than that—just at the opposite edge of the clearing. It looked like an oddly shaped tree trunk, but for some reason Gurganus couldn't take his eyes off it. Had it been closer to the season, had he dumped a pile of corn in the clearing to attract the deer as he'd done when he shot his record breaker ten years ago, well, he might've waited until after daylight before climbing down to investigate.

But tonight, so early in the off-season, with the woods so still and no sign of any deer activity at all, Otis Gurganus's curiosity got the better of him. And in no time he was back down the tree and heading across the clearing. He'd traveled only a few yards when his goggles finally registered what he'd been unable to put together from his stand. The sight of it stopped him dead in his tracks.

The oddly shaped tree looked like a man—a skinny green man leaning against a pole.

"Hey!" Gurganus called out impulsively. "This is private property!"

No response—only the sound of his own voice disappear-ing into the woods—and suddenly he felt his cheeks go hot; felt a flash of anger in his stomach as he reached down for his Sig Sauer and began running across the field.

But as he drew closer and the skinny green man became clearer, Otis Gurganus's fury quickly turned to terror. The skinny green man was not leaning against the pole. No, the pole was running up through the middle of his body—through his ass and out his shoulder! His legs were missing below the knees—made him look as if he was floating in the trees—and somewhere in the back of Otis Gurganus's mind flashed a clip from some zombie movie he'd seen as a kid back in the eighties.

The skinny green man smiled back at him—mouth open, teeth bared, the lips pulled back or missing altogether. Someone had tied the guy's head to the pole so that he appeared to be gazing down and to his left. His eye sockets, however, were empty; his eyeballs and his nose gone. *Breakfast for crows,* Gurganus thought in numb horror.

His heart was pounding wildly now; and standing there, staring up at the shriveled corpse not five feet away from him, Otis Gurganus suddenly felt a hot wetness running down the inside of his thigh. He registered it absently, as if it were happening to someone else. And years later, when he would tell this story to his grandchildren, more than coming upon a dead body all alone in the middle of the woods, the old man would swear that what *really* made him piss his pants was the glowing white symbols on the trespasser's rotting torso.

Chapter 15

He is on a spaceship that looks like his bed at his parents' house—is speeding through a ceiling of pasted plastic stars toward a fuzzy planet in the distance. He is almost there now—feels as if he can reach out and touch the yellow glow-in-the-dark circle through the windshield.

Then a message flashes on the console. The fuel gauge— STUPID FUCK! *it says in bright orange letters—and he understands.*

"This is the wrong planet!" he says, panicking. "I'll have to switch to impulse power!" He flicks some switches and presses some buttons when suddenly another message starts flashing—this time across the windshield:

DEFLECTOR SHIELDS DOWN—COME ON, BALBOA!

"I'm going to burn up on entry!" he says as the theme from Rocky *comes over the loudspeaker. The cabin is on fire and a heavy sinking feeling overpowers him as the flames lick up at his elbows. "Mayday! Mayday!" he wants to say, but the com-link is gone and the controls come off in his*

hands. I'm not going to make it, *he thinks, and all at once his burning spaceship brightens* . . . into the light of his bedside lamp—the theme from *Rocky* blaring away from his BlackBerry on the nightstand.

He'd fallen asleep while working.

Groggily, Markham reached for his BlackBerry, but his fingers weren't awake yet and he knocked it to the floor. He lay there for a moment, unsure of where he was until the missed-call ding brought him back to life—pissed him off and rolled him over. He found his laptop on the bed beside him; wiped off the screen saver and saw the time in the lower right hand corner: 7:15 a.m.

The ding of a voice mail came from somewhere on the floor to his left, and suddenly he realized he couldn't remember what he'd been dreaming about. Only a vague sense of anxiety and bright yellow helplessness.

Then the ring of the landline startled him. He answered it.

"Hello?"

"It's Schaap."

"Jesus, what—"

"I'm on my way to your apartment now. Get dressed and meet me out front as soon as you can."

"What's going on?"

"They found another body. Out in the boonies about fifty miles northeast of Raleigh. Bird's already being puddle-jumped from Fort Bragg as we speak. We go airborne in twenty minutes."

Chapter 16

In no time a black Bell Huey II had whisked Markham and his team from a nearby heliport, sped them through the North Carolina skies at 120 knots, and touched them down in Otis Gurganus's field just after 9:00 a.m. A storm was almost upon them, and the pilot had warned that the landing would be tight—ended up having to circle the small clearing twice to accommodate for the wind and to allow time for the state police helicopter to clear out.

During the flight, Schaap brought Markham up to date on what the FBI knew so far: the circumstances surrounding the discovery of the body, the preliminary time line of the murder, the similarities to the other victims, and the length of time the body had been exposed to the elements. They had a good idea who the guy was—had already laid some ground-work in conjunction with the missing person reports from February—but Markham didn't need any database to tell him that the victim had been out in the woods since the first crescent moon of March.

From the air, he'd not been able to see him; only the blue tarp and the half-dozen or so state troopers surrounding it.

And once they were on the ground, as the FBI agents approached from the Huey, the troopers, like children in a schoolyard, formed a curtain in front of the crime scene—held down their hats against the wind from the propellers and stared back defiantly, as if to say, *"Red Rover, Red Rover, don't you* dare *come over!"*

"Who's in charge here?" Schaap hollered.

"I am," a voice hollered back, and a tall man with a red face and a lump of chew beneath his lower lip stepped forward. "Sergeant Powell," he added. "You boys got your fingers deep in this one, don't you?"

Markham and Schaap held up their ID badges, introduced themselves, and thanked the state troopers as the Huey's propellers winded to a stop. The forensic team sprang into action, and the line of state troopers reluctantly broke apart.

Sergeant Powell looked annoyed.

"I've already secured the site, goddammit," he said. "Fucker's been out here for over a month it looks like. You boys ain't gonna find nothing that the animals ain't already dragged away."

"You've established a perimeter on the nearest access roads?" Schaap asked.

"How the hell you think we got in here?"

"I don't have time to get in a pissing contest with you, Powell," Schaap said. "All right with you then if my men have some room?"

Markham suppressed a smile as the red-faced trooper spat and signaled for his men to move away. Finally, the FBI agents had a clear view of what was waiting for them beneath the tarp.

"Jesus Christ," Schaap said amid the clicks and flashes from the forensic cameras.

The corpse was little more than a skeleton and appeared

to be impaled up through the rectum. The victim was male, Markham could tell, but his genitalia had been torn away, and his legs were missing below the knees. The rest of the body was intact—shriveled, hairless, the flesh mostly gone, and what little of it remained looked tanned and dried like leather. The victim's head was still lashed to the stake, the nose an open triangle, the hollow eye sockets gazing downward in what was not their original position. The head had moved as the body decomposed. And had it not been for the little crossbar under the victim's groin, the man with the tattoos and the missing pecker would have slid all the way down to the ground.

"Word's been on the wire for some time now about who you feds're looking for," Powell said, spitting. "Same guy who spiked 'em in Raleigh, I reckon."

"Same guy," Schaap said absently.

Markham stepped under the tarp, donned a pair of rubber gloves, and removed a small flashlight from his Windbreaker. He slowly circled the corpse, shining his light as close as he could on the victim's arms without touching them.

"All them tattoos," said Powell. "He's got one on the back of his head, too. Skin is covered in them. What's left of it, anyway. Looks like the animals got to him soon after your boy spiked him. More woulda been gone if he wasn't hanging like that. Dried him out quicker, I suppose. Tats will make it easier to ID him. Looks like the fella in the database. Kept his head shaved, it says, so whatever hair's there grew in after he disappeared. Prolly some after he died, too."

Markham held his light on the victim's sunken chest and studied the yellowed symbols for a long time.

A rumble of thunder in the distance.

The skies were darkening.

It would rain soon.

"He took the time to thoroughly bleach these out," Markham said finally. "The symbols are larger. Wrote only one line of each language, too."

"You mean them white marks is some kind of writing?" Powell asked.

"Yes."

"What's it mean?"

Markham clicked off his flashlight and turned back to the trooper, stone-faced.

"It means he's getting better."

Chapter 17

Two hours later Markham sat alone at his laptop, the rain beating heavily on the hunting-lodge roof as he studied the driver's license picture on the screen before him. The profile had been forwarded to him by the NC State Police. The guy had been on their missing persons list since mid-February.

William "Billy" Canning: thirty-eight, local boy originally from Smithfield, owner of a tattoo parlor in Cary—Billy's, it was called. No criminal record, last seen on February fifteenth by his lover Stefan Dorsey. Keyword search in the missing persons database brought up a description of the tattoos. They were a perfect match to the markings on the corpse. The body had already been airlifted to Raleigh; would have an official ID in less than an hour and then it was off to Quantico for analysis.

The handle on the outside door rattled, and Markham looked up to find Andy Schaap entering with his jacket over his head. He plopped a stack of rain-stained papers on the table and sat down in one of the big chairs.

"Those are the only records he's got," Schaap said. "Disorganized, takes cash mostly. Got a feeling there's nothing there."

Markham glanced briefly at the papers as his partner sunk deeper into his chair. Schaap slipped off his ring and began rolling it between his fingers.

"Sixteen," he said, his eyes fixed on the large deer head above the fireplace. "That's a big one. Sixteen points. You have to go by the spread, too—the distance between the antlers. Never understood the appeal of it—killing a beautiful animal like that. Wonder where they go when it rains. Raining like a bitch out there now."

"Gurganus tell you anything else?" Markham asked. "Talk about any hunters who acted strange while they were here?"

"No one he could single out specifically."

"His kid give you anything?"

Schaap shook his head and began bouncing his ring on the arm of the chair. Markham rose and went to the window—gazed out past the line of black FBI vehicles and into the woods.

"You really think he's been here before?" Schaap asked.

"Yes, I do. Easy enough to get lost out there during the day unless you know exactly where you're headed."

"But why go through the trouble of lugging the body all the way up here when he could find other places with easier access?"

"There's the rub," Markham said, turning. "This spot is pretty far out from Raleigh. That's quite unusual, isn't it? Serial killers like Vlad—the organized, visionary types of high intelligence—they usually don't stray this far from home. Usually like to hunt and dump in an area they know well."

"We know from Donovan that Vlad kept him alive for a few days. His vocal folds were fried. Indicates he'd been screaming a lot before he was killed. Vlad had to have kept him somewhere where the neighbors wouldn't hear. Someplace remote."

"And we know Canning disappeared sometime during the evening of February fifteenth to the sixteenth, which means Vlad had to hang on to him for over two weeks before he dropped him off here. That is, if he stuck to the crescent-moon visual."

"Jesus," Schaap said, slipping the ring back on his finger. "The body would've already been badly decomposed if he killed him in the same time frame as Donovan. You think there's a possibility that Vlad kept him alive for all that time?"

"The hair growth would point to yes, but we won't know for sure until the autopsy. The body has been out in the woods for over a month, but Quantico should be able to approximate the time of death, and whether or not Vlad put him on ice."

"This Canning is from Cary," Schaap said. "Same as Randall Donovan."

"Right. Canning was last seen on surveillance footage at a nearby gas station at around seven o'clock p.m. His car was found by his boyfriend outside his tattoo studio at eleven o'clock the next morning. If we work from the premise that Vlad lives closer to Cary than he does here, then the question becomes not only what links Canning to the other victims but also what links the actual places where the victims were impaled. A link that goes beyond their remoteness and a clear view of the nighttime sky."

"What do you mean?"

"The fact that Vlad was determined to dispose of Canning way out here where there's a good chance no one would find him for a long time tells me we're dealing with someone who doesn't care about us."

"Us?"

"You, me, the public. If you'll recall, in addition to being a demented sadist, the reason Vlad Tepes impaled his victims was because he wanted others to see them; wanted to strike fear in the hearts of his people and send a message to his enemies. If our boy thought he was Vlad the Third reincarnated, why wouldn't he have displayed Canning someplace where he was sure the public would find him? Furthermore, why wouldn't he have written the message on Donovan so it was visible to the naked eye?"

"But what about the message on Canning? That was visible to the naked eye. Even after all this time."

"Right. But maybe that's because Vlad didn't expect us to find Canning so soon. Maybe the bleaching on Canning's chest was unintentional. Maybe he didn't get it right until Donovan."

"So you think he impaled Canning all the way out here to hide him from us? To hide him but at the same keep to his crescent-moon schedule?"

"I don't know."

"Canning was a known homosexual," Schaap said after a moment. "Which means he fits the historical Vlad's victim profile just like the others do. Donovan, the crooked lawyer. The Hispanics, the drug-dealing gangbangers. Killing them is a message in and of itself, don't you think?

"Yes."

"But, this Canning being a homosexual—you think maybe we missed something with the other three men? Think there's a possibility that Donovan or the Hispanics might have had some kind of secret lifestyle?"

"I thought about that, yes; will explore that angle when we get back to Raleigh."

"Then, that could mean that the killer's fixation with staking his victims through the rectum—are you thinking what I'm thinking?"

"That our man might be a gay basher? The impalement, a deranged representation of male-on-male sodomy?"

"If you want to put it that way, yes."

"Who knows? There's no evidence that Randall Donovan was a homosexual. However, do I think he could've had some kind of secret lifestyle? Yes, I do."

"Well, regardless what team these guys played for, Vlad's sending a message to someone."

"I agree. But I think that's where we're getting off track."

"The connection to the Islamic crescent moon and star, you mean? The Arabic, the ancient Middle Eastern scripts and all that?"

"Yes. The impalements seem to me now to be entirely self-centered. Purpose-driven in their methodological detail, yes, but important only to Vlad and whatever he thinks is seeing him from the sky. And the locations where he leaves his victims matter just as much. But only to him."

"But the victims are supposed to see whatever's in the sky, too."

"That's right."

"Then do you think the phrase 'I have returned' could also mean Vlad's return to the murder sites? To those locales specifically?"

"It's possible, yes."

"That would make it much more personal," Schaap said. "And much more difficult to figure out the reason behind the murders."

Markham shrugged.

"But even if Vlad has been here before," Schaap said, "how the hell could he have found his way out there in the dark?"

"The dirt access road. He obviously knew about it."

"But still, he'd have to know exactly where to stop. I mean, I suppose he could've Google Earthed it; plotted the coordinates and used GPS and night vision like Gurganus does. At the very least he'd have to have a map. Never mind lugging a body three hundred yards and sticking him in the ground."

Markham was about to speak, then stopped.

"What is it?" Schaap asked.

Markham walked over to his laptop, minimized the Billy Canning file, and clicked on the Your Sky icon. "Maybe he *is* using a map after all."

"The stars, you mean?"

"I'm not sure," Markham said, staring at the Web page. "But I think we need to get back to the RA immediately."

Chapter 18

The General awoke after 10 a.m., but he was still tired. The Prince had kept him up late talking the night before. It had been a while since they'd communicated so openly, and they had a lot of catching up to do.

The General was used to rising before dawn, upon which he would work out in the old horse barn before heading off to Greenville—hundreds of push-ups and sit-ups and chin-ups, along with lifting some old cinder blocks that his grandfather had left in there. The barn was big enough for him to park his van inside, too. And on Mondays, Wednesdays, and Fridays he would open up the van's back doors and do reverse tricep presses off the rear of the inside bed. And when he was finished with that portion of his training, he would sprint back and forth across the barren tobacco fields until he could sprint no more.

He needed the strength of a warrior, sure; but he also needed the speed if his body was to be worthy of a second in command.

The General had placed an old quartz heater in the barn (which warmed him just fine if he stood right in front of it), but the sprinting could be dangerous in the winter. One time, just before Christmas, the General had actually rolled his ankle on a patch of ice. That had put him out of commission for almost two weeks, but even so the General still looked forward to his training.

It was an important part of the equation.

Of course, it would've made much more sense to work out in the cellar, but there was not enough room down there now that everything had been dedicated to the Prince. And then there was the attic, but even after all these years the General didn't like going up there. Besides, the Prince had indicated that he was saving the attic for something *really special*.

Today was Tuesday, and even though he would not have to do his tricep presses or his sprints, the General entered the horse barn feeling behind. He didn't bother turning on the heater and went straight for the chin-up bar that he'd installed between the beams of one of the horse stalls. The General had also hung a mirror on the stall's back wall so he could watch himself as he did his chin-ups.

The barn smelled wonderful this morning, the General thought as he took off his shirt. Like Pine-Sol. He had washed down the inside of the van before parking it inside the barn—left the back doors open so the inside would dry—and the clean, fresh scent seemed to permeate everything. He made a mental note to do that from now on, after he transported the impaled to the sites of sacrifice. He wouldn't need to hunt any more drifters on Route 301. True, the doorways lasted for three months—that was part of the 9:3—but the General already had the final doorway. The one through which the Prince would return in the flesh, the one through which the General would become spirit.

The General grasped the cold steel bar—paused briefly to admire his muscular torso—and then began his chin-ups.

He moved quickly but methodically. There was a lot to do

today—both at the farmhouse and later this afternoon with the rehearsal at Harriot. His other self, the young man named Edmund Lambert, would not go to class today. In fact, Edmund Lambert would stop going to classes from now on altogether. That was one of the things he and the Prince had discussed the night before. There was no need to keep up that part of his day-life now.

No, by the time the registrar's office caught up with him and notified Jennings that his work-study boy had been slacking, Edmund Lambert and the General would have no need of Harriot University and its theatre department.

The doorway in the mirror before him told him that.

Chapter 19

Schaap sat next to Markham at his desk, both of them studying the computer and nursing their coffee. The pressure behind Markham's eyes was back, and the little trick of flinging the bright red ball wasn't working for him today. Then again, had he been alone, he might've been able to concentrate better.

"It's impossible to get the coordinates exactly right," Schaap said with a mouthful of donut. "The computer program at Quantico will take care of adjusting the margin of error. Same program we used to establish the pattern in that long-haul-trucker case last year. They should be getting back to us within the hour."

Markham said nothing—tapped a couple of keys, and the map of Raleigh on the computer grew larger. He then superimposed on the screen a tracing he'd made of the constellation Leo—kept rotating it until two of the stars lined up with the murder sites in Clayton and Cary. He held it there for a moment, then, dissatisfied, discarded it for another tracing—this one of the constellation Cancer.

"But if I follow you," Schaap said, "you're thinking the phrase 'I have returned' could correlate to some cosmic occurrence that happens only once in a great while—like every thousand years or something?"

"Maybe not that long, but yes."

"Then 'I have returned' could also mean a return to visibility, just like Vlad literally returning to the murder sites?"

"Just a hunch," Markham said. "The return of which Vlad speaks could be taken as some kind of second coming—a resurrection, a rebirth if you will—that is governed by a pattern in the stars. There may be something going on up there—trajectories, alignments of planets, and what have you—that Vlad is interpreting as a herald, as sign of his second coming. Our astronomy consultant at NC State hasn't gotten back to me yet; and because of my limited knowledge on the subject, the most logical place for me to begin is with the zodiac—constellations that are seasonal and are most commonly associated with birth. There are a bunch of other constellations that could be candidates, too, but I simply don't know how they relate to the grand scheme of things."

"But why a constellation and not just a single star? An alignment of planets or something?"

"Because of the murder sites and how they plot out on the map. They are specific, a pattern on the ground that mimics how one draws pictures in the sky. In order to get the right picture one has to use the right stars. Almost like a massive game of connect the dots—a game that perhaps makes sense only to Vlad, but nonetheless can be understood if you see things through his eyes. The return of whatever is happening in the sky corresponds somehow to the return of whatever is happening on the ground."

"You don't think the murder sites themselves could line up with the stars of one of these constellations?"

"It's possible," Markham said, rotating the tracing. "But now that I look at everything on the map, I'm thinking that scenario is unlikely. Too easy to establish the pattern; would be like Vlad sending us an invitation where to meet him on the night of the crescent moon. I'm still going to try to weed out the major spring constellations, but I'm more apt to believe now that he's making his own constellation, his own return—a picture on the ground that mimics a dynamic in the sky but at the same time is deeply personal."

Schaap was silent—began fiddling with his ring, thinking.

"Christ, I don't know," Markham said. "But if you look at the stars as long as I have—and, I submit, as long as Vlad has—well, you can't help but see patterns all over the place. Hard not to connect the dots and make your own pictures."

"Well," Schaap said, rising, "I'll let you play. Be in my cell if you need me."

Markham nodded, and Schaap left. He rotated the constellation Cancer one last time and crumpled it into the trash. He leaned on his desk—closed his eyes and rubbed his forehead.

He was irritated—not because Schaap was right that he was wasting his time—but because he knew there was a link to the murder sites that was just beyond his reach. It was the same for the crescent-moon visual. He was off with the Vlad the Impaler angle. He could feel it. The messages on the bodies, the ancient scripts were just as much for something in the heavens as it was for something here on the earth. Billy Canning proved this.

Markham looked at his watch. Schaap's team had already questioned Canning's lover, Stefan Dorsey, this afternoon—

had most likely finished their sweep of the tattoo parlor, too—but Markham would need to question Dorsey himself. Would also need to spend some time at the tattoo parlor and see if anything spoke to him. But what could he possibly find there? Tattoos on the walls as numerous as the stars themselves?

Get off the stars, he said to himself. *Focus on the victims. Quit theorizing for now and get back to the facts, the things you know for sure.*

Markham stared at the map of Raleigh on his computer screen—thumbed his mouse and scrolled it over to the right, centering the map on Cary. He zoomed in. Canning was from Cary. So was Randall Donovan. Canning was a homosexual. But was Randall Donovan? And what about Rodriguez and Guerrera?

Randall Donovan. Schaap had questioned his wife again over the weekend, and the FBI had already analyzed the lawyer's computers and combed through his files. Found nothing unusual, but now, with the discovery of Canning and this possible wrinkle in Vlad's victim profile, he would need to speak to Randall Donovan's wife himself.

Yes, he thought, if he could establish that Donovan was a homosexual, he would know where to begin again with Rodriguez and Guerrera. If Vlad turned out to be some kind of gay basher, one might be able to narrow down where the bastard would go looking for his next victim. Not to mention, if he could figure out Vlad's game of connect the dots, he might also be able to narrow down where he intended to *display* him.

Markham turned off his computer and gathered his things, gulped down the last of his coffee, and turned off his office light. Tracy Donovan had been through a lot, he knew. Was devastated, from what Schaap told him. The lawyer's body had just been shipped back from Quantico, and the funeral arrangements were in full swing. Maybe he should wait a day or two before implying her husband could've been killed because he was a homosexual.

"I don't have time for courtesy," he muttered as he was leaving. "And neither does Vlad."

Chapter 20

Markham identified himself and was buzzed through the gate. He followed the driveway around a clump of trees and up to the house—one of those large, plantation-style repros with big white columns and lots of land surrounding it. The storm from the hunting lodge had followed him back to Raleigh, but through the rain he could make out someone sitting on the porch smoking.

It was Tracy Donovan. He recognized her blond hair and the trendy pink tracksuit from the countless family photos he'd sifted through the week before.

Markham parked his TrailBlazer at the end of a line of cars. There'd be no calling hours for Randall Donovan this week, Schaap had told him—only a small, private funeral for the lawyer's family and closest friends. That was smart, Markham thought. The scumbags this guy dealt with, who knows who might show up?

Markham felt beneath the seats for his umbrella—he was sure he'd brought one—and when he didn't find it, he exited the TrailBlazer with his briefcase over his head, ran across the soggy lawn, and bounded up the steps to the porch. Tracy

Donovan didn't move, didn't even draw from her cigarette, but only tracked him with her eyes as if his presence was inevitable to her.

"All those movies," she said finally. "I never asked myself why the FBI always shows up unannounced. You have that look about you. Like the others. Unannounced."

Markham pegged her to be in her mid-thirties; knew from her pictures that she had been quite attractive before her husband's disappearance—athletic, blond, blue-eyed with nice skin. But now she looked old and haggard; her dry hair pulled back like bundled straw, her face pale and blotchy with hollow red eyes.

The ashtray beside her was overflowing with cigarette butts.

"Forgive me, ma'am," Markham said. He shook off his briefcase and showed his ID, gave her the standard intro, and was invited to sit down. The rain was blowing from behind the house, the porch entirely dry.

"The children are inside," she said. "They're old enough to know what's going on, so I'll ask you like I asked the others to keep your voice down. The reporters—were there any outside the front gate?"

"No. They're still bothering you?"

"Since day one. But we've got our cameras on them, too. There's one by the gate, hidden in the topiaries. I bet you didn't see that now, did you?"

"No, I didn't."

"I take it my sister only let you in because she could tell you weren't one of them. She doesn't bother me with all that anymore. Been everything to me and the kids during all this. You've read those stories they printed about Randy? Calling him dirty and corrupt; lying down with dogs and getting up with fleas—that kind of thing?"

"Yes, I did. And I'm sorry that your family has to go through this. Truly, I am."

Tracy Donovan snuffed her cigarette and lit another. Markham noticed the blisters between her index and middle fingers. She'd been letting the cigarettes burn down to her skin—intentionally or unintentionally, he wasn't sure.

"You know," she exhaled, "Randy came from nothing. He grew up in Providence, Rhode Island, in a working-class district made up of Italians mostly—all of them suspicious of anyone who didn't have a vowel at the end of his name. There was this kid who used to pick on Randy in elementary school. Some punk from a broken home who didn't make it past the eighth grade. Made my husband's life miserable. Long story short, this guy grows up to be a small-time hood, gets busted on a narcotics rap, and is looking at twenty years minimum. But as fate would have it, guess who ends up being his attorney all those years later? That's right. Randy's first case with the public defender's office. Scumbag didn't remember Randy, but Randy remembered him. Most people you'd think would still hold a grudge, but not Randy. No, he did everything he could to get him a lighter sentence. Even kept tabs on him after he was paroled. That was Randy. Main thing for him was that everybody got a fair shake, no matter who you were. Didn't read about that little story in the newspapers, now did you?"

Markham told her about the discovery of Billy Canning—showed her his picture, explained the details of the murder, and said that it was only a matter of time before the press got wind of the story.

"I don't know if he's connected to my husband, if that's what you're getting at."

"Not exactly," Markham said.

"Then what?"

"I know you've been questioned a lot since your husband's disappearance, but I'd like to ask you a few questions about your marriage. Specifically, about your sex life with your husband."

Tracy Donovan smiled, but Markham noticed her hand begin to tremble, the smoke rising from her cigarette in thin, white squiggles.

"The police and the FBI already asked me that. And I'll tell you what I told them. Randy would never cheat. All of you wasting your time searching for love letters, for shady dealings on his computers when you should've been out looking for his—"

She stopped—took a long drag off her cigarette and exhaled slowly. "Only thing they found," she said after a moment, "were Internet records of some porn sites. No scandalous e-mails or pictures, no evidence of an affair or shady dealings with Colombian cartels out to kill him. Nothing you wouldn't find on any other forty-five-year-old, devoted father of two's computer."

"That's not quite what I wanted to ask you," Markham said. "But since you brought up the investigation of your husband's Internet activity, did the authorities mention what types of porn sites he was visiting?"

"What do you mean?"

"Did they indicate to you whether the sites were straight or gay?"

Tracy Donovan leveled her eyes at him—raised a trembling hand to her lips and took a drag off her cigarette. The ash needed to be tapped, but she ignored it.

"Special Agent Markham," she began slowly. "Are you asking me if I think my husband was a closet homosexual?"

"Billy Canning, the man we found up north, was a known homosexual. I don't know yet about Rodriguez and Guerrera, but we're trying to establish a connection between the killer's victims—a profile of the types of men Vlad likes to hunt."

Tracy Donovan smiled thinly.

"It just keeps getting better, doesn't it?" she said, her eyes beginning to well.

"Please forgive me for the line of questioning, but so far the FBI can find nothing to tie all four of the victims together other than a loose parallel to the victims of the historical Vlad Tepes. We're just trying to explore every avenue. Perhaps something we might have missed up front."

"Randy and I had quite an active sex life," Tracy Donovan said after a moment. "At least compared to what the girls at the country club tell me about their husbands. Usually two or three times a week. There are some DVDs back at the house in his top dresser. After Amber was born, we went through a bit of a dry spell, and it was Randy who suggested that we watch the DVDs to spice things up. All guy-girl stuff with the obligatory lesbian scenes thrown in for good measure. It seemed to do the trick; he was really into them at first and always got off pretty quickly. But we hadn't watched them in years. No need to, quite frankly. No, in the last few years Randy was, well, pretty randy, if you'll forgive the pun. Does that satisfy you?"

"And never once in your relationship did you ever suspect your husband might be a homosexual? Might be having an affair with another man, perhaps?"

"Randy was very neat around the house," she said dryly. "Was a snappy dresser and did sing the occasional show tune. He even teared up the first time he watched Disney's *Tarzan* with the kids—the part where Tarzan's ape mother dies. So I guess you're right. A raging queen my husband was, yes."

Markham looked away into the rain, and Tracy Donovan took another drag from her cigarette—let the ash fall on her bosom and absently brushed it away.

"For the record," she said after a heavy silence. "I loved being married to Randall Donovan. He was a good husband, a good father who always made time for his family." Her voice began to break. "He didn't deserve what happened to him, no matter what you and the fucking press might think."

Another woman with blond hair stepped out onto the porch. Tracy Donovan's sister. Markham recognized her from the photos.

"You all right, T?" she asked. "Anything I can get you?"

Her sister shook her head, snuffed her cigarette into the ashtray, and stood up.

"I have family inside," Tracy Donovan said. "The funeral is on Saturday. All I ask is that you let us alone until then to grieve in peace."

She made to leave, then stopped at the front door and turned back.

"One more thing," she said. "If it's your intention to slander my husband's name in the press any further, I suggest you think twice before leveling accusations about his private life in public. Randall Donovan wasn't the only Donovan in this family to pass the bar in North Carolina."

The women disappeared inside—slammed the front door loudly and left Sam Markham alone on the porch with only the rain for company.

Chapter 21

Markham hung up with Schaap and parked his Trail-Blazer in the loading area behind the shopping plaza. He sat there for a moment, eyes closed, listening to the rain. Schaap had just told him the results from Quantico had come back negative; no discernable correlation between the constellations and the coordinates of the murder sites. There were patterns that jibed between individual stars, but that was to be expected, Markham thought. Schaap would forward everything to their man at NC State, of course, but Markham felt in his gut that it was all just another dead end. Just like Tracy Donovan. Either she was totally clueless, he thought, or her husband was not a homosexual.

Markham opened his eyes, took a deep breath, and made a dash for the back door of the tattoo parlor—BILLY'S, someone had written on it in black Magic Marker. Driving through the parking lot, he'd noticed a Chinese restaurant at the opposite end of the shopping plaza. He could smell it now through the rain, and promised himself he'd get something to eat there later. He was starving, hadn't eaten a thing all day—

Anything but beef teriyaki, said a voice in his head. *You've had enough skewered meat to last you a lifetime, eh Sammy boy?*

Markham sighed and inserted the key into the lock. It was sticky, and he had to turn it a couple of times before the door finally gave. He stepped inside, felt for the light switch, and flicked it. He was in the back office. Homicide had removed all the business records and some other evidence the month before, but turned everything over (including the key) to the FBI upon the positive ID from Canning's lover. The business records were scarce, but Schaap's team would take care of the follow-up. That part of the investigation wouldn't take long. There simply wasn't much to look at.

Markham gave the office a quick once-over and stepped out into the studio.

Billy's Tattoo Parlor was a small, one-man operation with a large plate-glass window and an L-shaped display counter full of cheap, sterling-silver jewelry. There was a couch and a Barcalounger toward the front, and behind the counter, along with a pair of chairs and a padded table, was Canning's equipment. None of that stuff had been touched since the day he disappeared, Dorsey had told the FBI in a stream of tears, and Markham could clearly see the marks the forensic team had made in the dust upon their initial sweep of the parlor earlier that afternoon.

He wandered about looking at the images on the walls— thousands of drawings grouped by subject matter. He paused briefly at the signs of the zodiac, then came upon the letters and symbols—the obligatory Chinese and Japanese, of course, but also Hebrew, Arabic, Greek, even Egyptian. There were countless others, too, but no Babylonian cuneiform from what he could see, and certainly no arrangement of letters that even remotely approached the markings found on Donovan and Canning.

Markham worked his way in a horseshoe around the parlor and came to the section devoted to photographs of Billy Canning's work: a large, six-by-six-foot bulletin board covered in Polaroids of tattooed flesh—arms and legs and chests and backs, a couple of necks and a pair of breasts here and there. There were hundreds of them, and Markham's eyes darted about the photos haphazardly.

Canning was good, he had to admit, and the Polaroids were obviously of some of the artist's best work. His eyes came to rest on a large back tattoo of a pair of sword-dueling ninjas. He thought of Jackson Briggs—removed the picture and stared at it for a long time.

The superposition principle, said the voice in his head. *The ninjas are speaking to you, telling you to look closely, telling you not to miss anything. Like that time in the martial arts studio. Briggs was coming for your head with his ninja sword. Would have lopped it off like a pineapple if you hadn't stopped to look in the mirror.*

Markham's left shoulder began to tingle. He quickly skirted around the counter, grabbed one of the chairs, and sat down in front of the bulletin board. He let his eyes wander slowly across the collage of jumbled body parts, scanning back and forth in a manner that reminded him for some reason of Arnold Schwarzenegger in *The Terminator*. There had to be a thousand pictures, he thought, going back many years.

Markham's eyes began to ache with fatigue. What the hell was he looking for? The writing on Donovan and Canning? Was it possible Vlad had Canning tattoo the same thing on his chest? But surely Vlad wouldn't have been so stupid as to let him take a Polaroid of it.

He gazed down at the photo of the dueling ninjas in his hand. The size, the detail, the color—how long would it take Canning to do a tattoo like that?

Vlad kept Canning longer than the others, Markham thought suddenly. *Almost two and a half weeks. The hair growth. What if the autopsy comes back and says Canning was alive for most of that time? What if Vlad had his own private tattoo session with Canning before he impaled him?*

Pure supposition, Markham thought—but something about the image of the faceless Vlad forcing Canning to tattoo him gnawed at his gut.

Canning's car was found out back, Markham said to himself. *That means he had to have driven here after he went to the convenience store. But why so late at night? A private session? Could he have been two-timing Dorsey? Whatever the case, Vlad had to have known he was coming back here that night.*

Or, the voice in his head countered, *Vlad could've simply been following him. Canning could've come back here for any number of reasons—forgot his cell phone or something—and Vlad took advantage of the situation. Pretty dark back there.*

But the writing on Canning and Donovan is like a tattoo. He didn't do that to Rodriguez and Guerrera. It started with Canning.

The voice in his head was silent, and Markham stared at the photos. He would have to get Dorsey back in here to double-check if any equipment was missing. Would have to follow up with distributors on any recent orders in the Raleigh area, too. Christ, that would be a pain in the ass— just another wild-goose chase? Was he really getting that desperate?

Markham sighed and returned the photo of the dueling ninjas to the bulletin board. The guy in the picture was bald—reminded him of an album cover he'd once seen.

What was the name of the group?

He closed his eyes and rubbed his forehead. Then it came to him.

Sublime. That was it. *Picture of some skinhead-looking dude with the group's name tattooed across his back.*

Nineties music. Tattoos.

Markham didn't understand nineties music—felt disconnected from it—and didn't understand the ninties tattoo craze, either. Every stockbroker with his tribal band, every sorority girl with her "tramp stamp" sticking to the seat of her BMW.

Tramp stamp. That had been Michelle's bon mot.

Markham smiled.

He can see her now, on the beach, rising naked from the surf like Botticelli's Venus—her skin pristine and glistening in the sun, her hips swaying as she walks toward him.

"Where's your clamshell, Venus?" he asks. He is naked, too, lying on the sand. Michelle kneels over him and kisses his lips. She tastes salty.

"I think it's an oyster shell," she says, and reaches behind him and clicks on an old-school-style boom box—Blue Öyster Cult's "Don't Fear the Reaper."

"That's right," he says, then kisses her again. "Seventies and eighties all the way, baby. That's where we belong. Another world. Another time."

"I miss you," she whispers.

"I miss you, too."

A wave of sadness passed through him, and he opened his eyes.

He sat there well into the night, adrift on an ocean of tattooed flesh and feeling more lost than ever.

Chapter 22

It was still raining, and Markham spent the morning at the Resident Agency updating Sentinel and studying the Rodriguez and Guerrera file. The FBI had already questioned Mr. and Mrs. Rodriguez about a possible connection between their son and Randall Donovan, but not about Billy Canning. Markham had insisted on handling the Rodriguezes himself. He felt he should be the one to inform them their son had been murdered by a serial killer, but more important, felt he should be the one to ask them about their son's sexuality.

Of course, there had been nothing in the case file to indicate that the young man might have been a homosexual. However, Markham needed to exclude that possibility for himself before he could move forward with the victim profile. He also felt he had a good bead on the Hispanic culture from his stint in Tampa—and unless the Rodriguezes were an unusually enlightened family of Catholics, he had a feeling they wouldn't take kindly to an implication their son might have been gay.

It was a slim possibility, Markham thought; but nonetheless, that line of questioning needed to be handled delicately. He decided Mrs. Rodriguez would be the best bet—would be the most receptive to him—but still he needed to catch her alone, while her husband was at work. The case file said she had a part-time job in the mornings, which meant she would be home this afternoon when the kids got back from school.

Besides, Markham wanted to determine for himself if Mrs. Rodriguez might be hiding something—not just from him, but also from her husband.

Markham drove first to the Rodriguezes' old apartment in Fox Run—got a sense of the layout and gazed up through the rain at the large streetlights that peppered the parking lots. They looked out of place, an afterthought in the rundown, gang-infested neighborhood, but told Markham the property would've been well lit at night. Moreover, the apartment complex had too many balconies. It was raining on the night Rodriguez disappeared, but there still would've been a lot of people around to see the killer waiting. And there was only one entrance in and out of the place—too risky for Vlad to take him here.

Then there was the bus stop and the walk home. Not the safest area, but still well lit and well traveled. At the very least, someone would have heard the gunshots.

But the bus stop on the other end? That mysterious place from where Jose Rodriguez was really travelling on Wednesday and Saturday nights? Well, that was the big question, wasn't it?

The police figured out early on that Rodriguez's waitering

job was bogus, but had since been unable to pin down exactly where he'd been coming from on the night he was shot. On the other hand, there was a strong possibility that one of the restaurant owners was lying; his employees could be lying, too, for fear of getting involved and being deported. That's what bothered Sam Markham the most: that he couldn't rule out the possibility that perhaps Jose Rodriguez might have been telling the truth all along.

But Alex Guerrera had gone somewhere on Saturday night, too. He hadn't been seen by his roommates since the night before and had asked to use the car they shared but then canceled at the last minute. Odd, they thought, but that's all they could tell the police. No knowledge of a connection to MS-13 or any of the other Latino gangs that had sprung up in the area. There was nothing there, Markham felt instinctively, but he would talk to the cousin and track down the roommates if he got desperate.

It had stopped raining by the time he reached the Rodriguez family's new home thirty minutes later. The apartment complex was located in North Raleigh; typical three-floor multi-unit built in the early seventies, complete with a sign at the entrance that advertised LU URY RENTALS in faded letters and a missing *x*. The property had some nice tree coverage, was definitely no Fox Run—working-class, some Section 8—but Markham could tell from the cars that it was on its way down.

He drove to a building at the rear of the complex, parked in a space beside an old Malibu and emerged to find two Hispanic boys staring down at him from a second-floor balcony. The older one (Markham pegged him to be about fifteen) was leaning over the railing smoking; the younger (short, twelve or thirteen) had been fiddling with an iPod and stood up as he approached.

The complex was strangely quiet, Markham thought; only the sound of the wind in the pine trees. He looked up at the building number; watched the boys out of the corner of his eye, and pretended he was unsure he had the right place. Judging from the layout, he guessed that the balcony with the boys was most likely the balcony for the Rodriguez family's new apartment; the taller boy, most likely Diego.

"You looking for something, *jefe*?" asked the taller boy. Markham smiled and gazed up at the streetlights. "If you're looking for your boyfriend, you ain't gonna find him up there. Unless he's a bird."

The younger boy laughed and Markham turned back to them—produced his cred case from underneath his Windbreaker and flipped open his ID. He held it up by his face and smiled as wide as he could.

"Looks like you get to be my boyfriend today," he said. "FBI. Came a long way to ask you out, Diego Rodriguez."

The taller boy swallowed hard, took a final drag off his cigarette, and flicked it from the balcony. He disappeared inside. The younger boy followed, calling out to someone in Spanish.

Markham mounted the stairs and quickly reached the apartment door—was about to knock when he heard the security chain rattle inside and the dead bolt unlock. The door opened slightly, and a Hispanic woman squeezed her face through the crack.

"I'm sorry, sir," she said in a thick accent. "My brother and my husband is working. Only me and the children right now."

"I'm Special Agent Sam Markham," he said, holding up his cred case. "FBI Behavioral Analysis Unit. Are you Mrs. Rodriguez?"

"No. She my brother's wife. They all working now they live here."

"I see," Markham said. "I'd like to ask Diego a few questions."

"He in trouble again?"

"No, ma'am. It's about Jose."

The woman hesitated, pulled back from the doorway, and whispered in Spanish to someone inside. "I'm not going to make trouble for you," Markham said. "Just send Diego out, and I promise I won't come in. I'll wait over here."

He crossed to the stairs, leaned against the railing, and slipped his hands in his pockets. The Hispanic woman watched him for a moment, then closed the door. Markham waited, and soon became uncomfortable as he felt the presence of people looking at him through the peepholes of the surrounding apartments.

Finally, Diego Rodriguez emerged from the apartment. He was dressed in an oversized black T-shirt and a black baseball cap—tags still on and cocked to the side. He eyed Markham up and down and shuffled over, postured himself against the opposite wall and hooked his thumbs in his pockets.

Markham glanced quickly at the boy's fingernails; saw that they were cut neat and clean against his baggy knockoff jeans. *Scared mama's boy,* he thought, and knew at once that Diego Rodriguez would turn out all right.

"What time'll your parents be home?" Markham asked.

"They both working," Diego mumbled. "Six, six-thirty. Maybe seven."

"You know why I want to talk to you?"

Diego shrugged his shoulders.

"I don't know how much TV you watch," Markham said, "but your brother's murder has been turned over to the FBI now. You know what that means?" Diego said nothing. "Means now we have more people trying to figure out who killed him. Means now I have to ask you some questions like the police did so I get my facts straight."

"I didn't talk to Jose that much, and I don't know nothing more now than what I already told Five-O. Only interested in us again cuz of that lawyer that got smoked. They asked my father some questions about Colombians and gangs and drugs and shit. Shit is wack is what I'm saying. Me and Jose, we wasn't down with that. I told y'all that from the beginning, but no one wants to listen cuz some fool says the *pandilleros* done it. I don't know nothing 'bout that shit 'cept Jose was straight-up."

"You have some of the same friends?" Markham asked, reaching inside his pocket. "Does this guy look familiar to you?"

Markham handed him a picture of Billy Canning. The boy scanned it quickly.

"No," said Diego, handing back the paper. "Like I said, me and Jose wasn't close." There was a hint of regret in the kid's voice—almost shame, Markham thought—and he folded Canning's picture back into his pocket.

"You know where Jose might have gone on the night he disappeared?" he asked.

"If you think he went and seen that lawyer for something, you's even more wack than the police. Cuz that's the only reason we seeing y'all again. Cuz of that lawyer. They smoked that motherfucker the way they did Jose. That's the only reason why y'all so worried about Jose again after almost two months of us seeing no one."

"There's been a development," Markham said. "And I assure you I'm going to do my best to find your brother's—

Markham noticed something catch Diego's eye. He followed it and saw a little girl at the opposite stairwell. She cradled a cat in her arms.

"Go inside, Marla," Diego said. The girl didn't move. "You hear what I said? Or do you want me to give you another beating before Papa gets home?"

"Auntie said I could look for Paco, *tú pendejo.*"

Markham smiled in spite of himself. He knew from working in Tampa that *pendejo* meant dumb-ass.

Diego didn't move—only looked back at Markham cynically and said: "May I go now, sir?"

"Yes. But tell your aunt that I'll send your sister in after I talk to her, okay?"

Diego nodded and sulked into the apartment without looking back. Markham approached the little girl.

"That's a pretty cat," he said. "What's his name?"

"Paco."

"How old is he?"

"Papa says he's about a year old, but nobody's sure, really. He was a stray and was living here before we moved in. But he likes me best. You a policeman?"

"No, I'm with the FBI. You know what the FBI is?"

"I think so. It's like a policeman only you work for the President."

"That's right," Markham said, smiling.

"Is that black car over there yours or the President's?"

"I wish it was mine, but the President just lets me borrow it."

"Did Diego ask you to sit in it?"

"No. Why?"

"Cuz Diego keeps telling Hector he's going to buy a Ford Explorer someday after he gets his license. The Ford Explorer looks kind of like your car. Diego says he's going to get a black one like yours and give Hector a ride in it before anybody else. Hector is my cousin. He's older than me."

"That wasn't very nice, you know, what you said to Diego."

"I'm sorry, sir, but Diego let Paco out on purpose when it was raining just to be mean to me. The policemen, the ones who came after Jose died, they spoke Spanish and, well, you didn't look like you knew how to speak Spanish."

"I don't. Just a few words. Your English is much better than my Spanish."

"Papa doesn't like us to speak Spanish too much. Only when he doesn't understand us. He wants us to learn English so we can all go to college someday. Diego says he's not going to college. Says he's going to be rapper or a DJ, but even his English is better than Papa's. You won't tell Papa what I said to Diego, will you?"

"No. It's a secret between us. Your name is Marla?"

"Yes."

"I'm Sam Markham. Your first name and my last name sound a little alike, don't you think? Marla and Markham?"

"Yes, they do."

"Do you know why I'm here?"

"You brought back our computer?"

"Your computer?"

"Oh," said the girl, deflating. "I guess you didn't. I thought we were finally going to get our computer back. The policemen took it away when Jose died. Papa called about it a couple of weeks ago and they said they needed to keep it for evidence. Diego said they probably sold it and kept the money, but he doesn't really care cuz Hector has a computer. I don't get to use it very much cuz they're always hogging it. Do you know if the police still have it, Mr. Markham?"

"Call me Sam. And I will check on it. Did Jose use your old computer a lot?"

"Not that much," Marla said, scratching behind Paco's ears. "We spent a lot of time together when he wasn't working. He was my best friend."

"Did you know any of his friends?" Markham held up the picture of Billy Canning. "Does this man look familiar to you?"

"Who is he?"

"His name is Billy Canning. Do you recognize him? A friend of Jose's maybe?"

"No," Marla said, studying the picture. "But Jose had a lot of friends. You didn't come to the funeral, but there were a lot of people there. But I don't know this man, no."

"Did you ever see him with that other man, Alex Guerrera? Jose ever mention him to you? Someone just named Alex, maybe?"

"No."

"Did he ever chat with anyone on the computer that you know of? Ever tell you about anybody he met online? Someone named William or Billy?"

"Jose and Diego were always fighting over the computer, but Diego used it more. I don't think Jose went into chat rooms and stuff. He worked a lot, and Diego was always downloading music. Jose had a MySpace page like a lot of the older kids do, but Papa made Diego take it down after Jose died and the police printed it out."

"Yes, I saw that."

"Some men came by last week. Men dressed like you. They asked Papa and Diego a bunch of questions, and I overheard Papa telling Mama that some lawyer got killed and they think it might be related to Jose. I didn't hear anything else, but I'm sure they were talking about the *pandilleros*. Diego says he doesn't think it was the *pandilleros* who killed Jose. He said that from the beginning. But Diego is stupid because even Jose said he thought it was—"

Marla stopped.

"What, Marla? Did Jose say something to you before he died?"

The girl looked uncomfortably at her feet—bit her lip and held Paco tighter to her bosom. The cat squirmed, stuck out its paw and looked up at Markham helplessly.

"What is it, Marla?" he asked. "Do you want to tell me something but you're afraid? Afraid of the *pandilleros*?"

"No," said Marla. "It's just that, well, I promised Jose I wouldn't tell."

"Yes, I understand. But Jose is gone now and wouldn't mind if you—"

"No, I promised him *after* he died."

Markham looked at her curiously.

"In my dreams," she whispered, looking past him toward her apartment door. "I haven't told anyone except Father Banigas last week at confession, but Jose, after he died . . . well . . . sometimes he speaks to me in my dreams."

"I see," said Markham, smiling. "I know what you mean."

"You do?"

"Yes. I once lost someone I loved very much, too. And sometimes she speaks to me in my dreams just like Jose speaks to you."

"Who is she?"

"My wife. She died about eleven years ago. Her name was Michelle—began with an M just like your name."

"Were you sad when she died?"

"Very much so. I still am sometimes."

"Me, too. But not as much now that I know Jose is in Heaven. Is your wife in Heaven?"

"Yes, she is."

"Maybe she and Jose can become friends up there. Maybe she and Jose can do stuff together and talk about things now that he's in Heaven with her. I'm glad that you told me about your wife talking to you cuz I was worried that once Jose got into Heaven he wouldn't want to talk to me anymore. Or maybe God wouldn't let him, even."

"Marla, does Jose say anything else to you in your dreams?"

"Please," Marla said, frightened. "Don't make me break my promise."

"Listen to me," Markham said, sitting down on the stairs, "I had wanted to speak to your parents first, but what if I told you that Diego is right? What if I told you that Jose wasn't murdered by the *pandilleros*, but by someone else?" Markham held up the picture of Billy Canning. "The same some-one who murdered the lawyer and now this man."

"You mean the man in the picture is dead, too?"

"Yes, Marla, and that's why I need you to help me. You have to tell me what you know about Jose."

"But it's a secret that only the two of us were supposed to know. Papa and Diego would hate Jose if they found out. And if Papa and Diego find out that I knew about Jose's se-cret and didn't tell them, they'd hate me, too. Might kill me, even."

"I won't tell your father and brother that I found out Jose's secret from you. You have my word on that, Marla."

Marla was silent, unconvinced.

"Do you love your cat Paco?" Markham asked. Marla nodded. "Well, let's say someone very mean was going around hurting cats like Paco. And say that I knew some-thing that could save Paco from this person—a secret, maybe, that somebody told me. Something really important that I promised not to tell, but it could save Paco's life. Which do you think is more important, the secret or saving Paco?"

"Saving Paco."

"Well it's the same thing for Jose. There's nothing we can do for your brother now, but what you tell me might save other young men just like him; might even prevent other sis-ters like you from losing a brother and feeling sad. And you don't have to worry about anything. I promise you that your father and Diego won't know you told me. You don't have to worry about getting into trouble, okay?"

"But what about Papa and Mama? Jose's secret would kill them."

"No, it won't, Marla. I promise you. Nothing could be worse than losing Jose. And don't you think they'd want to prevent other parents from losing their sons, too?"

"But what about Jose?" Marla asked with tears in her

eyes. "What about what Papa and what everybody else would think of him? Jose told me that he heard a story of a boy like him whose father and family got so mad that the boy ran away and then committed suicide with this gun he found. Jose said that if I told, he would have to kill himself, too; said it would be like I killed him myself."

"But Jose is in Heaven now, Marla. And when you're in Heaven, you're happy no matter what happens down here on Earth, right?"

"Well . . ." Marla said, thinking hard. "If I tell you Jose's secret, do you promise, next time you see your wife that you'll tell her to tell Jose that it was okay because you said so? Will you tell her to tell him not to be mad at me?"

"I promise," Markham said. "I'll tell her the very next time I see her."

Chapter 23

The little girl whispered her secret in his ear—lit a fire under his ass and put him on West Hargett Street in twenty minutes. Markham didn't wait to speak to Mr. and Mrs. Rodriguez. Instead, he sent Marla back inside to tell her aunt he'd been called away and that someone else would stop by later to explain everything to her parents. Schaap was on his way back to the Resident Agency from the NC State campus. Most important for the FBI was that they get everything coordinated before the media got wind of Canning. Most important for Sam Markham was that he kept Marla Rodriguez's secret.

"To the grave, *señorita*," he said as he cruised down West Hargett Street.

He couldn't believe he'd gotten so lucky; couldn't believe that an eleven-year-old girl could have possibly kept secret the most important lead in the investigation thus far. Yet at the same time it all made sense: her love for her brother, her need to protect him from the wrath of her family. And then there was the lack of media attention because of the initial gang angle. It was almost as if the deck had been stacked against Jose Rodriguez from the beginning. But rather than feeling anger or frustration toward his little sister for not coming forward, curiously, Markham loved her for it.

Angel's, was what she told him. Angel's.

Markham parked his SUV in a lot about a block away from the club—recognized it immediately from the silver Mylar banners that hung vertically along the length of the building like angel wings. Despite its renovations, he could tell that the club had once been a pair of connecting storefronts. However, what stuck out to him the most was the orientation of the "dead" space—the parking lots, the sidewalks, the narrow alleyways between the buildings. Lots of places to hide and watch.

Angel's took up nearly the entire block. Billed itself as a "nightclub complex" and sported a marquee over the front door that read:

HOME OF RALEIGH'S FINEST
FEMALE ILLUSIONISTS.

Markham stepped inside and found a map on the wall to his left—color-coded with sections labeled *bar*, *dance floor*, *patio*, *video bar*, *pool hall*, and *theater*.

He approached the bar.

"Can I get you something?" asked the bartender. He was muscular, bald, and wore a tight black T-shirt. Markham quickly scanned the room—eight patrons, all male, two at the bar, the rest scattered at the tables. Half suits, half casual.

"Is the manager or the owner around?" he asked.

"You got a two-for-one special, friend," the bartender said, smiling. "I'm Paulie Angel, and welcome to my home."

Markham flashed his ID and introduced himself.

"I see," Angel said, nervous. "Perhaps we'd better talk in

the office." He signaled over Markham's shoulder. "You're up, Karl," he said, and a man rose from one of the tables and stepped behind the bar.

Angel led Markham out the back and across an enclosed courtyard. Once inside again, they quickly passed through the pool hall and entered an office at the end of a narrow hallway. Markham had taken in as much as he could, but what stuck out to him the most was the obnoxious neon sign at the opposite end of the hallway:

Starlight Theater

"All right," Angel said, settling in behind his desk. "What can I do for you?"

Markham sat down and slid him a copy of Jose Rodriguez's senior class photo. "You recognize this man?" he asked.

"Sure. That's Ricky Martinez."

"Ricky Martinez?"

"Yeah. She used to work here as one of our performers, only for a few months, though. Called herself Leona Bonita. Kickoff slot in our Wednesday and Saturday shows. I haven't seen her in a while, though. Left her shit in the dressing room and never came back for it. That happens sometimes with the younger girls. Tried calling her, but number is no longer in service. Stuff's pretty much been picked through. What's left is still back there. Something happen to her?"

"His real name is Jose Rodriguez," Markham said. "Seventeen years old. Found murdered two months ago."

"Jesus Christ," Angel gasped. "What happened?"

"Mr. Rodriguez and a man by the name of Alex Guerrera were both shot in the head and later discovered by police near a cemetery outside of town, their bodies impaled up through the rectum and planted in the ground."

The nightclub owner gasped, and Markham slid Guerrera's mug shot across the bar. Two years old, from a petty-theft conviction in Texas. "You recognize him?"

Angel shook his head, dismissed the photograph and went back to Rodriguez.

"You said she was seventeen?"

"That's right."

"Jesus," Angel said. "I hired her myself. Checked her ID—Ricardo Martinez, it said, I swear. Said she was a college student; was going to be a fashion designer and made her own costumes. I—how come we didn't know?"

"The confusion about the names, for one; but also because the police initially kept the details from the press. Rodriguez and Guerrera were thought to have been the victims of a gang-related drug hit; their deaths, the display of their bodies were very similar to what's been going on in South America. Consequently, there's been a conscious effort among law enforcement not to give this kind of thing too much media traction."

"But you said it's been two months. You're just getting around to us now?"

"It appears that Mr. Rodriguez's sexuality, as well as his alias of Ricky Martinez, was kept secret from everyone except a handful of people. He was terrified that his family would find out that he was a homosexual, but he was also a very smart young man. In addition to questioning his friends, the original police investigation looked into Rodriguez's cell phone records and his computer activity with the hopes of getting a lead on the drug angle. Nothing there. Consequently, there was also nothing there that tied him to this establishment or his secret lifestyle. The phone number he gave you was most likely a prepaid cell deal that his parents weren't aware of. I'll want that phone number and any records of his employment here if you still have them."

The nightclub owner nodded. He stared down at the photograph, upset.

"Two more men have been found murdered in the same fashion," Markham said, producing another pair of photographs. "You know either of these gentlemen?"

Paulie Angel glanced quickly at the picture of Randall Donovan—shook his head and said he knew him only from the news reports about his murder, about his supposed connection to Colombian drug money. But when he saw the second photograph, the nightclub owner let out a moan and held his head in his hands.

"Please don't tell me," he said. "That's Billy Canning, isn't it?"

"You know him?"

"He and his partner were regulars here for years. Disappearance was in the news. Police questioned me and some of the other club owners in town after it first happened. Questioned Stefan, too, from what I heard; thought he might have had something to do with it, they said, but we all knew it wasn't true. I know they were having problems, and we all thought maybe that Billy just bolted, that maybe—but what happened? Where'd they find him?"

"I'm not at liberty to tell you that just yet. Murder has not been made public, investigation still in its preliminary stages."

"I understand."

"But Donovan and Guerrera, you're sure you've never seen them here before?"

"Yes, I'm sure. But that doesn't mean they've never been here. Well, perhaps the Hispanic gentleman. You can ask Karl and the other bartenders if they ever saw him. Can ask our performers, too—there's a show tonight. But this Donovan? No, now that I think of it, I'd have to say definitely not a patron."

"What makes you say that?"

"I pride myself on keeping a hand in things," Angel said confidentially. "I'm here seven days a week. Of course, I can't say I know everyone who frequents our establishment.

But a guy like Donovan, well, I think if he'd been in here I'd know."

"Why?"

"He was well-known in Raleigh, even nationally they said on the news. Sure, a lot of those family types—the ones with the kids and the golf clubs and the reputations—they like to keep their real tastes hush-hush. But even before I learned of Donovan's murder, I never heard anything in our circles about him being gay."

"I see."

"Again, I'm not saying I'm an authority on the subject. But, here in Raleigh—in the grand scheme of things, I mean—the circle is pretty small. Word gets around, especially about the high-profile ones."

Markham was silent, thinking.

"Would you like to speak with Karl?" Angel asked. "He's the only bartender on call right now."

"Yes, I would. But first I'd like to see any business records associated with Rodriguez—your telephone number for him, pay stubs, a Social Security number for Ricky Martinez. I'd also like to see what's left of his act."

"Yes, of course. But, I have to be honest with you, Agent Markham. We pay most of our employees in cash. That includes our performers. Helps with accounting and whatnot, if you know what I mean." Angel smiled sheepishly. "I hope you'll take into consideration how helpful I've been when you look into our business records. Last thing I need right now is the IRS breathing down my neck."

"I understand," Markham said. "No worries."

Angel gave a sigh of relief and proceeded to make Markham a copy of his pay ledger. No pay stubs, no phony Social Security number for Rodriguez, just the name "R. Martinez" and the amount he was paid per show: fifty dollars.

Plus tips, Marla Rodriguez had told him.

Angel then led him behind the stage to the dressing room. The space was tight with the smell of body odor and stale hair spray; it was packed wall to wall with spangled dresses and bouffant wigs on Styrofoam heads. Angel brought down an old shoebox from atop the shelf. It was filled with makeup mostly, as well as a tube of glitter, a pair of cheap costume earrings, and a dirty bra and panties. Rodriguez's wig was still here, Angel explained, but his dress and other accessories were gone—had been "adopted" by the other performers, he figured. Nonetheless, he assured Markham that he would try to track that stuff down, too. Markham informed him that he would have to call the forensic team to collect what remained of Rodriguez's things. Some men from the Resident Agency would be by shortly, he added, but assured the nightclub owner that they would try not to cause too much of a scene.

Angel thanked him and slipped through the split in the curtains, leaving Markham alone backstage in the dark. He waited there until he saw the lights from the theater spill underneath the curtains and onto his shoes. Then, he stepped out onto the stage. Angel waved to him and disappeared through the door at the rear of the theater.

The Starlight Theater was barely a theater at all, Markham thought. High ceiling, black walls, with only a dozen or so colored spotlights beamed down at its narrow, two-foot-high thrust stage. An electric piano and a sound system stood in the corner to the right; to the left, a handful of tables and chairs.

Markham walked to the edge of the stage and gazed out into the house. He counted the tables, the bistro chairs, and the barstools at the back of the theater and estimated the space could hold about a hundred people. He stepped off the stage and wandered aimlessly about the house. He soon arrived at the bar at the rear of the theater and sat down on one of the stools.

It was then he noticed for the first time the large, glittered sign above the stage: a pair of singing lips and a microphone inside a group of stars—all of it cradled by the word STARLIGHT in the shape of a crescent moon.

A crescent moon and stars.

"Oh my God," Markham cried. "It's all right here!"

His mind spinning, his heart pounding in his throat, Markham looked up to find a disco ball on the ceiling. He was off his stool in a flash—went straight for the big spotlight at the right of the bar, where he discovered a control board. He flicked on the small reading lamp—rows of sliding dimmers and switches labeled with electrical tape. He scanned them quickly, figured out the workings of the light board and flicked the switch labeled *O-ride/Finale*.

All at once the theater was bathed in darkness and in light—a spattering of cutout stars on the curtains; a swirl of shimmering diamonds that slowly picked up speed across the walls. Markham looked upward and instantly became hypnotized by the revolving disco ball. A flashback of a dream, of speeding toward a planet on a spaceship made of fire. Then suddenly the universe and the fire became a crowd—a sparkling theater of silhouetted applause, of music and laughter.

Markham sat down at the bar and stared open-mouthed at the crescent moon above the stage.

He finally understood.

Chapter 24

"I'm telling you I found it," Markham shouted into his BlackBerry—traffic, a semi passing him on the interstate making it hard to hear.

"You don't think it's a coincidence?" Schaap asked on the other end.

"No. The murder sites mimic the dynamic of the Starlight Theater itself—the lips and the microphone inside the stars, the crescent moon. Vlad is literally responding to a message in the sky—perhaps even to a voice that he thinks is speaking to him."

"Then you're thinking the theater is where it all began?" Schaap asked.

"Yes. Maybe Vlad had some kind of epiphany there. Maybe something about Rodriguez's performance set him off. Christ, Vlad could be a performer at Angel's himself for all I know at this point. All I can tell you is that Rodriguez was the first because of his connection with the crescent-moon visual in the drag theater. I just know it."

"But how the hell did you connect Rodriguez to Angel's?"

"The possible homosexual connection to Canning," Marham lied. "I started canvassing the gay bars in Raleigh on a hunch. Started alphabetically and got lucky."

Silence on the other end—the sound of Andy Schaap thinking, not believing him. Markham felt a pang of guilt about lying to his partner, but he would take Marla Rodriguez's secret to the grave with him, no matter what.

"I also checked out the alley behind the club," Markham continued. "That's where the performers come and go. It's dark back there, hidden, and has an adjoining parking lot and a broken-down fence through which the killer could've slipped in and out. If Vlad hit them there, if he neglected to pick up his bullet casings—"

"Forensic team is already on its way," Schaap said. "I'll meet them there in—"

"No, I need you back at the RA."

"Why?"

"Just a hunch, but I think I may have discovered Vlad's constellation, too."

Chapter 25

"That's incredible," Schaap said, leaning in. "The stars line up almost perfectly with the murder sites."

Markham removed his tracing of the Starlight Theater logo from the map on his computer screen. He held it up next to his BlackBerry and compared it to the picture he'd taken at the club.

"But Sam," Schaap continued, "there are only three stars in that logo—one star, according to you, for each of the murder sites. If Vlad is following this schematic—that is, if he's mimicking the pattern of the Starlight logo on the ground— one could argue that his killing spree is over."

"You're forgetting about the pair of lips next to the crescent moon."

"You mean the lips could be thought of as a possible murder site, too?"

"I don't know."

"The lips are in roughly the same position as the star in the symbol for Islam. But, per your map, that would put a murder site almost in the center of Raleigh itself."

Markham set the tracing and the BlackBerry on his desk—leaned on his elbows and rubbed his forehead, thinking. "Those lips and the crescent moon," he said finally. "When I was sitting there in the theater it was as if something was speaking to me, too. I can't explain it, Schaap, but I don't think those lips are finished speaking to Vlad either."

"The 'I' in 'I have returned,' you mean? A figure literally speaking to Vlad from the stars? Like in the drag theater?"

"That's what I think, yes."

"But Vlad didn't start writing on his victims until Canning."

"Right. And the writing was different on Donovan—the phrase written over and over again and then washed off—which means Vlad is still evolving. Perhaps his pattern on the ground is evolving, too. Maybe the three stars in the logo are a starting point off of which he plans to build a bigger picture. I also wonder if he didn't know what he was doing yet with Rodriguez and Guerrera. Or maybe his plans got screwed up and he didn't have time to impale them alive."

"The gunshots you mean?"

"That's right. Vlad held on to Rodriguez and Guerrera for about forty-eight hours. He held on to Donovan and Canning for longer. We know for sure that Donovan died from the impaling itself, but I'm willing to bet Canning did, too. They were also murdered one at a time and put on display individually, unlike the Hispanics. It's why I now have a feeling that Rodriguez was the prize all along—at Angel's—and Guerrera showed up unexpectedly. Vlad had to improvise."

"Rodriguez and Guerrera were lovers, you think?"

"I don't know. We might never know unless we can tie them together."

Just then an agent poked his head into Markham's office. Joe Connelly was his name—a big, rough-voiced guy with whom Markham had talked about the Red Sox the week before. Markham was happy for some reason to find out that Big Joe was a Sox fan, even though he himself had never given a rat's ass about baseball.

"Kid's stuff is starting to come in," Big Joe said. "I'll leave everything in the conference room before the first batch goes out to Quantico."

"Thanks," Markham said. "Come on, Schaap, let's take a look."

Schaap followed Markham into the conference room. Spread out on the table were the remains of Jose Rodriguez's act—the shoebox and its contents that Markham had seen earlier, all tagged and placed inside clear plastic bags—as well as a large wig on a Styrofoam head and a CD in a plastic case. They had also been tagged and bagged.

Markham and Schaap each put on a pair of rubber gloves.

"So," Schaap said, holding up the plastic bag containing the wig. "He called himself Ricky Martinez when he wore this shit?"

"No," Markham said, fingering the other items. "Angel said his stage name was something else—something Spanish."

"Here it is," Schaap said. "A piece of masking tape underneath the wig on the forehead. Leona Bonita, it says. I don't speak Spanish, but I know the word *bonita* means beautiful, right? Remember that Madonna song, "La Isla Bonita?" Song used to get on my fucking nerves—" Schaap stopped.

It was Markham. He looked as if he'd seen a ghost.

"What is it, Sam?"

"Leona Bonita," he said. "It means beautiful lion."

"So?"

"Leo the lion is one of the constellations that return to the nighttime sky in the spring. It's also one of the constellations that would've passed through the Hispanics' sight lines on the night they were left in the cemetery."

"You think there might be a connection there, too? Because Rodriguez called himself Leona Bonita?"

"The crescent-moon visual, the stars at the club, and then the beautiful lion literally singing beneath them—maybe that's why Vlad didn't bother writing the messages on him."

"What do you mean?"

"Maybe Vlad saw him as part of the message—perhaps the most important part. The figure speaking to him in the stars—the lips with the microphone beside the crescent moon—they could represent to Vlad the mouth of Leo the lion."

"Jesus Christ."

"And if Vlad thought it was Leo speaking to him through Rodriguez, he would have no need to write on Rodriguez because the kid was part of the message itself."

"That would mean that Vlad was also communicating to Leo via the impalement of Rodriguez and Guerrera. Sending some kind of message like, 'Look at me, Ma'—some kind of human sacrifice, maybe?"

"Yes."

"But if Vlad is sacrificing his victims to Leo, to whom does the 'I' in 'I have returned' refer? Vlad or the constellation?"

"Perhaps both."

"You mean he sees himself as Leo?"

"I don't know. Perhaps he's speaking to Leo on behalf of someone or something else; perhaps he is challenging the constellation. Whatever his reason, I know Vlad wants the figure in the stars to see his victims impaled—either Leo, whatever that constellation represents to him, or something else connected to it."

"A god or some mythological figure?"

"Perhaps something like that, yes—that is, if I'm right about Leo to begin with."

"But the impalement," Schaap said. "How the hell does that connect to the constellation Leo?"

"I don't know, Schaap," Markham said. "I haven't got that part figured out; could be spinning my wheels again."

"I'm not saying—"

"But I know in my gut that it began with Rodriguez at the drag theater, and then somehow Guerrera got into the mix. It also began at the cemetery, the first murder site. Perhaps there's something there I missed. Something that—"

Markham stopped, furrowed his brow for a moment, then suddenly bolted from the room—peeled off his rubber gloves and tossed them onto the floor as he dashed back into his office. He put on his Windbreaker.

"Where are you going?" Schaap asked, running after him.

"Back to the cemetery. Meantime, you begin with Leo. Dig up everything you can about the astrological sign and its origins, its history and its place in different cultures and whatnot."

"The writing you mean?" Schaap asked. "Those cultures represented by the Arabic and the Egyptian and shit?"

"Yes. There's got to be a link to the constellation there, as well as a possible link to the impalements."

"But why are you going back to the cemetery?

"I think I missed something. Something so obvious I should be taken out back and shot."

"What?"

"Another message," Markham said.

And then he was gone.

Chapter 26

Now he was Edmund Lambert again.

He pulled his pickup into the Harriot Theater parking lot and turned off the ignition. He sat there for a long time just watching the rain drizzle down the windshield. He would need to watch the final dress rehearsal of *Macbeth* tonight; would also have to be there tomorrow night before the opening to make sure the trap was working smoothly. But then that was it. Finally, the General would be free again to conscript the next soldier into service—*soldiers*, he had to keep reminding himself. Yes, in order to balance the equation, he owed the Prince two of them.

That would make things 6:2—or 3:1, depending on how you wanted to look at it.

He had begun with the tattoo artist—the sinful sodomite named Canning. The General thought the Prince wanted him to be the first, for the sodomite named Canning had seen the last of the doorways with his own eyes, had even been allowed to touch it—to run his fingers over it and kiss it.

But on the night the General followed Canning to Angel's,

when the show began and the Spanish drag queen appeared on the stage looking so much like a lion, the General was overcome with a feeling similar to his anointing in Iraq; felt as if his whole body had collapsed into itself, just like the day on which he was officially chosen to become the Prince's second in command.

And then there was the song; the song that the boy sang and prowled about to on the stage—yes, the General thought, the Prince was speaking to him as in the old days!

"How could you think, I'd let you get away?

When I came out of the darkness, and told you who you are."

But still the General needed to be sure. And so he consulted the Prince in the Throne Room and was pleased to learn that he had read the messages correctly. And once he began stalking the boy, once he discovered that all the drag queens used the back entrance, he knew what needed to be done.

The end of the month drew closer, and on the night before the drag show, the General pulled up his van to the old plank-board fence that separated the nightclub's alleyway from the parking lot of an empty warehouse. He loosened one of the fence boards, slipped through the opening, and decided the space behind the Dumpster would be the best place from which to strike.

The following night, everything seemed at first to go according to plan. The General tailed the drag queen's bus as he had done many times and waited in the parking lot behind the club; stood listening on the opposite side of the fence and got into place behind the Dumpster when he heard the applause inside. It started to rain, but the General only smiled. Divine providence, he thought, for the rain would keep any potential witnesses inside.

However, about twenty minutes later, when the General

saw the young sodomite come out of the club with a stranger, all at once he began to panic. The men were arguing in Spanish. The General couldn't understand everything they were saying, but heard the word *dinero* thrown back and forth a few times. He'd picked up enough Spanish in the Army to know that *dinero* meant money—but the men kept getting louder, until finally the stranger forced the drag queen to his knees and unzipped his fly.

The General watched and listened as the drag queen took the stranger in his mouth, and in a rush of adrenaline he suddenly felt his plan slipping away. He'd have to kill them both if he was to take the drag queen tonight—he might not get another chance before it was too late—but the stranger was not part of the equation! Taking him also might throw off the 9:3 and ruin everything!

Then, without thinking, the General felt himself being propelled out from behind the Dumpster. He fired in quick succession—*Thhhwhip! Thhhwhip!*—dropping the two men with a silenced bullet to each of their heads before they even saw him.

The rain was coming down hard now, and the General quickly dragged the bodies through the hole in the fence and loaded them onto the plastic tarp in the back of his van. The chloroform he had made from a recipe on the Internet, the rope and the pipe he had stolen from Harriot—all of it was useless to him now! And once he was safely out of the city, he became fearful that he screwed up the Prince's plan beyond repair, for even though the Prince loved his second in command above all others, he did not tolerate failure from *anyone*.

He shouldn't have brought the gun. That had been his mistake.

The General was almost in tears by the time he got back to the farmhouse. He pulled the van around back, unlocked the bulkhead to the cellar, and dragged the tarp containing the bodies down the stairs and into the reeducation chamber.

The General then rushed into the Throne Room—threw himself on the floor and punched himself again and again in the face until his eyes watered and the blood began to trickle from his nose. "Forgive me! Forgive me!" he cried.

But the first drifter had only been on the throne for a week—had hardly begun to smell at all—and the Prince's voice came through the doorway loud and clear.

The General listened carefully for a long time—closed his eyes and allowed the Prince's voice to penetrate his entire body. That was how the General had to listen: *with his entire body*. For the Prince's voice was not a voice at all; instead, he spoke to the General in flashes of pictures and sounds that scrolled through the General's mind like TV channels being changed with a remote control. The General assumed it had been that way for all the warrior-priests—those chosen few who had been allowed access through the doorway. And not only did the General understand the pictures and sounds, when the doorway was fresh, the Prince's "voice" blocked out all other thoughts from his mind.

Back in the present, sitting there in his truck, Edmund Lambert recalled what the Prince had told the General on that night. And even now he felt silly for having worried so. He should've known right away that Leona Bonita and the other sodomite were part of the message itself. They already understood the 9:3, the 3:1. Yes, they would be waiting at the doorway when the Prince called them into service; they would recognize him at once and embrace their destiny.

Edmund Lambert exited his pickup and headed for the rear of the building, cut through the small breezeway that connected the theater to the academic buildings, and hurried down the steps that brought him past the large bulkhead for the props cellar. He smiled. It was there that he'd found the dentist's chair last semester—from an old production of *Little Shop of Horrors,* someone had told him. Jennings still hadn't missed it, and the General had since modified the lever mechanism and outfitted the lower half with leg brackets constructed from scrap metal he'd stolen from the scene shop.

Edmund continued on to the electrics shop door, slipped his key into the lock, and paused briefly as he remembered what the General did to Rodriguez and Guerrera. True, their sacrifice lacked the ceremony befitting his role as a warrior-priest—no need for his robes or the strobe light; no need for the songs like with the corrupt attorney and the adulterous, body-profaning sodomite—but still, the General enjoyed his time with them.

His only regret was that they never got to meet the Prince.

But they would meet him soon enough, Edmund said to himself as he entered the electrics shop. The others, too. And all of them would be waiting for him by the doorway when he called them to service.

However, Edmund knew the Prince's enemies would be waiting for him, too. They would see him coming from the sky and try to thwart his return. But the General and the Prince weren't too worried about them. No, the Prince wanted his enemies to see him coming; for the Prince was worshipped, and worship gave him strength. And that was something his enemies did not have.

The cemetery.

It began there. His enemies understood the sacrifice as part of the 9, but the cemetery was important to the General, too—part of the 1 or the 3, depending on how you looked at it.

Yes, Edmund thought as he sat down in front of the electrics shop computer. The cemetery proved to all of them that the Prince had an ally to be feared.

One who had given up everything.

One who was worthy of a second in command.

But most importantly, one who would be rewarded for all his hard work.

Chapter 27

Willow Brook Cemetery was large for Johnston County. It sat on roughly six acres surrounded by lush farmland, and contained family plots dating back to the late 1800s. Markham knew the cemetery's namesake brook lay somewhere behind the copse of willow trees to the south, but he could never hear it babbling during his nighttime visits. He'd also read somewhere that the adjoining field had been purchased by the county, which planned on expanding the cemetery along its eastern border.

The stormy skies looked purplish by the time Markham arrived at the cemetery's western entrance. He drove past it about a hundred yards and turned right onto the narrow country road that ran parallel to the northern edge of the property. He followed the low fieldstone wall until it banked south again, upon which he parked his SUV at the corner and immediately made for the field. Now he ran along the eastern wall. The grass was high—his shoes, the cuffs of his trousers instantly soaked—but he made good time; covered the two hundred yards like an Olympic sprinter and stopped at the spot where Rodriguez and Guerrera had been impaled.

Markham had been to the cemetery only once during the daytime, but had been able to determine the victims' exact location by the pattern of stonework behind them in the crime scene photographs. First thing he'd done the week before was to wedge a bike reflector in the wall to help him find his position at night—he'd forgotten to retrieve it on his last visit—and thus pried the reflector loose and hopped over the wall.

It was raining harder now, the cloudy skies flirting with nightfall, and Markham patted his inside jacket pocket to make sure he'd remembered his Maglite. He had, but he hoped he wouldn't be at the cemetery long enough to need it. He stuck the reflector between the stones on the inside of the wall and began walking back and forth among the gravestones in twenty-yard lengths, row by row—one eye on the gravestones, the other on the reflector.

He found what he was looking for on his third pass: a small, inconspicuous headstone about four rows back and facing west.

It bore the name of LYONS.

"So that's why you didn't write on Rodriguez and Guerrera," Markham whispered. "Whoever is in the sky watching you didn't need your messages to understand."

Suddenly, the ring of his BlackBerry startled him. He answered it.

"Hello?"

"It's Schaap."

"Go ahead."

"The forensics team finished its sweep of the alley behind Angel's."

"And?"

"They found the shells, Sam. Under the Dumpster, two of them, nine millimeter. Same caliber as the bullets the ME pulled from Rodriguez and Guerrera. All we need now is the ballistics test to make it official."

"Then that's where it happened," Markham said. "Rodriguez and Guerrera were lovers. They had to be. Vlad killed them together in the alley—but he was careless."

"Safe to say then that Vlad is hunting homosexuals?"

"The evidence would seem to point that way."

"You don't sound convinced."

"I missed something here at the cemetery," Markham said after a moment. "There's a headstone with the name of Lyons directly west from the spot at which Rodriguez and Guerrera were impaled."

"Holy shit. And Rodriguez calling himself the beautiful lion, that means—"

"Yes. We were right about Rodriguez being part of the message itself—about Vlad not needing to write on him and Guerrera."

"Then what's bothering you?"

"I'm thinking that if I missed this here, I might have missed something else, too."

"But the headstone is only meaningful now because you know of the connection to Leo—because you know what to look for."

"Right," Markham said, walking. "That's why I need to get back to Donovan's."

"Tonight?"

"Yes. I need to figure out for sure how the lawyer fits into the picture. Now tell me, did you find out anything yet about the constellation?"

"Only stuff about the physical layout of Leo itself—major stars and whatnot. Been busy with the forensics team, the evidence collection."

"I understand, go ahead."

"Well, there are basically two visualizations of the constellation Leo, both of which contain the same base stars. The traditional version, the one you were using, consists of nine stars with a triangular-shaped body and a sickle-shaped head. However, a more recent visualization, by H. A. Rey, alters and expands the constellation's traditional shape into fifteen stars and depicts the lion figure walking."

"H. A. Rey? The same guy who wrote the *Curious George* books?"

"Very good, Mr. Former English Teacher. Rey published a book in the fifties in which he came up with more concrete, almost cartoonlike visualizations of the traditional constellations by adding stars or connecting them in different patterns."

"Let's go with the nine-star version for now. Older and more recognizable. Anything on how it might relate to the ancient writing?"

"Not yet. I got the name of a professor in the classical studies department at NC State—some guy with whom we've worked in the past—but we probably won't hear back from him until tomorrow."

"Okay. I'm going to head over to Donovan's and then I'll meet you back at the RA. I have a feeling it's going to be a late night."

"Check. And I'll alert Cary PD you're back at Donovan's."

"Thanks." Markham reached his TrailBlazer and slipped inside. "One more thing," he said, turning the ignition. "I remember from my research that Leo Minor is one of the constellations near Leo, too. It's made up of only three or four stars, I believe, but I'd like you to look into that as well."

"Leo Minor? Why Leo Minor?"

"Just a hunch," Markham said, driving off. "But there are three stars in the Starlight Theater logo. Also, the name on the gravestone is plural."

Chapter 28

Markham hit an accident on the belt line, so it was just after eight-thirty by the time he turned into the Donovans' driveway. The skies above were almost black, the rain coming down in sheets, and the enormous, five-bedroom Mc-Mansion appeared out of the gloom like some giant toad waiting to snatch him up with its tongue.

He parked his SUV in front of the three-car garage and sat for a moment, gathering his thoughts. The gravestone and the connection to Leo were huge, as was the discovery of the shell casings, but still he felt empty and unsatisfied. All still theory, no concrete proof. And Christ, he was tired; had to piss like a racehorse, too. He grabbed his briefcase but did not bother putting it over his head as he exited the TrailBlazer—he was still soaked—and made no attempt to avoid the tiny puddles that had formed along the Donovans' brick walkway.

The house was dark inside, but Markham didn't turn on the lights. He knew the layout well from the week before and went straight for the bathroom off the kitchen. He urinated with the door open, steadying his breathing to the blinking clock on the microwave. He was off about Donovan being a closet homosexual. He could feel it. So what the hell did he expect to find here?

But now that you can tie Guerrera to Angel's, a voice said in his head, *now that you know he was with Rodriguez on the night he died—well, you don't have to be Sherlock Holmes to solve that mystery.*

Maybe Guerrera was blackmailing Rodriguez. Maybe he followed him to Angel's and threatened to tell his family. Could've been in the wrong place at the wrong time.

It's possible. But that's three out of four victims we can tie to Angel's for sure. Most likely Vlad would have thought Guerrera was gay if he saw him in the alley with Rodriguez. Odds are that Donovan played for the other team, too.

Markham responded by flushing the toilet.

All right then, the voice in his head continued. *What if Donovan wasn't gay?*

"Then that means Vlad had a different reason for killing him," Markham said to his reflection in the mirror. He washed his hands and splashed some cold water on his face, dried himself, and went upstairs.

He began in the master bedroom, rifled through the lawyer's top dresser drawer, and removed the porn DVDs. There were three of them—higher-end, more "conceptual" fare made in the early 2000s starring no one he'd ever heard of. Then again, he hadn't seen a porno since college. The only DVDs on his shelf were from the Criterion Collection, a film distribution company that released "important classic and contemporary films" to cinema buffs. Markham didn't consider himself a cinema buff by any stretch, but nonetheless most often gravitated toward movies with a more intellectual bent. One of his few indulgences outside of work; one of the few hobbies that he allowed himself to get excited about since the death of his wife.

The cases for the Criterion DVDs were numbered on the spine, which made cataloguing and collecting them quite simple—that is, if you could find them. Some had gone out of print, which made them quite valuable to collectors. Indeed, Markham's latest acquisition had been an out-of-print copy of John Woo's *The Killer,* number eight on the Criterion list. He'd paid a pretty penny for it from a dealer, too, but it was worth it—not because *The Killer* was anything to write home about, but simply because it filled the space on his shelf between number seven and number nine.

Markham stared down at the porn flicks and suddenly wished he was back at his town house unpacking his DVDs. He'd found the lawyer's stash the week before, but thought it best at the time not to mention to Tracy Donovan that he'd already been snooping around her house.

He opened the cases and checked the labels; traced his fingers over the discs and wondered if Donovan could have switched out the movies for some gay porn instead. Then he returned the DVDs to the drawer and left the bedroom feeling foolish. He wandered through the children's bedrooms, through the big bonus room where Tracy Donovan kept her treadmill, and in and out of the upstairs bathrooms. He didn't bother with the family photos in the living room as he'd done the week before; didn't shine his flashlight into the kitchen cupboards or behind the boxes in the attic.

He ended up in Randall Donovan's office and sat down in the lawyer's big leather chair—propped his feet up on the desk and listened to the rain for a long time in the dark. The air hung cold about his wet clothes; the empty rooms above his head like a guilty conscience. The books, the lawyer's papers had already been searched by the FBI; the safe in the wall, empty. Anything of note had been removed and shipped off to Quantico. He'd already printed out the updated inventory list from Sentinel, so what was there left for him to find?

Markham flicked on the desk lamp and removed the Donovan file from his briefcase. He scanned the evidence inventory and saw that Donovan's hard drive was still being analyzed at Quantico. He would have to tell them what to look for now—perhaps something the FBI missed on their initial sweep; something subtle that might stand out in light of his new theory about the connection to Leo. The same went for the Rodriguezes' computer. That had been shipped off to Quantico, too.

If they don't find anything, Markham thought, *I'll bring back Marla Rodriguez's computer myself. Don't forget the beautiful lion's little sister.*

The beautiful lion . . .

Markham found himself staring down at the Donovan file—a flash of an image, vague, unclear, colored with something Alan Gates had said last week at his town house. He flipped through the file, found his copy of the initial police report and read the description of the crime scene—the results of the fingerprint analysis of Randall Donovan's car. Forensics had found nothing, but it wasn't the killer's fingerprints that Markham was interested in.

"Donovan's car," he read out loud. "A red, 2004 Peugeot 307 coupé convertible."

Import, expensive and hard to find. Just like your Criterion DVDs.

Peugeot . . . Peugeot . . .

Markham ran from the office, quickly negotiated his way in the dark to the opposite end of the house, and was out the kitchen door in less than ten seconds. He flicked on the garage light. Randall Donovan's red Peugeot was at the far end, on the other side of a white BMW. Markham headed straight for it—leaped over a stack of boxes and stopped dead before the grille.

"You've got to be kidding me," he said to himself, panting.

The Peugeot logo seemed to sparkle back at him.

The answer had been on the hood of Randall Donovan's car all along.

Chapter 29

Thursday, April 13

Cindy Smith arrived an hour before her six-thirty call to find the flowers from her mother already waiting for her in her dressing room—a dozen white roses and a note reading, *"Break a leg, kiddo! Love, Mom."*

Cindy smiled. *Too expensive, she shouldn't have done that, blahdy-blahdy-blah—but oh God, how glad I am that she did!*

Cindy felt *on*; felt ready and rested and relaxed. She had slept until noon that day and blew off her one o'clock biology class for the gym. Cindy hated biology—hated anything having to do with science and math in general—but would most likely be able to squeak out an A-minus if she buckled down for the final. Cindy hated A-minuses. She'd maintained a solid 3.8 for three years now and wasn't quite sure how an A-minus would affect her GPA—suspected it would drop a point or two and felt a sudden wave of anxiety at seeing the 3.79 on her transcript.

You're too much of a perfectionist, she heard her mother say in her head.

Right you are, M, Cindy replied, and arranged the flowers in the vase so she could see every one.

Cindy removed her script from her backpack and placed it directly in the center of her dressing table. Then she lined up everything parallel and at right angles around it: her makeup, her hair spray and hairbrush, her cough drops and her coffee mug. *"Cluttered desk, cluttered mind,"* she had heard someone say once. *OCD kiss ass*, she knew that two-faced slut Amy Pratt would call her behind her back. But Cindy didn't care. After all, Amy Pratt had been called worse behind her own back.

Cindy changed into a Harriot T-shirt and sweats and turned on her iPod, scrolled to the folder titled PRESHOW, and ate her supermarket sushi in the green room. She'd splurged for opening night; felt sorry for not eating her mother's left-over lasagna but didn't want anything too heavy messing with her stomach.

The music pumping through her earphones was from the movie *Amadeus*. One of her professors had shown a clip from it in theatre history class, and for some reason Cindy had fallen in love with it. She downloaded the entire sound-track that very afternoon and had since listened to it every day. The music grounded her—made her feel more like her-self, she thought (whatever that meant)—and had even helped her nail her first big audition at Harriot. Now, *Amadeus* was a staple of her preshow ritual, part of a complex good luck charm, and Cindy was convinced her performance would suffer without it.

Superstitious? *Beyond superstitious,* Cindy thought. And although she wasn't that hungry, she knew she'd also have to eat an orange later in the dressing room. Cindy had picked up that little habit the year before from a guest artist who

swore it made him focus better onstage. Cindy wasn't sure if
the orange helped her or not, but nonetheless it had become
part of her preshow ritual, too.

You down with OCD? Yeah, you know me!

Cindy finished her sushi and lay down on the green room
couch. She closed her eyes and let the music enter her blood-
stream as she focused on her breathing and began going over
her lines. She had just finished her big scene with Macbeth,
the one after he murders Duncan, when something startled
her—movement, a chair scraping on the floor.

Her eyes sprang open.

It was Bradley Cox.

He sat at the green room table with his earphones plugged
into his laptop—caught Cindy's gaze just as she opened her
eyes and jerked his chin to say hello.

Such a dickhead, Cindy said to herself.

She had no idea how long he'd been sitting there, but
knew he'd moved his chair on purpose to get her attention
and fuck with her while she was focusing. He'd loosened up
over the past week; had tried making casual conversation
with her during the technical rehearsals and (and Cindy
could not believe this) had even tried *flirting* with her backstage before final dress. The bruise she'd left on his ego had
finally healed, she thought. Only took two fucking semes-
ters.

Cindy nodded her hello and closed her eyes—tried to
relax into the music again but quickly became irritated with
herself when she realized her costar's presence was making
her uneasy. She turned up her music, but her iPod wasn't
loud enough to drown out what she heard next.

"Hey, Amy," Cox called. "You hear about this shit?"

"What?"

Cindy opened her eyes to see Amy Pratt entering the
green room. The fiery redhead threw down her book bag and
stood behind him, rubbing Cox's shoulders as she looked at

his laptop. Cindy's stomach flipped with disgust as she thumbed her volume down to hear what they were saying.

"Says they found some guy dead in the woods," Cox said. "North of Raleigh. Says he was stuck in the ground with a pole up his ass. Been dead for over a month. Cops think it's a serial killer. Vlad the Impaler, they're calling him."

Cindy had seen the breaking news report earlier that afternoon as she was getting off the treadmill at the gym. She couldn't hear the newscaster above all the hip-hop and the drone of the elliptical riders, and only got the gist of the story when she opened her AOL homepage on her computer back home. She glanced at the article quickly: some guy found impaled, details still sketchy, might be connected to the murder of some lawyer in Raleigh.

"Ew," Amy Pratt said, reading. "That's sick. People are so fucked up nowadays."

"Maybe you should give him your number, Amy," Cox said. "Word on the street is you like it up the ass, too."

Amy giggled and slapped him playfully on his shoulder—but she kept massaging him and whispered something in his ear. Cox smiled, then looked over at Cindy and nodded. Cindy pretended to turn down her volume.

"You say something?" she asked.

"Just wanted to know if you were ready for tonight," he said smugly. Cindy didn't take the bait—knew that he and Amy had an inside joke going and wanted her to say "yes" so they could pretend she was agreeing to whatever it was that Amy had just whispered in his ear. Their version of the *"Douchebag says what?"* game.

Childish, asinine, easy to defuse.

"You mean am I ready for the show?" Cindy asked.

"Yes," he said, smiling wider. "I mean for the *show*."

Amy smiled wider, too—thought it brilliant, Cindy could tell, the way Bradley had salvaged their little joke by emphasizing *show*.

Okay, whatever, Cindy said to herself. She didn't feel like playing, but at the same time she didn't want to leave the green room and let Mr. and Mrs. Dipshit win.

"Just go with your heart, Bradley," she said, deadpan. "Therein resides the only answer you'll ever need."

Bradley looked momentarily confused—as if he couldn't figure out if he'd just been insulted—then sighed and rolled his eyes over to Amy.

"Guess I'm not good enough for a straight answer," he said. Cindy could tell he was about to follow up with a snide remark, when the break she was looking for came over the intercom.

"Testing, one-two-three," said the stage manager. "It's ten minutes 'til our official call. Don't forget to sign in on the callboard."

And in a flash Cindy was off the couch. She'd signed in nearly an hour ago but couldn't pass up the opportunity to get away. She turned up the volume on her iPod and hurried down the hall, past a group of students and straight for the electrics shop. She hoped the door was unlocked—wanted to find a quiet corner to finish going over her lines before going back to the dressing room.

I should've had one of the star dressing rooms upstairs, Cindy thought, while simultaneously chastising herself for being such a diva. *Who cares if Mr. Dickhead and his boys have more quick changes—*

The doorknob pulled away from her hand just as she reached for it—startled her and caused one of her earphones to fall out.

It was Edmund Lambert.

He stood in the electrics shop doorway looking down at her—black T-shirt, his face dusty but unfazed. He'd been checking the trap to make sure everything was running smoothly, Cindy knew. *Even more OCD than I am*, she thought, and felt her face go hot at the thought of liking him all the more for it. She hadn't had much time to speak with him over the last week—they kept missing each other because he was out in the house with Jennings or under the stage in Hell—and she hoped he couldn't see how happy she was to finally talk to him alone.

"I'm sorry," she said. "I was going to see if the door was unlocked. Needed a place that was quiet to focus before the show."

"I can lock the doorknob, if you want," Edmund said. Cindy was confused. "So no one will bother you. The doorknob is only locked on the outside. Jennings gave me the keys. You can leave whenever you're finished. See?"

He locked the door and turned the inside knob; demonstrated by closing the door, then opening it from the inside.

"That'd be awesome, Edmund. Thank you."

He smiled and let her in, unfolded a chair, and placed it in the corner behind a rack of coupling cables. He was so cool around her—but in a good way, Cindy thought; not aloof, not superior, yet not awkward or trying too hard to be smooth like Bradley Cox. Edmund Lambert was just . . . well . . . *present* was the only word Cindy could think of to describe him. He listened to her when she spoke; really listened for the sake of listening only. No hidden agenda. No underlying intention of wanting to bang her. He was just there, taking her in with his steel-blue eyes. And when he smiled—which she had never seen him do with any of the other girls—well, she never had to question whether or not that smile was genuine.

But what Cindy *really* liked about Edmund Lambert was how she felt when she smiled back.

"I'm going to watch the show tonight," he said, "but I'm not part of the running crew. Won't be back until photo call on Sunday unless something goes wrong with the trap. Means you'll have to get a stage manager to let you in here from now on."

"I should be all right tomorrow," Cindy said. "I can find another place if it's locked—but this is great. Just opening-night jitters, I guess."

"You shouldn't be nervous." Cindy loved the way he said *nuh-vuhs*. "You're doing a great job. You steal the show from Bradley Cox."

Edmund was so matter of fact in his compliment, yet at the same time so devoid of any pettiness toward Cox, that Cindy felt herself blushing.

"Thank you," she said. "I really appreciate it. And this, too. Letting me warm up and focus in here, I mean."

"No problem. I'll be back in about twenty minutes, but I won't disturb you if you're still here. Break a leg tonight, Cindy."

Edmund was almost out the door when Cindy called after him: "Did you decide yet if you're going to the cast party to-morrow night?"

"Probably not. I have a lot of work to do around the house this weekend."

"Well, it might be fun if you made an appearance. I won't be there long, either. Just a couple of drinks and I'll have to stick around for Brown Bags. I know you've never been to a cast party here, but do you know what those are? Brown Bags, I mean?"

"Yes. I've heard people mention them in the scene shop. The awards the seniors make for people in the cast. Inside jokes written down on brown paper bags, right?"

"Yes, that's right."

"I hear sometimes they can get pretty mean."

"Yeah, they can, but it's all in fun, I guess. You have to have a good sense of humor. I'm sure mine will be pretty brutal if Bradley has anything to say about it."

Edmund said nothing.

"Anyway," Cindy continued, "maybe you could come along and save me—not from my Brown Bag, I mean—but, well, I pretty much don't like the people who are going to be there. I'd rather talk to you than any of them, to be honest."

"If you don't like them, then why you going?"

His question was sincere and nonjudgmental—almost childlike in his curiosity, Cindy thought. "Because I'm weak," she said. "Because I've gotten the reputation of being a snob, and I don't want to give people the satisfaction of being able to say, 'See? I told you she thinks her shit doesn't stink.' " Edmund smiled vaguely and looked away from her for the first time. "I hope you don't think less of me for admitting that to you."

"Not at all."

"I don't know, maybe we could just hang out together, have a couple of drinks and just chill. Might be nice just to talk. You know, away from the theater, the show, all the stuff on our minds when we're here."

Edmund stood by the door, thinking. Cindy suddenly felt uncomfortable.

"If it's too much of a big deal," she said quickly, "like, if your girlfriend will get pissed off or something—well, I mean, I totally understand."

"Let me see how things go tonight," Edmund said finally. "Okay?"

"Okay."

He smiled and was gone.

Alone in the electrics shop, Cindy suddenly became aware of her breathing and the steady thumping in her chest. Did she really just do that? Did she really just ask a man out on a date for the first time in her life?

But he didn't say yes, said a voice in her head.

But he didn't say no, either, replied another voice.

But he wanted *to say yes,* said the first voice. *Couldn't you tell?*

You saw it in his eyes, too, then?

Yes, I did!

Cindy didn't sit down in the chair Edmund had set out for her. She was too excited, felt a hundred pounds lighter, and began pacing behind the cable rack. She tried going over her lines, tried saying them out loud and imagining Edmund Lambert as Macbeth instead of douchebag Bradley Cox, but the voices in her head kept analyzing what had just passed between them, making her nervous but proud at the same time.

Edmund Lambert was going to come.

She just *knew* it.

Then, out of the corner of her eye, she spied his book bag on the chair by the electrics shop computer. She'd seen him with it many times and recognized the Army-issue camouflage.

She got an idea.

Cindy ran to the door and peeked out—saw a freshman, a pudgy kid who played one of Macbeth's soldiers, heading toward the green room. Jonathan was his name—or at least, that's what she thought his name was. She couldn't remember; had never spoken to him before and wondered if she was confusing him with another freshman in Macbeth's army. No time to worry; no time to feel guilty for using him.

"Jonathan?" Cindy called out impulsively. He stopped. She had gotten his name right, *thank God!* "Could you come here for a minute, please?"

The pudgy soldier sauntered over awkwardly, suspiciously.

"Would you mind doing me a favor?" Cindy asked.

"What kind of favor?"

"I got lucky getting in here to go over my speeches, but I need something from my dressing room. Would you mind holding the door for me while I go and get it? Otherwise it'll shut and I'll be locked out."

"What, do I look like your bitch now?"

"Please, Jonathan. I don't want to prop the door open.

Someone might close it or steal the room from me. And it'd be a huge help, you have no idea, if you're here to tell anybody who tries to do that I'll be right back."

"All right," he sighed. "But make it quick. I got stuff to do, too, you know."

Cindy thanked him and dashed down the hall.

Chapter 30

Twenty minutes later, Edmund Lambert returned to the electrics shop to find the white rose from Cindy Smith sticking out of his book bag. He knew it was from her; had seen one of the assistant stage managers carrying the vase into her dressing room earlier that afternoon when he arrived at the theater.

Edmund removed the flower and sniffed it—stroked the petals with the tip of his nose and wondered if it was a sign from the Prince.

He'd read the news on the electrics shop computer; had even gone to CNN.com to watch the video. The police had found Billy Canning, and the press had already tied him to Randall Donovan. They would no doubt unearth the connection to Leona Bonita and Angel's very soon, too. In fact, Edmund suspected the police might already know about Angel's; had probably pieced it together as soon as they found Donovan.

The General had been fortunate in the beginning. The police had bought his telephone call about the Latino gangs, but the General didn't know why they never connected

Rodriguez to Angel's. All part of the equation, he'd concluded. It'd been the same for Billy Canning. And, after all,
the Prince hadn't been worried about the police finding him
all the way out there in the woods anytime soon.

"Touch the doorway," Edmund heard the General say in
his mind. He closed his eyes and saw the sodomite staring
up at him from the chair in horror—his eyes filled with tears,
with the disbelieving desperation of one who had sinned.
"Touch the doorway," the General repeated.

"Please, God," the sodomite cried as he raised a trembling hand—his one *free* hand—and touched the General's
chest. "Please, I did what you wanted me to do, now please
let me go."

"Will you know him when he comes for you?" the General asked, guiding the sodomite's fingers along the outside
of the doorway.

"Please, I did what you—"

"Will you *know* him when he *comes* for you?"

"Yes," the sodomite said weakly. "Yes, now please let me
go."

"And what will you tell him, soldier?"

"Jesus Christ, I—"

"*What* will you *tell* him, soldier?"

"I accept my mission."

"And why do you accept?"

"The nine to three," the sodomite whimpered, his tears
flowing freely. "It is my destiny as written in the stars."

The General strapped down the sodomite's free hand and
began gathering up the tattoo equipment. The sodomite
screamed again to be set free, but the General ignored him.
Besides, the sodomite hardly had any voice left at all. He'd
been in the chair for over a week.

And despite the circumstances, even the Prince was impressed with the sodomite's work on the doorway—or at
least he seemed to be. The power of the first doorway, the

one on the throne, was already beginning to weaken by that point. The General had only allowed the sodomite's right hand to be free and kept his Beretta pointed at his head the entire time he used his needle. That was one of the reasons the tattoo had taken so long to be completed; for even though the General was strong, his arm often grew tired from holding the gun for long stretches at a time.

The General often wondered if the police knew about the stolen tattoo equipment—older equipment, which the General had taken from a storage closet at Canning's. He also wondered if the sodomite's lover ever suspected his beau was having an affair at the tattoo parlor behind his back. Granted, the Prince hadn't allowed the affair to go on long. Just long enough for the sinful sodomite to touch and kiss the doorway; just long enough for him to let his guard down and become attracted to the young man who called himself Ken Ralston.

But now, over two months later, the General understood that with the discovery of the corrupt lawyer the FBI was involved. And thus the General also understood that, now that the authorities had ditched the drug cartel connection and were calling him a serial killer—Vlad the Impaler, how ridiculous!—well, now things would have to be different.

No, the General would not be able to go back to West Hargett Street tonight. Instead, he would have to spend the evening in consultation with the Prince.

The rose. Cindy Smith. The cast party Friday night.

Perhaps the Prince would like the General to recruit his soldiers elsewhere?

Edmund took a deep breath. He needn't worry about all that now, for unlike the beginning, when the General had to decode and interpret the messages from the Prince on his own, now the General could ask the Prince directly, and the Prince would answer him with his visions.

As long as the doorway remained open.

Edmund returned the rose to his book bag and sat admiring it for a long time—its stem, a long wooden stake planted in the earth; the flower itself, the scrubbed-white flesh of the next soldier.

A sign, he heard the General whisper in his mind. *The female most certainly has given us a sign.*

Chapter 31

Markham sat at the Resident Agency conference table with a sea of paperwork stretched out before him. He had been there all day; had gone home at 2 a.m. the night before and only punched four restless hours of sleep on the clock before returning to the Resident Agency at eight.

The story broke about four hours later, and was all over the news by three that afternoon—Rodriguez and Guerrera, Donovan and Canning, all connected in their grisly, graphic glory. The FBI had learned that the groundskeeper who'd discovered Donovan in the baseball field was going to talk. He'd already made a public statement and was scheduled to appear on *Nancy Grace* that evening. Gurganus would roll soon, too, he knew. They always did.

Word had also gotten out about the writing on Canning's chest via "a reliable source inside the investigation." Markham thought most likely one of Sergeant Powell's boys had been paid off, and unless the FBI didn't deal with this information swiftly, the vultures were going to be a pain in the ass about it. Fortunately, an FBI spokesperson had temporarily dodged the question during a press conference earlier that afternoon.

However, rather than seeing all the media attention as a roadblock, Markham relished the idea of getting the vultures to work for him for a change. And so the FBI decided to release an incomplete image of the writing found on Billy Canning's torso. They would also alter the image to include a line of what they said "appeared to be Romanian." This would satisfy the press and let them run with the Vlad angle while the FBI followed their real leads.

Their real leads.

Markham stared down at them on the table. It had taken him, along with Schaap and their consultant in the classical studies department at NC State, over twelve hours to put it all together—feverish bouts of research and discussion broken up by long stretches of waiting while this or that theory was followed up on. This last follow-up had taken the longest of them all. Markham had been waiting to hear back for almost two hours. But that was all right, for this last followup was indeed going to be the *last*—the most important piece of the puzzle; the proof that all his research had not been for naught.

"Here it is," Schaap said, entering. "I got one of the boys preparing the JPEG scan as we speak."

He handed Markham a copy of a black-and-white photograph.

Markham studied it for an entire minute without speaking.

"I'll call Alan Gates," he said finally.

But he did not move.

No, for the moment Sam Markham was content to just sit there gaping, unable to believe his eyes.

Chapter 32

The General stepped into the farmhouse, set the alarm, and checked his watch. If the second act had started on time, he thought, Macbeth was about to get his head cut off. The General thought this fitting, as he himself was about to consult the Prince's head in the Throne Room.

All part of the equation. Everything connected.

The General was happy to finally be home. True, the young man named Edmund had only stayed to watch the trap open for Duncan's descent into Hell, but still it had seemed like a long time. Jennings had stopped by to see how things were going and told Edmund to go home; said he was a good worker and gave him a key to the tool closet—"for the summer theater season," he added.

This sat well with Edmund Lambert, even though he would soon have no more need for the tool closet. In fact, he would be *long gone* by the time summer theater began. After all, it was during the summer that the Prince was prophesized to return—as in the old days, in the burning sun of noontime, bringing war and pestilence and destruction with the deadly harvest of the summer solstice.

And the Prince's army would return with him; would be waiting by the doorway, ready to serve and pave the way for what was to come.

But someone would be waiting for the General, too. And once he was able to pass through the doorway, they would be together again. In this world or that? Well, the General wasn't sure.

The General smiled and went upstairs, undressed in the bathroom, and stepped into the shower. And as he scrubbed off the remains of his day-life, his mind soon wandered to the young woman named Cindy Smith.

He turned up the water as hot as it would go and stood there watching as it reddened the flesh beneath the large tattoo on his chest and stomach. And when the doorway became numb with the pain, he closed his eyes and imagined Cindy Smith in her spirit costume, rising up from the trap and stepping through his flesh from the depths of Hell. He opened his eyes and gazed down at the doorway, half expecting to see her there with him in the shower, and saw instead that he had grown erect.

He would need to consult the Prince about all this; would need to look for her in his visions, in the flashes of images and sounds. He hoped he would find her there, and began to wonder if the she wasn't part of the equation, too.

Chapter 33

Alan Gates had been dreaming about pigs when the telephone startled him awake. The clunky old ringer was set on high, but his wife kept on snoring. She was used to it; had always been a heavy sleeper, but had been conditioned over the course of their thirty-five-year marriage to snore through her husband's occasional late-night interruptions.

It was all part of being married to "the life," just one of the many sacrifices that Debbie Gates had made for her husband over the years. And in all that time, he never once took her for granted; still thanked God every night for his blessings even as he thought it was only a matter time before the Old Man Upstairs pulled the rug out from under his feet—just as He'd done to so many others in his line of work.

A deeply religious man, Alan Gates had indeed been blessed over the last forty years. Had come out unscathed from two tours in Vietnam and quickly made his way up through the ranks of the FBI in the seventies and early eighties. He could've long ago been promoted to director if he'd gunned for it; could have retired by now, too. But the unit chief slot at Quantico was where his heart was; and when he thought about it, he considered himself as much a part of the Behavioral Analysis Unit as the glass and steel and brick in which it was housed.

However, the fact that his wife had learned over the years to sleep through his late-night telephone calls always made him feel uneasy—even more so now that the kids were moved out and married. Heaven forbid if he was away on a case and needed to get in touch with her. Heaven forbid if there was ever an emergency. And if the Old Man were to decide that it was finally time to pull that rug out, Gates was sure He'd do it while he was away and Debbie was asleep— a fire or some other tragedy in which, if only she'd woken up, she could've been saved.

Something like that would be most in line with the Old Man's MO, for over the years Gates had come to the conclusion that not only did God have a sick sense of humor but also that He judged a man's character by how well he could take a joke.

Gates fumbled for the receiver and squinted at his bed-side clock. *11:17 p.m.*

"Yes?"

"Alan? It's Sam."

"Go ahead."

"Sorry to bother you so late, but I'm here with Andy Schaap at the RA in Raleigh. We've found something. Something we need to get moving on right away."

"Give it to me."

Gates listened carefully as his number-one agent explained his theory. And when Markham was finished, Gates hung up and lay in bed staring up at the ceiling. His wife had slept through the entire conversation—had already started snoring full force again by the time he donned his bathrobe and closed the bedroom door gently behind him.

He would make his telephone calls downstairs in his study, but would first make a pot of coffee to clear his head.

The necessary arrangements wouldn't take much time. He could be back in bed in less than half an hour if he wanted. But Alan Gates decided it would be better if he remained in his study. After all, there was no way he was going to fall back to sleep now.

Not after what Sam Markham had just told him.

Chapter 34

Cindy Smith hated that she enjoyed getting bigger applause than Bradley Cox—actually despised that diva side of her personality—but at the same time wasn't about to lie to herself and pretend it didn't matter. It did. *Oh, how it did!* And when the audience began their standing ovation on *her* bow; when their applause died down ever so slightly for her costar—*slightly, yes,* Cindy thought, *but noticeable enough that even Bradley's parents had to hear*—the young actress felt as if her heart would burst with pride.

But when she looked toward the wings and saw that Edmund Lambert was nowhere to be found, Cindy felt her heart deflate. She was sure he would've been there watching, applauding, smiling—especially after what had passed between them just before intermission.

"Thank you for the flower," he said, catching her in the stairwell on the way back down to her dressing room.

"Thank you for looking out for me," Cindy replied.

Then, a long silence in which she saw the corner of Edmund's mouth turn up, his eyes narrowing as if he was studying her. Cindy felt her cheeks go hot, felt as if an electric generator had been turned on in the stairwell—the low hum of a charged circuit suddenly connecting them at their chests. He wanted to kiss her. She just knew it. And oh God how badly she wanted to kiss him back!

"You're very special," he said finally, his steel-blue eyes locked with hers in that way that made her retinas tingle. "I never realized just how special until tonight."

Then he smiled and was out the stage door.

Cindy felt as if she were on fire; made her way back to her dressing room and changed into her next costume with the hum of the electric generator never leaving her. It powered her all through the second act. And even before she took her bow, she knew her performance had been a triumph.

But now, as the lights dimmed and the cast left the stage to resounding applause, Cindy's victory felt curiously hollow. She was on autopilot, it seemed, and caught herself paying only half attention to George Kiernan as she searched for Edmund among the crowd outside her dressing room. He never showed. And when Amy Pratt asked her to join the rest of the cast downtown for a beer and some cheese fries, Cindy politely declined and drove back to her house feeling more alone than she had in a long time.

She lay awake well into the night, straddling the thrill, the satisfaction of her bravura performance along with the hollow disappointment that Edmund Lambert hadn't returned to the theater after she saw him leave. She had a crush on him. A bad one. And her awareness of how deeply his absence affected her only made matters worse.

Had she misread his signals? Had she come on too strong with the rose? Perhaps she was overreacting—being "melodramatic" as her mother would say. After all, there had to be a simple explanation, hadn't there?

Nonetheless, Cindy still felt the electric circuit she had closed with him humming quietly beneath her thoughts. And once again she found herself sitting in front of her computer. She didn't bother with her Facebook page, but instead went straight for Google Earth and typed in the address she'd found in the campus directory. A couple more clicks and Cindy zoomed in the satellite imagery as close as it would go. She went back and forth between plus and minus until she was satisfied, but still the photo was grainy and unclear—a blurry white square at the end of a long dirt road; some smaller squares surrounded by clumps of trees and patches of green farmland.

Impulsively, Cindy clicked on the *Get Directions* link, typed in her home address, and discovered it would take about thirty-five minutes to get there.

"A simple explanation," she whispered. "Perhaps you needed to get home for something. A sick mother, maybe, all the way out there on your farm."

You're a sick mother, replied a voice in her head. *A fucking stalker, if you ask me.*

Cindy sighed and clicked for maximum zoom-in; sat looking at the house for a long time and wondered if maybe, just maybe, Edmund Lambert was sitting in front of his computer, zooming in on her house, too.

"The cast party," she said. "I'll know for sure if you come to the cast party."

Or maybe someday you can just pay him a visit at his little farmhouse and have a party of your own.

Cindy smiled.

That sounds like something Amy Pratt would say, she replied in her mind, and climbed back into bed wondering whether or not the redheaded slut might just be on to something.

Chapter 35

An emergency teleconference ordered by Alan Gates himself.

Sam Markham was tired and sat staring at his notes with his head in his hands. The Resident Agency's conference room was small and cramped with almost two dozen agents seated double deep around a narrow oak table. They were already looking at him suspiciously, their message loud and clear: *"This better be good, Quantico boy."*

But Markham didn't give a shit. He felt confident about the cards he was holding, but at the same time felt guilty for not telling Schaap that it was Marla Rodriguez who'd blown the case wide open for him. Nonetheless, he would keep his promise to her. He owed her that and much, much more.

"You need anything, Sam?" Schaap asked, sitting next to him.

"I'm good, I think."

"Still feel like we're on the *Twilight Zone.* You hear from Underhill again?"

"Not since we talked yesterday. He said he'll tag along with Gates this morning."

"He's got to be close to retirement now, am I right?"

"I hope not," Markham said. "He's the best forensic psychiatrist around. Still teaches at Georgetown. Developmental science, personality disorders. A lot like Gates, in that respect. They'll have to drag him out kicking and screaming."

"All set," said an agent, handing Schaap the remote control. Schaap pressed a button, and the large teleconference screen flickered on to reveal the face of Alan Gates.

"Good morning, gentlemen," he said. "You're the last to come online, Agent Schaap. Do you have your visual and your PowerPoint feed ready?"

"Yes, sir," Schaap said, holding up the remote.

"Thank you all for coming on such short notice," Gates said. "Because of the nature of this investigation, time is of the essence. As you know, this conference is a joint linkup involving the FBI Resident Agency in Raleigh, the FBI Field Office in Charlotte, and the BAU here at Quantico. This is Agent Markham's show, so if you have any questions, please raise your hands and wait for confirmation from him."

The feed on the screen split into two: Alan Gates and a long shot of the conference room at the Charlotte Field Office. Markham quickly surveyed the faces watching him there—suspicious, cold, yet childlike in their expectations of him.

"Joining me now," Gates said, his feed widening, "is Dr. David Underhill, chief forensic psychiatrist for the Behavioral Analysis Unit's support team. Doctor Underhill has been working with Special Agent Markham to develop a preliminary psychological profile of the killer known as the Impaler. It's all yours, Sam."

The rustling of papers, the shifting of butts, and Sam Markham began.

"Thank you, Alan," he said, leaning forward like a senator. "We're pretty tired over here, so I ask for your patience if I become inarticulate."

Silence, still not much sympathy in the air, but screw it, the soft sell was over.

"You've already been briefed on how I discovered the killer's connection to the constellation Leo, as well as the crescent-moon visual and the murder sites being a mirror of the physical dynamic of the drag theater. Also, you should have in front of you a copy of the altered text that will be released to the press later this morning. You'll notice that this version contains not only the original Arabic and Hebrew but also a partial of the Greek. It is this line that our linguistics experts modified into the Romanian with the hopes of satisfying both the media and any amateur sleuths who might give us trouble. They don't know yet about the writing on Donovan, so we needn't worry about addressing that."

A hand went up in the Charlotte Office—their NCAVC coordinator.

"Go ahead, Charlotte," Markham said.

"Do you think the Romanian might compel the Impaler to come forward and correct us?"

"I don't," Markham said. "Our boy was never concerned about public recognition of his crimes to begin with—never corrected the media with the original gang and drug angles, nor did he seem to care if we ever found Canning. The best we can hope for is that the Romanian will keep him in the dark about the true nature of our investigation."

"I assume then," the NCAVC coordinator sighed wearily, "that you are at some point going to tell us exactly what that true nature is?"

Markham had disliked this guy almost immediately—his cynical tone, the deep vocal resonance, and the way his right eyebrow was constantly raised like Mr. Spock's.

Yes, you Vulcan prick, he thought—but instead said, "Let's first establish whom we're up against. Dr. Underhill?"

"Taking into consideration the context and methodological detail of the Impaler's crimes," Underhill began, "it's safe to say our boy is a textbook visionary killer who believes some outside force is commanding him to kill. Indeed, his highly disciplined behavioral pattern—the custom measurements of the stakes, the precision of the writing, the scrubbing of Donovan with Comet—is quite common in cases in which the subject is suffering from some kind of severe delusional disorder. Most telling, however, is how all this relates to the killer's selection of his victims in conjunction with the messages gleaned from the drag theater. You see, our boy not only thinks that he is receiving messages but also that he needs to send them back. Sam?"

"Given my initial premise of the killer's connection to the constellation Leo, and that most likely three of the four victims were homosexuals, I originally suspected our victim profile would be based on a common sexual orientation. The fact that the historical Vlad impaled homosexuals only seemed to bolster this theory. However, during my investigation into Randall Donovan's background, I could find no evidence of a secret homosexual lifestyle, and certainly nothing that connected him to the other three victims—that is, until I began to look for a connection somewhere else. First slide, please."

Schaap clicked the remote, and the screen wiped into a pair of JPEG scans.

"Here we have both a map of downtown Raleigh and the Peugeot logo from Donovan's car: a silver standing lion. Agent Schaap and I discovered that the route Donovan took to his office would have brought him very close not only to Angel's but also to any number of intersections the killer might have taken to get to West Hargett Street. Thus, in light of the connections to the constellation Leo and the evidence we are about to show you, it's our opinion that the Impaler first zeroed in on Randall Donovan because of the unusual car he drove: a Peugeot 307 with a lion logo on its hood."

A gasp from somewhere in the Charlotte Office, and a hand went up at the Resident Agency. It was Big Joe the Sox Fan Connelly.

"Question here from the RA," Markham said. "Clear slide and go ahead, Joe."

"I'm not sure I understand. Are you saying that the connection between the victims has to do with a purely visual, almost superficial connection between them and the constellation Leo?"

"Not necessarily the constellation itself, but what it represents: a lion. Thus, the Impaler selected each of his victims because they bore a common visual—a mark of the lion, so to speak, that says to the killer, 'This is the one.' "

"Then the Impaler chose Donovan at random, simply because he had the mark of the lion on the hood of his car?"

"Yes and no," Markham replied. "To a certain degree, the lawyer was in the wrong place at the wrong time; meaning, he crossed paths with the Impaler when he was out looking for his next victim on West Hargett Street. But the fact that Donovan had a lion on his car is only part of the equation. We must remember that the Impaler needs confirmation from an outside entity to go ahead with his killing. This kind of delusional behavior is indicative not only of sacrificial types of killings but also of the type of killer who believes he'll be rewarded somehow for doing as he is told."

"But my kid wears a frigging *Lion King* T-shirt all the time," Big Joe said. "Are you saying I should tell him to stop until we catch this guy?"

"I'm not saying that at all. The prevalence of lion imagery in our culture would make such an exclusive criterion impractical. And since we know that the Impaler is very patient and calculated, we can assume that the mark of the lion has to combine with another set of criteria—the first of which is the context of the presentation of the mark itself. The Impaler would not only have to identify the mark of the lion while he is hunting but its context must seem to him as out of the ordinary, perhaps almost supernatural. The serendipitous appearance of the lawyer in his rare Peugeot on West Hargett Street, as well as Jose Rodriguez's Leona Bonita act in the drag theater, are only two examples of such contexts."

"So the mark of the lion is some kind of visual omen?" Joe asked. "Like a black cat crossing your path or something?"

"That's a good way of putting it, yes," Markham said.

A hand went up in the Charlotte Office—Mr. Spock again.

"But what about the act of the impalement itself?" he asked. "I assume that you've explored the deeper psychological underpinnings; the impalements being a symbolic representation of male-on-male sodomy. And given the fact that perhaps three, if not all four, of the victims were gay males, are you willing to classify the killer as some kind of twisted gay basher? Perhaps a frustrated or latent homosexual who selects his victims from Raleigh's gay population?"

"Again," Markham said, "I can find no evidence that Randall Donovan was gay. Perhaps the Impaler began his search among the homosexual population, but then moved beyond that criterion. I think it's too early to make a call on the Impaler's sexual orientation, especially when taken in the context of the sacrificial nature of the killings, as well as how our boy thinks he will be rewarded for all his hard work."

"I understand that," said Mr. Spock. "But if the connection between the victims lies in the mark of the lion and not in their sexual orientation, how does Billy Canning fit in? Of all the tattoos on his body, none of them were lions."

"Point taken," Markham said. "But again, the mark of the lion is only the first criterion in the Impaler's selection process. With regard to Canning, there are many possibilities as to why the Impaler would've selected him in conjunction with the lion imagery. Perhaps Canning tattooed a lion on the Impaler's body. I visited the tattoo parlor again last night. There's a bulletin board filled with Polaroids there. Most were faceless close-ups of his work—a few lions, yes, but nothing that I could tie directly to the Impaler. The Polaroids have been collected into evidence, of course, and we'll analyze them in conjunction with our working physical description—"

"You actually think the Impaler would've allowed Canning take a picture of him?" Mr. Spock asked.

"No, I don't. Our boy is too careful, too meticulous to leave a calling card like that. If the Impaler *did* allow Canning to take his picture, I submit he abducted him at the tattoo parlor so he could snatch the Polaroid back. Who knows at this point? In my opinion, the most likely scenario is that the Impaler was inspired to kill Canning via a lion image he saw at the tattoo parlor itself. But the presentation of it would have to have been in a context that was out of the ordinary. Perhaps Canning suggested the lion tattoo. That would have been a good enough sign for the Impaler."

"Most visionary killers are extremely narcissistic," Underhill said. "They consider themselves to be chosen ones, if you will, and sometimes believe themselves to be another person or supernatural figure altogether. The lion imagery is only part of the code our boy uses to communicate with whomever he thinks is commanding him to kill."

"Yes," said Markham. "And once he begins looking more closely at an individual, that person has to meet another criterion in order to be worthy of sacrifice. From the Impaler's point of view, a homosexual would be a fine candidate, but not the only kind of candidate. No, the Impaler's victims could come from almost any walk of life, as long as they are the kind of male the outside entity would desire."

"That's what we're all so anxious to hear," said Mr. Spock. "If this outside entity is not Vlad the Impaler, then who is he?"

Markham smiled.

"I'm getting to that," he said—but stopped himself short of adding, *You Vulcan prick.*

Chapter 36

Cindy Smith awoke that morning at ten o'clock and went straight for her computer, turned it on, then decided to hop in the shower while the old relic booted up—fully aware, of course, that she was prolonging the anticipation.

More like self-torture, she thought as she scrubbed the last of the previous night's makeup from her face. She felt foolish but at the same time alive with excitement—the hot water washing over her, the electric generator (still humming) now steaming and sizzling and sparking beneath her smooth, pink skin.

Plus, Cindy said to herself, *if he hasn't written yet, this will give him more time. My e-mail address is on the contact sheet for* Macbeth. *My phone number, too. Maybe he'll call.*

You're really acting pathetic, a voice said in her head, but Cindy ignored it, toweled herself dry, and put on her bathrobe. And just to prove to the voice that she could still play it cool, she padded downstairs to the kitchen and grabbed a cereal bar and a glass of orange juice.

When she returned to her bedroom and finally signed into her e-mail, Cindy found four messages in her inbox—two general notifications from the university, which she immediately deleted; an opening-night congratulations from George Kiernan to the cast and crew; and an e-mail from her father titled simply, *The show.*

But there was nothing from Edmund Lambert.

Nothing at all.

Her stomach sinking, Cindy deleted her father's e-mail without opening it. She already knew what it would say: some version of, *Hope the show went well. Sorry I won't be able to make it. Things are pretty hectic around* her *as usual. Keep up with your studies and talk to you soon. Dad.*

Cindy never forgot that first e-mail from her father saying he was going to miss her main-stage debut; how he made the mistake of writing "her" instead of "here"—*"Things are pretty hectic around HER,"* he'd said.

A Freudian slip, Cindy thought.

Of course, in the three years since her first role at Harriot, Cindy's father never made that mistake again, but his absence at every one of her shows spoke volumes. *Don't ever forget you come second,* Daddy Dearest was really saying. *Always second after new wife and new kid.*

Yeah, things sure were pretty hectic around "her."

And, of course, Cindy knew deep down that the *keep up your studies* tag at the end—always at the end—was just a slap in the face in case she didn't get the gist of the previous sentence. For Daddy Dearest was not only saying, *Make sure you have a backup plan when this silly-waste-of-time acting thing doesn't work out,* but also, *Don't expect me to waste any of* my *time on your bullshit.*

Cindy sat staring at her empty inbox for a long time, when suddenly the sinking feeling in her stomach rose to the back of her throat. She swallowed hard, and for a moment felt as if she would cry.

Who are you getting so upset over? asked the voice in her

head. *Daddy or Edmund Lambert? At least Daddy Dearest took the time to e-mail you.*

Impulsively, Cindy reached for her book bag, found the *Macbeth* contact sheet inside her dialects binder, and traced her finger over Edmund Lambert's e-mail address. There was no number listed for him; only the number for the Harriot scene shop.

"You wouldn't call him anyway," Cindy said out loud. "Not after the thing with the rose. But you could always e-mail him."

Maybe they're one and the same, the voice in her head persisted. *Daddy and Lambert. Maybe that's why you're so attracted to Mr. Soldier Boy—older guy, Daddy issues. What would Freud have said about* that?

"Fuck you," Cindy whispered, and shut off her computer.

She closed her eyes and took a deep breath—tried to shut out all thoughts of her father and Edmund Lambert and forced her mind to focus on the day ahead. Her dialects class was canceled because of the show, but she still had her private singing tutorial at noon. She'd get her ass reamed for sure if word got back to Kiernan that she blew it off. But her voice lesson was in the music building, which meant she'd really have no excuse to stop by the theater at all today; no excuse to wander past the scene shop and perhaps run into Edmund Lambert. She could always hang out for a bit in the computer lab; linger just a little longer at her locker with the hope that—

You see? said the voice in her head. *You just can't keep your mind off of him. So fucking pathetic.*

"Okay," Cindy said, "if he hasn't e-mailed or called me when I get back, I'll e-mail him before I head off to the gym. After that, he can just keep up with his fucking studies."

Pathetic and obsessed, said the voice in her head.

Cindy laid the contact sheet atop her keyboard, making

sure that it was centered and its edges were perfectly parallel with the edges of the keyboard underneath.

Curiously, she felt better.

Obsessed, repeated the voice in her head.

"Beyond obsessed," Cindy answered, smiling.

Then she got dressed.

Chapter 37

As Markham shuffled his notes, he became keenly aware of how the anticipation in the room suddenly ratcheted up a notch—could almost feel the other agents zeroing in on him and adjusting their antennae.

"Now then," he said, "I'll ask all of you to entertain the line of reasoning that led us to whom we believe to be the 'I' in 'I have returned.' The Leo slide, please."

Schaap obliged, and Markham rose from his chair, thrust his hands in his pockets, and walked casually to the far end of the conference table.

"On the screen," he began, "is the traditional version of the constellation Leo. Schaap and I, with the assistance of our consultant in the classical studies department at NC State, began our research into the ancient cultures represented by the writing found on Donovan and Canning. Our consultant quickly pointed out that, in all of these cultures, not only do we see strong astrological traditions dating back to the beginnings of their written history but also the lion figuring prominently in their respective mythologies.

"Next we began to look specifically for mythological traditions connected to the time of year when Leo is the most visible: spring, when the lion returns once again to become visible among the stars. In other words, we took the phrase 'I have returned' as literally as possible. Schaap?"

"The most obvious place to look first was with the Ancient Egyptians," he said. "Pretty much everybody is familiar with the way their gods are portrayed. You know, half animal, half human. But before we even began looking for a spring connection, our classical studies expert suggested we look somewhere else."

"Right," said Markham. "Given the history of each of the ancient cultures at the center of our investigation, as well as the documented borrowing and cross-fertilization of religions and mythologies between those cultures, our consultant said an Egyptian deity would be a stretch. Meaning, if we worked from the premise that the Impaler used each of the six ancient scripts to literally speak to a lion god or a mutation of such within those cultures—or perhaps, even to speak as the god himself—a through-line of an Egyptian deity would not work."

"Now you're losing me," said Big Joe Connelly.

Markham was about to answer, but Alan Gates interrupted him: "May I, Sam?"

"Sure," Markham said, taken aback.

"You see," Gates began, "many scholars believe that, specifically with regard to Middle Eastern religions, one can trace similarities and borrowings from one religion to the next. For example, in the Christian religion, some scholars believe that the story of Jesus Christ's resurrection was adapted from the Egyptian myth of Osiris, who was also believed to have been murdered and resurrected. Legitimate scholarship or academic conspiracy theory, depending on your point of view. Nonetheless, if I follow Agent Markham correctly, he's saying that if one were to look for such a god emanating from the Egyptians—that is, a lion god that could have permeated and/or mutated within all the ancient religions represented by the scripts on Donovan and Canning—well, you're saying such an Egyptian god doesn't exist, right, Sam?"

"That's exactly right," Markham said. "Especially since there is a better candidate that not only can be traced between all the mythologies in question, but that also fits nicely with a return in the spring. Next slide, please."

Schaap clicked the remote, and the screen wiped into a drawing of what appeared to be two separate stone tablets. The first tablet was divided into three rows, each containing a procession of half-human animal-headed deities. A lion-headed god with strange ears in the center of the bottom row was slightly larger than the rest of the figures. The most terrifying image, however, was at the top: the head of a roaring lion peeking over the border of the tablet itself. The other tablet showed the rear of the lion. It stood on eagle-clawed hindquarters with a pair of large wings on its back.

"What you're looking at," Markham said, "is an artist's rendering of the front and back of the Hell Plaque, or Lamashtu Plaque as some scholars call it. The original is in the Louvre, is made of bronze, and dates from the Neo-Assyrian period between the tenth and seventh centuries BC. It's believed to be a type of healing artifact that was hung over the bed to ward off sickness. Most scholars agree that the lion-headed figure with the donkey ears at the center of the plaque is the demon Lamashtu, who in ancient times was thought to bring pestilence and disease. The lion-headed figure peeking over the top of the plaque in both the front and rear views is believed to be her husband, the demon Pazuzu, who was invoked to make Lamashtu go away.

"Upon its discovery, however, the artifact was originally thought to have represented the Babylonian goddess Ereshkigal on her journey through the underworld. The lion-headed figure at the top was thus believed to be the Babylonian god

Nergal, Lord of the Underworld and Ereshkigal's husband. Some scholars still cling to this original notion, and thus it is Nergal to whom I'd like to draw your attention. Next slide, please."

A drawing of a winged, sphinxlike figure with a long-bearded human head labeled *Nineveh, 800–700 B.C.*

"In some manifestations, Nergal is often portrayed anthropomorphically—with a man's head and the body of a winged lion. Next slide, please."

Another drawing, from a stone tablet, with a lion-headed deity between two other gods—a procession of some kind, in which one of the more human-looking gods holds a long spear. Markham could feel the agents lean forward.

"In this case," Markham said, "the portrayal is reversed, more Egyptian, and we see Nergal with the head of a lion, wings, and the body of a man. I'll hold off on commenting on the long spear for now. But, in addition to presiding over the Underworld, Nergal appears in his early manifestations to have been a solar deity, as well as a god of war and pestilence. He also became associated with the destruction brought on by the summer solstice, the dead season in the Mesopotamian planting cycle, and was often referred to as the Raging Prince. His main center of worship in Ancient Babylonia was the city of Kutha, now known as the archaeological site Tel Ibrahim in Iraq.

"Like the Ancient Egyptians, lions and lionlike gods figured prominently in Ancient Babylonian mythology. Indeed, many scholars specifically trace Nergal's mutation throughout nearly all Middle Eastern religions, including Judaism, in which he was first identified with Satan, only later on to be demoted to one of Satan's demons. In fact, Nergal is mentioned by name in the Bible's Second Book of Kings.

"However," Markham continued, "given the obscurity of the god Nergal in the collective consciousness, Schaap and I were somewhat skeptical until our classical studies expert convinced us that only Nergal could give us the through-line we were looking for. Many scholars argue that the ancient Greeks adapted Nergal into Ares, their god of war—better known as the Roman Mars—and associated him with the red planet just as the Assyrians did when they assimilated Nergal into their culture. Furthermore, our man at NC State went on to tell us that scholars believe the cult at Kutha followed an annual worship cycle of Nergal in the spring to ensure a bountiful harvest and to pacify the god into showing them some mercy during the summer."

"The spring," said Big Joe Connelly. "The return of Leo to the nighttime sky."

"That's right," said Markham. "And so we too must come back to Leo."

The screen wiped into a complex astronomy chart.

"Now," Markham said, "upon closer examination of Leo and its pattern across the sky from winter into spring into summer, Schaap and I found something interesting. If you look carefully at the chart on the screen, you'll notice the sun gets progressively closer to appearing in Leo until it enters the constellation around the middle of August. The summer solstice, the very moment when Nergal is said to wreak havoc on mankind, occurs on June 21st this year. Since the hottest of the Mesopotamian months are July and August, that the sun and Leo should be connected at this time is only fitting. You'll remember, scholars believe Nergal in his early Babylonian manifestation was a solar deity. However—next slide, please."

A close-up of Mars in the constellation Leo with the dates *June 3–July 22, 2006.*

"If you look at the trajectory of Mars, that very planet that the Ancient Assyrian astronomers came to identify with Nergal himself, you'll see that this year Mars, the god of war, will appear in the constellation Leo at the height of the summer solstice. Mars transits Leo only once every two years.

"If one were to look at the current progression of Mars toward Leo in conjunction with how the murders have progressed in methodological detail, it opens up the possibility that, in the Impaler's mind, he and Nergal are progressing toward each other, too. Perhaps the Impaler is trying to join with the god. Or more likely, in my opinion, perhaps he sees himself as a sort of Leo Minor, progressing with him toward his return. Leo consists of nine stars, Leo Minor is often represented by only three. Both return to the springtime sky at roughly the same time. And since the gravestone I discovered at Willow Brook is both plural and directly west of the spot at which Rodriguez and Guerrera were sacrificed, perhaps our boy sees himself as a servant to Nergal, a right-hand man, if you will, facilitating his return—which, of course, will all go down during the summer solstice. Now, what exactly will happen when Nergal returns? Well, your guess is as good as mine at this point. Clear slides for questions, please."

Silence, everyone thinking—some confused, some disbelieving.

"You really think the Impaler could've made all these connections?" Mr. Spock asked finally.

"Yes, I do," Markham said. "After all, when you look at the bigger picture from the Impaler's point of view, it's all about connections, isn't it? What is a constellation if nothing more than a primitive game of connect the dots? Singularly, the stars don't make sense. One must see them in relation to one another in order for the picture to come into focus. I have a feeling our boy looks for dots everywhere; messages that he connects to what he surely sees as the return of Nergal."

"Such thought processes are common in extreme cases of

paranoid delusions," Underhill added. "I hesitate to diagnose our boy as a schizophrenic, but there's a strong possibility he might be suffering from such a psychosis. His delusions of grandeur are one thing, but in addition to the messages he believes he's receiving, he may also have auditory, perhaps even visual hallucinations—hears voices, sees visions in which the god tells him to do things."

"But the act of impalement," Mr. Spock said. "Even if what you're saying is true, other than that long spear in one of the slides, I still don't see how this god Nergal connects to the killer's desire to impale his victims."

"Neither did I at first," Markham said. "Like you, when I was first assigned to this case I was given a brief overview of the history of impalement as a form of execution. If you'll recall, impalement was common in the Middle East during ancient times—next slide, please."

A photograph of a stone tablet labeled, *Neo-Assyrian, 6th century BCE*.

"On this relief we see three men being impaled by a pair of soldiers. It's a depiction of the Babylonian conquest of Judea, in which hundreds of Judeans were impaled by the king Nebuchadnezzar in the late seventh century BC. Incidentally, the Persian king Darius would return the favor later in the sixth century BC, when he is said to have impaled three thousand Babylonians. This Babylonian connection in and of itself is a compelling enough tie-in to Nergal. However, it was our man at NC State again who sealed the deal for us. No pun intended. Schaap?"

An audible gasp filled the conference room as the last of the slides appeared.

"What you're looking at," Markham said, "is a photograph of an ancient cylinder seal and its impression. Seals such as this one from Ancient Babylonia were usually engraved with a type of picture story, and were thus used to roll reliefs onto a soft surface such as the clay you see before you. This seal is believed to date back to about two thousand years before the birth of Christ. It was seized along with some other artifacts by Italian customs agents about a month ago, and is thought to have been stolen from one of the many unguarded archaeological sites looted at the beginning of the U.S.-led invasion of Iraq. Although the other artifacts with which the seal was found were stolen from the Baghdad Museum, officials there are not exactly sure from which site the seal was stolen—perhaps an unknown site somewhere near the dig at Tel Ibrahim.

"Although crudely rendered," Markham continued, "the seal is a stunning discovery. Made of limestone, it's unusually large for this type of artifact; about two inches in length with a two-inch diameter. The imagery is unprecedented in that it seems to represent some kind of sacrifice being paid to the god Nergal. The procession of lion-headed figures holding the spears with the dangling humans are thought to be his priests; the fierce-looking creature at the end, the one with the human head and the winged body of a lion, is Nergal himself. Relatively little iconography of Nergal has survived, making this perhaps one of the most important archaeological discoveries for Ancient Babylonian scholars in recent years."

"Extraordinary," said Dr. Underhill. "A marriage of the lion imagery and the impalement; almost an instruction manual of how to sacrifice to the god. And as Nergal was the ruler of Hell, perhaps the impaled victims on the seal are undesirables, criminals, or even heretics in the eyes of the cult at Kutha."

"Perhaps," Markham said, "but the Babylonian concept of the Underworld was different than, say, the Christian concept of Hell. Nevertheless, it wasn't a pretty place; and most likely the Impaler's concept of Hell would be influenced by contemporary Christian notions, as well as the fact that Nergal mutated into one of Satan's demons." Big Joe raised his hand again. "Go ahead, Joe."

"Then, if as you say, Nergal was the ruler of Hell, do you think then that the victim profile has something to do with Hell, too? I mean, do you think the Impaler sees his victims as sinners?"

"That's exactly what I think," Markham said, "which brings us to the last of the Impaler's selection criteria: the act of sin. Homosexuality, in the Impaler's eyes, is a sin; and Randall Donovan might represent to him corruption or greed or dishonesty. If we look at the Impaler's victim profile as males who bear the mark of the lion and who have sinned, all four victims are thus connected. All four of them are worthy of hell from the killer's perspective; and thus are worthy of sacrifice to him, the Prince of Hell."

It was Alan Gates who spoke next.

"Your consultant at NC State, did he indicate to you if the seal depicts an actual ritual at Kutha, as opposed to some ancient Babylonian myth lost to history?"

"No," said Markham. "Not much is known about the ancient city or the types of rituals performed there. However, it is believed that the temple at Kutha came to be seen as a physical representation of the Babylonian Underworld itself. The temple doors, the doorway to hell, if you will."

"How did the seal end up in Italy?" asked Big Joe Connelly.

"Interpol isn't exactly sure. Many of the smuggling operations out of Iraq are pretty complex. Interpol's been trying to trace the artifact's route since it was discovered last month, but they've reached a dead end in Jordan. It was our man at NC State who led us to the picture of the newly recovered seal. He was part of the original *National Geographic* team that went over to Iraq to assess the damage to the country's archaeological treasures back in 2003, and he now receives a monthly update of recovered items from both Interpol and the Baghdad Museum."

"So you think the killer was inspired by this artifact?" Mr. Spock asked.

"Yes, I do," Markham said. "The similarities between the imagery and the killer's MO are too compelling to ignore. Furthermore, the seal is the only known artifact in the archaeological record where we see a depiction of human sacrifice to the god Nergal."

"But you said the authorities learned of the seal's existence only a month ago," Mr. Spock said smugly. "The Impaler murdered Rodriguez and Guerrera at the end of January—well over *two* months ago."

"That's exactly my point," Markham said. "I think the Impaler knew about the seal long before the authorities did."

Chapter 38

The General had just finished taping his latest Vlad the Impaler article to the wall when he thought he heard a voice say:

"Edmund?"

The General stopped and listened.

Nothing. Only the silence of the cellar, only the beating of his heart in his ears. His mind was playing tricks on him, he thought, but still he listened until the throbbing in his ears subsided.

He was overtired; had been up late speaking with the Prince the night before. The Prince hadn't shown him any visions of the young woman named Cindy Smith, and even now the General had to admit he was disappointed that the Prince seemed uninterested in her. Instead, the Prince had wanted to talk about his army; about those who would follow him through the doorway when he returned. Just like in the old days.

Yes, the Prince had been uncharacteristically nostalgic the night before; had taken the General's hand and led him across the scorched earth—the two of them watching together as scores of enemies were impaled on the battlefields, or along the roads that led to the Prince's temple at Kutha. He even allowed the General to touch the temple doors; allowed him to push them open and gaze down into the depths of the abyss—an ever-changing whirlpool in the colors of sin; of darkness and flame and flesh and destruction. The sodomites had been there, as was the gold-coveting lawyer. All of them understanding now, all of them smiling and waiting eagerly for the Prince's return.

And then the Prince had led the General into the stars; flew with him across space and time and into the heart of the nine and the three, that very place where the Prince had hidden himself for thousands of years—forgotten by most, but still watching and waiting for a warrior-priest to worship him again and be rewarded.

A warrior-priest like the General.

It had been a long night, the General thought as he scanned the clippings on the wall. And the Prince's instructions had been clear: no more recruiting on West Hargett Street. But still, the General thought, the Prince did not say anything negative about the young woman named Cindy. He just did not address her, seemed to have more important things on his mind—

"Edmund?"

The General heard the voice clearly this time—a woman's voice, unmistakable, echoing close but far away—and suddenly his heart was in his ears again.

This can't be happening, he said to himself as he dashed from the reeducation chamber and through the darkened hallway. He stopped in the entrance to the Throne Room and stared at the Prince's head. Nothing. No sense of calling; no flashes and sounds, no feeling of that force he so often felt when the Prince wanted to speak with him. The Prince was sleeping. The General understood this—the Prince always slept during the day—but the doorway was fresh, was always open, and now that there were others inside, perhaps—

"Edmund?" the woman's voice called again. *"Are you there, Edmund?"*

The General recognized the voice immediately, and all at once his heart was filled with a mixture of both joy and terror.

Quiet! he cried out in his mind. *He'll hear you!*

"Edmund, I'm afraid!"

"Mama, please!" the General whispered, and now he was Edmund Lambert again.

He rushed into the room and stood before the figure on the throne, gazing back and forth between the Prince's head and the golden doors that he had carved for the body below it. The smell of booze and rotting flesh was stronger now, but the Prince was still asleep. No, there was no one beyond the doorway now except—

"Edmund, it's been so long—let me see you!"

"Mama, please, you'll ruin—"

"You don't have to be afraid. He's sleeping now. He doesn't suspect—"

Mama, quiet! Edmund screamed in his mind.

"Please, Edmund. Let me see you like he does. Let me know it's really you who has come for me. I'm so afraid!"

Anything to silence her, Edmund thought—and before he could think better of it, he saw himself reaching out for the Prince's head.

It was the General who usually wore the Prince's head; had many times removed the plaster skull from inside and slipped it over his face—a smell of mold and leather and sweat and blood that reminded him of the helmet Edmund wore in Iraq. It was hot and hard to breathe inside the Prince's head. And even though the General had made a hole at the rear of the Prince's gaping mouth through which to see, it had taken him hours of prowling the cellar before he got used to wearing it.

But all of that had been for nothing; for once the General acquired the first of the doorways, when he wore the Prince's head it was as if he was transported to another world—a world in which the smells and heat and claustrophobia of the Prince's head did not exist. No, there was only the doorway and the world beyond; for when the General donned the Prince's head, he saw through the eyes of the nine and the three—those all-knowing, all-seeing eyes of the lions in the sky.

It was Edmund Lambert who first saw the lion's head; years ago, when he was twelve, at the taxidermy shop to which his grandfather had taken him after his first deer kill. Even then, young Edmund Lambert had been fascinated by it—Leo, the shop owner called it, a monstrous African lion that had been shot on safari back in the 1930s. That too had been a message from the Prince—*their first face-to-face encounter*—but young Edmund Lambert had simply been too stupid to understand.

But after Edmund read *Macbeth* and understood he needed a head to communicate with the Prince, it was the General who broke into the taxidermy shop and brought Leo back to the Throne Room. And so only the General was allowed to wear the lion's head, and only then in service of the Prince.

But now, it was Edmund Lambert who slipped the Prince's visage over his face; and all at once he could feel the Prince's power flowing through his muscles. It always felt like liquid electricity to the General; but to Edmund Lambert, the energy coursing through his veins made him feel weak and fearful—like a child sneaking into a haunted house.

Thhwummp!—a rush of brightness—and the doorway was open.

Yes, there was his mother! Clear and bright and floating with the swirling colors of sin behind her. She was dressed as she was on the day she died, at once both near and far away, but she did not call to him anymore—only dropped to her knees and cried with joy when she saw him. And there was Edmund—a finger to his lips as his other hand reached out and touched her face. A secret touch that spoke of little time but said, "Don't worry, Mama."

Flash-flash—a sliver flash like the strobe light at the farmhouse—and now there was someone else with them, someone helping his mother to her feet and drawing her back into the swirling colors. Another woman, dressed in white. A young woman with long black hair and a smile that looked like—Cindy Smith's?

"Ereshkigal," his mother said before she disappeared. "Ereshkigal will help us."

Flash-flash and another rush—this one of darkness—and suddenly Edmund was back in the Throne Room with the lion's head in his hands. He'd torn it from his face without realizing, and quickly fumbled it back onto the shelf. Then he bolted from the cellar—up the stairs, through the kitchen and out the back door.

He kept running until he was safely inside the barn—closed the doors behind him, tore off his shirt, and fell to his knees before the mirror in the horse stall, the temple doors of Kutha rising and falling with his breaths.

He was terrified, but that was all right for now. The Prince had not awakened—would not be able to hear him in here even if he *was* awake. No, this doorway, the last of them all, was not yet open.

Ereshkigal, he heard his mother say in his head. *Ereshkigal will help us.*

That had been unexpected—perhaps even more unexpected than hearing from his mother. He knew the latter would have to happen eventually, especially if she ever sensed him near the doorway or perhaps saw him with the Prince.

But Ereshkigal? The Prince's beloved?

Of course, Edmund knew the story of how the Prince had raped her and taken her throne by force. And when he thought about it, the fact that Ereshkigal might want to help them made perfect sense. Perhaps that was why the Prince did not want to talk about Cindy Smith. Perhaps the Prince was keeping something from him after all.

Then again, Edmund thought, the General had been keeping something from the Prince, too—a promise he'd made long before he was anointed, but a promise nonetheless of which the Prince would surely disapprove.

But could this be a trap? Could the Prince be testing the General's loyalty?

"The General is *still* loyal," Edmund said out loud. "His loyalty is split is all; and there is no reason why this can't be part of his reward."

But the Prince demands ultimate devotion. You know that. There is to be no one but the Prince. He has shown you that in his visions, in the sacrifices at Kutha—

"The General made his promise before he was anointed," Edmund said. "That is surely one of the reasons why the Prince chose him. For his loyalty."

The voice in his head was silent, and all at once Edmund Lambert was the General again. He watched himself in the mirror until the temple doors became still. Cindy Smith? But how could she be Ereshkigal? How could she be both in this world and that world at the same time?

The General envisioned the young actress as Lady Macbeth; saw her in her spirit costume rising from beneath the stage to take her husband into Hell. The General kept replaying this scene over and over again in his mind. Could the answer have been right there in front of him all along? Was it written in the stars that he, the General, should have been the one to design and build the doorway through which he would join with Ereshkigal in the Underworld?

Something deep behind the temple doors on his chest told him yes. A parallel with his day-life, part of the equation, everything connected—but he would need to think on it. There was still much about the doorway that he had yet to understand—so much so that, oftentimes when the Prince revealed things to him in his visions, the General didn't know what to make of them. Even *after* consulting with the Prince.

Of course, there would be no consulting the Prince about all this. And even though the Prince spoke to the General inside his head, he could not read the General's thoughts unless the General wanted him to.

No, when it came to this part of the equation, the General was on his own.

But that was all right. He'd figured out how to balance other parts of the equation on his own. And so he would figure out how to balance this part on his own, too.

Eventually, a voice answered in his head.

The General smiled. He understood the concept of eventually. It had been that way from the beginning, all those years ago when he promised his mother he would save her. It had taken him almost two decades of eventually to balance that part of the equation.

But then again, the General thought, what's a couple of decades compared to eternity?

Chapter 39

Alan Gates hung up from a call with his Interpol liaison feeling frustrated and helpless. He hated having to deal with anyone at the United Nations—hated having to deal with anyone outside the FBI *period*. True, things had gotten better since 9/11; clearer channels and more cooperation all around. Nonetheless, even with this new wrinkle surrounding the objets d'art seized in Rome, he knew things were going to come to a screeching halt again in Jordan. Yes, now that the United States was involved, those bastards would take great pride in sabotaging Interpol's investigation.

The suspect in question was a Dutchman named Bertjan van Weerdt, a black-market antiquities dealer whose specialty was European art seized by the Nazis during World War II, and against whom Interpol had been building a case for almost a year. Why or how van Weerdt had gotten mixed up in one of the many smuggling rings to come out of Iraq following the U.S.-led invasion was still a bit of a mystery. He'd already been turned over to the authorities in The Hague, and even though Interpol had him by the balls, van

Weerdt wouldn't give up the name of his contact in Jordan—said he knew the man only as Abdul and could provide no further information. Gates had a feeling van Weerdt was telling the truth. He knew the type—no loyalty, anything to save his own skin—and could already see the trail ending at the Jordan consulate with or without the Dutchman's help.

Of course, Gates would fly one of his men to The Hague to run van Weerdt through the obligatory round of questions. But that was going to take time, and time was something they didn't have.

The implications of his protégé's theory were staggering. Never mind the killer's time line; never mind his connection to the constellation Leo, the god Nergal, and his obsession with the mark of the lion. No, given the date on which Interpol nabbed van Weerdt in Rome, what bothered Alan Gates the most was that, if in fact the Impaler *had* drawn on the stolen Babylonian seal for inspiration, there were really only two possible scenarios in which he could've come into contact with it. Either he was involved in the smuggling ring himself, or he'd seen the seal somewhere else—perhaps at an archaeological dig in Iraq or a private collection that eventually got mixed up with the stolen items from the Baghdad Museum. The latter left open too many variables. And so, until anything told them differently, the FBI would have to begin from the premise that the Impaler had seen the ancient seal somewhere between its theoretical departure from Iraq and its appearance in Rome.

Of course, Special Agent Schaap—in conjunction with both the Raleigh PD and ICE—would check out the anomalies with immigration and customs, as well as any leads involving violent offenders of Middle Eastern descent in and around the Raleigh area. But it was what Markham said at the end of the teleconference that made Alan Gates's stomach turn.

"One last thing," Markham said. "Back in 2003, three U.S. soldiers from the Army's 3rd Infantry Division were brought up on allegations of attempting to smuggle out of the country priceless artifacts that Iraqi antiquities officials said were looted from the Bagdad Musuem. The names of the soldiers were never released and the charges later dismissed. And even though incidents of smuggling by U.S. military personnel are extremely rare, it at least proves that a serviceman could not only have come into contact with the ancient Babylonian seal, but also that he could've been connected to the smuggling operation in Jordan."

"You're saying you think there's a possibility that the Impaler might be a veteran of the Iraq War?" Mr. Spock asked.

"Perhaps," said Markham. "There's the planet Mars connection—the god of war, the ultimate soldier crossing paths with the lion figure in the sky. Our profile for the killer thus far indicates that our boy is a highly disciplined individual. He goes to a lot of trouble to make sure he doesn't leave any DNA at the crime scenes. If the Impaler was in the military, they'd have a sample of his DNA and a record of his prints if he'd been on special assignment. Never mind that he'd have to possess quite a bit of physical strength to pull off his little shenanigans.

"Then there's the fact that the kind of gun used to kill Rodriguez and Guerrera was a nine-millimeter, the rounds from which show marking consistent with the Beretta M9. Ballistics can't be one hundred percent sure, of course, but the M9 has been standard issue for the U.S. military since 1990. Given Raleigh's relative proximity to both Fort Bragg and Camp Lejeune, it's another connection to Iraq that I think can't be ignored at this point."

"I'll take care of getting the clearance on all that," Gates said.

"Thank you, Alan. For the rest of us, in addition to getting on Interpol and ICE, I suggest we put together a team to cover Bragg and Lejeune and begin working from there—fast-track the necessary paperwork to requisition medical records and look for servicemen in the Raleigh area who have a history of mental illness. It's a long shot, but if you've got a better place to begin, I'm all ears."

Then came the silence—all of their minds spinning, Alan Gates knew, with variations on the same theme. The fact that the Impaler might be in the military had blindsided them more than anything Markham had said that day. And for Alan Gates, it was a prospect that both saddened and terrified him: sad because he felt an unspoken kinship with the killer; terrified because he also identified with him.

He'd seen it all firsthand. Sometimes he still saw it. In the middle of the night, the dream fading, the warm wet blood on his face and hands chilling into the sweat of his nightmare. Thankfully, gone were the nights when he woke up screaming, or when Debbie had to sleep in the guest room because his tossing and turning and talking in his sleep scared her close to death. But still, the dream always returned.

Curiously, however, he never remembered the dream itself; only pieced it together afterward when he figured it had to be about the worst day of them all—the day his best friend Ronnie Blake stepped on a land mine; the day First Lieutenant Alan Gates watched him die in his arms even as he wiped from his eyes the blood and shit from Blake's blown-out bowels.

Those were the kinds of days that made a man snap, made him come back "a tick away" as they used to say. Gates had been close, could have snapped with the best of them were it not for his faith in God. Yeah, the Old Man Upstairs had bailed him out of that one just as he had bailed him out of Nam without a scratch.

But then there were the guys who snapped in a different way. The guys who came back "normal." The guys who never dreamed, never cried, held a steady job and golfed and banged their wives and colored Easter eggs with their kids. That is, until one day . . .

One day.

The doctors and the smart men with the degrees had names for that day—theories and fancy terminology that he learned at Georgetown and had to indulge over his many years with Behavioral Analysis. But in the end Alan Gates didn't care why a man snapped; didn't preoccupy himself with the minutia as to why one kid could grow up to be a healthy member of society after being raped repeatedly by his uncle, while another felt the need to kill little old ladies because his grandmother got him the wrong color bicycle for Christmas.

No, when it came right down to it, Alan Gates was good at what he did because he not only understood what it meant to be a tick away from his own *one day*, but also because he was able to wrap his mind around the kind of snap that made the one day into a string of days. Sure, he could think like the killers he hunted, but he was also able to see and feel the waves of the water in which they swam. It was the latter that separated the men from the boys. The tick of the clock that took him further, but at the same time kept him sane. It was that way for Markham, Gates knew. His tick was Elmer Stokes.

After all, thinking like a killer was one thing, but feeling like him was another.

The superposition principle.

Markham, Gates said to himself as he looked at the clock over his office door: *1 p.m. Already on his way. So much to do, so little time. Tick tock, tick tock, tick tock.*

Gates thought about his platoon in Vietnam, and in his

head he ran through the names and faces of those who'd made it and those who hadn't—of those he knew were still living, and those he knew had since died.

And then Alan Gates did something he'd never done before.

He got down on his knees and said a prayer for a killer.

Chapter 40

Cindy Smith was beyond thrilled that she had waited in front of her computer just that little bit longer before heading off to the gym.

Direct and to the point, she said to herself, reading. *But at the same time mysterious. Just like the handsome soldier himself.*

Cindy smiled and read the e-mail again:

Hello Cindy: Jennings doesn't need me at the show tonight, but I'll stop by your dressing room afterwards to pick you up for the party. I guess it's meant to be after all. Yours truly, Edmund Lambert

"I guess it's meant to be, after all," Cindy said out loud for the twentieth time. "But *what* is meant to be? Going to the party? Or going to the party with me?"

Cindy sighed and chastised herself for not playing it cool even in private. She shut down her computer and slipped her script into her book bag.

"I'll be home late, Mom," she called on her way out the door. "Don't forget the cast party is tonight."

"Be careful," her mother replied from the kitchen. "And no drinking and driving."

"I know," Cindy said. They exchanged *I love yous*, and then she was gone.

"I guess it's meant to be," Cindy said to herself as she started up her car. "Yeeess, *Meester Lem-behrt.* Now I have you right vehre I vahnt you."

Chapter 41

As Markham walked across the tarmac, he felt a wave of panic pass through his stomach when he imagined how thin the FBI's resources would be stretched in the days to come. There was the European and Middle Eastern can of worms now, not to mention the coordination of all the military records. He'd already followed up on the name Lyons itself but came up empty. He wasn't surprised. That would've been too easy.

Markham reached the mobile stairs unit and checked his watch—*2:07 p.m.* He was seven minutes late for his flight. *Late—period*, he thought. Yes, the clock was certainly ticking. The crescent moon would hit around May 3rd, which meant the Impaler would go looking for his next victim any time now if he already hadn't. In fact, there would be *two* crescent moons in May, the second on the 31st.

Oh yes, Markham said to himself. *The merry month of May will be the Impaler's busiest month yet.*

But would he go hunting again on West Hargett Street? And furthermore, where would he display his next victim if the FBI didn't stop him in time? That was the question.

It was Dr. Underhill who offered the best answer.

"The military connection makes a lot of sense," he said at the end of the teleconference. "But in addition to checking out the patient records, you may want to look at specific units that identify themselves with lions or other big cats, perhaps even winged creatures like eagles and hawks. After all, Nergal was not only the god of war—the ultimate soldier, if you will—but also a lion with wings."

"Do you think we should narrow down our suspect pool further by focusing on servicemen whose birthdays fall under the sign of Leo?" Markham asked. "Identification with a destiny written in the stars?"

"Couldn't hurt," Underhill replied. "But maybe our boy is mapping out his own sign, his own identity on the ground. Given the nature of the sacrifices, the theory of a servant, a sort of Leo Minor helping to resurrect the god makes the most sense to me. And if that is in fact the case, maybe the Starlight Theater visual was the starting point for a picture on the ground that mimics his military insignia—a creature or something with which he identifies. Just a hunch."

A good hunch, Markham had thought, but as constellations were by their very nature subjective in their rendering, with only three stars to build off it would be impossible to match up the Starlight Theater schematic with the military insignias.

Markham climbed onto the plane and said hello to the flight attendant. No FBI plane today, but there were only a handful of passengers making the trip with him on the charter flight to Connecticut. He found a seat over the wing, stowed his carry-on, and sat down by the window. The flight attendant closed the hatch and came by to make sure he'd fastened his seat belt. He hadn't, and she smiled and pointed to remind him.

Attractive, Markham thought, even though he'd never been a fan of blondes, and wondered if she was the type of

woman who would ask him about the plaque above his bedroom door. She smiled again at him as she strapped herself
into the seat by the cockpit, and Markham decided she wasn't.

Waiting.

More than anything else about his job Sam Markham
hated the waiting. And as he stared past the flight attendant
into the open cockpit, he imagined the days ahead of him
tumbling out in a series of big black numbers.

The news conference had gone well, he thought. That was
a plus. The FBI would now be able to work quietly behind
the scenes while the media chewed on the phony Vlad angle.
And it would only be a matter of time before Geraldo and
Nancy Grace and all the others would start throwing around
the gay-bashing theories, too. But that wouldn't bother the
Impaler. No, Markham thought, the Impaler wouldn't give
two shits about what the public thought as long as Nergal
was happy.

The plane started to move and he punched open his e-mail
on his BlackBerry. Alan Gates had already gotten the ball
rolling with the three soldiers who'd been brought up on smuggling charges at the beginning of Iraq War. Markham had received the e-mail on the way to the airport. He read it again.

> I got their names. Two are presently serving their third
> tours in Iraq, while the other has been confirmed to
> be living in Seattle. I got a man with him now. None of
> them are our boy, but they may know something.
> Good work today. —AG
>
> PS: The preliminary autopsy report just came back on
> Canning. Looks like our boy kept him alive for a
> couple of weeks before he skewered him.

Markham felt his stomach turn. Did the Impaler hold
Canning hostage so he could tattoo him? Was that why he

abducted him in the first place? If so, that meant there were more leads to follow: the thefts or purchases of tattoo equipment in the—

Stick to what you know, said the voice in his head. *You've got your hands full as it is, Sammy boy.*

This was true. Schaap had already come back with a working list of military units and ranked them according to their assignments in Iraq, as well as by their associated insignias and mascots. There were plenty of lions, of course, but a bunch of hybrid animals, too: the winged soaring black panther of the 82nd Airborne's 3rd Combat Brigade out of Fort Bragg, the fishtailed lion of the 8th Marines Regiment out of Camp Lejeune, the Screaming Eagle of Fort Campbell's 101st Airborne. So many that Markham had never heard of; so many that his head felt as if it was spinning when he left the Resident Agency.

The flight attendant motioned for him to turn off his BlackBerry. He did and closed his eyes. Perhaps it was good that he was getting away. There was nothing he could do now but wait. No one else for him to question until all the data came back and he could get some boots on the ground. Besides, he needed to sleep; needed to clear his mind and come back fresh with a new perspective.

Yes, said the voice in his head. *A nice little vacation to see your wife's killer get pumped full of chemicals. Now that's what I call fun in the sun!*

The plane stopped again and Markham opened his eyes, slipped his hand under the seat in front of him and removed some papers from his briefcase. He read them.

An examination of how the god Nergal transitioned over the centuries from a solar deity to the lord of the Underworld (as well as his association with the planet Mars) cannot be explained without an examination of his relationship to Ereshkigal, the Babylonian goddess of the Underworld.

The love story of Nergal and Ereshkigal is unique in that it takes place in Irkalla, the Mesopotamian Land of the Dead. Two different versions of the myth exist—the first discovered in Tel El-Amarna, Egypt, dates from around the fifteenth century BCE and contains roughly 90 lines of text; the second, much longer version (approx. 750 lines) dates from seventh century BCE and was found on the site of the ancient Assyrian city of Sultantepe.

In the first version, Nergal descends to the Underworld with an army of demons, rapes Ereshkigal and seizes her throne, then remains there to rule as king. In the later tradition, Nergal seems to make two trips to the Underworld, and instead of an army of demons, he takes down a special throne that will protect him from being seized by ghosts. Ereshkigal then seduces Nergal by showing him a glimpse of her body while taking a bath, and the two then fall into a passionate love affair. Otherwise, the basic story lines are the same.

In both versions, the celestial gods hold a banquet, and since Ereshkigal is the queen of the Underworld, cosmic law dictates that she cannot journey to the heavens to join them. She sends an envoy to fetch her portion, and Nergal, god of war and pestilence, is rude to him. The other gods deem that Nergal must be punished by Ereshkigal for the insult. Nergal descends to the Underworld, overpowers Ereshkigal, and the two fall in love. Thus, the chief difference between the two versions is that in the first, Nergal comes to the throne by violence. In the second, the conflict leads to a love affair.

A significant portion of the Nergal and Ereshkigal myth is missing from both the Tel El-Amarna and the

Sultantepe versions. However, as mentioned earlier, not only do we have what appears to be the mythological record of how the god Nergal went from becoming a solar deity to the lord of the Underworld, we also have a cultural record that expresses views about human sexuality, as well as Neo-Babylonian and Late Assyrian relationships between men and women.

Let's examine the . . .

The plane started down the runway; and by the time it lifted off, Markham's eyelids had grown heavy—the urge to sleep overpowering him as the plane climbed higher and higher.

The thoughts, the images that flickered before his eyes were of the lion-headed god Nergal—but the lion god *is also Elmer Stokes, complete with a buzz cut and a dirty white T-shirt as he chases Michelle through the parking lot of the Mystic Aquarium.*

Markham runs after them in the darkness, around a maze of corners and through pools of light cast down from streetlamps. Then the flash of a giant bathtub, up ahead in the distance, and the lion god and Michelle disappear.

There is only the parking lot now and the silhouettes of thousands of impaled bodies stretching out toward a fiery horizon. He can hear Michelle speaking somewhere behind him—"Would you like something to drink, ma'am?"—but he tells her to go on without him.

He does not wish to leave—not today, not when he is so close—and lets the images and the low humming of the plane's engines, the Babylonian spirits, carry him forward to the temple at Kutha. He can see it in the distance, no, behind him—where is it?

He sits down on the asphalt, his back against something hard—Michelle's car? He turns around to look and discovers that he is alone on an obsidian ocean—in a rowboat be-

neath a stormy sky. He searches for the shore but cannot find it.

No, now there is only the Impaler—up ahead in the distance, seated Indian style on the water and moving away quickly, silently, leaving no trace of wake behind him.

He feels himself sinking, but doesn't resist. The sky and the ocean are one now, heavy and sinking with him as the curtain of sleep descends—as the Impaler's wings unfold from his back and lift him high into the air . . . higher and higher, smaller and smaller until the both of them disappear like smoke into the seamless black.

PART III
INTERSECTING

Chapter 42

Annie Lambert loved her son Edmund more than any-thing in the world, but sometimes even she couldn't help pinching his nipple and twisting it until he screamed—when he was a poop head, sure, but especially when he called him-self "Eddie."

His grandfather had been behind *that*; even went so far as to teach the boy to write E-D-D-I-E in capital letters, hy-phens and all, in the dirt when the boy was five years old. Her son's name was Edmund—*Edmund, Edmund, Edmund!*

And besides, Edmund knew better, too. He'd been writing his name the right way since he was three years old, and Annie vowed that she would twist little Edmund's nipple until the boy learned to obey her and *only* her.

True, Annie Lambert had given her son the name Ed-mund primarily as a dig at the old man. A private joke with herself, really, and she never thought in a million years that her father would find out Edmund was a character in Shake-speare—let alone a bastard one at that. But Claude Lambert *did* find out. How? Well, Annie never worked up the courage to ask him.

As with everything else, however, Claude Lambert didn't get mad or act any different toward his daughter than he had all her life. Quiet, cold, uninterested. No, the old man only got *even*. As he always did. Through other people.

Yes, teaching her son to write his name E-D-D-I-E was par for the course for old Claude Lambert. Just like the cookie crumbs on the settee in the parlor, the spilled bottle of her mother's perfume, the blueberry stains on her pillowcase from a stolen pie on Thanksgiving.

When she was about six or seven, Annie Lambert thought a ghost had suddenly moved in with them, and would swear up and down that it wasn't she who took the lipstick. "It was the ghost, Mama!" she would scream as her mother whipped her naked behind with her cat-o'-nine-tails. And then, when she was a little older, for many years she thought it was her brother James who'd been framing her, and would sometimes hide behind the furniture in an attempt to catch him breaking the handle off a china cup or stealing a piece of her mother's jewelry.

She never caught him—never caught anybody, for that matter—and often felt as if she were going crazy in that old house—as if the rooms were all crooked and the back of her head was about to crack open. Sometimes she'd hear a high ringing in her ears and she'd bang her head against the wall to make it stop. And a couple of times she got so upset that she took her father's straight razor and carved the word *"NO"* into her arm. Things settled down for a few months after that. No little mishaps around the Lambert household for which she got blamed. But then something would happen and the cycle would begin all over again until Annie hurt herself bad enough to make it stop.

Then one day without warning, when she was about twelve or so, *everything* stopped—the bad things, the blaming, the beatings, the banging her head and the cutting. And only years later—just before Edmund was born—when she saw the nod her father gave her brother when they read the guilty verdict at the trial, did something click inside her head. She couldn't explain it, even to herself; only that, after all those years, she knew deep down that it had been her father behind the frame game all along.

Annie Lambert never understood why her father didn't love her, or why he didn't even like her just a little. But when it came right down to it she had to admit that she didn't like him much, either. Claude Lambert was older than most of the fathers in Wilson; was a widower of forty with no children when he met Annie's mother at the bowling alley. She was only twenty-three, and Annie calculated (when she was old enough to do such things) that her mother and father must have tried to have children for about three years before Annie was born. Her mother told Annie flat out when she was nine that her father had wanted a son. Luckily, she said, they'd a quicker time of it with James, who came along a year after Annie. "And that was that," her mother said.

Over the years, Claude Lambert was never outwardly mean to his daughter. Quite the opposite, he hardly ever spoke to her. And he certainly never laid a hand on her—except sometimes when he'd been in the cellar too long. On those rare occasions, he'd come into her room late at night, flick on the lights, and calmly tell her to sit up. He'd take her face in his big rough hand and squeeze her cheeks together and stick his fingers in her mouth to feel her teeth as if he were examining a horse. His eyes always looked bulgy and red, and his breath always smelled like licorice, but his fingers always tasted like metal. He'd feel around inside her mouth for a few seconds, then would kiss her on the forehead and wish her good night.

"Bonne nuit, ma cheri," he'd say. And that was that.

But after Annie's mother died from the breast cancer, old Claude Lambert was even more remote. Sometimes he would stay out in the field after dark, just sitting on his tractor and staring off into the sky. Most often, however, he would just stay down in the cellar, in his workroom boozing or mixing up those stupid experiments. Sometimes, mostly on Friday nights, his old friend Eugene Ralston would join him down there.

Claude Lambert and Eugene Ralston—or "Rally," as he was called—went way back. They'd known each other since they were boys, had been best men at each other's weddings, and even stormed the beaches at Normandy together during World War II. Rally had saved her father's life that day, Claude Lambert insisted. Rally swore it was the other way around; but when James would ask them specifics about what happened, the two men would clam up and say some things were just better left in the past.

Annie had known Eugene "Rally" Ralston all her life, and sometimes thought of him as just another part of the old farmhouse—just like the kitchen sink, or better yet the saggy front porch. Rally was a mechanic, a certified bachelor with no children of his own, and for as long as Annie could remember he would show up on Friday nights after work all dirty and smelling of motor oil. Sometimes, her mother would make Rally clean up in the slop sink in the mudroom. The washer and dryer were in there, too, and she would give him some of her husband's clothes and tell him he couldn't set foot in her kitchen until he was clean and his coveralls were in the washer.

Eugene Ralston was a short, pudgy man with thick gray hair plastered so tightly to his head that it reminded Annie of the shiny marble foyer at the library. He was always combing it, and he was always telling jokes—but slowly, and often repeated himself in such a way that the joke wasn't funny anymore by the end. And when he laughed, no sound came out—just a choppy wheeze that Annie thought sounded like the cartoon character Muttley.

Annie hated how Rally smelled, but when she thought about it, she had to admit that she liked him a lot better than her father. He always asked her about school and if there were any boys who needed their legs broken. And when she and James were little, he would often bring them Hot Wheels cars that he said he got from one of his "connections" at the auto shop. Annie had no interest in the cars, but appreciated that Rally saved the more "girlie-lookin' " ones for her.

Rally always brought flowers for Annie's mother, too; and sometimes fancy sugar cubes and bags full of stuff that he said he got from one of his connections. This particular connection, Annie learned, was some pharmacist fella who paid him in miscellaneous supplies—all legal, all aboveboard, he used to assure Mrs. Lambert. Annie's mother would serve them supper and shake her head and say the men were gonna kill themselves with those stupid farm experiments. And when Annie's mother died, it fell to Annie to cook everyone dinner, after which her father and Rally would retreat to the cellar just as before.

Indeed, as a child, it didn't take Annie long to realize that the only time she ever heard her father laugh was when he was with Rally. And when her mother was still alive, on those nights when the men went down into the cellar, pretty soon Annie would begin to hear this strange music—usually some lady singing in French—and then her father and Rally would start laughing and talking in what sounded to her like baby talk. The two of them would emerge from the cellar around midnight, snickering and smiling stupidly with their eyes all red.

They were drinking moonshine down there. Annie was sure of that. Her mother had told her so—had even warned Annie never to go down there when Rally was over. That was the rule; that was the "men's time," she used say. But Annie didn't listen, and crept down into the cellar one night when she was nine, after her mother and James had fallen asleep watching TV in the den.

Annie came upon them in the workroom, just as they were pouring some liquid into some strange-shaped glasses with spoons across them. They swirled the glasses and clinked them and said something to each other in their nonsense talk. They had been down there for a while at this point; and the whole cellar smelled like licorice and cigarette smoke and other stuff that the little girl didn't recognize. The light in the workroom was yellow, the old black-and-white TV in the corner tuned to static with the volume off. The French lady was singing, the men laughing, and when they turned and saw Annie standing in the doorway, Claude Lambert smiled wide and said:

"Va-t'en, fée verte, tu n'es pas invitée."

Rally laughed his Muttley laugh—but Annie just stood in the doorway, gaping.

"I said go away, green fairy," her father repeated. "Come down here again and I'll cut off your head and use it for a flower vase."

"Oui, oui, le fée verte!" Rally shouted, and the two men howled with laughter.

Annie thought their eyes looked like Ping-Pong balls made of fire, their smiles like the Cheshire Cat's from her *Alice in Wonderland* book. Annie bolted from the cellar; was so terrified she didn't even realize she'd peed herself until she was under the covers in her bedroom.

From then on, when Rally showed up on Friday nights, Annie stayed with her mother and James in the den. Even James wasn't allowed in the cellar, which seemed to suit him just fine. True, her brother had always been a sullen boy with nothing much to say, but Annie could tell from the look on his face that, when Rally was around, he was afraid of going down into the cellar just as much as she was.

Rally continued his visits long after Annie's mother died, even after Edmund was born, and started stopping by on Saturday nights, too. However, things always seemed quieter in the cellar. There were still the same smells, the same music and nonsense talk, but it was different somehow. Things were different with her father, too. They'd never had much to say to each other, but now, when he returned from the fields or when he came up from the cellar, Claude Lambert would hardly even look at her; would only ask whether or not supper was ready or if the laundry was done.

In fact, the longest conversation Annie ever had with her father was on the night she told him she was pregnant. But even then Annie did most of the talking.

She had to admit that she was partly to blame for getting herself knocked up, and wondered sometimes if she hadn't done so subconsciously simply to get a rise out of the old man. She didn't even like Danny Gibbs really. Only went out with him in his '69 Camaro to make Mike Higgins jealous, and because Higgins was going out with Wendy Morris on the same night. That was dumb, yes, but what was even dumber was getting into the backseat with him and his bottle of Southern Comfort. It all happened so fast; kisses, groping, and the clamminess of his pressing in the dark—then the protestations, the suddenness of her hands pinned behind her head and her legs spread apart.

"It ain't your choice now," Danny whispered in her ear.

Then came the pain.

Oh yes, Annie Lambert's first time had hurt badly, but was over so fast that she wondered in her drunken haze whether or not it had really happened at all.

The blood on her panties when she got home told her it had. But Danny Gibbs also told her he loved her; asked her to the senior prom that very night and said he couldn't wait to see her again. Annie said nothing and bolted from his car to make her twelve o'clock curfew. She took her shower and rinsed her panties and got into bed; didn't bother waking her father, who was passed out with Rally in front of the television. And had her brother James not been at a tractor pull with his cousin that evening, Annie might have had to spill the beans right then and there.

Later, alone in the dark, Annie Lambert cried herself to sleep amid a haze of confusion and shame, blaming Danny Gibbs for what happened even as she asked her mother to forgive her from beyond the grave. And by the following Monday, Annie had resolved to put the incident behind her; had accepted what she thought was her guilt in the matter and vowed never to be so stupid with a boy again.

But when Danny Gibbs came up to her locker before first period, Annie told him to get lost and then slapped him in the face when he called her a slut. Danny knew better than to brag to his friends about his little rendezvous with Annie Lambert in the back of his Camaro; for although her brother James was two years his junior, the six-foot-two sixteen-year-old had made a name for himself as the toughest kid at Wilson High.

And had Annie not missed her period a couple of weeks later; had she not started throwing up in the mornings soon after that, the slap she gave Danny Gibbs might have been the end of it. A visit to the school nurse, however, confirmed what she already knew, and Annie sat her father down in the kitchen and told him through her tears everything that happened. And after a long silence, rather than flying into a rage as she thought he might, Claude Lambert surprised Annie with the most words he'd ever spoken to her in a single sitting.

"I reckon I'm to blame, too," he said. "Always left the disciplining to your mother, even though I knew it was up to me to get you straight in your head. I should have talked to you more; or different, at least. That might have helped, but I didn't see any of that coming. Shouldn't have let you run so wild these past couple of years, neither." Then, another long silence, after which he said simply: "Don't worry, Annie. I'll take care of it for you."

And that was that.

Then again, the old man didn't have to work too hard on her brother to get him to go after Danny Gibbs with the shotgun. Didn't really have to do anything other than drop a couple of hints about "family honor" and "the duty of a man," upon which James walked right into Danny Gibbs's trailer and blew his head off while he was playing Atari.

Everybody who knew the Lamberts thought James was a carbon copy of his father inside and out. Heavily built with big hands and a brooding, quiet demeanor. And he worshipped the old man like Jesus Christ himself; would've shot a hundred Danny Gibbses if the old man had asked him to. Theirs was a relationship to which Annie would forever be an outsider; a riddle wrapped up in hours of backyard catch and deer-hunting trips up to Virginia. Sometimes Rally would tag along on those trips, but mostly it was just the two of them, father and son.

Looking back, Annie concluded that early on she must have accepted her father's lack of interest because she had her mother—father loves son more, mother loves daughter more, everything vice versa, everything simple as that. And even though deep down she was secretly grateful for what her brother did to Danny Gibbs, Annie also knew deep down that Claude Lambert had sacrificed his son's future not only to redeem his family's name, but also to make things up to her.

At least, she *hoped* that was the reason.

And strangely, Annie accepted the whole Danny Gibbs incident with little or no emotion whatsoever; watched it all unfold before her like the plot of one of those silly soaps her mother used to watch in the afternoons. Annie's mother was all for her involvement in the drama club, and used to say stuff like, "You're a better actress than them TV sluts. Like that time you dumped out that moonshine and filled the jar up with water? They shoulda given you the Academy Award for your performance afterwards."

Of course, Annie had been telling the truth when she denied dumping out the moonshine, but it was the way her mother always forgave her afterwards—the slightly bigger pieces of pie at dessert, the kisses and hugs at bedtime, the walks by the pond to pick flowers just the two of them— well, it made having to take a beating because of the ghost or James or whoever it was framing her all worth it.

And Annie was able to turn all that nonsense with the head banging and the cutting and the ringing in her ears into a positive anyway; was able to somehow channel the same kind of emotion she used when she was protesting her innocence into the emotion she used when she was pretending to be a character in a play. She didn't know how she did it. It just came natural, she told her drama teacher. And whatever "it" was, it landed her the lead in *Romeo and Juliet* when she was in ninth grade and then the part of Abigail in *The Crucible* when she was in tenth. Her drama teacher told her she was the best actress she'd ever seen; and when Annie told her mother that, her mother replied: "Well, that doesn't surprise me. You've been practicing since you were six years old."

Her father and James, however, never came to see Annie's plays. They thought the drama club was stupid and a waste of time. But her mother always came. Even after she got sick. She usually brought her friends with her from the Women's Club and the five of them were always the first to stand when Annie took her bow. Those had been the happiest days of Annie's life. Annie loved Shakespeare the best; and after her mother's death, she saw a performance of *Macbeth* at Harriot University and read all the plays and practiced the speeches with her drama teacher after school in preparation

for the big auditions she was sure to get once she got into
Harriot University herself

Oh yes, it was only a matter of time before she'd have left
little ol' Shitwoods, North Carolina, high and dry for a big-
time stage career in New York. And had it not been for
Danny Gibbs, well, who knows how big she could've been?

Instead, five years and nine months later she was a single
mother whose only job was to take care of her child and look
after her father's house. And Annie excelled at both; got
plenty of money from her father, and would even sometimes
go into Raleigh on Friday nights with her girlfriends from
high school. No, the Lamberts had never been rich; but then
again, they'd never been in need of money, either. Claude
Lambert had a good thing going with the tobacco farm and
gave Annie more than enough to start saving for Edmund's
college fund. He still rarely spoke to his daughter, but often
voiced his opinion that it was foolish to send little Eddie to
college when everything he'd ever need was right here on the
tobacco farm.

"His name is *Edmund*," was all Annie would say, and just
kept right on socking the money away. She started taking
classes herself and, by the time Edmund was five, was only a
few credits away from her associate's degree in business.

And when Annie thought about it, things were actually
pretty good in that old farmhouse. Definitely much better
than the time before she got pregnant and James went to jail.
After all, Claude Lambert did seem to love his grandson
very much, and would actually ask Annie's permission to
take him for a ride on the tractor or to catch an inning or two
with Rally at the baseball field. He taught the little boy how
to throw a knuckleball before he was five; taught him how to
fish and how to identify different kinds of trees—stuff Annie
figured her father had done with James, too.

But the business with the name? The E-D-D-I-E in the
dirt?

Well, Annie Lambert understood at once that it was all over for her.

That little Edmund should have learned to write his name at the age of three really came as no surprise to Annie. Her son was a very smart boy; was walking at eleven months and talking in complete sentences at the age of two. Where he got it from, was anybody's guess.

But it was the way in which the E-D-D-I-E in the dirt snuck up on her—yes, that was what did her in. A message that had been there all along; a message that pushed her over the edge once she finally remembered.

It was a week after Edmund's fifth birthday. The boy was playing by himself in the yard when Annie stepped out on the back porch to call him in for sandwiches and lemonade. There was something wrong with her father's tractor. She could hear it making a grinding noise out in the field. And when Edmund didn't come when she called, Annie went out looking for him.

She found him behind the old horse barn, stick in hand, staring down at the big E-D-D-I-E he had just written in the dirt. Annie saw red; knew, of course, that it was her father's doing.

"You poop head!" she cried, reaching out for her son's nipple.

Then she stopped.

A dark flash—a shadow—then the horse barn again, and the blurry blob of something true; something that crossed before her eyes even as it began spinning invisibly in her stomach like a saw blade.

"Medicine," Annie whispered absently, and looked down at her son in a pile of broken china cups and stolen pies and smashed lipsticks.

C'est mieux de mourir que de se rappeler, Annie.
It's not true.
But the E-D-D-I-E in the dirt told her different.

M-E-D-I-C-I-N-E.
It's better to die than remember, Annie.

She felt a crack inside her head, the backyard shifting crooked across her eyes, and then came the high ringing in her ears. She could hear Edmund asking her what was wrong, but Annie only smiled and told him to fetch the coil of rope from inside the barn. Edmund obeyed, and after lunch, Annie gave him three extra sugar cookies for finishing his entire baloney sandwich.

"You look funny today, Mama," the boy said. "Like one of them robots on TV who can look like a real person."

Annie smiled.

"Let's go in Mama's bedroom and watch TV," she said. "And be a good boy and carry that rope for me, okay?"

Edmund gathered up the rope and followed his mother upstairs into her bedroom. She laid him down on the bed and turned on the television. It was already tuned to MTV.

"If you're patient," she said, "if you wait like a good boy, 'Born in the USA' will come on and you can jump on the bed and sing it as loud as you want, okay?"

Little Edmund clapped his hands and shouted, "Woohoo!" He loved jumping on his mother's bed, but he loved "Born in the USA" even more. He knew almost all the words by heart, even though he had to fake a bunch of them because he couldn't understand what Bruce Springsteen was saying.

Annie kissed her son on the forehead. "I love you," she said matter-of-factly, and then picked up the rope and mounted the stairs that led up from her closet to the attic.

Little Edmund waited patiently like a good boy for what seemed like forever, when finally, just as his mother had promised, 'Born in the USA' came on. Edmund jumped up and down on the bed and sang at the top of his lungs, but it wasn't nearly as much fun without his mother watching. And when the song was over, when the scary video came on with the man with the funny hair who kept asking, *"How could you think?"* over and over, Edmund climbed off the bed and went looking for his mother.

"Why are you hanging from the ceiling, Mama?" he asked when he reached the top of the attic stairs. But when his mother didn't respond—when Edmund pushed her and she just kept on swinging—the little boy got scared and began to cry.

"Your body is the doorway," the man with the funny hair said in the bedroom, and Edmund ran downstairs to the kitchen and dialed 911. He told the lady on the other end that his mother was dead and hanging from the ceiling and that it wasn't his fault. Then he ran outside, across the tobacco field to where his grandfather and a group of men were still working on the broken-down tractor.

Through his tears, Edmund told his grandfather that his mother was dead. The little boy knew all about death from watching his grandfather bury his pet rabbit Batman in the backyard earlier that spring. Edmund didn't know if his mother would be buried in the backyard next to Batman, but knew all the same that dead meant you didn't wake up.

Even when you were pushed really hard.

Chapter 43

All his life, it seemed, Edmund Lambert had been searching.

Searching. At first, he supposed, for his mother; then afterward, for something he could never quite put his finger on. Still, he knew it was there. Waiting on the other side of his dreams. Eventually it would come for him, he thought. One morning when he least expected it. With the sunrise. A new dawn through an open doorway that whispered, *"Finally, Edmund. Finally."*

By the time he was ten years old, Edmund could not remember much of his life before the day he found his mother swinging from the rafters. Jumbled pictures, mostly, that brought with them the vague sense of someone else—a character on a TV series that he used to watch before bedtime; a happy little boy whom Edmund envied.

But the TV series that aired afterwards? Well, the little boy on that show was someone Edmund Lambert didn't envy at all.

The series began with an episode about the little boy's mother, about her funeral and the high collar she had to wear to hide her neck; then, the program focused on the sadness the boy felt in the weeks that followed. These shows would sometimes take place in the boy's bedroom, in the dark with the boy in bed telling his mother how much he missed her. Those were the toughest to watch, but things really took a turn for the worse when the grandfather on the show found the dead mother's yearbook.

"So you and your mother had a secret," he said, pulling the yearbook up from the floorboards. "You known who your daddy was all along, is that right, Eddie?"

"She made me promise not to tell you, Grandpa," the boy said. "Mama said Daddy was Daddy even though he was dead like Batman is out back. And she said I could kiss him good night cuz I asked her if I could cuz I can't kiss Batman no more cuz he was in the ground and all dirty even though he was up in Heaven, too."

"I see," said the old man. Claude Lambert sat down on the floor thinking for what seemed to Edmund like a long time. Then he opened the yearbook, flipped to Danny Gibbs's photograph, and ripped out the page. Carefully, he tore out the young man's photograph—crushed and rolled the little square between his thumb and forefinger until Danny Gibbs was no bigger than an aspirin. Edmund watched his grandfather in silence.

"Come here, Eddie," the old man said finally.

Edmund obeyed and sat on the floor beside him.

"You remember how I taught you to spit?"

"Yes," said the boy.

"Well, I want you to fill your mouth just like I taught you when you was little."

"Why?"

"Just do as I say now, Eddie."

Edmund obeyed.

"Your mouth full?" asked his grandfather. Edmund nodded. And in a flash Claude Lambert seized the boy's face—

squished his cheeks together with one hand and forced the tiny wad through his lips with the other. Edmund began to squeal, to cry, and then to choke. He tried to spit the picture out, but Claude Lambert's big hand slapped over his mouth and nostrils so the boy couldn't breathe.

"Swallow, boy," was all he said. "Swallow."

And eventually little Edmund Lambert did.

Later, even though it was hot that night in the farmhouse, Claude Lambert built a big fire in the fireplace. He threw the yearbook on top and sat down on the floor next to his grandson—sweating, watching it burn.

"*C'est mieux d'oublier*," he kept saying over and over, until Edmund asked, "What do those words you're saying mean, Grandpa?"

"You don't remember ever hearing them before? When you was dreaming?"

"No."

Claude Lambert smiled. "I reckon that's a secret under the floorboards, too."

"Will you tell me?"

The old man was silent again for what seemed to Edmund like a long time. "I'll tell you, Eddie," he said finally, "but only if you promise to keep that secret just between us. Like you done with your mother."

"I promise."

"And you gotta promise me you won't cry no more like a baby."

"I promise, Grandpa. I'm a big boy now."

"That you are," said his grandfather. "That you are." He turned the boy to face him—held him firmly by the shoulders and stared deeply into his eyes. "You see, Eddie, them words is magic words that I invented a long time ago when I was mixing up things in the cellar. It took me a long time to invent them, to get them just right, but them words is a secret that's never to be spoken in real life except by me, and maybe someday by you in your head. You see, Eddie, with them words, I can talk to you in your dreams."

"What do you mean?"

"Well, let's say you're having a bad dream. A dream where you're lost or some monster is chasing you. You ever have dreams like that?"

"Sometimes."

"Well, I can say those magic words in my dreams and then come to you in your dreams and tell you everything is all right so you won't be afraid no more. And then you can grow stronger. You can fight off all those bad things and become brave like a big boy. You understand?"

"I think so."

"It's like, if I say them words in your dreams you'll forget all the bad things you dreamed about, but at the same time you remember them deep down and they end up becoming a part of you and make you stronger. It's kind of like you eat the bad things without knowing it. Like, when you eat your dinner—a nice cheeseburger—when you're eating the cheeseburger, all you taste in your mouth is the cheese and the burger and the bun, right?"

"And the mustard and ketchup."

"Right, and the mustard and ketchup. But once all that stuff is in your stomach, your stomach does the work of taking out everything that's good and using it so it makes you stronger. And it does all that without you even knowing it."

"I learned about that on TV, Grandpa. It's called digestion. It's why your poop smells bad, Mama used to say. Cuz once your stomach finishes taking out all the good stuff then it starts pushing out all the bad stuff, right?"

"I keep forgetting how smart you are, Eddie," said Claude Lambert, smiling. "That's why I came up with them words. So you can take in all the good stuff and poop out all the bad. Like today. You were really upset and scared, but you can take some good out of it. I can say the magic words to you—

or you can say them to yourself in your head even—and you can grow bigger and stronger because you know how to digest the pain."

"Is that why you made me eat Daddy?"

"Yes. Now you can forget him, but at the same he'll be a part of you and you can grow stronger cuz you ate him. The magic words help you do that in your dreams and for stuff you can't eat—kind of like teeth and a stomach for bad memories. I used to say words like that to your Uncle James and your mother in their dreams, too, and look how tough and brave they ended up. Well, your Uncle James at least. Don't know what went wrong with your mother."

Edmund felt his throat tighten, the tears welling in his eyes. He swallowed hard.

"*C'est mieux d'oublier*, Eddie," Claude Lambert whispered. "Them words mean, 'It's better to forget.' Say the words over and over and see if you feel better."

Edmund furrowed his brow and did as his grandfather asked of him—repeated the words back and forth until they sounded right—and pretty soon he felt his tears subside and the tightness in his throat leave him.

"You see?" said his grandfather. "Them words is magic."

Silence, Edmund thinking.

"Do you think God lets you dream in Heaven?" the boy asked after a while.

"Why do you ask that?"

"Well, maybe if I get really good at using them magic words, I can speak to Mama in her dreams the way you speak to me in mine."

Claude Lambert narrowed his gaze, gripped the boy tighter, and pulled him so close that Edmund could smell the liquor on his breath.

"Your mother ain't in Heaven, Eddie," the old man said quietly. "She killed herself. And when you kill yourself you go to Hell. Don't you ever forget that."

Chapter 44

Fighting. Always fighting. But what came first, the medicine or the fighting, Edmund Lambert could not remember. The medicine made him feel better, but not as good as the fighting. And when the pain from the fighting threatened to keep him awake at night, the medicine would make him sleep right on through until morning without having to pee once.

However, for almost three years following the death of his mother, Edmund was entirely unaware of the medicine—had no idea that his grandfather was secretly slipping it to him in his food, or sometimes in the milkshakes he would mix up special for him in the blender. The milkshakes were rare, but the medicine was rarer, and sometimes on the nights when his grandfather gave it to him (and even then not every night), Edmund would dream about someone called the General.

The dreams of the General were unlike the dreams Edmund had normally, and only after he awoke and stared for a long time at the ceiling would he remember that he had dreamed of anything at all. Also, the inside of his head, the space right behind his eyes, felt thick and gooey; the memories mostly big gaps of blackness that brought with them pressure in his sinuses and the vague awareness of the passage of time.

Sometimes, the General would appear between the big gaps in swirls and flashes of color—but Edmund could never see his face, could never see any part of him at all, for that matter. Yet all the same he knew he'd been there—more of a feeling of a person than an actual person was the only way Edmund could describe it. And sometimes he thought he could see the word "general" floating around in the swirls and flashes of color, but Edmund was never sure if he had just made that up afterwards because he knew the General had been there. The General was kind of like the air, Edmund thought. You never realize the air's there until you think about it, and even then you can't see it.

Early on it occurred to Edmund that the General might be a ghost. Ghosts were like the air. You couldn't see them most of the time, but you knew they were there because they made you afraid. And the farmhouse was certainly old enough. Edmund had learned somewhere that ghosts liked old houses. And of course there was the attic where his mother died. Ghosts lived in attics, Edmund knew. But surely his mother wasn't a ghost; she couldn't be both in Hell and in the attic at the same time.

Edmund understood his mother was never coming back the way she was when she was living, but often he found himself wishing he could find some way to get her out of Hell and back into the attic as a ghost. Ghosts were dead people who got stuck in old houses instead of going to Heaven or Hell; and even if you were dead and stuck in an old house, that had to be better than being stuck in Hell.

"If someday I can find a way to make you a ghost, Mama, I will. I promise."

Yes, Edmund thought, if his mother was a ghost and lived in the attic, at least he wouldn't be afraid of it anymore. His grandfather always said he was being a baby, but the old man never made him go up there. Edmund was thankful for that, especially since his grandfather often made him do things he was afraid of—things like making him stand in the fast-pitch batting cages or making him practice his curveballs in the backyard after dark or making him go down into the cellar by himself.

"C'est mieux d'oublier."

Edmund didn't mind the cellar when he was with his grandfather. And he especially liked spending time with him down there in his workroom. There were lots of tools in the workroom, but there were also some machines. Edmund loved the machines the best. His favorite was the grinder. It looked kind of like the old vacuum cleaner that they had upstairs but without the hose. And it was smaller; was mounted on the biggest of the three workbenches and had this fuzzy wheel on its side—only the fuzz was made up of thousands of thin metal wires that would cut you if you stuck your finger in them when they were spinning (Edmund had found this out the hard way when he was little).

Sometimes Edmund's grandfather would let him stick tools or other metal objects in the fuzzy wheel to polish them or to smooth them out. He told Edmund that you could change out the wire wheel for other wheels if you wanted, but Edmund never saw him do that. Edmund loved using the grinder, but what he loved most was how when you flicked on the switch it made a whirring noise that sounded like a jet engine starting up. The grinder also blew out warm air from a little vent on its side. Edmund loved how the air felt against his face; he loved how it smelled, too—kind of coppery, like someone was burning a stack of pennies.

There were other smells in the workroom, however, that young Edmund didn't care for very much at all; smells that came from all the bottles and jars that were stored on the shelves above the small workbench in the corner. Most of the bottles and jars had labels on them—single letters or combinations of letters and numbers and dashes that made no sense to Edmund. They were symbols for chemicals, his grandfather told him; stuff that "was gonna make them all rich someday," he used to say. There were also beakers and burners and weird-looking glass tubes, along with stacks of paper and a bunch of books about plants that Edmund couldn't pronounce.

Wormwood.

That was the only word in the big mess of it all that Edmund really understood, or at least remembered—and that was only because he heard Rally talking about it one time in the kitchen and thought it sounded funny.

"You mean the wood is full of worms, Uncle Rally?" Edmund asked.

"Naw," he said. "It's just what they call it. Ain't no wood at all. Just a plant that you can use for a bunch of different reasons, like keeping pests away and stuff. Gonna make us all rich when we get the formula right, Eddie."

Edmund knew Rally was not his real uncle, but still he liked him a lot. He always brought him stuff from his auto body shop—toy cars and trucks, mainly, which he said he got from something called a distributor. Edmund didn't know what a distributor was, but always appreciated the cars and trucks just the same.

"The whole shebang has to do with farming and tobacco crops," his grandfather added. "You just mind your own business, Eddie, until the money starts rolling in."

Edmund wasn't allowed to go down into the workroom when Rally was around. And after Edmund's mother died, Rally and his grandfather hardly ever went down into the cellar just themselves—at least not when Edmund was awake. And Edmund certainly never heard them acting funny and playing music down there like he did when his mother was still alive.

True, sometimes Rally and his grandfather would disappear down into the cellar to fetch something, but Edmund was never left alone upstairs for long. And true, sometimes in the mornings, after he'd slept all through the night without having to pee once, Edmund would smell that faint licorice smell by the cellar door in the kitchen. But most of the time, Rally's visits were uneventful; a night of watching TV that (after they had drank too much of Claude Lambert's moonshine) usually devolved into them bitching that if they could just figure out the right equations to balance the formula, if they could just get their hands on the right chemicals and the right equipment so they could run the right experiments and get those bastards to listen to them oh *blahdy-blah-blah-blah* (Edmund had picked up that last phrase from his mother).

When it came right down to it, however, Edmund didn't give two shits about his grandfather's farming experiments. But still, the old man always warned the boy to mind his own business and not to go messing with his stuff and to never go down into the workroom alone unless he told him to and if he ever caught him touching any of his stuff he'd get his ass run up against the grinder until it cut him a second butt crack.

All that was fine with Edmund, who never wanted to go down into the cellar alone anyway. The cramped darkness always gave him the feeling that someone was down there with him—a ghost, Edmund was sure; most likely the General.

"C'est mieux d'oublier," he'd say to himself over and over again, but still the fear and the feeling that the General was with him would not go away.

It was like that for most of his childhood, Edmund would recall. But the first time he told his grandfather about the General was after he'd dreamed of him a second time. Edmund was six years old.

"Did a general from the Army ever live in this house, Grandpa?"

"Why do you ask that, Eddie?"

Edmund explained that ghosts were dead people who got stuck in old houses because they couldn't get into Heaven or Hell.

"Hmm," said Claude Lambert after he was quiet in that way that seemed to Edmund like a long time. "So the General's been messing around in your dreams, huh?"

"What do you mean?"

"Well, you see, the General's someone who died on the property over a hundred years ago in this thing called the Civil War. You ever hear about the Civil War, Eddie?"

"No."

"Well, I'll explain it to you someday when you'll understand better. But all you need to know right now is that the Civil War was this war that took place way back when our country was split in two halves—a northern half and a southern half. This property was part of the southern half back then, and the General was fighting for the southern side, and he got hurt really bad in this big battle nearby and they brought him here to try and fix him up. They couldn't, though, and the General ended up dying."

"No fooling, Grandpa?"

"No fooling, Eddie. There was a different house on the property back then that got burned down. But the General ended up dying right here where we're sitting."

"No fooling?"

"Nope."

"So the General really is a ghost, then?"

"I'm afraid so, Eddie."

Edmund swallowed hard. "Is he buried somewhere out back?" he asked. "The General, I mean—near Batman, maybe?"

"Naw. They took his body away. Probably buried him in a cemetery near where he lived. But I guess his ghost decided to stick around all these years."

"Does he live in the attic now?"

"No. In the cellar. That's why you're not supposed to go down there and mess with my stuff unless I'm with you. The General is scared of me, you see. Won't bother you when I'm with you, or when I send you down there alone to fetch me something."

Edmund was silent—thinking, terrified.

"You don't need to be scared, Eddie," said the old man. "The General ain't a bad fella if you don't piss him off. Just nosy most of the time. Likes to poke his nose into your business. Especially when you're sleeping—but only when you're really tired and when it's hard for you to wake up."

"You swear you're not making this up, Grandpa?" the boy asked. "You got that look on your face like you do when you and Rally is fooling me. Like that time you told me you guys caught a shark in Randolph's Pond but then when I told you sharks couldn't live in fresh water you and Rally said that you was only fooling."

"I swear I'm not fooling, Eddie. You're too smart a boy to fool. Besides, I would never fool about someone like the General. The General is one dangerous fella when he wants to be. Can make you do things in your dreams that you don't want to—or at the very least he can scare you real bad. He'd never try that shit with me, though. Yeah, he's scared of me cuz I'm bigger and stronger than he is—doesn't dare come into my dreams cuz he knows I'd kick his ass. You see, Eddie, only I can control the General."

"The magic words," Edmund said suddenly. "*C'est mieux d'oublier*—you said you can come into my dreams and help me, right Grandpa? *C'est mieux*—"

"Ssh, Eddie. Remember, you're not supposed to say them magic words out loud."

"But you said the General is too strong for me. Will you help me with the magic words? Will you come into my dreams and kick his ass like you do in yours?"

"You're really that afraid of him, huh?"

Edmund swallowed again.

"All right," said his grandfather. "I'll tell you what, Eddie. Next time the General starts messing with you I'll come in there like I told you and I'll say the magic words and that'll chase the General away. Okay, Eddie?"

"Thanks, Grandpa!" said the boy, and he flung himself into his arms.

It was about two years later when Edmund learned of the medicine and began to make the connection between it and his visits from the General.

Claude Lambert kept the medicine hidden someplace in the cellar. Even as a child Edmund thought this strange, as it was labeled just like the jars and bottles in the workroom. M-E-D-I-C-I-N-E it read in big block letters that looked just like the letters with which he had written his name in the dirt behind the old horse barn.

Edmund couldn't remember if his grandfather had taught him to write the E-D-D-I-E or if he had just picked it up from spending time with him in the workroom. However, Edmund *did* remember the first time he saw the old man bring up the medicine bottle from the cellar. It was the same afternoon he got sent home from school for fighting—second grade, Edmund got the worst of it—and his head still stung from where his classmate had whipped him with a jump-rope handle.

"What's that?" the boy asked.

"Special medicine," said his grandfather. "You don't remember ever seeing this?"

"No."

"I gave it to you a couple of times when you was little and your mother was still alive. I been giving it to you now and then in your food without you knowing. When you was hurt or sick or afraid of something so as to make you feel better. Like that time when you stuck your finger in the grinder. I gave it to you in secret then, but you felt better in the morning. Remember that?"

"I think so," Edmund said. He'd slept like a rock that night, if he remembered correctly. And his finger felt a lot better in the morning—*but didn't the General visit him that night, too?*

"But now," said his grandfather, "you're a big enough boy that you can take your medicine straight without me keeping it secret. Your mother and Uncle James got the medicine when they was kids, too—James, more so. Your mother usually refused it; liked the pain better, I guess."

"You're not mad at me for fighting then, Grandpa?"

"Naw," said Claude Lambert, taking a spoon from the drawer. "I'm not mad at you, I'm proud of you. Other kid did something to piss you off, right?"

"Yes."

"Well, he probably deserved it then." The old man poured the medicine. "Fighting is good for you, Eddie. Gotta learn to take your licks as well as give 'em—but only when someone gives you shit. Never go picking fights, understand? Ain't no grandson of mine gonna be a bully. You ain't one of them bullies at school, are you, Eddie?"

"No, sir."

"Good boy. Just like your uncle. Next time we go visit Uncle James, you can ask him about how he used to be when he was your age. He was a fighter, too. A good one."

Edmund didn't really like his Uncle James. In all the years he visited him at the prison with his grandfather, James Lambert never looked at him directly—would only tighten his lips and raise his left eyebrow now and then to give the boy a once-over. And he hardly ever spoke; would only nod his head on the other side of the visitor's glass as the old man talked, and always ended by asking if his father brought his chew.

"What he do to get in jail?" Edmund asked.

"I'll tell you when you're a little older," his grandfather said, smiling. "You take this medicine now, Eddie. Only a spoonful. Never too much, never too often. It's bad for you if you have too much too often. And it tastes shitty, too, but pretty soon the back of your head'll be numb and you'll forget all about the kid with the jump rope. Best of all, when you wake up in the morning the pain will be gone."

Edmund sniffed the spoon. It smelled a little like the licorice smell that was in the den sometimes when Rally was around. But it also smelled like Pine-Sol, Edmund thought, and tasted even worse—although he had never tasted Pine-Sol.

But Edmund swallowed the medicine anyway, and pretty soon his head felt numb just like his grandfather had promised. They sat together watching TV for a while. Then, a blink forward in time, and Edmund woke up in the dark. He was in his bed, under the covers, and it was really late—he could tell by the feel of things around him. His head was no longer numb, but it didn't hurt nearly as much as before.

But now something different was bothering him. Edmund thought long and hard, staring up at the ceiling. He couldn't see the ceiling, but he knew it was there. Just like the thing that was bothering him.

Then it came to him.

The General, he said to himself. *Where's the General?*

Yes, that was it. He had woken up feeling the same as he usually felt after he dreamed of the General, but when he looked for him between the big gaps of black and gooiness he could not find him, could not sense him anywhere.

"C'est mieux d'oublier."

And with those words, instead of the General's presence, flickered strange and distant images of him battling what he somehow understood to be a big black blob of pain—punching and kicking it violently until the big black blob disappeared.

Memories of a dream? Most likely, but the boy couldn't be sure, couldn't tell the difference between actually dreaming about the blob or just making it all up now that he was awake. No, all Edmund Lambert knew for sure was that the pain in the back of his head from the jump-rope handle was gone.

Grandpa gave me the medicine before without me knowing it, Edmund thought. *That's why the General must be able to get in my dreams—cuz I'm sleeping so heavy. That's why I need Grandpa to kick his ass out. Maybe the General was there tonight, too, but Grandpa got to him first. Maybe the General is like the pain. Only Grandpa can protect me from them both.*

And so the boy would willingly swallow the medicine many times in the years that followed—only after his fights or when he got hurt, and even then not every time.

Timing was part of it, his grandfather said. The timing had to be right.

Yes, in the end Claude Lambert was true to his word.

Never too much, never too often.

"C'est mieux d'oublier."

Chapter 45

There were really only two times that Edmund suspected his grandfather of giving him the medicine for reasons other than fighting or getting hurt: once in the summer of 1991 when Edmund was eleven, and once a year later in the fall, just after he turned twelve. Both times were without his knowing, and only years later did Edmund begin to suspect that Claude Lambert might have pulled a fast one on him.

The first time was in the farmhouse, in a supersweet milkshake Claude Lambert mixed in the blender. He made it "special" he said, to go with the two large pepperoni pizzas he'd picked up after he and Edmund got back from the Little League All-Star game in Cary. Edmund didn't play in the game that year because he was too young, but the coach of his Sunday league team in Wilson wanted him to go to meet another coach so they could clock Edmund's pitches with a radar gun they'd be using for the game.

Edmund and his grandfather had a bit of a ways to travel, but got to the baseball field in Cary early. And just as the older kids began warming up, one of the coaches took some time out to use the radar gun on Edmund's pitches—said he was really impressed with his arm and that he pitched just as fast, if not faster, than the older kids. The coach handed his grandfather his card and invited the two of them to watch the game, too. They did, but Edmund quickly became bored. He didn't like watching baseball; and when he thought about it, he didn't really like playing it much, either.

Edmund wasn't quite sure what the whole trip to the baseball field in Cary had been about until he got home and his grandfather handed him the milkshake.

"All that pitching you done in the backyard is gonna pay off for you someday, Eddie," said Claude Lambert, sitting down. "You'll be moving up next year to the higher division. Gonna keep on moving up, too, if you play your cards right."

"Past Little League, you mean?"

"Right you are," said his grandfather. "Little League, high school, college, straight on through to the majors, I reckon."

"I thought you didn't want me to go to college."

"If you can go for baseball, well, that's a different story."

"But what if I don't want to go to college? What if I don't want to play baseball no more and just want to work on the farm with you?"

"Don't be stupid now, Eddie. Baseball's a God-given talent that you can't deny."

Edmund had never thought of it that way. But still, the idea of playing baseball for the rest of his life didn't sit well with him.

"Did you pick up *Young Guns 2* like you promised?" he asked, changing the subject.

"Yeah, I picked it up," said the old man. "But it's getting late and you better not fall asleep during it. You know I don't like them cowboy movies."

"I won't. I promise."

"All right then," said his grandfather. "Drink your milkshake before it melts."

But Edmund did fall asleep before the end of the movie. He woke up on the couch just before sunrise with the thick and gooey feeling behind his eyes. He looked for the General but could not find him. At the same time, however, the gaps of blackness told him someone had been there in his dreams—someone who had been fighting with him on a baseball field; someone with a scratchy voice who was forcing his arm to throw pitches. Yes, fighting and baseball, that's what the dream had been about—but at the same time Edmund couldn't be sure if he'd really dreamed it or if he'd just made it up afterward because of his conversation with his grandfather.

He told the old man about the dream at breakfast, and straight up asked him if he had given him the medicine like he used to when he was a boy—without his knowing.

"Now why would I do that?" his grandfather replied. "You was tired and ate too much pizza, is all. But maybe your conscience was trying to tell you something, Eddie. Maybe it could've even been God trying to tell you something. After all, baseball's a God-given talent. All that nonsense about not playing—that's downright blasphemy."

Edmund didn't think it was God who had talked to him in his dreams—didn't think not wanting to play baseball was blasphemy, either—but he decided not to argue. All that didn't seem to matter now anyway. College was a long way off, and for some reason he felt better about playing baseball than he had in a long time.

Besides, his grandfather was going to let him keep *Young Guns 2* an extra day.

The other time Edmund suspected his grandfather might've slipped him some medicine without his knowing was on their first deer-hunting trip upstate, after he and the old man took a piss next to each other in the woods.

"What you got on your prick there, Eddie?" Claude Lambert asked.

"I guess I'm getting my pubes is all."

His grandfather zipped up his pants and looked down at Edmund's crotch.

"I'll be a son of a bitch," Claude Lambert said, smiling, and told Edmund to zip up his fly and head back to the cabin.

"What's in there?" Edmund asked when his grandfather came out of the bathroom with the flask.

"You're a man now, Eddie," said Claude Lambert. "And a man deserves a drink." He handed him the flask. "Drink up. There's just enough for you."

"It smells awful," said Edmund. He knew that smell well; had smelled it many times on his grandfather's breath. The licorice moonshine.

"Right you are," said Claude Lambert. "And you might feel a little loopy. But it's all part of being a man."

But there's something that smells different about the licorice, Edmund thought. *Something stronger; something that smells a little like Pine-Sol.*

"It'll help you sleep, too," said his grandfather. "We gotta catch some shut-eye before we head out to the stand. Gotta be rested for our twelve-pointer now, don't we?"

Edmund drank the flask dry. And sure enough, not only did he start to feel loopy, but soon he fell asleep. He was still groggy, the inside of his head still thick and gooey when his grandfather woke him later to head out to the deer stand.

"That stuff you made me drink feels a lot like the medicine," Edmund said.

"Yeah," said his grandfather, "but it also feels different though, doesn't it? And *you* feel different now after taking that drink, don't you, Eddie? Different than after you take the medicine. Makes you feel more like a man, wouldn't you say?"

Edmund couldn't tell if he felt more like a man, but he

did feel pretty calm about going out into the woods to kill his first deer—not sort of afraid, as he had felt before. No, now he felt as if killing the deer was just something he had to do—sort of like he was on a mission, he thought—but at the same time he kept seeing these strange shadows in his head that he knew had to do with guns and being a hunter and *"C'est mieux d'oublier."*

"You'll see what I mean when the time comes," said the old man.

And even though his grandfather kept saying over and over again how proud he was that his grandson took his first drink like a man, once they settled themselves in the stand Edmund quickly fell asleep. He had no idea how much time had passed when he felt his grandfather's elbow in his side. And when he opened his eyes, he immediately noticed that the woods had grown darker.

Then he saw it: a single buck in the clearing.

The boy's heart pounded him instantly awake.

Without a sound, the old man handed him the rifle. Edmund judged the buck to be about fifty yards away, and trained the scope on it steadily just as his grandfather had taught him the previous fall, when he let the boy practice on some wild turkeys that had been poking around the woods at the edge of the farm. Edmund hadn't been able to hit any of the turkeys, but he and the old man had gone target shooting over the summer, everything in preparation for this moment.

Edmund took a deep breath and slowly exhaled, bracing himself for the rifle's kickback—he still wasn't used to it; it still made the inside of his shoulder ache for days—when suddenly, without thinking, he squeezed the trigger and— *Bam!*

The buck dropped to the ground.

Claude Lambert snatched the rifle, and the two of them scrambled down from the stand. They closed the distance quickly, slowing down the last ten yards or so and approaching cautiously. And just before they reached the buck, the old man handed the rifle back to his grandson. "One more in the back of the head in case he ain't dead."

Edmund shot the buck again.

"An eight-pointer," his grandfather said when they were upon it. "Not bad for your first time. You done that without thinking, Eddie. Like a real hunter does."

His heart still pounding, Edmund gazed down at his kill.

"Gonna make a nice mount," Claude Lambert said, more to himself. "I done good making you a hunter. Done good to get your mind straight on things, too."

He immediately tagged the buck on its ear and motioned for the boy to help him. They turned the carcass over and propped it up on its back, its head resting against a large tangle of exposed tree roots. Then, the old man removed a hunting knife from his belt, knelt down, and began cutting the buck just beneath the breastbone. He worked quickly, using his index and middle fingers as a guide, and opened the deer lengthwise along its belly. Edmund had seen his grandfather field dress deer many times back on the farm, and as he slowly cut away the stomach and intestines, the boy knew the old man was taking care not to puncture the organs and contaminate the meat.

But something was different this time. Edmund could feel it throughout his entire body, vibrating pleasantly and with an eerie sense of calm expectation. It was as if he had watched this scene many years ago in a movie—a movie starring a boy who looked just like him—but he couldn't quite remember exactly what the boy was about to do.

"C'est mieux d'oublier."

Now he was watching, but was also being pulled downward to his knees with the boy. He could hear a voice commanding them both—could not hear actual words, but nonetheless understood what the voice was telling them to do.

Then a blink, a rush, a coming together, and Edmund and the boy were one again.

The vibrating was gone, but the calm remained.

And now there was only the buck's bloody beating heart held out to him in his grandfather's hands.

"Take it, Eddie," said the old man. "You know what to do."

Edmund took the heart from his grandfather and brought it to his lips. He did not pause to ponder its warmth, its wetness, and without hesitation sank his teeth deep into the twitching muscle, tore out a bite, and swallowed.

Chapter 46

When he was grown, Edmund would realize that the hunting trip was not only the last time his grandfather gave him the medicine in secret, but also the last time his grandfather gave him the medicine *period*. However, over the course of the two years following the hunting trip, Edmund began to wonder why his grandfather never offered him the medicine even after some of his really bad fights. Like the one with the catcher that got him kicked off his junior high school baseball team.

Granted, Edmund threw the first punch, but the catcher had called Edmund a faggot because he didn't feel like pitching hard that day. Edmund flew off the mound in a fury, but another player stepped in front of him just as he reached home plate, making Edmund's punch go wild. The catcher, who was a big, fat kid, easily sidestepped their scuffle and tagged Edmund in the face—pushed the other player out of the way and tackled Edmund to the ground. He got in a few more punches before Edmund could connect with one of his own. And surely Edmund would have gotten the best of him had the coach and the other players not stepped in. But because Edmund had thrown the first punch, he was told to gather up his things and never come back.

Claude Lambert had been really disappointed in his grandson for getting kicked off the baseball team. He even went down to the school and tried to reason with the coach, but the coach wouldn't hear of taking Edmund back. Didn't matter how good the kid was, he said. That kind of unsportsmanlike conduct simply would not be tolerated.

The old man went on a two-week bender after that. And oftentimes, Edmund would come home from school and find him down in the cellar by himself, the smell of licorice mixed with cigarette smoke wafting up the stairs and that weird French music playing in the background. It had been ages since Edmund had heard that music, and he couldn't remember ever seeing his grandfather that way—depressed, distant, quiet. Rally seemed to look at him differently, too, and for weeks the two men only spoke to Edmund in spurts of yeses, nos, and maybes.

Eventually, the old man forgave him—never actually said anything, but Edmund could tell by the way he and Rally looked at him normally again. Edmund would get in many more fights that year, but still Claude Lambert never brought the medicine up from the cellar. The boy even went looking for it one night when his grandfather was passed out in the den—something he swore he would never do—but could not find it anywhere. Edmund still got spooked when he went down into the cellar alone, but strangely, not only did he find himself longing for the medicine, but more than anything else, Edmund also found himself longing for the General.

Edmund hadn't dreamed of the General since even before the hunting trip; hadn't talked about him with his grandfather since he was a boy and began to wonder if he had ever dreamed of him at all. And so he asked the school librarian about any Civil War battles fought in Wilson. She said she didn't know of any and told him to look it up in the encyclopedia. Edmund did, and discovered that no Civil War battles had been fought in Wilson County *ever.* The closest one seemed to be the Battle of Bentonville, near the present-day town of Four Oaks—about forty miles away, by Edmund's calculations, and certainly not close enough to warrant carrying the General all the way to his property.

He asked his grandfather about it.

"I reckon the General must've been someone you made up," the old man replied. "You always had a hyperactive imagination, Eddie."

"But you were the one who told me about the Civil War stuff."

"I don't remember," said his grandfather. "I probably said all that just to make you feel better even though it wasn't true. Like *c'est mieux d'oublier.* I used to say them words to you thinking they was magic. But look what happened? Them words ended up not being magic at all. If they was, you wouldn't have gotten yourself kicked off the baseball team, now would ya? My own damn fault, I reckon. Wrong fucking equation and back to square one."

Edmund had no idea what his grandfather was talking about, and asked, "But what about the medicine? You used to give it to me to make me feel better when I was hurt, but now you won't anymore."

"You've had too much of it," his grandfather said simply. "Ain't good for your head no more, I reckon. Besides, there ain't none of it left."

Chapter 47

Edmund got the idea to kill the cat from the buck his grandfather had mounted for him years earlier. He didn't know why the image of the cat skewered on the deer's antlers suddenly flashed in his mind while he was doing his geometry homework; and he most certainly didn't know why it should be his *first* buck rather than all the others he and his grandfather had hung up in the den over the years. Perhaps, Edmund thought, it was because he had been daydreaming about pussy; about Erin Jones and their first time in the back of her cramped Honda Civic. She was sixteen, he was fifteen. His first time, not hers. Fun, but nothing special, and not nearly as exciting as he had thought it would be. But the idea of the cat suddenly excited him more than the memory of doing it with Erin Jones; excited him even more than the idea of doing it with Karen Blume, who had been the star of his jerk-off sessions for pretty much his entire sophomore year now.

Searching. Searching.

The cat? Was that what he had been searching for?

It felt like the answer, and for an entire week Edmund Lambert could not get the image out of his mind.

Edmund and his grandfather had about a half dozen cats roaming the property—all outdoors, all former strays. Two of the new ones were still feral, and only came out from under the back porch when Edmund set out their food. They hadn't been fixed like the others, hadn't even been named yet, and Edmund knew it was only a matter of time before another litter popped and he and Rally would have to cart them off to the shelter. Well, it was really Edmund who would have to take care of all that. Rally would just tag along for the ride like he always did. Claude Lambert preferred more and more to stay in the farmhouse—in the cellar, mostly, or in the den watching TV. The two men were well into their seventies now, retired, and Edmund had begun to think of them both as pretty fucking useless; had grown bored with them, and would often look for any excuse to get out of the house.

But the cats? Well, that was one reason to stick around.

Edmund knew how to catch the wild ones. He'd done it before with a can of tuna fish and a bottomless wooden crate with a hinged lid that his grandfather kept in the old horse barn. There were no more horses in the horse barn—only his Uncle James's old van and some other junk behind which Edmund kept his stack of nudie books. Edmund rarely went in there anymore to look at them. No, in the last year or so, he had begun to feel confused when he looked at the pictures that had both men and women in them; would sometimes find his eyes drifting to the men, to their buttocks and their chests. Edmund didn't think he was a "sodomite" as his grandfather and Rally called them. He still liked girls, still liked doing Erin Jones and hoped someday to do Karen Blume, too.

But still, sometimes, late at night, when his mind wandered . . .

There was no confusion about what Edmund wanted to do to the cat, however. And so one day while his grandfather was at Rally's auto shop (which had been bought out by a nephew after the pudgy old man retired), fifteen-year-old Edmund Lambert latched the top of the crate closed and tied a clothesline through a hole in the lid; rigged everything up so the crate hung from a tree limb about three feet off the ground. He tied off the other end of the line on a chair leg a few yards away on the back porch. Then he clicked the top of a tuna fish can a few times, opened four of them, and set them beneath the crate.

All the cats came out of hiding immediately, but only the ones with names rushed to feed while Edmund was still there. Edmund didn't want them. No, his grandfather and Rally liked those cats and would miss them; might ask questions and grow suspicious.

So Edmund sat on the porch and waited; untied the clothesline from the chair leg and held the crate aloft until the feral cats approached. And once all six of the cats were jostling for position around the tuna fish cans, Edmund let the crate drop. Three, including a feral one, got away immediately, but the others were trapped—meowing and hissing and batting against the inside of the crate in a panic. Edmund felt excited, but at the same time as if his actions were not his own. Like that time with his grandfather in woods when he ate the deer's heart; felt as if he were standing a few feet away watching a robot who had been programmed by somebody else.

Either way, he knew exactly what to do.

Edmund walked over to the crate and picked up the pitchfork he'd leaned up against the other side of the tree. He undid the latch and, with some quick maneuvering, was able to corner the feral cat while the other two escaped. The cat hissed and screeched and clawed at the pitchfork points that held it down. And then, without thinking, Edmund skewered the creature through its back and belly. The cat let out a wail—started trembling and clawed at itself as it tried to escape. But Edmund pushed harder, then lifted the cat into the air as if he were baling hay. The cat shrieked and began to spasm, its movements impaling it farther down the pitchfork. The other cats were wailing now, too, watching from the woods and from underneath the porch. Edmund held the pitchfork at arm's length as the cat began to twitch—a soft hissing coming from its mouth—and the blood began to drip down the handle and onto Edmund's hand.

And then it was over.

Edmund twisted the pitchfork's handle into the soft dirt, and when it would stand upright on its own, he stepped back a few feet and studied his work. His heart was beating wildly, and he felt exhilarated overall, but something was missing. Impulsively, he dipped his fingers in the cat's blood and brought them to his mouth. The blood was warm and tasted coppery, and for some reason Edmund thought of the wind from his grandfather's grinder in the workroom.

But something was still missing. And the more Edmund thought about it, the further away the answer seemed to be.

Later, after he buried the cat in the woods, Edmund lay in his bed wide awake, thinking and listening to the other cats outside as they mourned their fallen comrade. He felt no guilt, only confusion. And then the searching again—still there, creeping back in, the answer tomorrow maybe.

No, killing the cat and tasting its blood—at least *that* cat and *that* blood—wasn't it. And Edmund Lambert felt as empty as he did before.

Chapter 48

Edmund's first time with a man was with a lawyer named Alfred, an older gentleman he met in an AOL chat room called RaleighMen4Men. It was in the spring of 1998, during his senior year of high school, while he was still going hot and heavy with Karen Blume. Edmund liked Karen; well, he liked banging her, but didn't really enjoy spending time with her, and often found himself thinking strange thoughts when they were together.

He wondered what it would be like if he *did things* to her: things like he had done to the cat; things like he had done to some of the other animals he'd captured over the last couple of years—squirrels, mice, a possum or two, and that stray dog. And of course, there were more cats. So many cats.

Edmund had also fixed up his uncle's old van, and his favorite fantasy involved drugging Karen and driving her out into the woods, where he would park the van and set up a little workshop with the tools he had brought along to play with her. But at the same time Edmund suspected that doing those kinds of things to Karen Blume wouldn't be worth the risk and wouldn't satisfy him in the long run.

No, something was missing. Something was always missing.

Edmund didn't know why he started going in the Men4Men chat room; didn't know why searched the male-modeling sites until he found a picture that sort of looked like him. Edmund called himself "Ken" and asked a lot of questions of the men online; even sent his picture to a few of them. But just like the phony photo and the phony name, Edmund felt as if his actions were not his own, and watched himself with the same detached curiosity as if he were watching a character on a TV show.

And of course there was the searching. Always the searching.

Edmund and Alfred had gone back and forth on AOL for about a month before Edmund agreed to meet him one afternoon in the philosophy and religion section at Barnes & Noble. The plan was simple enough: if each liked what he saw, Edmund would follow the lawyer to a hotel room a few miles away. Alfred was married, he said—had one child already and another on the way—and the only time he could get away was during the weekdays. It also worked out well for Edmund, who had been suspended from school again for fighting. He was one step away from being expelled, his counselor said, and would have to go to summer school to finish up his coursework. Indeed, it was Edmund's counselor who had made the case for Edmund to be allowed to graduate; reminded the principal that Edmund had a 3.8 GPA and had tested the previous year at the genius level. If the boy could just get his temper under control, his counselor said; if he could just focus, it would pay off for him in the long run.

School had always been easy for Edmund Lambert. Girls, sports, the respect and envy from the other boys—it all came just *so goddamn easy* to him. But the searching? Yes, only the searching was hard.

Like Edmund, Alfred the lawyer said he wasn't gay—just

liked to "experiment now and then," as he called it. And after the awkwardness of their initial meeting at the Barnes & Noble, Alfred and "Ken" experimented with each other a number of times over the next few weeks. Alfred began calling himself Ken's "mentor" and taught him the differences between having sex with a woman and having sex with a man.

But afterward, especially when Ken was Edmund again and he was banging Karen Blume in her basement, when he thought about the sex with Alfred, Edmund had a hard time sorting out the differences between the two in his head. No, the only difference Edmund could see was that, when he was with Alfred—*and when he was Ken in general*—his fantasies of doing what he did to the animals were much more vivid, much more exciting. And one time after they had sex, when Alfred asked Ken what he was thinking, the young man came right out and said: "I'm wondering what you would look like stuck with a giant pitchfork."

Alfred broke it off with Edmund soon afterwards; made some excuse about the wife catching on and said they had to cool it for a while. Edmund understood. He knew that he had spooked him; knew that he would never see Alfred the lawyer again. But it was all for the best, Edmund thought. He had grown tired of Alfred anyway, and thus exited his first homosexual affair with the same sort of mechanical detachment with which he'd entered into it.

The urge to kill, however, had been strong—the strongest yet with a human being. Edmund didn't know why, and wondered whether Alfred sensed it, too. Yet something had held him back. What? He couldn't put his finger on it right away, and only after he thought about it long and hard did he find the answer. An answer that surprised him.

"C'est mieux d'oublier," he heard his grandfather say. *"C'est mieux d'oublier."*

Chapter 49

"The Army or prison," Claude Lambert said. "Those are pretty much your options now, Eddie."

Edmund looked at his cheekbone in the pickup truck's side mirror. The swelling had gone down some, but his face would still bruise up nicely. The punch had been hard—he got blindsided by the other guy's friend—but in the end, Edmund had gotten the best of the both of them. He always did now.

"The way things is going," said his grandfather, turning off the highway, "I give you a year before you end up killing someone like your Uncle James done."

The old man was pushing eighty years old, but still it bothered Edmund how slowly he was driving.

"You don't like me fighting anymore then?" Edmund asked.

"I suppose it's partly my fault," Claude Lambert said, ignoring him. "Taught you how to fight but not how to control it—didn't think about that part of the equation. I reckon the Army will take care of that. It's where James had been planning on going, too, but . . . well, you know what happened there."

The fight in the bar had been Edmund's doing. He went there after he asked his Uncle James what really happened on the afternoon he murdered Danny Gibbs.

"I reckon it's simple," James Lambert said from the other side of the visitor's glass. "Sometimes you just gotta to do what's right cuz a higher power's telling you to."

"A higher power?" Edmund asked. "You mean like the General?"

"Don't know nothing 'bout no General. But I reckon what you're saying is right if you was in the Army or something."

Suddenly, Edmund felt emptier and more alone than he had felt in a long time.

"*C'est mieux d'oublier*," he said impulsively, and waited for a reaction.

James Lambert was silent for a long time—his expression like stone.

"You best not be visiting me no more," he said finally, looking him straight in the eye for the first time in eighteen years. Then he motioned for the guard and left.

That was the last time Edmund ever saw him.

He drove around afterward for hours and ended up at an eighteen-and-over bar in Greenville. He'd purchased a tube of Chapstick first and coated the back of his hands so he'd be able to wash off the *X* with which the doorman would mark him as underage. Edmund did so in the men's room, stepped up to the bar, ordered three shots of Southern Comfort, one right after the other, and then just started swinging.

"You're lucky the bar and them two other guys you floored ain't gonna press charges, Eddie," said his grandfather, parking the truck. "A good thing you ordered those shots, I reckon, too. Underage drinking and losing licenses—no one wants this to get any bigger than it already has."

Edmund was silent as he looked up at the sign for the Army recruiting center.

"*Sometimes you just gotta do what's right cuz a higher power's telling you to.*"

A sign—what he had been searching for all along?

"But the Army will fix you up right, Eddie," said Claude Lambert. "Best thing for your head now, I reckon."

Chapter 50

Searching.

But drifting now, too.

Basic training, then the assignment to Air Assault at Fort Campbell. More assignments here, more assignments there. Commendations and promotions—E2 up through E5. Sometimes Sergeant Lambert was with women, sometimes he was with men, but the drifting, the new places and new faces helped with the searching; made him forget about it completely for weeks at a time.

His grandfather had been right. The Army kept him focused; kept the fighting in his belly; kept the fantasies of doing to his lovers what he had done to his animals out of his head. Even when he was with the men, for a long time it seemed to Edmund that the only animal he ever thought about was the golden, seal-tailed lion on the crest of his 101st Airborne's 187th Infantry Regiment patch.

Perhaps that was why he took the ancient cylinder.

Edmund came upon the stash of stolen Iraqi artifacts in October of 2003, while on patrol in Tal Afar, a city north of

Mosul. The 101st Airborne's 187th Infantry Regiment was making a big push to secure the city for the upcoming elections, and Edmund was in charge of a door-to-door sweep to root out insurgents. He killed one man inside the house where he found the cylinder; he'd thought at first the house's occupants were terrorists, then later realized the two remaining men were part of a smuggling ring.

The house secure, the men arrested, for the briefest of moments Edmund was left alone with the open crate. He didn't know what the tiny cylindrical object on the top was at first, but knew it had to be valuable because of the other objects beneath it—stone tablets, figurines, a solid-gold jeweled bowl just like the bowl the soldier from the 3rd Infantry Division tried to smuggle back to Fort Stewart.

Edmund had heard about that little incident back in May; knew he could get in big trouble if he was caught stealing, too. But that had been at the start of the war; that had been before the contacts had been put in place in Qatar—contacts who were willing to pay cash on the spot for stolen ancient Iraqi artifacts.

Or so Edmund had heard.

Yes, as hard as it was to get that kind of stuff back to the United States, word on the street was a man with the right connections could make a lot of money in Qatar if he was willing to take the risk. And although Edmund Lambert had never even stolen a candy bar in his life, when he picked up the tiny stone cylinder and saw the lion heads that looked so much like the lion on his 187th patch, impulsively he pocketed it before his soldiers returned.

Afterwards, on his way back to the base, Edmund realized that for the first time since his enlistment his actions had not been his own—a feeling that reminded him so much of those days back on the tobacco farm in North Carolina. And when he was alone in the latrine, when he studied the carving more closely and figured out what the lions on the cylinder were *doing*, well, Edmund Lambert simply could not believe his eyes.

At first he didn't know the identity of the bearded man with the body of the winged lion; didn't know why the lion-headed men were presenting him with impaled bodies, either. And although Edmund had seen similar objects during his time in Iraq, he wasn't quite sure what the little cylinder was until he looked it up on the Internet. An ancient Babylonian seal, he discovered, most likely depicting the god Nergal.

And, after extensive research, Edmund concluded that the winged god to whom the impaled bodies were being presented *had* to be Nergal. The Raging Prince, the Babylonians called him; the Furious One; Lord of the Underworld—part man, part winged lion—just like Edmund himself in his 187th Infantry Regiment uniform.

The lion and the wings on the *seal*—just like his patch. Yes, it was all connected somehow. Edmund could feel it.

He figured the ancient artifact would fetch him a lot of money if he dumped it off in Qatar, but he had no desire to part with it—he didn't tell anyone about it and studied the seal whenever he was alone. Eventually, Edmund was able to close his eyes and see the carved figures in as much detail as if they were right there before him. He kept the seal on his person always; carried it in his pocket for months while on patrol. His good luck charm, he thought; it got him out of a number of scrapes when others only a few feet away bit it for good.

But toward the end of January 2004, a week before he was scheduled to come home, Edmund Lambert's luck changed—for better or for worse, he wasn't sure at first.

His grandfather was dead.

Edmund spoke with Rally on the telephone, and received the news calmly, with little or no emotion, as Rally explained how he found the old man facedown in the cellar.

"Looks like he drank too much of that stuff," he said, his voice tired and strained with tears. "Heart just gave out is what the coroner is saying."

"I see," Edmund said.

"The sheriff was there, too, Eddie, and—"

Rally was suddenly quiet.

"You still there?" Edmund asked. "Rally?"

"Yeah," Rally said finally. "I'm still here, Eddie. But do you know if the Army tapes these calls?"

"I don't think so. Why?"

"Well, I'm not sure how to tell you this, but, well, all your grandfather's stuff in the cellar—in the workroom—you know what stuff I'm talking about?"

"The stuff for the farm experiments?"

"Well, yeah, but . . . you see, that's what he told you all that stuff was for when you was growing up. So you wouldn't tell no one, and so your ma and grandma wouldn't worry and give us shit. But, you see, Eddie, that stuff down there we was making for other reasons."

"The moonshine, you mean?"

"Yeah, the moonshine was part of it. But there were two different batches of the moonshine, mainly. One, you drank for fun. Well, you remember. You seen us drink it."

"Uh-huh."

"Well, we called it moonshine, but it wasn't really moonshine the way most other people make it. It was something else, from a recipe that'd been in your family before they moved to North Carolina. The other batch of that stuff was kind of like that, at its base, you know, but mainly different in that it was stronger and had different effects when you drank it. And, well, let's just say you could use it for more important reasons other than just drinking it for fun. We'd been close to getting the formula right for a long time. But before we could market it, we had to have the right patents to protect ourselves."

"Rally—"

"Some of that stuff, the ingredients for the second batch, I mean, was illegal, Eddie. A lot of it we'd already used up—and we ain't nearly been doing it as much as we used to—but, when I found the old man, well, there was still some of the illegal stuff that I needed to get rid of. I woulda dragged the old man upstairs and put him in the den so the sheriff wouldn't have found it, but I'm too weak now, Eddie. And they found the stuff in his system. I mean, I got rid of what I could—Christ, Eddie, eighty fucking years old and I'm running around like a chicken with my head cut off. I can't breathe good no more and my back don't work and I'm—"

"Rally, calm—"

"—worried it's only a matter of time before they trace it back to me. I thought it best to leave everything else, all the equipment and books and stuff, so they could see he cooked it up and done it to himself—"

"Rally, calm down. I don't know what the hell you're talking about."

"Look, Eddie," the old man said, exhausted, "I really don't want to talk about this on the phone—especially you working for the government. When you coming home?"

"I'm scheduled to process out in a week."

"You can't get here no earlier?"

"I'll see what I can do."

"Eddie, I'm only telling you about all this so you won't be shocked when you get home. I thought the old man would've told you himself by now."

"I understand," Edmund said. "You just keep him on ice until I get back to you."

He hung up feeling irritated and confused, but at the same time curiously empty. He supposed he had loved his grandfather, but he never told him so. If he did love him, it was a love colored with fear. Where the fear came from, Edmund was never sure. Claude Lambert never laid a hand on him;

was never violent, never even raised his voice at him—not even when he got kicked off the baseball team.

Indeed, looking back, it suddenly occurred to Edmund that after his fight with the catcher Claude Lambert never touched him *at all*; never hugged him or tousled his hair like he used to when he was a boy. It was almost as if his grandfather was afraid of him, too. True, sometimes when his grandfather had spent too much time in the cellar, he would squish Edmund's cheeks together and stick his finger in his mouth and feel around his teeth. Edmund asked him why once, and all his grandfather would say was that he was checking to see if he was healthy. But for some reason Edmund didn't believe him.

And perhaps that was it, Edmund thought. Maybe the fear of his grandfather came from the knowledge that he would never really know the man who had become his guardian. Of course, there were plenty of things about Edmund that Claude Lambert didn't know, either. And often Edmund wondered if that was where the searching came from—a quest for the thing that would finally close the distance between them.

But now that his grandfather was gone that could never happen; now that Rally had told him the truth about what was going on in the cellar, Edmund didn't know quite how to feel about the whole thing.

Only that the searching was still there.

Chapter 51

"I've arranged for you to fly home, Lambert," said Edmund's commanding officer. "We can have you manifested on the next bird to Kuwait."

"No thank you, sir," said Edmund. "I'd like to finish up my time here. I've squared it so we can delay the funeral. It's only a week, and my men need me."

This was true. The 187th was scheduled for a raid on an insurgent stronghold that evening in the southern part of Tal Afar. The intel had come in that morning, and Edmund had organized the mission himself—needed to move fast before the enemy changed position again.

But his men were angry with him; thought the whole thing poorly timed. Edmund couldn't blame them. With less than a week of their tour remaining, no one from the 187th wanted to be the last to bite it. There was no question as far as Edmund Lambert was concerned. He knew what he had to do.

"Are you sure your head's on straight for this?" asked his commanding officer. "You've got a lot of men depending on you tonight, Lambert."

"Yes, sir," Edmund replied. "My grandfather and I weren't very close."

Later that night, Edmund and his unit set out in a convoy of unarmored Humvees that were to bring him and his men along a main road to the outskirts of the city, about a quarter mile from their target. The remainder of the distance would be covered on foot.

Everything had been going according to plan until the convoy passed through an intersection about a hundred yards from the drop-off point.

Edmund watched in horror as the Humvee at the head of the convoy was hit dead-on in a hissing streak of white. Then came the explosion, and Edmund knew the gunner was dead. Two men scrambled from the disabled vehicle. One of them was on fire.

Another explosion—screams of *"RPG!"* and *"Medic!"*—and all at once Edmund and his men were under attack from small-arms fire and rocket-propelled grenades.

Time seemed to rush forward in leaps—the *poppity-pop-pop* of returning fire; the metallic thunder of Edmund's gunner above his head shooting wildly. Then the pump of boots on the hard-pack street—screams of *"Down there, down there!"* and Edmund found himself crouched behind the corner of a building, the green of his night-vision goggles illuminating his surroundings.

More gunfire, and Edmund peered down the side street as a Humvee rolled past him, the gunner firing at the fleeing insurgents. It was a trap. Edmund and his men had seen this before. Edmund radioed for the Humvee to hold its position. It did, and kept firing down the street as an IED exploded up ahead.

Then they were running—Edmund and three of his men on the main road—rounding the corner of the next block; the back and forth of orders, the salute report, the request for rerouting and reinforcements on the radio.

They were in the southern neighborhoods—close to the city's small wooded park, beyond which were pockets of farmland and then the desert. Intercept them before they get to the park, Edmund thought; take up position and mow them down before they lose them in the trees and then on to who knows where.

Edmund waved his men ahead in three-to-five-second rushes, covering each other as they cleared and passed the narrow alleyways between the houses. Edmund was at the end of the line, was about to take up his next position when his NVGs picked up something strange approaching in the alleyway. Instinctively, he stepped forward and raised his weapon—but when his mind finally registered what he was seeing, Sergeant Edmund Lambert froze.

It was a large male lion.

Edmund had heard the stories at the start of the war; knew that in the days leading up to and immediately following the U.S.-led invasion, the sight of animals wandering the streets of Baghdad was quite common. Most had either escaped or were freed by looters from the Baghdad Zoo, which had been home to a large number of lions. Many of the big cats had been rounded up by American soldiers in armored vehicles; others were rescued from the Hussein family's personal menageries, as well as from the appalling conditions of many private zoos.

Yet the rumors among the locals had persisted; sightings of man-eaters believed to have once belonged to Saddam Hussein's son Uday, who was notorious for feeding his lions with the flesh of his enemies.

Rumors. Just rumors.

But here, north of Mosul, so far away—this couldn't be happening.

The lion was closer now.

It stopped about ten feet away and looked back over its shoulder down the alleyway. Edmund registered in the back of his mind that the lion looked well fed. And at the same time he realized he was not afraid, he felt a crack inside his head—the lion, the alley shifting crooked across his eyes, along with a high ringing in his ears. He was vaguely aware of the sound of gunfire and shouting behind him, but felt himself being pulled forward, as if a hand had been placed on the barrel of his rifle, gently pushing it down. He let it fall but didn't hear it hit the ground as the ringing in his ears grew louder.

The lion turned back, lowered its head, and stepped closer—looked meekly up at him with eyes both sad and full of greenish white fire. Edmund felt as if the air around him had turned to lime Jell-O, his movements heavy and not his own. A dream, a swirly dream of shadows, of bright green crumbling brick and a presence—no, *two* presences—whispering somewhere behind him.

"Be a good boy and carry that rope for me, okay?"

"C'est mieux d'oublier."

Then Edmund saw the word G-E-N-E-R-A-L—a flash of silvery letters, stitched in cursive across a dark blue background. It was as if the word was sneaking up on him from behind; as if he was catching only a glimpse of it before it faded back into the black.

"C'est mieux d'oublier."

Then another crack.

Now, there was only the lion again, staring up at him from the green. Edmund stroked its mane, his hand tracing slowly down to caress its face. Another flash of memory, and Edmund's fingers were inside the lion's mouth. He registered somewhere the feel of its teeth, but at the same time saw his fingers as his grandfather's, the lion's mouth his own.

The lion licked Edmund's hand—not his hand, but his

good luck charm; the ancient Babylonian seal between his thumb and forefinger.

"C'est mieux d'oublier," Edmund whispered, and suddenly felt a hot wetness in his groin—felt it running down his legs—and realized his face was cold and moist, his breathing labored as if he was sobbing.

Sobbing?

Edmund could not remember crying since his mother died, since that TV show with the happy little boy who looked just like him got canceled.

"Be a good boy and carry that rope for me, okay?"

"It's not my fault," Edmund said—and all at once the alley shifted again, this time with a whoosh, and the green of his NVGs grew brighter. The lime Jell-O dissolved, the air grew thinner, and now there was only the sound of someone calling his name.

Edmund looked down at his hands. The Babylonian seal was gone, and the lion was moving away—did not look back as its heavy paws carried it quickly around the curve of the alleyway and out of sight.

"Come back," Edmund heard himself whisper. "Come back."

He felt someone touch his shoulder—heard his name, closer now—but the world had already begun to iris into black.

Edmund awoke in the infirmary, groggy, but clean and dry and stripped down to his underwear. The lights, the colors—especially the whites—seemed brighter, and Edmund could hear the tapping of fingers on a keyboard.

"He's awake, Doctor," said a female voice to his left.

Edmund turned toward it, but a bright light met his eyes—a man's voice now, soothing, and a gentle hand on his eyelids propping them open. Then the light was gone, and in its place, big orange dots and lots of questions. Lots of answers, too—most of them "I don't know" in a scratchy voice that sounded nothing like his own. Words from the doctor like dehydration, heat exhaustion, fainting, and semi-comatose—questions about what he ate, "I'm going to give you so many ccs of this and so many ccs of that," and more words that Edmund didn't understand.

And then he remembered—asked suddenly, "Where's the lion?"

"The lion?"

"Yes," said Edmund. "The lion who killed my mother."

"You're hallucinating, soldier," the doctor said.

Silence. A dull prick on his forearm.

"Carry that rope for me, Doc," Edmund whispered, fading. "It's better to forget."

"That's right," the doctor said. "It's better to forget."

Chapter 52

Two soldiers were killed in the ambush, two were wounded, but Edmund's team got eight insurgents thanks in part to Edmund's intimate knowledge of the area and his quick rerouting of his troops toward the park. And even though Edmund didn't participate in the gun battle, even though no one ever knew what happened to him in the alleyway, his men didn't blame him for the loss of their comrades.

But Edmund couldn't have cared less if they had. All that, his former life, was over. All that—the Army, Iraq, war, insurgents, death—all nonsense, all meaningless to him now in comparison to his anointing.

Sergeant Edmund Lambert was given a clean bill of health but declined to speak with an Army counselor. He made two more patrols and killed one Iraqi before flying back to Fort Campbell. He never mentioned the lion or the General ever again, and never once mourned the loss of his good luck charm. The lion wanted it. The lion wanted everything. But most of all, the lion wanted him, too.

It was all so clear to him now. Indeed, the answer had

been there ever since he was a child, but Edmund had simply
been too stupid to see it.

The General.

G-E-N-E-R-A-L

Yes, Edmund thought, if he broke apart the word General
(or, wrote it on a piece of paper like his grandfather had
taught him, *dash-dash-dash* and whatnot) and rearranged
the letters, one would get Nergal with a leftover E, as in:

G-E-N-E-R-A-L = E + N-E-R-G-A-L

Or, if one preferred, on could write the equation this way:

E + N-E-R-G-A-L = G-E-N-E-R-A-L

Either way it was the same. The leftover *e*, of course,
stood for Edmund. There could be no doubting that now. The
evidence was clear, irrefutable, beyond coincidental. Edmund knew this with every fiber of his being; knew it in a
way that made him feel as if he had never known anything
before.

The god Nergal had visited him in his dreams all those
years ago—had bestowed upon him the code, the equation,
the *formula*—and had since waited patiently for Edmund to
understand. And how many times had he heard those words
from Rally and his grandfather? Equation and formula? Nergal had been speaking to him all that time through the old
men, too!

And now, finally, Edmund understood what the god was
saying: Edmund and Nergal on one side of the equal sign,
the General on the other. Yes, only with Nergal could Edmund become the General.

The totality of the equation said so: E + N-E-R-G-A-L =
G-E-N-E-R-A-L

But N-E-R-G-A-L needed E(dmund) to become the G-E-N-
E-R-A-L, too. But Nergal was already a general—the
supreme general; the most fearful of them all, in fact. So
what was Nergal getting at? Perhaps the formula meant Nergal needed Edmund to become a real, living breathing gen-

eral again. Yes, perhaps Nergal needed Edmund to help him return to the land of the living. But how?

The images on the seal! It was all there! How else could one balance the equation? Nergal wished to return, to become flesh again, and he had chosen Edmund as his vehicle—had actually given him instructions on how to do it! That was why he sent the lion to take back the seal. The lion was Nergal's emissary, and by returning the seal—that very thing that in ancient times was used in secret correspondence—Edmund had accepted the god's offer. Worship and sacrifice were the keys to bringing him back!

He had not been hallucinating. The lion was real, and everything happened there in the alleyway just as Edmund remembered it. Edmund was sure of that. The proof was there in the formula.

E + N-E-R-G-A-L = G-E-N-E-R-A-L

And what was it that Rally had said on the telephone? Something again about getting the "formula" right? Well, that had to be another message from Nergal, too; and now that Edmund had finally gotten *his* formula right, he would never be so stupid as to ignore or misinterpret his messages ever again.

The messages were everywhere and in everything. Edmund understood this now. He just had to look more closely to be able to read them.

And Edmund knew he needed to look more closely at Rally, too. There was a message there, an answer that needed to be extracted from all his doublespeak about formulas and whatnot; an answer that had been there all along, but again Edmund had simply been too stupid to see it.

Edmund understood this in his gut, although he could not articulate it in his mind; could not reach out and touch that flash of silver stitching against that dark blue background no matter how hard he tried.

G-E-N-E-R-A-L

To see the word written that way—*A memory? A dream? Something real or imagined? Something he was projecting now that he knew the formula?*

But along with the silver stitching of *G-E-N-E-R-A-L* came other flashes—distant shadows and voices that brought with them a thick gooiness that reminded Edmund of the medicine. He could not see to whom the voices belonged, but understood there were only two of them—understood this in the same way he had understood the General's name all those years ago as a child. But the voices were speaking in French; whispers and mumblings and back-and-forth echoes that Edmund didn't understand.

Edmund knew his ancestors had moved from New Orleans to North Carolina after the Civil War. Was it his family he was hearing? Was it Nergal speaking through his ancestors of his destiny?

C'est mieux d'oublier. . . .

Rally. He needed to talk to Rally. Perhaps Nergal would speak again through him as he had on the phone with the word "formula." *All in good time,* Edmund thought. Nergal would reveal everything eventually, but it would be up to Edmund to make sure he read the messages correctly.

Chapter 53

After his honorable discharge was finalized, Edmund made it back to Wilson in time for his grandfather's funeral—a small ceremony, complete with a rent-a-preacher at the family plot in Clayton. Edmund, Rally, Rally's nephew, and about a half-a-dozen others were the only ones in attendance—no extended family to offer their condolences, no close friends to tell Edmund what a wonderful man his grandfather had been.

But Edmund was thankful for that. He would be able to cut things clean from his former life now that Claude Lambert was dead; would be able to begin preparing for the Raging Prince's return in private, in secret, without having to worry about family members and friends sticking their noses where they didn't belong.

However, there were still two loose ends that needed tying up before Edmund could begin: Rally, and that pesky little problem about what the police had found in the cellar. The latter resolved itself gradually, but neatly, and began with a brief meeting in the sheriff's office to answer some questions about how much Edmund knew. Edmund played dumb, just shook his head and kept saying, "I had no idea," and "I haven't lived there since I was eighteen."

No crime had been committed, the sheriff explained, other than illegal possession of a couple of controlled substances: opium and something called concentrated thujone.

"We had to bring all that over to the state lab in Raleigh," the sheriff said. He was a tall, portly man with a moustache that Edmund thought made him look like a fat Adolf Hitler. "Looks like your grandfather was cooking up some kind of homemade absinthe. You ever heard of that stuff?"

"No, I haven't," Edmund replied.

"I didn't either until this whole mess got dumped in my lap. Shit is illegal here in the States, but you can still get it in Europe, they tell me. Something you drink by dissolving sugar cubes in it until it looks all cloudy and shit. Christ, Eddie, I'm no expert on any of this—just going by what the lab is telling me. Shit is highly alcoholic—like over a hundred and twenty proof, they're saying—and made primarily from this stuff called wormwood. Was popular among the French artsy-fartsies in the late 1800s and early 1900s, and was thought to have some kind of hallucinogenic effects. But a lot of that's been proven now to be bullshit. Anyway, I guess there's a movement going on to legalize absinthe here in this country. Tastes like licorice, they say."

"That would make sense," Edmund said. "I remember the smell of licorice in the house when I was a kid. But my grandfather just called it moonshine. I guess the recipe had been in his family for years. The Lamberts originally hailed from New Orleans, and I remember him saying that his great-grandfather or somebody used to own some kind of saloon there."

"The lab tells me your grandfather's stuff was different, though. Had opium and that concentrated thujone and some other ingredients that could make it really dangerous if consumed too often."

Never too much, never too often—be a good boy and carry that rope for me—

"You're sure you don't know where he got all that shit?" the sheriff asked.

"I'm sure," Edmund said. "But I remember him saying a couple of times that he wanted to patent his moonshine and market it someday. This movement you're telling me about here to legalize—what's it called again?"

"Absinthe."

"Absinthe," Edmund repeated. "Well, maybe the old man had the same thing in mind. Maybe he was ahead of his time."

"It all looks pretty innocent to me," the sheriff said, chuckling. "He was making it in such small quantities. Clearly no intent to distribute. Christ, if I went around chasing every redneck cooking up moonshine for private consumption, I'd be one hell of a lot skinnier, that's for sure." Edmund pretended to laugh. "And shit, last thing I need right now are the fucking Staties and the DEA breathing down my neck. Can't prosecute a dead man last I checked. I only knew your grandfather superficially through Rally's nephew. Other than this bullshit, he seemed to be an upstanding citizen as far as I can tell. Don't know about you, but I'd be happy if all this just went away."

"Me, too," Edmund said, smiling.

Edmund signed some papers that allowed the sheriff to retain Claude Lambert's books indefinitely. He couldn't tie them directly to the illicit absinthe production, he explained, as the books were mainly about botany and general chemistry. But still, he thought it best that Edmund sign a release in case everything came back to bite him in the ass. He made no mention of Claude Lambert's notebooks.

Rally must have taken them, Edmund thought. He assured the sheriff that he would do everything in his power to cooperate with the investigation—even allowed the fat Adolf

Hitler lookalike and a couple of his Gestapo to take one more look in the cellar that evening. And then, much to Edmund's surprise, in the weeks that followed the whole thing just "went away."

But then there was the problem of Rally—a problem that resolved itself much more quickly and, for Edmund Lambert, much more satisfactorily.

"I want to talk to you in person," Edmund said on the telephone the day after the funeral.

"About your meeting with the sheriff?" Rally replied. "You didn't tell him I was involved, did you Eddie?"

Even though Rally was over eighty, upon his return from Iraq Edmund was surprised to see how frail and skinny he'd become since last he saw him—three years earlier, on a random visit to his boyhood home. And he looked skittish, too; his once bright, smiling eyes all wide and pink and seemingly incapable of holding Edmund's gaze for long.

"I didn't tell him anything," Edmund said. "Don't worry about that. But I want to talk to you about the General."

"The who?"

Edmund was silent for a moment, then whispered, *"C'est mieux d'oublier."*

More silence, this time from Rally.

"When you coming by?" the old man asked finally.

"Now."

"Makes sense," Rally said, distantly. "I reckon it was only a matter of time."

Edmund noticed the tension in his voice was gone—he sounded more like the Rally he used to know—but before Edmund could respond, Rally hung up.

Edmund arrived at Rally's twenty minutes later.

The old man lived alone in a double-wide on what he often bragged added up to ten acres of "primo farmland."

Most of the land, however, was uncultivated, and the trailer itself was set back about a hundred yards off the road against a thick swath of trees. For as long as Edmund could remember, Rally had said that someday he was going to build his dream house there. And it wasn't like he couldn't afford it, Claude Lambert used to say. But for some reason, the old man never seemed in much of a hurry to get out of his trailer. Edmund suspected this was because Rally thought he didn't need a house when he already had the Lamberts' to hang around in.

Edmund parked his pickup beside Rally's, his headlights scattering the more than two dozen cats that the old man allowed to roam free amid the junk that littered his property—old auto parts mostly, including the shell of a beat-up Chevy Nova propped up on cinder blocks. Some of the cats, Edmund knew, were former residents of his grandfather's tobacco farm; others, most likely their offspring. Rally had often adopted them over the years, more so after Edmund joined the Army and Claude Lambert's health began to decline.

There were no more cats now on the tobacco farm.

Edmund smiled at the memories of what he used to do to the cats way-back-when before his anointing. How stupid he'd been back then; how blind to the messages that were right there in front of him. And now, the fact that Rally's cats were gathered out front to greet him when he arrived, well, surely this must be a message from Nergal, too.

Edmund exited his truck and climbed the three rickety steps that led up to Rally's screen door. The inside door was open a crack, and Edmund could see a light on in the living area. He knocked. No answer.

A pair of cats began meowing and rubbing against his legs.

Edmund knocked again. "Rally?" he called. "Hey, Rally, it's Edmund."

No answer.

Edmund kicked the cats away, opened the door, and stepped inside.

He took in everything in less than a second. Nothing much had changed in the years since he last visited Rally's trailer with his grandfather—the mess, the odor of mildew and burnt frozen dinners and motor oil, the junky sixties-style furniture, the racing pictures on the walls and the model automobiles on the mantel above the propane fireplace.

No, the only thing that was different was Rally himself.

The old man sat slumped in his La-Z-Boy—the shotgun still propped between his legs, his brains blown out all over the wall behind him.

Time suddenly slowed down for Edmund Lambert—his heart pounding, a faint ringing in his ears as the room grew brighter, the colors and outlines of the objects around him more vivid. He felt numb—just stood in the doorway, staring at the grisly tableau for what seemed to him both an eternity and only a matter of seconds.

Then Edmund heard what sounded like a clicking, and felt his legs carrying him forward as if controlled by someone else. He stopped at Rally's feet.

The blood was still trickling from the old man's nose, but Edmund knew that trickle would have looked quite different a few minutes ago. He had witnessed a similar suicide in Iraq; an insurgent who, rather than be taken alive, stuck the muzzle of a .45 in his mouth and blew out the back of his skull. The blood from his nostrils had gushed like a pair of fire hoses, his body deflating like a balloon. It had been the same for Rally, Edmund could tell: the lower part of the old man's face and neck, his chest and the right side of his coveralls all soaked with blood.

But where was that clicking coming from?

Edmund peered around the side of the chair and discovered two large cats lapping up the blood that had run down between the cushions and out from underneath the recliner. The cats didn't even bother acknowledging him, and Edmund stood there watching them for some time.

Edmund turned back to Rally and caught something out of the corner of his eye—on the end table, under the lamp, on the opposite side of the recliner.

It was his grandfather's old medicine bottle. He recognized it immediately—M-E-D-I-C-I-N-E the label read, yellowed and peeling up at the corners. The cap was still on, but Edmund could tell by the way the lamplight filtered through the glass that the bottle was empty. It stood atop a stack of old-fashioned, composition-style notebooks. Edmund recognized those as his grandfather's, too.

Edmund picked up the bottle, unscrewed the cap, and sniffed.

Licorice and Pine-Sol. *Absinthe?*

But the other batch of that stuff, Rally said in his mind, *well, let's just say you could use it for more important reasons other than just drinking it for fun. We'd been close to getting the formula right for a long time.*

The formula. E + N-E-R-G-A-L = G-E-N-E-R-A-L

And then Edmund saw it.

The name patch on Rally's coveralls—on his left pocket, the silver stitching against the dark blue background.

The silver stitching that spelled out *Gene Ralston.*

G-E-N-E-R-A-L-S-T-O-N

The first seven letters. G-E-N-E-R-A-L

But how could that be? Rally was not the General!

C'est mieux d'oublier.

His mind suddenly racing, Edmund backed away from the bloody corpse, bumped into a chair, and stood staring at the patch in a daze, his breath coming in little puffs.

Gene Ralston = G-E-N-E-R-A-L? he asked himself over and over. *No, that couldn't be it! Rally was not included in the formula! Rally was not part of the equation!*

Edmund dropped the notebooks and the bottle on the floor and fell back into a chair—closed his eyes and tried to focus on the image of the silver stitching in his mind.

Gene Ralston.

He could see it hovering there in the darkness, against the blue background, but still he only saw the word *General*—from an angle, out of the corner of his eye, as if it were sneaking up on him from behind. There were the French voices mixed in there, too. And there was something else—no, *someone* else. Someone terrifying.

Nergal, Edmund thought. *Nergal was there, too!*

E + N-E-R-G-A-L = G-E-N-E-R-A-L!

It was Nergal. There could be no doubt about that. Nergal was terrifying. So was Edmund now. And with him Edmund was the General. Together they would—but—

Edmund pressed the heels of his hands to his eyes, scrunched his forehead, and tried to remember. He thought he could feel the old gooiness creeping back in, but the image of the silver stitching would not expand, would not stretch out into Gene Ralston or anything else that he could recognize. And then all trace of the gooiness disappeared.

C'est mieux d'oublier.

Edmund opened his eyes and scooped up one of the notebooks from the floor—snatched a pen from amid the mess on the kitchen table and opened the notebook to the first page. His grandfather's writing, symbols and words that Edmund didn't understand. Everything appeared to be written in French, but Edmund couldn't be sure—felt like he couldn't be sure of *anything* anymore.

There had to be a message in here somewhere. Nergal was speaking to him. Edmund could feel it, could see it in his mind—

$E + N\text{-}E\text{-}R\text{-}G\text{-}A\text{-}L = G\text{-}E\text{-}N\text{-}E\text{-}R\text{-}A\text{-}L!$

That was the formula!

Edmund scribbled the letters G-E-N-E-R-A-L-S-T-O-N on the inside cover of the notebook—quickly took out the word NERGAL, and was left with E-S-T-O-N.

The answer came to him immediately.

"Of course!" Edmund said—his mind, his body relaxing at once into the bliss of total understanding. "Move the letter E the end, and you get the word stone."

Edmund wrote it down next to Nergal.

NERGAL STONE, or STONE NERGAL, depending on how you wanted to look at it.

"The Nergal Stone," Edmund said, smiling. "The stone seal depicting the sacrifice to the god Nergal. Gene Ralston equals the Nergal Stone! Just like the god who visited me all those years ago, the formula, the message pointing me toward the seal had been there all along! Right on Rally's coveralls!"

One of the cats poked its head out from around the recliner—licked its chops and gazed up at Edmund quizzically.

"I understand," Edmund said with tears of joy.

He drove back to the farmhouse and hid the medicine bottle and the notebooks under the floorboards in his mother's old bedroom. That was the proper place for secrets, he thought.

Then he drove back to Rally's and called the police. That was the sensible thing to do, he figured; it was best to just tell the truth about how he found Rally dead in his La-Z-Boy. Surely, if they investigated further, they would have a record of his phone call an hour earlier. Surely, if they investigated further, they would be able to establish Rally's time of death shortly afterwards.

Edmund told the sheriff that the old man had sounded depressed when he talked to him on the phone—was babbling nonsense, he said, and what a shame he hadn't gotten there sooner. He gave this as his official statement and then left—not before, of course, offering once again to be of whatever assistance he could. No, Edmund thought, it didn't take a fat Adolf Hitler lookalike to tell the scene was a suicide; but telling the truth (well, *almost* the truth) was smart just to be on the safe side.

But why was Edmund even worried about all that? After all, he had nothing to do with Rally's death.

Or did he?

What was it Rally had said on the phone? *"I reckon it was only a matter of time."* Yes, Edmund thought, Rally had understood *c'est mieux d'oublier*; had obviously heard those words before and seemed almost resigned when he spoke again afterwards.

And hadn't Rally seemed afraid of Edmund since his return from Iraq? Afraid of something that went beyond the old man's connection to the illegal absinthe production?

Edmund thought about this on the ride home—scoured his memory banks, searching for an answer—but saw only the General there; the silver stitching of the formula, and the signs and messages that had been there from the God of War since the day he was born.

And when he arrived back at the farmhouse, Edmund concluded that perhaps Rally had sensed the change in him; sensed that the time had come, and that Nergal had returned to claim what was rightfully his.

Indeed, Edmund thought, perhaps because Rally had worn the Nergal message in his name—the Nergal Stone in the Gene Ralston that had been like a tattoo on his chest for all those years—perhaps Eugene "Rally" Ralston recognized deep down the terror that had returned with him from Iraq.

"I have returned," Edmund said to himself as he pulled up to the farmhouse. He sensed Nergal speaking in him, too, and looked down at his chest, to the left pocket of his shirt and half expected to see a patch there. There wasn't one, of course, but Edmund saw the potential for his own Nergal Stone underneath. Something more lasting. Something that could not be destroyed or torn away like Rally's silver stitched name patch; something as durable as the carved Nergal Stone itself.

A tattoo. Yes. But of what?

The answer would come to him eventually, he thought. And once he was certain the business with Rally and the illegal absinthe was finally over, he would need to start readying the farmhouse. He knew what needed to be done, but he wasn't exactly sure how. That would all be revealed eventually, too, he thought.

In Nergal's messages.

But would Edmund Lambert be smart enough to decode all the messages? Would he be worthy enough to stand shoulder to shoulder with Nergal in the end?

Edmund took a deep breath and told himself not worry about all that; for when he looked down past his chest to his stomach; when he thought about the searching and looked for it deep inside his belly, a breeze whispered back at him through a window in his mind.

"Finally, Edmund. Finally."

Yes, after all these years, the searching was over.

After all these years, the answer finally had come.

PART IV

EXITING

Chapter 54

Names, names, and more names—thousands of them scattered before him—but Andy Schaap held out hope.

The cemetery.

Yes, he thought as he bounced his ring on his desk. *The cemetery was the beginning for the Impaler. The first star in his personal logo. The star off of which the rest of his constellation would be built.*

But why the cemetery? Because the Impaler had a connection there that went beyond the name of Lyons. Schaap was sure of it. Someone important to him was buried there; someone who was connected to the identity on earth that needed to be remapped in the eyes of the lion in the sky. Planting Rodriguez and Guerrera outside the wall directly east of the Lyons plot was only part of the equation, as was the cemetery's connection to the other murder sites that made up the Starlight Theater logo.

All theory, of course, and nothing really on which to base his assumptions other than a gut reading of the evidence so far. But Andy Schaap was sure he was on to something; and this little side investigation was going to be his baby. He'd gotten hold of the cemetery records soon after Markham left. That was good. That meant he could follow his leads alone; might even get a little credit for all the hard work he'd done.

Sure, he knew he was becoming a little jealous of Sam Markham. But didn't Markham also keep things to himself when he was on a case? Isn't that how he caught Jackson Briggs? Hell, he still never told anyone how he really did it.

Besides, there was nothing Markham could offer from Connecticut anyway. At least not until the medical records were obtained and the lists of servicemen and their units checked against them.

There were over two-thousand residents buried beneath the soil in Clayton's Willow Brook Cemetery, and Schaap's first order of business was to begin testing those records against a list of men who fit Underhill's unit profile. And once those lists were complete, once he got all the names of servicemen living in the Raleigh area, his computer program would rank them in order of probability.

It was complicated stuff, Schaap thought; and without each list to test against the other, just using the cemetery records alone would be like shooting blind from the white pages. No, the cemetery records would only narrow down the unit lists. But even then, it would be slow going. Schaap had seen those names already—Davis, White, Brown, Anderson, Jones—*common* names that seemed to taunt him with the futility of his plan.

But fuck it. He would spend the whole night there if he had to, checking his lists against each other and developing a preliminary cross-section of candidates. Then, once he ran that list through a computer program that would rank them according to *location*—that is, remote areas in and around Raleigh that theoretically would provide the Impaler with good "working conditions"—Schaap would have a better idea where to begin. But he didn't have much time before

Markham returned Sunday afternoon; not much time to keep his little side investigation secret.

But Schaap *would* keep it secret. As long as humanly possible, he decided.

After all, isn't that what Sam Markham would do?

Chapter 55

Edmund and Cindy arrived at the cast party at exactly 11:30 p.m. They could've gotten there sooner, but Cindy insisted on showering at the theater after the show. She even came right out and admitted to Edmund that she wanted to look nice for him. He was dressed in a button-down shirt and jeans that made his butt look beyond sexy, Cindy thought. All she said, however, was, "You look very handsome." Edmund smiled and said he would wait for her in the green room. He ended up waiting almost half an hour. But Edmund said he didn't mind. He was used to waiting.

The party was at Amy Pratt's—a rundown, student-district rancher that had been passed down among the theatre majors for as long as anyone could remember. It was designated "the party house" every year because of its large, fenced yard and L-shaped deck out back.

The party house was already packed when Cindy and Edmund snaked their way into the kitchen amid a sea of second glances and whispers. Cindy had expected that; had even warned Edmund to be ready for a scandal on Monday.

Edmund said that they'd have to come up with something really juicy to get the rumors going.

Cindy had laughed at that, and so did Edmund. Cindy had never seen Edmund smile and laugh so much, and it made her feel beyond ecstatic to know that he was already opening up to her; made the ass-chewing she got from her director about her being unfocused during the show all the more worth it.

Kiernan was right: her mind had been on Edmund Lambert all day.

"Holy shit," said Amy Pratt when she saw Cindy and her date. "Edmund Lambert? Edmund *Laaam-bert*? What the fuck are you doing here?"

"Hello, Amy," he said. "I hope I was invited."

"Of course!" she said as she reached down into her bag of plastic cups. "I'm gonna give you and your date here a cup for free cuz I'm already wasted and you look fucking hot and you never come see me, how's that?"

"Thank you," Edmund said.

"*Buuuut*," Amy said, snatching the cups back at the last second, "you're gonna have to promise to ditch this ho and dance with me after Brown Bags, okay?"

Edmund smiled and nodded and Amy gave him the cups.

"How much longer until they start?" asked Cindy.

"Bradley-boy and the other seniors are still in my bedroom writing them out," Amy said, rolling her eyes. "I peeked in and he told me to get out of there—my own fucking bedroom, can you believe it? Someone—and I'm not saying who—but someone told me that Bradley and some of the other guys started doing shots in the dressing room after the show. Bet ol' Georgie Porgie would love to hear that one. Bradley telling me to get out of my own fucking bedroom!"

Cindy shrugged and led Edmund outside onto the deck. Edmund quickly negotiated the mob around the keg, filled up their cups, and retreated alone with Cindy to a corner of the yard—drinking and laughing and making conversation just as Cindy had hoped they would.

Cindy discovered that Edmund was a Cancer. She was a Gemini, she told him.

"I don't really believe in astrology," she added, "but, if I remember correctly, I think Cancer and Gemini are like the two most incompatible signs possible. What do you think of that?"

"I wouldn't worry about it," Edmund said. "I should have been born a Leo, but I came out two weeks early because my mother wasn't taking care of herself. At least, that's what my grandfather used to tell me."

Cindy didn't know if Gemini and Leo were compatible signs, but Edmund assured her they were, and Cindy asked him to fill her cup again. Edmund obliged.

She could not remember if she was on her third or fourth beer (*it felt like her fourth*) by the time Bradley Cox and the rest of the seniors stumbled out onto the deck. She and Edmund had been deep in conversation about his mother, about how she committed suicide when he was a child. Cindy was on the verge of tears, but Edmund told her not to feel sorry for him and that everything happened for a reason. She wanted to hug him—wanted to kiss him, too—but even though she had good buzz going she held back until Edmund said: "Please, don't take it as a downer, Cindy. It's just something that happened. Besides, tonight is about new beginnings, isn't it?"

Oh yes, Cindy thought. *Now I'm going to kiss him.* She could see in Edmund's eyes that he wanted to kiss her, too. But then—

"Okay, motherfuckers," shouted Bradley Cox. "Gather round, gather round. It's that time."

Cindy sighed and gulped down the last of her beer as the rest of the students began crowding onto the deck. Cox and his cohorts—six seniors total, all men—stood on chairs at the far end opposite the keg. Cindy declined when Edmund motioned to get her another beer.

"I'm buzzing too much already," she said. "Just hold my hand if it gets too bad, will you?" Edmund smiled and took her hand anyway, and Cindy felt a surge of excitement and pride—especially when she saw some of the other students notice.

"We got a shitload of bags to di-perse," Cox slurred, "to dis*burse*, I mean, so everybody shut the fuck up and don't make a big deal. Cuz they's gonna be *mean,* motherfuckers!"

The crowd cheered.

"Seriously, seriously," Cox chuckled, "this is all in fun, so nobody start crying and shit—seriously, mine's like the worst, I'm sure."

"Get on with it!" someone shouted, to which Cox replied: "That's what your mom said before I blew my load in her face!"

Everybody laughed except Cindy and Edmund.

"Okay, okay, seriously," Cox said, and began reading from the top of his stack of lunch bags. "This first Brown Bag goes out to the guy playing Mentieth. It's called the 'Perils of Inbreeding Award.' Jonathan Reynolds: To the porky freshman with one of the most fucked-up grills we've ever seen, your teeth look like a leftover makeup effect from *Deliverance.* In fact, every time you speak on stage, we keep expecting you to add, 'He's *suuure* got a purty mouth!' Who knew that backwoods rednecks lived in eleventh-century Scotland? Your mom and dad, apparently. Hard to keep a se-cret like that in the house when you're brother and sister!"

Some laughter, some groans, and the pudgy freshman who played Mentieth pushed through the applauding crowd to accept his award.

"Witty, aren't they?" Cindy whispered, her tongue thick with beer. "Mine will come at the end. Watch. They usually go from smallest parts to biggest. With Bradley at the helm, it's going to be pure poetry all night, I'm sure."

Edmund smiled and squeezed her hand.

And Cindy was right. The awards went on for about half an hour, the seniors taking turns reading them. Juvenile insults, profanity, and bathroom humor mostly—nothing even remotely clever—and Cindy could tell that some of the underclassmen got their feelings hurt. The worst was the young man playing Macduff, who got the dreaded "Freshman Fuckup Award," and whose Brown Bag stated in no uncertain terms that his was the worst performance ever to grace the Harriot stage.

Cindy felt sorry for him, but her sympathy was short-lived when she heard her award was to be next. It was pretty much what she expected. The "Monica Lewinsky Award" they called it this time: an eloquent, heartfelt missive about how Cindy got her role because she sucked George Kiernan's dick, and that her *"Out, out, damn spot!"* had something to do with a cum stain on her Harriot sweatshirt.

Cindy didn't even look at her Brown Bag after she walked up to accept it; was just happy to get it over with and folded it into her purse when she joined Edmund at the other end of the deck. He looked upset.

"They shouldn't say stuff like that about you," he said. "It's disrespectful."

"Who cares?" Cindy said, aware of the stares from the crowd. "They're just a bunch of idiots. It's not nearly as bad as it could've been, trust me. Really, it doesn't bother me at all. Don't let it ruin our night, okay?"

Cindy smiled and tugged on his shirt. Edmund, stone-faced, narrowed his eyes at her—seemed to look right through her, Cindy thought—then gazed past her toward Cox and his friends.

"And now the moment you've all been waiting for," said

the guy who played Banquo. "The 'My Wife Won't Sleep With Me Award.' Bradley Cox: We know how many times you begged Cindy Smith to go out with you this year. And we know how many times she rejected you, so it's no shocker that you should be playing her bitch on stage—'Will you fuck me if I kill Duncan, honey? Will you fuck me if I kill Banquo, sweetie?' "

Laughter from the crowd.

"Art imitates life," Banquo continued. "So what's next for you, Bradley? Wait a minute, wait a minute." He pretended to answer his cell phone. "Uh-huh. Uh-huh. Okay I'll tell him. That was your agent, Bradley. They've got an audition for you: an understudy role playing sloppy seconds to Edmund Lambert in *Psycho Meets the Egocentric Bitch*!"

A chorus of *"oohs"* as the heads whipped around to see Cindy and Edmund's reactions. Cox stepped across from his chair onto Banquo's—pushed him off as he snatched up his Brown Bag and waved it over his head.

"Thass-right," he shouted, smiling, slurring. "I ain't got in yet, but word from her ex at Sigma Chi is that it ain't worth shit anyway!"

Gasps, uncomfortable laughter, and all heads turned to Edmund and Cindy.

Then Edmund stepped forward.

"Come here, Bradley," he said calmly.

The crowd grew silent.

"Edmund, don't," Cindy whispered, her hand on his arm. Edmund ignored her, just stood staring at Cox, motioning with his finger for him to come.

"Dude, relax," said the guy playing Banquo. "It's all in fun."

"All of you then," said Edmund. "All of you who wrote that stuff about Cindy can come over here and apologize to her."

A murmuring in the crowd—some saying *"Relax, dude,"* and *"Calm down"* while others barked out, *"Fuck him up, Lambert!"*

"What's your problem, man?" asked Banquo. "It's just a joke."

"Now's your chance," said Edmund. "If I have to come to you, then your chance to apologize is gone."

"Dude—"

"No!" said Cox, stumbling off his chair. "Fuck him— fuck *you*, Lambert—you and your bitch there. Can't take a joke, then you can go fuck yourself after you fuck her."

Another gasp, and the students began backing away off the deck.

"Everybody just calm down," said Banquo, but Edmund was already heading across the deck—calmly, methodically, the students parting before him like the Red Sea.

"That's right, come on, you little bitch," said Cox, stumbling drunkenly. "Six of us against one of you—gonna fuck you up good 'n tight, soldier boy."

Although Cindy remained on the opposite end of the deck, she had no trouble seeing what happened next.

Banquo and another senior bailed immediately—jumped over the railing and ran before Edmund could reach them— and thus only three of Cox's constituents backed him up in the end.

Edmund floored them with a flurry of punches and kicks as Cox stumbled past him with a wild haymaker. Cox had been the first to swing—Cindy saw that clearly—but it took him too long to recover from his missed punch; and by the time he turned back, Edmund met him square in the face with a head butt.

Cox howled in pain—the blood gushing from his nose and onto his T-shirt like water from a faucet. Cindy felt as if her stomach was filled with cement; and time seemed to slow down. Cheering and screams, someone shouting, *"Call*

911!" while someone else (*Amy Pratt*, Cindy thought) shouted, *"Let them fight!"*—the sounds, the people, the light from the tiki torches swirling all around her in a haze.

And then suddenly there was Bradley Cox—his bloody, sobbing face presented before her in a sleeper hold.

"Apologize to her, Bradley," Edmund whispered in his ear.

"Fuck you," Cox spat—whimpering, struggling. "I can't fucking br—"

"Apologize," Edmund said again, squeezing harder.

Cox squealed in pain.

"Okay, okay," he said. "I'm sorry, okay? Now let me go you fuck—"

Edmund's grip tightened, and Cindy heard him whisper something in Cox's ear that she could not make out—something that sounded like French—and then Cox dropped to the deck, semiconscious, babbling incoherently in spurts of spitting blood.

"He's dead!" someone shouted, while another cried out, *"Good night, Irene!"*

But when Cox quickly came to—when he looked around, dazed, and asked for a beer—the crowd of students applauded.

"Serves you assholes right!" one girl yelled; *"Woohoo!"* and *"Way to go, Lambert!"* cheered some of the guys.

"Come on, Cindy," Edmund said, taking her hand. "Let's get out of here."

Cindy followed him through the crowd—the smiling faces, the cheering and pats on their backs whizzing past her like a dream. She saw two of the boys Edmund had floored, both of them still on the deck holding their stomachs and moaning. But when a pretty girl Cindy didn't know reached out and touched Edmund's arm like he was a rock star, incredibly, Cindy felt a wave of jealousy.

Edmund led Cindy out through the gate and across the

front lawn. Cindy thought she heard Amy Pratt call out from the house, *"Don't leave, Edmund!"* but could not be sure. She could not be sure of anything anymore. And only when she found herself in the passenger seat of Edmund Lambert's pickup, only when she realized that they'd come to a stop in the Harriot Theater parking lot, did the reality of what had just happened finally begin to sink in.

"I guess we gave them something to talk about," Edmund said after a long silence—sincerely, without the slightest hint of irony. "I'm sorry if I ruined our date, but those guys shouldn't talk that way about—"

Before she could second-guess herself, Cindy leaned in and kissed him.

The pickup's cabin seemed to swirl around her as she melted into his arms—a voice in the back of her head whispering, *Finally, Cindy. Finally.*

Chapter 56

Markham sat in the cramped witness gallery staring not into the execution chamber, but at the back of his hand. A security guard had stamped it with ink that glowed under black light. "No glow, no go," was all he'd said. Markham wasn't even sure what the stamp read, could see no trace of it in the harshness of the fluorescent lights, and felt his throat tighten when he thought of the bizarre coincidence, of his connection with Randall Donovan.

I have returned, I have returned, I have returned.

They had taken his wallet, his keys, and his BlackBerry and gave him a yellow WITNESS badge to wear around his neck. They also ran a handheld metal detector up and down his body. "You can only take in your watch," the security guard had said. "To mark the time, if you'd like."

"To help with the sense of closure," Markham knew his in-laws would say.

He had hardly spoken to them since his arrival in Connecticut late that afternoon. They had all gathered first at his childhood home in Waterford—Michelle's parents, her brother, a cousin with whom she'd been close growing up—but even before they arrived Markham felt as if he didn't belong there. His parents still kept his old bedroom as it had been when he was in high school, but the idea of grabbing a nap before Michelle's family arrived had seemed inappropriate to him, as if he didn't belong in there, either.

And so Markham had passed the time quietly with his mother and father in the den until the people started filtering in. They would all wait there, ludicrously snacking on "heavy hors d'oeuvres" as his mother called them and making small talk until the appointed time. Markham tried not to think about the Impaler; tried to play his part and convince himself as well as the others that somehow the death of Elmer Stokes would bring closure to his wife's murder. But soon he found himself alone on the back porch, sipping a glass of red wine as the futility of it all grew heavier and heavier around him.

And now, in the witness gallery, there was only his hand and the invisible glow in the dark stamp that gave him permission to watch.

Permission, Markham said to himself over and over again. *A stamp of approval from the gods that now is the time to bear witness to the sacrifice.*

Markham and the others had arrived at the prison just after midnight. They waited in a holding area where the warden briefed them on procedure and protocol, and then were escorted into the narrow witness gallery.

"You've all met with the prison psychologist," the warden had said, "so you know you must remain seated on the risers at all times. No excessive or loud talking is permitted, and no emotional outbursts of any kind will be tolerated. Not even from immediate family members. Any such behavior will result in your being promptly removed from the witness gallery. After the execution is completed, we will wait approximately thirty seconds for you to view the motionless remains."

And now, staring at the back of his hand, Markham wondered if the Impaler would also see the connection between the invisible writing and Randall Donovan. He gazed from his hand through the one-way glass and into the execution chamber; could see from his vantage point the windows that connected the other three galleries surrounding it. Behind one of them, he knew, sat Elmer Stokes's mother; behind another were the press and "official" state witnesses. Markham didn't know who was behind the fourth window. *The guards?* he thought. *You mean the GODS,* a voice countered with a heavy New England accent. And then in his mind a blanket of stars, the universe, and an image of himself in the execution chamber looking out the window as if it was a porthole on a spaceship. Markham knew what was waiting for him out there in space: the SWAT teams keeping the crowds both for and against Stokes's execution in line; and farther out, back in Raleigh, the crowds of faceless servicemen, one of whom he was sure was his man.

Elmer Stokes was escorted into the execution chamber at exactly 1 a.m. He had grown thinner since the last time Markham saw him—balder, too—but still wore his hair square in a buzz cut. Markham thought Stokes seemed genuinely at peace with it all; seemed happy to "finally pay back the lady's parents," as he had said in his final statement earlier that afternoon. Markham knew Stokes had requested steak for his final meal, and he had to force himself to stop searching for meaning in it—the hidden message encoded in the transposed letter "e" that made a *steak* into a *stake*.

Elmer begins with E! shouted a voice in his head, and Markham felt his brain squirm in his skull—his thoughts a jumbled mess of nonsense and fatigue. He closed his eyes;

and mercifully, when he opened them again, he found Stokes being secured in the chair. His mind seemed to drain at once into the reality of the present, and he noted on his watch that it took nearly fifteen minutes to finish prepping the Neanderthal for his injection.

At first, Stokes was alert and awake. He spoke to the attendants and even seemed to chuckle at one point. Markham couldn't hear what they were saying, but felt nothing as he cataloged the scene before him like a scientist. After a while, however, Stokes seemed to grow distant and sad, his head turning toward the window to his right. And when the drugs finally began to flow, Stokes mouthed the words *"I love you"* to that window—and his mother behind it, Markham assumed.

But still Markham felt nothing. He could hear his mother-in-law quietly weeping somewhere to his left, but felt not the slightest inclination to look at her. Instead, he found himself staring into the execution chamber, running through the formula for the lethal injection in his mind— *Sodium Pentothal, pancuronium bromide, potassium chloride . . .*

Then Stokes's eyes closed, and Markham leaned forward, watching the big man's chest rise and fall, rise and fall—at first slowly, then much faster as he went under. Markham didn't mark the time or how long it took until everything stopped, but only stared ahead in silence for several minutes until the attendants drew the curtains.

Elmer Stokes, the Smiling Shanty Man, was pronounced dead at 1:34 a.m. It took almost eleven years for this day to arrive, Markham would realize afterward, but only thirty-four minutes for the whole thing to go down in the end.

It was over, but he felt no different.

He had expected that—the numb emptiness, the surreal

charade—but what he hadn't seen coming was the gnawing envy he suddenly felt for Elmer Stokes.

Sam Markham wanted to sleep, too. To sleep and not pull back the curtains until he was sure his wife was waiting for him on the other side.

Chapter 57

.

Cindy Smith reached out her arm and found nothing but air. Her head hurt and her throat was parched, and for a moment she had no idea where she was. She bolted upright and caught sight of the ghost light on the stage below—its single bulb casting shadows that ran across her body like prison bars. She sat there for a moment thinking—her memory, like a leaky faucet, coming back to her in drips.

She was on the second tier of the *Macbeth* set, behind the railing on the stage right side. That's right. She and Edmund had come up here after kissing in the parking lot—but where was he? Cindy looked around and found her handbag beside her. She took out her cell phone. 3:42 a.m.

"Christ," she sighed, closing her eyes.

It had been her idea, she remembered suddenly, guiltily—*she* who'd asked Edmund to open the theater so they could have some privacy in case any of the other students spotted them in the parking lot on the way home from the party.

The party, Cindy said to herself. *There was a fight at the party.*

But Cindy didn't care about that, and instead fast-forwarded to the memory of Edmund leading her up the stairs—the outline of his muscular back through his shirt glowing an eerie blue in the shadows from the ghost light. Then they were together, pawing at each other in the darkness—her back against the hard platform, the warmth of his skin, the sour smell of stage paint all around her. She had been drunk, but that wasn't why she wanted him. She understood this even now, but thought it strange that Edmund wouldn't take off his shirt even as she felt his hardness probing between her thighs.

Suddenly, Edmund froze—whispered something in her ear that sounded like *"arrest a gal"*—and then slid off. Cindy felt a wave of embarrassment and shame as she remembered how she all but begged him to continue "Come on," she'd said, "put it inside me." But now she couldn't remember exactly what Edmund said next—mumbled something about stars and not having permission.

"Permission?" Cindy had slurred. "You're too much of a gentleman." Then came the fuzzy memory of them dressing—of *him* dressing *her*—and the warmth of his embrace as they drifted off to sleep. But Edmund hadn't slept. Cindy knew that now.

"Edmund?" she whispered—but only her voice echoed back from the black. And suddenly Cindy was not only angry but also very afraid.

She stood up and grabbed her handbag, dashed down the escape steps behind the set, and felt her way through the wings to the side entrance. Her head was throbbing, her sense of balance off, but she found the doorknob and burst out into the night.

The cool air felt good on Cindy's face—sobered her up but did nothing for her anger. She quickly descended the outside stairs and ran into the parking lot. Edmund's pickup was gone, but her piece-of-shit Pontiac was right where she had left it before the show.

"Asshole," she muttered—but once she was inside her car, her anger left her at once. On the passenger seat was a white rose, taken from her dressing room while she was asleep, she knew. Lying across it was a folded piece of notebook paper. She flicked on the dome light and read the note.

Dear Cindy: Please forgive me for leaving, but I need to be sure things are what they seem before we go any further. I will see you after the show tonight. I hope you're not angry with me. Edmund

Cindy sat there for a moment, confused, reading the note over and over again. Edmund had written it in pencil, but it appeared as if he'd written another name first, then erased it and wrote Cindy instead. What was it?

Looks like the name begins with E, Cindy thought, but she couldn't make out the rest of it in the Pontiac's dim dome light. But the note itself—what the hell was *that* about? And what kind of guy would leave a girl all alone in a darkened theater?

Cindy sat in the driver's seat, playing over the night's events in her mind until the windows of her Pontiac began to fog. Amy Pratt was right. There was something kind of creepy about Edmund Lambert. The note, the talk about things being what they seem—so strange, yes, but at the same time . . . well . . .

Cindy sighed and closed her eyes; tried to block out the realization of just how much that strangeness intrigued her—how much it *turned her on*. Jesus Christ, she almost had sex with Edmund Lambert after only a single date! This from the girl who in high school made her boyfriend wait over a year to get in her pants—and that was only because she was drunk and it was the senior prom and he begged her.

But now, tonight, it was she who had begged Edmund Lambert. What the fuck was going on with her? And what was it about Edmund Lambert that made her act so unlike herself—made her throw herself at him just like that slut Amy Pratt would do?

Cindy opened her eyes and stared down at Edmund's neat block-lettered print. She needed to get to bed and sleep off what had the potential to be a bitch of a hangover; she had to pull the lunch shift at Chili's, too, before heading off to the show.

"He needs to be sure things are what they seem," Cindy whispered, reading the note again. "Whatever the fuck that means."

What things "seem" like, a voice said in her head, *is that he ditched you in the theater. Didn't wake you or stick around to walk to you to your car. That's fucked up.*

"But the note," Cindy replied. "And the flower. It's not like he just left me. Maybe he tried to wake me—"

Are you kidding? You're gonna give him a pass on this?

"And the way he defended me at the party—"

Oh, my God! You're truly one needy, pathetic bitch!

Cindy closed her eyes and told the voice in her head to fuck off. It was right: she should be furious with Edmund Lambert—but she wasn't. And there was this odd feeling in the pit of her stomach: a dull sense of inevitability that at once both terrified and excited her—made her feel strangely liberated but at the same time like she was going bonkers inside a padded cell.

Damn right, crazy OCD bitch. Talking to yourself in your car at four a.m.—

"Out, out, damned spot!" Cindy screamed, her hands clawing at her tangled black hair—when suddenly in her mind she heard George Kiernan shout, *"That's it!"*

Chapter 58

The General thought Edmund Lambert handled himself very well with Ereshkigal; for if in fact Cindy Smith *was* Ereshkigal, the General mustn't allow himself to be seduced as the Prince had been all those years ago. True, that had been the beginning of Nergal's love (if you could call it that) for the goddess; but it had also been the end of his rule in the land of the living. And it was to the land of the living that Prince Nergal wished to return; to once again take his throne in the sun and be worshipped.

But the Prince needed the General to return as much as the General needed the Prince. The General was the last of the doorways, and through him not only would Nergal become a living, breathing god again but also the General would be able to travel back and forth through the doorway to Hell. The General still wasn't clear how it would all work in the end—such things were still beyond him—but it *would* work. He was sure of that. The Prince had revealed it to him in his visions; and before that, the equation had told him so, too. 9:3 or 3:1, depending on how you looked at it.

Yes, it was *how* you looked it that was the key. And thus,

in order to determine exactly how Ereshkigal fit into the equation, the General figured that the answer must lie in how he looked at her as well. He thought about this long and hard during the ride home from Greenville; but only when he pulled past the crumbling fieldstone columns at the head of his driveway did the answer, in a flash of insight, finally come to him.

Of course! he thought. *Ereshkigal had to be part of the equation if one were to look at things from the other side of the doorway!* Only with Ereshkigal could the equation of 3:1 be balanced in Hell—the General, his mother, Ereshkigal on one side of the colon, the Prince on the other. And perhaps the colon itself was a symbol for the doorway, which meant the numbers indicate their relative positions after the Prince's return.

But how would this work out in the end?

No need to worry about it now, the General thought giddily. No, the most important thing was that Ereshkigal *did* fit into the equation after all. Indeed, the answer was so obvious that the General actually began to laugh at how stupid he'd been for not seeing it earlier.

"But I still need to be careful," he whispered to himself as he entered the farmhouse. The concept of careful was inherent to the equation itself. The General already knew, for instance, that he would need to bring the throne through the doorway for his own protection. That was part of the legend. And so, he thought, he would also need the throne to protect his mother and carry her back while the Prince was busy with his return. That was the plan; that would be tricky enough—but now there was Ereshkigal, too. He would need to keep his meetings with her and his mother secret until the very last moment. The Prince was jealous of anyone talking to his princess; but even more so, the Prince was jealous of allegiance to anyone but him.

After all, wasn't that why the Prince took Edmund Lambert's mother from him in the first place? So there would be no one left for the boy to worship other than the Prince?

At first, when the General began wearing the lion's head, he'd hoped that—once the Prince saw how loyal he was—he would eventually grant Edmund Lambert's mother freedom from Hell. Prince Nergal had never done such a thing before—no, he was greedy and covetous of his souls—but perhaps, just perhaps, he might make an exception in the General's case.

But as time went on, more and more the General began to think that the Prince would never allow such a thing. He needed an alternate plan; and even though he still wasn't sure how it would all go down in the end, with the introduction of Ereshkigal the General felt confident that the Prince would have to yield to the 3:1 *himself.*

Perhaps that was written in the stars, too, the General thought. *Perhaps that was why the Prince never wanted to talk about Cindy Smith.*

"No use getting ahead of myself," the General whispered, and he went upstairs and showered. It would be daylight soon, and the Prince would be sleeping if he wasn't already. The General had consulted with him before heading off to the cast party, upon which the Prince gave no indication that he was aware of Edmund's secret meeting with his mother and Ereshkigal. Quite the opposite, the Prince's visions indicated that he was excited about the cast party, and wanted the General to report back to him.

And so, once he was clean and dry, the General sat naked by his bedroom window until the sun was up and he could see no more stars in the sky. That meant the Prince was asleep. The General wanted to sleep, too, but first he needed to consult with his mother and Ereshkigal; needed to look for them in the swirling colors and confirm that his reading of the 3:1 was correct.

He went down into the Throne Room and stood before the lion's head, listening until he felt like Edmund Lambert again.

Mama? he called out in his mind. *Mama, are you there?*

"Yes, Edmund," he heard her say after a moment. "I'm here."

Edmund removed the Prince's head from the shelf and slipped it over his own. For a moment nothing happened; then all at once he felt as if the air was sucked from his lungs and his body was surging forward.

Thhwummp!—a rush of brightness—and the doorway was open.

There she was again! Radiant, floating in the swirling colors. She was alone this time, coming toward him, arms outstretched and smiling.

"C'est mieux d'oublier," she said.

"I'll never forget," Edmund replied, taking her hands. He was about to kiss her when—flash-flash—his mother's face changed. A low moaning seemed to rise up all around him, and suddenly Edmund realized he was staring into his grandfather's eyes. "C'est mieux d'oublier," the old man said, deep and guttural. Edmund was about to speak when— flash-flash—everything became the god Nergal.

"WHERE IS SHE?" he roared—hovering, wings spreading, teeth gnashing.

"No!" Edmund cried—flash-flash—and the moans became screams, louder and louder as Nergal grew until he filled the entire sky—a black orange sky above hordes of chanting soldiers; a smoking battlefield with lines of the impaled stretching as far as the eye could see. Edmund could smell it and taste it and feel it—

"WHERE IS SHE?"

Now Edmund could see the souls of the sacrificed rising toward Nergal's mouth, snaking and twisting their way around his monstrous fangs like tendrils of cigarette smoke. And there was his mother among them, screaming and pleading for help!

"Mama!" Edmund cried—but she could only call her son's name one last time before slipping through the god's teeth and disappearing into his throat.

"You can't take her again!" Edmund screamed, but the Prince flapped his wings and knocked the young man backwards onto—

The cellar floor? Something hard and cold on his naked back. A glimpse of the throne through the lion's mouth, of the headless body seated before him and—

No, he was up and moving now. Through a maze—a dark maze that brought him to the temple doors at Kutha.

"WHERE IS SHE?"

Now a whirring sound and wind—the god's breath! Edmund could feel it and smell it! A hot smell like burning pennies—

And then he was in the workroom, staring through the lion's mouth at the grinder on the workbench.

It was turned on to *high.*

"Please, no!" Edmund screamed, his voice coming back to him in echoes both hollow and deafening.

"WHERE IS SHE?" the god bellowed inside the lion's head, and Edmund was suddenly both at Kutha and in the workroom; could feel his hands on the temple doors and on the workbench at the same time as he stared through the lion's mouth in disbelief.

"Please, no," he sputtered—his actions not his own, the scene before him terrifying in its inevitability as he saw the temple doors crack open and felt the wind of the grinder's wheel against his skin. He was hovering above it now, his chest only inches from its spinning steel bristles.

"I'm sorry, please, I—

The temple doors swung open as the grinder bit into his flesh. A bright burst of pain passed before his eyes, and Edmund howled in agony—his cries matched only by the Prince's incessant *"Where is she?"* and *"C'est mieux d'oublier."* It was all one now inside the lion's head, as was the white liquid fire squirting from the abyss beyond the doorway. It splattered him like acid milk and then turned red as the grinder tore open the flesh between his pectoral muscles. The blood spattered everywhere, and Edmund felt a hot wetness run down the backs of his thighs. And as the spinning bristles, like thousands of little teeth, chomped farther and farther down the center of his torso, incredibly, amid his pain Edmund registered somewhere that he'd shit himself.

Thhwummp!—a rush of darkness and yellowy light, and now there was only the workroom through the lion's mouth. The grinder continued to whir somewhere behind him, but Edmund was moving again—legs trembling, chest screaming as the blood ran down his stomach and soaked his genitalia. The cellar began to spin; and in what seemed like a leap forward in time, Edmund found himself on the cellar stairs, sobbing and panting uncontrollably as the shit and blood trailed off behind him. He felt weak, but at the same time as if he was being dragged upstairs by an unseen hand.

He ended up in his grandmother's parlor, kneeling beneath the mirror that hung above the fireplace. The General had recently tilted it downward so he could sit naked on the floor and admire the doorway.

But now it was Edmund Lambert who gazed up at his reflection. And when he saw himself kneeling there with the lion's head atop his shoulders; when he saw the 9 and the 3 that Billy Canning had so intricately tattooed on the temple doors split apart by a thick red gash, the young man knew with chilling certainty that the General had severely underestimated the Prince.

"WHERE IS SHE?" Edmund cried in the voice of the Prince himself—but, in the gaping bloody maw that was to be his doorway to Hell, the young man could not find his mother anywhere.

Chapter 59

It was almost 2 p.m. when Andy Schaap emerged from the wooded subdivision in Wilson. He drove about a half mile then pulled into a Bojangles' parking lot, where he crossed another name off his list and rested his head back, wondering what Sam Markham would think had he known what he was up to.

Indeed, all day he'd been expecting his partner to call him. Schaap had decided not to lie to him; would say that he was following up on his lists but wouldn't go into detail unless Markham asked him. Of course, Schaap had no way of knowing that Markham had fallen asleep in his childhood bedroom early that morning and would sleep a vampire's sleep until the sun went down. But Schaap would've understood; he was tired, too. The last couple of days had been exhausting for both of them.

Names.

Christ, there were so many from the cemetery—*over three thousand* that his computer program had linked to Iraq War veterans living in and around the Raleigh area. The program had already weeded out servicemen who still lived on base; and thus Schaap focused first on men not only who had served in units with lions or lionlike creatures as their symbols but also who lived in areas remote enough for the Impaler's operation.

Schaap gazed down at the list in his hands—just over one hundred names. A much more manageable number, yes, but still daunting for one person. And so far he'd come up empty—had knocked off only nine names that day and met the tenth with a groan when he saw the address was located over an hour away near Fayetteville.

Schaap thumbed through a series of pages and found another list the computer had generated by cross-referencing the cemetery records with a list he'd received that morning from the U.S. Army. The program had also ranked the names by unit symbol and location.

He ran his finger down the page until he found a name in the city of Wilson.

"Here we are," he said. He leaned over to the passenger seat and checked the address against the satellite imagery on his laptop. "Sergeant Edmund Lambert. 101st Airborne, 187th Infantry. Eagle and a seal-tailed lion. Nice, Wilson boy. That'll make you number ten and then we'll call it day."

Schaap programmed Lambert's address into his GPS and drove away—decided against a snack of Bojangles' chicken and biscuits and vowed to treat himself to a Dubliner steak when he got back to Raleigh.

After all, he'd earned it.

Chapter 60

The General awoke on the parlor rug. He'd collapsed there on his stomach, unconscious for hours inside the lion's head. He pulled it off immediately and sat up, the gash on his chest crying out as he tore himself free from the caked blood and shit beneath him. His wound began to bleed again, but the General only sat there, staring up at himself in the mirror amid the mess that Edmund Lambert had created.

Oh yes, the young man had certainly made a mess of things. But how could he have guessed that the Prince would've awakened during the day? And how could he have guessed that the Prince would find out about his plan?

No use wondering about it now, he thought. The Prince was powerful, and he found out. That's all that mattered. And now it was up to the General to prove his loyalty once again and set things right.

However, as the General sat there thinking, it occurred to him that in all of the Prince's ranting and raving he never showed him visions of Ereshkigal. Perhaps he was still unaware of how she fit into the equation. Perhaps, because she too was a god, she had the power to cloud—

Again, no use wondering about it. He needed to square things with the Prince. The Prince had shown him mercy and allowed him to live, which meant perhaps he saw Edmund's communication with his mother as a temporary slip. Yes, the General thought; the Prince still needed him as much as he needed the Prince. He could still hide his thoughts about his mother and Ereshkigal. And as long as he didn't communicate with them through the doorway again, perhaps there was still hope.

The doorway.

The General looked down at the bloody gash between the numbers 9 and 3. The doorway was cracked open, but something was wrong now; something needed to be fixed. The General could feel this instinctively. He picked up the lion's head and went back down into the cellar. The grinder was still whirring, and he stepped in the workroom and shut it off before heading into the Throne Room.

The smell of rotting flesh was strong in here today, but it did not bother the General. He stood there, gazing down at the headless corpse on the throne, then back and forth between the carving of the temple doors and the bloody tattoo on his chest. Impulsively, he slipped the lion's head over his own and waited for the rush of light that told him the door was open.

Nothing happened.

It was as he suspected, the General thought, removing the head. The doorway was broken now. It had lost its power, most likely from a combination of Edmund's use of it during the day and the Prince coming through it to control Edmund's actions. But the General couldn't be sure. There was still so much about the doorways that he didn't understand. The gash on his chest told him so. It was a message from the Prince as in the old days. A wound that needed to be healed between them; a gap that needed to be closed between the 9 and the 3.

Yes, the General thought. The Prince required a new doorway. That would heal the wound between them and set the equation right again. That would prove to the Prince that the 9 and 3 were together again.

As the General returned the lion's head to its proper place, he felt a wave of remorse pass through him. He hoped the Prince, wherever he went during the daytime, could feel how sorry he was. He assumed he could; for the Prince and the General were tied together in the stars. Always had been, and both of them were in too deep to turn back now.

What was the line from *Macbeth* that Bradley Cox said so poorly? *"I am in blood stepped in so far that, should I wade no more, returning were as tedious as go o'er."*

Macbeth. Bradley Cox. Part of the equation? Everything connected?

There was something there.

Flash-flash—A memory? A dream from the night before?—and suddenly the General understood why the Prince had wanted him to go to the cast party.

Bradley Cox.

The Prince had wanted Bradley Cox—the self-worshipping actor, the vain and promiscuous sinner. That had to be it. But the young man named Edmund had let his recklessness and his obsession with Ereshkigal get in the way. And now it was too late. Now, if he were to take Cox as a soldier, because of their public confrontation, the authorities would focus on Edmund first.

Or would they?

The General knew from his previous consultations with the Prince where he desired the next soldier to be sacrificed. And surely, the authorities would never find him *there.* Plus, the General could make it look as if Cox had disappeared; could make it look as if he committed suicide or perhaps drowned in the Tar River while swimming drunk. Yes, the General thought, as long as the authorities didn't find Bradley Cox's body they might never connect his death to Vlad the Impaler. And even if they did, the General and the Prince would be long gone by the time they figured it all out.

It made sense—but the General needed to think about this. It was all coming at him too fast. He couldn't be sure anymore—he had grown too dependent on the doorways for confirmation of the Prince's messages, needed time to sort it all out. Perhaps Cox should be the doorway itself. Perhaps—

The gash on his chest cried out, and the General understood. He was wasting his time guessing. First things first: he needed to begin with cleaning up his mess.

The General left the cellar and went up two flights to the upstairs bathroom. He turned on the shower and stepped inside. His wound stung painfully under the hot water, but the General gritted his teeth and took it—washed himself thoroughly, then stood there thinking until the hot water ran out. The cold felt good on his skin, helped numb the pain in his chest and stomach. And when his mind had cleared somewhat, the General toweled off and bandaged himself with some gauze and medical tape he'd originally purchased to help his tattoo heal. How ironic.

Once his wound was properly dressed, the General donned a pair of jeans and a T-shirt and went downstairs to the kitchen and made himself a protein shake. He stood there at the sink, drinking and thinking how pleasant it felt to have the line of coolness running behind the burning gash at the center of his torso. There would be no workout in the horse barn today, he thought; no running across the tobacco fields, either, and no push-ups for a long time if he ever wanted his wound to heal.

"But the wound *will* heal," the General whispered. "Eventually."

He rinsed out his glass and headed into the parlor. The room smelled awful, and the General immediately opened all the windows. Then he rolled up the rug and lugged it out onto the back porch. It was ruined, he decided, and would have to be burned in the yard at some point. The General went back into the kitchen, fetched the mop and bucket from the broom closet, and filled it with hot water and Pine-Sol.

He began in the parlor, following the trail of blood and excrement and mopping carefully as it led him through the front hall and kitchen and back down the cellar stairs to the workroom. The General felt calm and at peace. One step at a time, he thought—the beginning of eventually, of solving the equation. Following the trail told him so. Yes, one could find the Prince's messages in anything—even in one's own blood and shit—if one looked closely enough.

"*C'est mieux d'oublier*," the General whispered as he mopped the workroom floor. He dumped the bloody-shitty water down the drain in the corner and rinsed out the bucket in the slop sink. And when he went back upstairs and looked at the clock on the kitchen wall, he realized he'd cleaned up the entire mess in just over half an hour.

Satisfied, the General took a deep breath and realized that his T-shirt was sticking to his chest. The temple doors were bleeding again. He would have to take another shower and replace the gauze and medical tape.

Before heading upstairs, however, the General returned to the parlor—was about to close the windows, when suddenly he caught sight of a black SUV coming up the driveway.

The General froze as a crippling wave of fear shot through his body. The SUV looked dangerous, and there was no time to change—no time to wash the blood from his chest! He began to tremble—had to fight the urge to flee—when suddenly something unexpected happened.

It came to him in a *flash-flash* inside his head, and all at once the General's fear disappeared.

Chapter 61

Andy Schaap parked his TrailBlazer alongside the white truck at the end of the driveway. He got out and peeked through the driver's side window. He didn't know what he expected to find—*Blood spatters on the dashboard?*—and felt foolish when he saw the truck was clean.

Nonetheless, Schaap couldn't deny the feeling he got when he pulled onto Sergeant Lambert's property. The old tobacco farm was the most secluded of the homes he'd visited so far. And had he not been taken so off guard by the little spark of hope clicking away deep inside his stomach, perhaps Andy Schaap might have been more careful.

Indeed, he wanted first to go looking in the old horse barn, perhaps even check out the crumbling tobacco sheds he passed on his way in. And if he had, things might have turned out differently that afternoon. Instead, however, Andy Schaap followed protocol—took out his cred case and headed up onto the front porch.

The old, weather-beaten planks creaked painfully beneath his feet as he came upon a little handwritten sign over the doorbell that read, *Please ring*. Schaap pressed the button.

The sound that came from inside was loud—like a buzzer on a game show, he thought—but afterwards there was only silence, no sign of life within.

Schaap rang the bell again and called out, "Hello? Anybody home?"

Nothing.

Schaap opened the screen door and peered through the inside door's small, beveled-glass porthole. The house was dark inside, but he could make out an empty hallway with a large staircase at the far end. Something about this place gave him the creeps, but he certainly would need more that that to justify his entering without a warrant. He rang the doorbell again—listening, watching for movement inside—when suddenly he heard a creak on the porch behind him.

Schaap turned just in time to see the man coming up the stairs—a tall, muscular man in a tight black T-shirt. In one moment, Schaap felt a smile form at the corner of his lips; in the next, he saw the man's gun.

"Freeze!" he shouted, dropping his cred case as he went for the gun beneath his jacket. "FBI!"

But the man coming for him did not freeze.

"Your body is the doorway," he said, raising his gun.

Time seemed to slow down for Andy Schaap; and amid his terror, he felt the clicking in his stomach travel up his spine and into the back of his head.

That's a Beretta M9, he said to himself.

A split second later the bullet struck him between the eyes.

Chapter 62

The General squatted down next to the dead man and snatched up his ID—"Andrew J. Schaap," he read out loud. "Federal Bureau of *c'est mieux d'oublier*."

The General took a deep breath and propped the agent's lifeless body against the doorjamb. He felt strangely calm—his movements both his own and someone else's as he took off his T-shirt and tied it like a tourniquet around the man's bleeding head.

His instincts had been correct. He'd known almost immediately that this man was some kind of authority. The man looked it, sure, but the General had also seen the bulge of the gun under his jacket and the ID case in his hand as he approached from the SUV.

The General stepped to the edge of the porch and gazed out across the fields. He could see a portion of the road through the trees at the edge of his property, and he cocked his ear toward it and listened. No one was coming. No more FBI agents on their way.

At least not yet.

But how did the FBI find him? Surely, it had nothing to

do with Cox—the FBI coming to his house over a fight at a college party? No, that didn't make any sense. And the fact that the Prince had not been angry with him for fighting with Cox only proved this point. If the FBI thought Edmund Lambert was Vlad the Impaler, why would they send only one man out to capture him? That didn't make any sense, either.

In a flash, the General was off the porch and inside the TrailBlazer. He found a laptop and some paperwork on the passenger seat and picked up the first page. Names. Lots of them. All in the Armed Forces. Edmund Lambert's name was eighteenth on a list with a handwritten title, *By City.*

The General flipped and scanned some more pages and found another list, this one labeled *Unit Probability/Cemetery* in the same handwriting. Four names, out of order but in the same general area, were crossed off. The General read the addresses and hit the back button for the open Google Earth page on the laptop's screen. The address on this page matched one of the addresses on the list. The General hit the back button again, and that address matched another name, too.

"Bad luck," he said. "Not even a prime suspect. Just a name on a list created from matching up names in the cemetery to members in the Armed Forces. But how did the FBI know I was in the Army?"

Your gun, a voice answered inside his head—but the General did not believe that. He'd read just how popular the Beretta M9 was with the gangbangers in the newspaper article about Rodriguez and Guerrera. And just as the General dismissed this as a possibility, the voice in his head spoke again.

It appears from the names and the order in which the FBI agent was following them that he was trying to give structure to the randomness of his suspect pool.

"Yes, it does."

That means the FBI has only recently begun exploring the military angle—a fact proved further by this man coming out here all alone.

"No," the General said, gazing over his shoulder and out the TrailBlazer's back window. "No one seems too worried about Agent Schaap just yet."

The General considered this and wondered if the FBI even knew Special Agent Schaap was out here. He felt in his gut that there was still time, that there was no need to panic, and that, even if others in the FBI had copies of these lists, they might not know exactly in what order this man Schaap was questioning the men on them.

"But surely the FBI will come looking for this man," the General said. "It's only a matter of time before they track him here. His cell phone, a LoJack in his car or something."

No, the General thought. He couldn't stick around the farmhouse forever.

However, the voice in his head said, *the doorway can now be repaired. The stars have smiled upon you and brought a doorway—well, right to your doorstep!*

With a surge of joy, the General gathered up the FBI agent's belongings and dashed from the SUV into the house. He dumped everything on the kitchen table and then dragged the FBI agent's corpse into the parlor—fished out his keys and set his body against the fireplace. He paused only briefly to look at himself in the mirror above the mantel. The gauze on his chest was soaked with blood, but the General felt no pain—only a tingling sensation, which he took as a sign that the doorway was already beginning to heal.

Yes, he thought, everything was back on track. The equation would be balanced again. And in a blur of excitement, the General was back outside.

First he rinsed off the blood on the porch with a garden hose. The he ran across the yard and into the old horse barn, where he started up his van and drove it around to the back of the house. He dashed back to the front yard and moved the TrailBlazer into the horse barn. The FBI would come for their man eventually, the General knew; would search his property and find everything—the TrailBlazer, the body, not to mention the reeducation chamber, the Throne Room, and all his equipment in the cellar.

But when *would they come?* That was the question.

The General suspected the FBI agent's laptop would give him a better idea.

He locked the barn doors from the outside and quickly surveyed his property as he ran back toward the house. No, the FBI wasn't looking for Andrew J. Schaap just yet. Indeed, the way things looked from the outside of his house, no one would be able to tell that the FBI agent had ever been there.

However, all that mattered to the General now was how things should look on the *inside* of his house when Andrew J. Schaap's friends finally came a-calling.

Chapter 63

Markham awoke around 5:15 in the evening—would've kept on sleeping, in fact, had his mother not knocked on his bedroom door and told him supper was ready.

"Well, it's going to be breakfast for you," she added. "Steak and eggs, so call it what you want."

"Steak," Markham said to himself when she was gone. "Go figure."

He lay there for a long time staring up at the glow-in-the-dark plastic stars that his father had pasted on the ceiling when he was a child. But rather than think of the Impaler, Markham's stomach growled in anticipation of the meal waiting for him downstairs.

He was starving. But even more so, he was amazed he'd slept almost the entire day. He remembered waking only a couple of times to pee, but the heaviness behind his eyes always dragged him back to his bedroom. And the fact that his parents had left him alone meant he must've been snoring up a storm.

He thought of Michelle; how, in the middle of the night,

she used to tap him lightly on his shoulder to make him roll over. But she never complained about his snoring—never once—and only shook her head and smiled at him in the morning as if he'd done something stupid the night before.

God, he missed her.

Indeed, after the execution Markham felt as if he missed her more than ever. He'd planned on traveling to Mystic on Saturday to visit her grave, but decided once he was back in his bedroom that he would do so early Sunday morning before he left for Raleigh. The cemetery was only about twenty minutes from his parents' house, but curiously, he didn't want to leave his old bedroom. It seemed to ease his pain, seemed to gas him into a deep and cleansing sleep broken only by glimpses of consciousness in which he swore he was a boy again—the sunlight streaming in around the window shade from a time long before he knew his wife and her killer even existed.

Markham showered and shaved and arrived at the kitchen table dressed in jeans and a faded University of Connecticut sweatshirt that he had found in his dresser drawer. His parents greeted him with looks of both concern and relief, but Markham knew neither of them would mention anything about the execution. It was a mutual understanding among the three of them that went back as long as he could remember. They never asked what was bothering him; seemed to accept that their son, even as a child, would talk to them only if he wanted to. And true to form, Sam Markham rarely did.

"Looks like you've been burning the candle at both ends, Sammy," his father said, holding up his newspaper. "This fella they're calling Vlad the Impaler—he's the reason you're on assignment in Raleigh, I take it?"

A former Navy man and retired real estate investor, Peter Markham had a somewhat gruff, no-nonsense manner that his son had grown to appreciate only after he joined the FBI.

Then again, Markham knew that was because his father had grown to appreciate him only after he joined the FBI—despite the circumstances surrounding his change of careers.

Peter Markham had never supported his son's desire to be an English teacher. Of course, he'd never come right out and said anything, but young Sammy had always been able to intuit his father's opinions by what he *didn't* say—like the way he never asked him how he was doing in his classes; like the way he never even asked him if he'd gotten laid yet. "It's your life," was all Peter Markham would say, his mind unable to wrap itself around the concept of a former all-star high school athlete like Sammy Markham wanting to teach poetry and shit. Besides, when it came right down to it, how much could a fella make doing that stuff anyway?

"Sammy's not allowed to talk about his work," said his mother. "You know better than to ask him, dear."

"I'm not asking about his work, Lois. I'm just asking if this Vlad boy is *his* boy."

Lois Markham rolled her eyes and slipped two eggs onto her son's plate.

"It's all right," Markham said. "I've no problem telling you I'm working on this case, Dad. But pretty much all we know is what you guys have read in the paper there." This was a lie, but he didn't care; knew this was the best way to get his father off the subject, and added, "But you have to keep all this between us. Don't go mentioning anything about me to the boys at the gun club. Okay?"

"What the hell do I look like?" said Peter Markham, cutting his steak. "I know better than to shoot my mouth off. You see, Lois? That's all I wanted to know."

Lois sighed and sat down at the table with a look of knowing resignation that her son had seen many times over the years. As close as he had been with his father growing up, Markham knew deep down that he was more like his mother—more reserved, more intellectual, and (*oh God, don't fucking say it!*) more *sensitive.*

Lois Markham had worked for a time in real estate with her husband, but for most of her adult life she'd been a stay-at-home mom. She dabbled in painting and poetry before her son was born, and used to take little Sammy with her to the theater and to classical music concerts. Peter Markham would never have been caught dead at the theater—used to say that all that artsy-fartsy stuff was gonna turn his boy into a sissy—but somehow Peter and Lois Markham made it work for over forty years.

"I'll tell you this, however," said Peter Markham with a mouthful of food. "The only way you guys'll catch this nut-bag is if he screws up. I'm not knocking what you do, Sammy, don't get me wrong. But all them serial killers that I've read about, they screw up eventually, am I right?"

"Not all of them," said Markham. "Some have never been caught—"

"I know, I know," his father said, waving his fork. "Jack the Ripper was one, sure. But nowadays it's just a matter of time. I guess you could say that they screw up all along, but it takes a smart guy like you to see the screw-ups that no-body else sees. You understand what I'm saying?"

"All right, Peter," said his wife. "Let's talk about something else, shall we?"

"What? I'm just telling my son I'm proud of him. I *am* proud of you, Sammy. You know that, don't you?"

Markham nodded but said nothing. He chewed his food slowly as his mind drifted to the Impaler. What the hell was he doing in Connecticut having dinner with his parents when he should be back in Raleigh? He was due to fly out tomorrow afternoon around two o'clock, but the idea of spending another night here, the idea of waiting well into the day tomorrow, suddenly seemed unbearable to him.

The family ate the rest of their meal peppered with small talk—politics, the Yankees, a woman Lois knew who left her husband for a younger man—but Markham's mind soon turned to Andy Schaap.

Still working on his lists, he thought. *Christ, I'd give anything to trade places with him right now.*

After his parents retired to the den to watch a movie on HBO, Markham excused himself and stepped out onto the back porch. He dialed Schaap's number on his Black-Berry—tried him first at the Resident Agency, then left a voice mail on his cell asking how things were going and to call him back ASAP with an update.

Then he sat for a long time just staring out the screened porch windows to the jagged silhouette of woods behind his house. It was chilly, and he could not see the stars, but he had no urge to go outside to look at them. Instead he closed his eyes and imagined what the sky would look like had he been camping out in the backyard with his father as they so often did when he was a child. Back then, little Sammy Markham didn't know where to look for Leo, but tonight he saw the lion through the eyes of a little boy—bright and shining above all the other constellations—and began to wonder if the Impaler ever camped out in the backyard with his father, too.

Chapter 64

The General almost fell off his ladder when the FBI agent's BlackBerry went off. He was working in the attic with his grandfather's old circular saw, and had he not paused to wipe the sweat from his brow, he most certainly wouldn't have heard KISS's "Detroit Rock City" blaring up at him from the attic floor. The General would never have pegged Andrew J. Schaap as a KISS fan, but then again, a lot of things had taken him by surprise today.

"I feel uptight on Saturday night," Paul Stanley wailed, and the General nodded absently. He was uptight, too. Things were taking longer than expected, and even after all these years, he was still afraid to be in the attic alone. But the work up there had to be done. And soon.

True, judging from Andrew J. Schaap's lists and the files on his computer, he and the Prince still had time to get things done before the rest of the FBI arrived. But what to do next and where to go once the work in the house was complete—well, that remained to be seen in the Prince's visions.

The FBI agent was working alone. There was no doubt

about that, and no doubt that he had only recently put two and two together and was working systematically down a list of names. The General had not been able to sign into the Sentinel case management system (something he shouldn't do anyway, IP addresses and all that), but still, from what files he could access, the General was nothing short of blown away.

The FBI knew almost everything—his relationship with the Prince, the stars, the ancient texts, the mark of the lion, Nergal, and the connection to Iraq. But what really stunned the General was the account of how the ancient Babylonian seal was found in Italy—the same seal that Edmund Lambert had offered up to the lion on the eve of his anointing!

Incredibly, the ancient artifact had been found. How? The General couldn't even begin to imagine. Maybe the lion dropped it, or maybe the seal had been discovered in the lion's stomach by someone who had killed it for meat. Maybe it was found in the lion's shit—

Or maybe, said a voice in his head, *just maybe the lion never took the seal at all. Maybe you imagined the whole thing and dropped the seal in the alleyway. Maybe one of your comrades found it and sold it in Qatar himself—*

But the General only laughed at this idea. The lion in Tal Afar had been real—there could be no doubt about that. The seal, that very instrument that the ancient Babylonians had used to seal their secret messages, was a secret message in and of itself. And that Edmund Lambert, the man who would become the General, should have selected it from all the other stolen artifacts proved that he was not only worthy but also the only mortal capable of understanding the Prince's messages.

Furthermore, the fact that Andrew J. Schaap and almost the entirety of the FBI's investigation had been literally dumped on his doorstep proved to the General two things: one, that the Prince's return was indeed inevitable; and two,

that it was up to the General to put all the information he had
been given to good use.

"But who is this Sam Markham?" he'd wondered when he
first searched the FBI agent's laptop. "Who is this man who
seems to know the Prince better than anyone?"

Oh yes, the General had thought, this Sam Markham was
a very smart man; for the files on the computer made it
abundantly clear that it was he who had singlehandedly put
everything together.

But the General did not have the time to ponder this.
More important matters required his immediate attention.
And now, hours later, the BlackBerry was ringing on the
attic floor; now, perhaps, Andrew J. Schaap's friends had
begun looking for him. The General didn't know if they
would activate the vehicle-tracking device that he figured
was hidden inside the TrailBlazer. And would they be able to
get a bead on their man's cell signal? He would have to dispose of the TrailBlazer and the BlackBerry soon. The General had his own cell phone, which he hardly ever used; only
kept it with him when he was at Harriot in case the alarm
went off and the security company had to call him.

However, the fact that the BlackBerry had not rung until
now told the General that the FBI was not looking for their
agent just yet. He had time, he still had time—

*But was Agent Schaap supposed to have been at another
meeting tonight? Did this Sam Markham find out anything
more about the Impaler?*

The General hopped off the ladder and removed the pistol
he'd tucked into the back of his jeans. He set it on the floor
and sat down next to the cell phone. The message dinged
into voice mail, and he stared at the word *BlackBerry* for a
long time, wondering if there was a message in it.

No matter, he thought. The new doorway was already
being prepared in the cellar. It was only a matter of time before it would be ready to be placed on the throne, and then

the General would be able to communicate with the Prince again directly.

"Communicate," the General said absently, and pressed the menu button on the BlackBerry. He didn't bother trying to get into the FBI agent's voice mail, and instead scrolled down the to the missed calls list.

"Sam Markham," he read. "The smart little friend from the Federal Bureau of *c'est mieux d'oublier*."

The General sprang to his feet, flew down the two flights of stairs, and ended up in the workroom. He sat down at his computer and googled "Sam Markham" and "FBI."

Bingo, first hit, an article from a Tampa newspaper about a serial killer named Jackson Briggs—the Sarasota Strangler, they called him. Some petty, self-involved moron who brutalized little old ladies, then strangled them, all while dressed up as a ninja. Sam Markham had been the one to take him down.

"Looks like they brought out the big guns for us," the General said, hitting the print button. "Only a matter of time before he figures out what his friend was up to."

He clicked a few more links, and found a photograph of Markham standing with a group of FBI agents. He was an attractive male, the General thought. Chiseled features, penetrating eyes, a strong jaw—someone with whom the young man named Edmund Lambert might have liked to copulate back in those days when he searched for meaning in such things.

The General hit the print button again. The newspaper article and the photograph of Sam Markham most certainly would have to go on the reeducation chamber wall. After all, Sam Markham was part of the equation now, too. How? He wasn't exactly sure.

But the General had an idea.

Chapter 65

George Kiernan didn't come backstage to give the cast their notes after the show on Saturday night; only sent a message via the stage manager that he'd meet with them in the house an hour before the matinee on Sunday. That wasn't good, Cindy thought. That meant he was *really* pissed off. And as she left the theater, Cindy was afraid she might run into him in the parking lot.

Later, as she was driving home, she started to feel kind of bad for him. She knew his elderly mother came to the shows on Saturday nights. Cindy always thought this was just the sweetest thing, and oftentimes imagined herself on Broadway many years from now with her own elderly mother sitting in the front row, smiling up at her. Besides, Kiernan had warned everyone on Friday to take it easy at the cast party and have their shit together the following night. They had really let him down, and Cindy didn't like to let people down.

She couldn't deny that she was just as much to blame as everyone else. She was tired and felt off during her performance. She had e-mailed Edmund twice that day—before and after her shift at Chili's—and was at first disappointed, then angry, then finally worried when he didn't reply. She couldn't find his number in the campus directory and had no idea how to get in touch with him other than the Internet. She knew where he lived, of course, but his house was out in the sticks—too far to visit and be back in time for the show. Oh yeah, there was no denying it: her bizarre-o date with Edmund Lambert had really fucked with her head, not to mention all the gossip going around the department about the fight at the cast party.

It was all good for Cindy, though, who was looked upon as a goddess by her female cast mates—even Amy Pratt, who asked her point-blank if she and Edmund had sex. Cindy told her they hadn't, and Amy seemed genuinely relieved. Go figure. Rumors were flying, however, but Amy assured her that she would set the record straight. Besides, she said, the majority of the gossip was about Bradley Cox and his crew getting their asses whipped. And Cindy didn't need Amy Pratt to tell her that said gossip was really fucking with Mr. Macbeth's head.

On top of it all, Cindy thought, Bradley-boy was going to get it bad from George Kiernan. Never mind that he was obviously hungover; never mind the noticeable swelling at the bridge of his nose and the way it affected his speech during his performance. Bradley Cox had actually *missed an entrance* on Saturday night.

Cindy was the one waiting for him onstage when it happened—early on in the first act, when Macbeth returns home after his first confrontation with the Witches. Cox had been getting into it with one of the cast members, Amy told Cindy during intermission—something about Lambert being lucky Cox had been drinking so much, otherwise he would've kicked soldier boy's ass. But when he finally realized he was supposed to be onstage, he tripped and stumbled on his entrance. That's when the audience laughed at him.

Cindy remembered that part clearly. The rest was kind of a blur.

"Thy letters have transported me beyond this ignorant present," she said, helping him recover his footing, "and I feel now the future in the instant."

Cox stared back at her dopily—his lips frozen in an O, his tongue groping for his line as the audience whispered and tittered in the long pause that followed.

"Thou look'st strange, *my dearest love*," Cindy said, improvising, hoping he'd pick up on her clue. Nothing. Cindy panicked and said, "Thou meanst to tell me the king is coming?"

"My dearest love!" Cox blurted. "Duncan comes here tonight!"

More laughter, but they ended up getting through the scene all right. The rest of the show, however, suffered. The rhythm was off, a couple of flubbed lines here and there—nothing major, really, but to George Kiernan the show would have seemed unworthy of a dress rehearsal.

As for herself, Cindy hoped her quick thinking would buy her some mercy from Kiernan during his note session tomorrow. But at the same time she knew how bad her *"Out, out damned spot!"* speech had gone—and even she couldn't blame Bradley Cox for that. No, Cindy thought. It was her own fault for staying out so late—and for letting Edmund Lambert mess with her head.

True, Edmund didn't seem like the kind of guy who liked to play games. But as Cindy turned onto her street, she was finally ready to admit to herself how hurt she'd been when he didn't stop by after the show. He let her down—didn't make good on what he said in his bizarre-o note—and Cindy had to fight the urge to turn around and head straight for Wilson and ask him why. If she didn't have the matinee tomorrow, she thought, she probably would have.

No, you wouldn't, taunted a voice in her head. *You're too much of a wuss to do something like that.*

Fuck you.

Will you relax and try playing it cool for once? Christ, the guy said on opening night he'd be there for photo call tomorrow. Remember?

Cindy didn't respond.

Give him a break, will you? Maybe something came up. Why don't you wait until you talk to him before you start flipping out?

Cindy sighed and pulled into her driveway.

Chronic fucking OCD, I swear.

"All right," she said, turning off the ignition. "If soldier boy doesn't show up for photo call tomorrow, we'll see whether or not I don't take a drive out to Wilson."

Chapter 66

In his bedroom, Markham had just finished downloading a song onto his laptop. An agent from the National Center for the Analysis of Violent Crime had entered it into Sentinel as being on the CD Jose Rodriguez used for his Leona Bonita act. "Dark in the Day," a remake of a popular tune from the eighties. Markham remembered the song from high school, but couldn't place the name of the band.

"How could you think I'd let you get away?
When I came out of the darkness and told you who
you are?"

Markham looped the song on his computer's media player and listened to it over and over again. The lyrics. He couldn't shake the connection, couldn't help but see the totality of the message through the Impaler's eyes, and felt a chill run up his spine when he imagined himself sitting in the audience, watching Rodriguez prowl about the stage in his lion drag.

"I thought I heard you calling. You thought you heard me speak.
Tell me how could you think I'd let you get away?"

Markham let the song cycle through one more time, then rolled over and saw his BlackBerry blinking on the nightstand. He checked it—a couple of e-mails and a text message from Andy Schaap. Finally.

Your voice mail was cracking up, the message read. Didn't get all of it. What's up?

Markham texted back: Any progress?

A moment later: Where r u?

Still in ct.

Ct?

Odd, Markham thought, and typed: ct = Connecticut.

Then an entire two minutes went by before Schaap replied: Duh sorry. Tired. Nothing new. Still getting names. What's your eta?

Tomorrow @ 4pm.

Another long pause before Schaap texted back: Need ride?

No. Car @ airport.

K. Have a safe trip. C u @ RA when u get back.

Markham stared at his BlackBerry for a long time. The texting with Schaap bothered him for some reason. He couldn't place it. No, he'd never communicated with him this way before—Schaap always called him—but the questions, the lingo—

"Christ," Markham said. Now he was overanalyzing things—looking for something to worry about in this limbo of waiting to get back to Raleigh.

Schaap was tired, too, that's all. But maybe that's what worried him. Could he depend on Schaap not to miss anything?

Fuck it, he heard Andy Schaap say in his mind. Yes, he'd figure it all out when he got back to Raleigh. He shut down his computer and turned off his bedside lamp—stared up at the fully charged stars on his ceiling and wondered how after all these years they could still glow so brightly.

And soon, despite his having slept nearly the entire day, Sam Markham was again dead to the world.

The General smiled and plugged in his cell phone charger next to the one he'd taken from the TrailBlazer. He hardly ever used his own cell phone anymore, but for what he was planning next, the General would need it just as much as he still needed Andrew J. Schaap's BlackBerry.

Chapter 67

Cindy heard the ding of the text message just as she was drifting off to sleep. She didn't recognize the number, but read the message anyway.

Cindy: Sorry I didn't get back 2 u sooner and I'm sorry I didn't c u @ the show. My uncle came by unexpectedly and I have been very busy.

"That's it?" Cindy said, the anger beginning to boil again in her stomach. She'd been furious when she returned home to find Edmund still hadn't answered her e-mails; had toyed with the idea of sending him another note (a nasty one, at that) but thought it better to wait until morning when her head had cleared.

But now? *What the fuck was this all about?*

Cindy was about to reply when the ding of another message stopped her.

Everything is fine, tho. I'll call you tomorrow (I got your cell # off the contact sheet for Macbeth).

"Tomorrow, and tomorrow, and tomorrow," she heard Macbeth say—and then, out of nowhere she thought of *Gone with the Wind*; saw herself as Scarlett in the final scene, tears in her eyes, alone on the stairs, violins and swelling music and—

"After all . . . tomorrow is another day!"
What the fuck?
Then another message.

Hope the show went well n sleep tight. I missed u
2day. E

Cindy realized her heart was beating a mile a minute, and she chastised herself for her silly, sappy relief at ever doubting Edmund Lambert in the first place.

He'll call me tomorrow.

She felt herself melt down into her mattress—texted back, Sounds good. Miss u 2 ☺—and fought off the urge to just call him right then and there. He'd probably understand, but that would not look cool. *Beyond stalkerish*, she thought. Besides, if he wanted to talk to her, he would've called, right? *Plus,* she needed to sleep; there was no way she could spend the whole night talking to Edmund with a pissed-off George Kiernan and a matinee waiting for her tomorrow.

"Fuck it," she said, and was about to call him anyway, when another text popped in her inbox.

U need to rest. Go to sleep and c u after the show
tomorrow.

Cindy started to text back, After all, tomorrow is another day!—but settled on Sounds good ☺ instead.

She waited for a reply, but when it didn't come, she saved

Edmund Lambert's number and closed her phone—closed her eyes, too, and drifted off to sleep feeling more like Scarlett O'Hara than ever.

It felt wonderful.

Chapter 68

An hour after Edmund Lambert's good night text to Cindy, the General saw the light go off in Bradley Cox's apartment. He didn't know if the young man was alone; didn't know if the redheaded female with whom he sometimes copulated was staying with him. But the General didn't care. He would take them both if he had to.

The timing of things demanded it.

Of course, the General would've much rather had the luxury to plan as he'd done with the other soldiers. At the same time, however, he was worried because of the uncertainty of what was to come. The time line of things most certainly would have to change. Of that, the General was sure. And he would need to leave the farmhouse and the doorway behind very soon—it was too risky to stay there to balance the equation, to complete the nine—but where would he go?

The doorway would tell him. Once it was finished draining, and once he had taken care of Cox, he would know what to do next.

The General had driven the FBI agent's TrailBlazer and parked it in a lot across from the young actor's apartment building—a two-level, student shithouse with a half-dozen single-bedroom units on each floor. The General had gotten his address and telephone number from the contact sheet. Cox lived in the corner unit on the first floor. His silver Mustang with the tinted windows was parked in front. The General had seen him pull up to theater in that car many times.

The General waited patiently in the TrailBlazer, his eyes never leaving Cox's front door as groups of drunken students stumbled in and out of the shadows on their way home from the bars downtown. The General had a number of ideas as to how he would get into Cox's apartment, but the timing of his arrival in Greenville was bad: early Sunday morning, the bars closing, a very good chance of him being seen.

And so the General would have to wait. But that was all right. The General was used to waiting.

Chapter 69

Bradley Cox was in bed staring up at the ceiling when the ring of his cell phone startled him. He reached for it immediately, but the line was already dead when he answered it. He looked at his alarm clock—*3:12 a.m.*—then looked at the missed-call list. He didn't recognize the number—*704 area code, Charlotte*, he thought—and was about to dial it back and tell the owner to go fuck himself for calling so late, when he heard the ding of a text message.

If this is Amy again, he thought, *I'll tell her straight up to fuck off for good.* He was in no mood for a booty call—especially not after tonight's horror show at the theater. She had called earlier that evening to ask him if he wanted some company, but he told her in no uncertain terms that he wanted to be left alone. And then the young actor did something he hadn't done since elementary school: he cried himself to sleep. He woke up around 1:45 a.m. and turned off his light. But a face hovering there in the darkness just beyond his busted nose had kept him wide awake until now.

Edmund Lambert.

Yeah, that son of a bitch had fucked things up royally for

him. And the motherfucker was going to pay. Cox had it all planned. He would get a couple of guys from his father's construction firm—big redneck-types who just loved this sort of thing—and they would pay a courtesy call to Edmund Lambert when the time was right. Might even deliver their candy-gram straight to the motherfucker's front door. Oh yeah, the three of them would tune old soldier boy's ass good 'n tight.

He'd played the scenario over and over again in his mind, and the image of Edmund Lambert's face beaten to a bloody pulp actually made him smile. Sure, he knew he was going to catch holy hell from Kiernan, but his little plan made an ass chewing from the old man all worth it. Indeed, he had just begun to feel better when the ring of his cell phone pulled him from his fantasy.

Cox scrolled out of the missed-call list and checked the incoming text message.

It's Cindy Smith, the message read. R u up?

Cox shot upright—his heart beating fast, his "player instinct" kicking in at once.

No matter who *a chick is*, he said to himself, *when she texts you at three in the morning that means only one thing.*

Booty call.

But Cindy Smith?

In an instant, Cox forgot all about Edmund Lambert—his mind racing now with how to play the situation properly. As much as he hated to admit it, he'd had it bad for Cindy Smith—still did, as a matter of fact—but never told a single soul. What bothered him the most was that he didn't know what he'd done to fuck it all up with her. Yeah, he'd been a rude dick to her a couple of times, but that was only after she turned him down. And he'd been genuine and gentlemanly in his desire to take her out—had already known that he was gonna have to put in his time if he wanted to bang her and made up his mind that she was definitely worth it.

But now?

The show. He'd seen the look in her eyes when he fucked up tonight: the compassion, the way she bailed him out without thinking, without contempt as his cast mates snickered in the wings behind him.

Maybe everything happens for a reason, he thought. *Maybe that's what was needed to finally bring us together.*

"All right," he said, thinking quickly. "If we talk on the phone, I won't even ask her to come over. If she comes over, I won't even touch her. Even if she wants to. That's the way to play it."

He took a deep breath and texted back, Yeah. What's up?

A moment later, Can we talk? I'm in my car outside.

"Holy shit," he said—his fingers moving before he could think twice about what to say. Just come in, he wrote. B right back.

His mind was on fire—but he needed to do three things: take a piss, put on some clothes, and brush his teeth. He leaped out of bed, turned on the lights, unlocked the front door, and headed straight for the bathroom—took a leak in the sink as he brushed his teeth, and then put on a pair of dirty workout shorts he found on the bathroom floor. He had just finished rinsing out his mouth when he heard the front door open and close.

"Just take a seat," he called. "I'll be right out." He splashed some water on his face, dried himself off, and fixed his hair in the mirror.

Oh yeah—Bradley Cox was ready.

"Sorry," he said, coming out of the bathroom. "I was still pretty gross from the—"

Cox froze when saw the man in the ski mask coming for him—was about to scream, but the foul-smelling rag in his face silenced him immediately.

Chapter 70

Markham sat down beside his wife's grave and began to cry. The emotion came upon him without warning, frightening him with its rapidity, but soon he gave in, weeping openly until it passed.

He wiped his eyes on his sleeve and breathed deeply—gazed around at his surroundings and tried to imagine Michelle sitting there with him. The Elm Grove Cemetery had been one of their favorite places—an impeccably landscaped park set on the Mystic River less than a half-mile from the Aquarium. They often strolled here on Sunday mornings; actually had a picnic once by the water on a sunny-cool Sunday like today—a bit morbid, they agreed, but comforted themselves with the knowledge they were imitating their Victorian ancestors, whose Sunday outings often included a stroll through the local cemetery, too.

"Did I really used to talk like that?" Markham asked. "Words like *stroll* and *outing*?"

A breeze whispered its consent in the trees. Markham smiled.

"I don't know who that guy is anymore," he said. "Buried here with you, I guess. Weird thing is, I look back and I don't like him; don't pine away or long for him—don't even see him anymore, really. There's only you back there now—still whole, yes, but with these other pieces, like parts of a shadow that I assume is me. I think that's what's so hard now. More and more lately it seems like the shadow-pieces are trying to make you into shadow-pieces, too."

You think too much, he heard his wife say. *You'll always miss me, but the missing will change as you change. It's the cliché of not moving on that bothers you.*

"Yes," Markham said. "I think I thought my self-awareness of the cliché, the whole *I'm-going-to-join-the-FBI-to-avenge-my-wife's-death* syndrome would keep something alive—you, me maybe. Christ, I don't know anymore. It's all the same now in the shadows; something's lost in there—in the work, everything I'm doing. Gates called me out on it, you know—back at my town house in Quantico. Was one hackneyed phrase away from calling me a shell of a man. He settled for something subtler about my work defining who I am."

It's the cliché, Michelle repeated, *combined with the futility of knowing none of it will bring us closer together. Let it go. Clichés are clichés because they're true. Stop being so smart about it all.*

"I don't think you'd like the new digs," Markham said, smiling. "Hardwood floors, yes, but the rest is pretty standard contractor grade. No wainscoting or built-ins—none of the character of the old place. Nice pond in back, though. Lots of ducks. You'd like them."

Let it go.

Markham sat for a moment listening to the breeze, then asked, "Would you care for a stroll down by the river, madame?"

I'd be delighted, Michelle replied.

He rose to his feet and started off toward the water, when suddenly he felt his BlackBerry buzzing in his pocket. He stopped and checked it. An e-mail from Schaap.

Think this has anything to do with our boy?

was all it said, but a link had been inserted into the body of the message above the words Sent from my Verizon Black-Berry. Markham clicked it—an article from the *Raleigh Sun* dated Tuesday, November 1, 2005.

Halloween Theft at Taxidermy Studio

By Jonathan Vaughn—Staff Writer

DURHAM—Somebody might have had their heart set on being a lion this year for Halloween, say Durham Police, who are currently investigating a break-in at Rowley's Taxidermy Emporium.

According to Detective Charles Gray, chief investigator on the case, the robbery took place just after 3 a.m. this morning. "The thieves knew exactly what they were going for," said Gray. "They entered at the rear of the establishment and used their vehicle to break down the door and tripped the silent alarm. Unfortunately, they made off with the lion's head before we could get there." Gray went on to say that no other items were reported missing, and that the owner's safe, which was empty at the time of the robbery, remained untouched.

"That's the worst part," said Tom Rowley, owner of Rowley's Taxidermy Emporium. "Of all the things in the store, what they could hope to gain by taking old Leo is beyond me."

A family business owned and operated in the same location for over 50 years, Rowley's Taxidermy Emporium is part taxidermy studio, part museum, and the animals inside have become old friends to both locals and curious tourists alike. Leo, a monstrous African lion's head, had been a fixture on the wall behind Rowley's counter since the early 1980s.

"It was one of my father's most prized possessions," Rowley said. "[Leo] had been in our house for years and was a gift from a friend who he served with in World War Two. It was shot on a safari back in the 1930s. These kinds of things are getting harder and harder to find, and to this day a lot of the kids used to come in here just to look at him."

Durham Police Department spokeswoman Sheryl Parks said she does not believe the burglary to be related to the break-in at nearby Lynn's Craft Store in mid-October, in which thieves made off with over $1,000 in cash. Parks, however, did advise business owners in the area to install loud alarms. "It is our experience that an audible alarm is a better deterrent than a silent alarm."

"That sounds like a good idea," said Tom Rowley. "It's just sad that we live in a world where we have to worry about stuff like this."

Markham was about to read the e-mail again when Michelle interrupted him.

No shadow-pieces in there now, she said. *Everything so clear when you're working; everything so alive. So what if your work defines who you are? You might be a shell of a man, Sam Markham, but I'd still do you in a heartbeat.*

Markham laughed, swallowed the tears that threatened to follow, and powered off his BlackBerry.

Then he took his wife's hand and strolled with her down by the river.

Chapter 71

"Where the hell could he be?" George Kiernan muttered, glancing at his watch.

1:51 p.m.

At first he'd been furious and started his note session chewing ass as planned. But soon his fury turned to panic when the minutes ticked by and Bradley Cox still didn't show. The rest of his cast, including Cindy Smith, had gotten off light. He had bigger fish to fry now, and that son of a bitch Cox was going to get it. Kiernan would have him thrown out of the department unless he was dead, he told the rest of the cast, and sent a pair of assistant stage managers out looking for him.

But now, almost an hour later, the director was sorry he'd said that. Yeah, now George Kiernan was really worried about the kid. He took a deep breath and closed his eyes; he was sweating badly and could hardly keep the script in his hand from shaking as the costumer finished letting out the waistband on Bradley Cox's pants.

At 1:40 he'd resigned himself that it was going to happen, but only at 1:50 did he actually begin to believe it. *The show must go on*, he said to himself over and over—but that *he* should have to go on in the title role of Macbeth? That was something George Kiernan would never have dreamed of in a million years. It wasn't department policy to employ under-studies—not enough time for rehearsals, and the pool of actors was simply too small to cover even just the big roles adequately. And who wanted to get involved with parents bitching that their kid was entitled to go onstage "at least once" for all his hard work? Besides, George Kiernan couldn't remember a student in a major role ever missing a perfor-mance while he was chair. Sure, things come up once in a while during tech week—but after a show had already opened? After it was too late to adapt and switch people around? Well, that kind of thing just didn't happen in the Harriot University Department of Theatre and Dance.

But it *had* happened. And as George Kiernan caught a glimpse of himself in the mirror, he decided then and there that the department's understudy policy would have to change.

"There's no one at his apartment," the stage manager said, rushing into the dressing room out of breath. "The landlord got us in. There were some clothes on the bed, but his cell phone was gone and the dead bolt locks from the outside. His car is gone, too—looks like he just took off."

"Christ almighty," Kiernan muttered, his mind spinning. *Sure,* he thought, *Cox was a bit of a snake—a bit of a pussy, too—but just bailing on them after a shaky performance?* That didn't seem right.

"We called the police," the stage manager continued. "Under the circumstances, they said there's nothing they can do unless he's gone for twenty-four hours. And then a family member has to—"

"All right, all right," Kiernan said. "Tell the cast I'll be going on for him script-in-hand—no, tell them all to meet me backstage left. I'll break the news to them myself. Also, notify everybody on headset that I'll be making a curtain speech before the show begins. When I'm clear, just call everything else as you normally do."

The stage manager just stood there, frightened.

"Don't worry," Kiernan said, winking. "We'll get through it."

The stage manager nodded and was off.

Kiernan took another deep breath and asked the costumer if he could have a moment alone. She left, and the director sat down at the dressing table, thumbing absently through the script given to him by Cindy Smith. She'd already written down all of Cox's blocking in the scenes with Lady Macbeth, and Kiernan figured he could remember the rest of it from his own promptbook, which was too thick, too heavy to carry around onstage.

He studied his face in the mirror—felt his breathing level off and his heart slow down. And when the announcement from the stage manager came over the intercom, the director calmly walked out of Bradley Cox's dressing room and stood in the wings before his cast like a general.

Chapter 72

Cindy held Edmund Lambert's hand as Kiernan laid out the battle plan for the matinee. With the absence of Cox, she'd grown nervous, but at the same time was beyond excited at being so close to Edmund—especially since he'd been waiting for her outside her dressing room when she arrived at the theater. They'd spoken to one another only briefly, but kissed long enough for her to know that everything was all right again.

"Now you need to focus," he'd said, pulling away. "But I'll be watching."

It was going to be the best show yet, Cindy thought, and felt beyond ecstatic when she played over in her mind how Edmund had looked at her.

But now when he looked at her he seemed agitated. And he kept glancing at his BlackBerry as Kiernan gave them a pep talk about focus and teamwork.

"I thought he would have canceled the show," Edmund said as Kiernan made his curtain speech. "Or at least the photo call."

He actually seemed disappointed, Cindy thought.

"Not George Kiernan," she said. "The show must go on. Just don't get jealous in that part where Macbeth tries to kiss me, okay? Even though it's George Kiernan, I'll still try my hardest to resist."

Edmund smiled thinly. Cindy kissed him and then ran to places for the opening scene—a silly scene, Cindy had always thought, in which the director had the Witches arrange all the characters like pieces on a chessboard. Edmund thought it was a silly scene, too, she learned at the cast party—just one of the many things they had in common. "A scene like that takes Macbeth's fate out of his hands," he'd said. "If only he'd read the messages correctly things wouldn't have turned out so badly for him."

For some reason talking like that with Edmund had turned her on.

His speech finished, Kiernan stepped back into the wings and took his place with the rest of the cast—directly opposite Cindy on the other side of the stage. He gave her a thumbs-up and she replied in kind. The audience was still murmuring as the music started and the lights dimmed, and Cindy felt as if the air were charged with electricity, as if she would explode from excitement at any moment. Yeah, she thought, in a sick way she was thrilled all this was happening.

"This is fucked up about Bradley," whispered the actor playing Macduff.

"Yeah," replied Jonathan, winner of the Perils of Inbreeding Award. "Maybe Vlad got him."

"Or maybe Lambert finally finished the job."

The two boys snickered, and Cindy told them to shut the hell up.

Yeah, even though it was Bradley Cox they were dissing, a comment like that was beyond uncalled for.

Chapter 73

Markham landed in Raleigh about twenty minutes early. As the plane taxied down the runway, he turned on his cell phone to find the text message from Andy Schaap already waiting for him.

Checking on names, the message read. Might be out of range 4 a while, but let me know when u land. Will call u when I get back to the RA l8r.

"Enough with this nonsense," Markham said, and promptly dialed his partner's number.

It rang only twice and then went straight into voice mail.

"I'm back," Markham said. "Got your article about the lion's head. Good work, and I'll follow up at the taxidermy shop myself first thing tomorrow. There are some other things I want to discuss with you. Don't know if you read the latest updates, but the set list from Rodriguez's CD was uploaded into Sentinel last night. I think there might be a connection with one of the songs in particular—"Dark in the Day" by that eighties band High Risk. Only going with my gut, but I'd like to bounce a couple of things off you. Let's

plan on dinner at the Dubliner around seven. Call me back
ASAP."

He hung up feeling on edge, but by the time he reached
his TrailBlazer he was furious. It didn't make sense,
Markham thought, this frustration with his NCAVC coordinator. Perhaps he might feel better after a stop at the Resident Agency to see what Andy Schaap was up to.

Still, something was off. Something was wrong.

Markham could feel it.

Chapter 74

KISS's "Detroit Rock City" kicked in just as the General turned off the Mustang's ignition, and for a moment he thought he'd tripped an alarm or something. He glanced down at the BlackBerry—the name Sam Markham in bright white letters on the screen—and waited patiently for the song to stop. And when it did, the General gazed across the parking lot to the apartment building where the famous Quantico profiler was staying.

The General had reconned the Resident Agency earlier that morning; had to circle the outside lot only once to realize it was too risky to grab out Markham there. His apartment would be much better. The General had found the address on Schaap's computer, but after he left the theater he decided to first drive back to the farmhouse to check on the progress there. Satisfied, the General switched his pickup for Bradley Cox's Mustang and arrived at the apartment building forty-five minutes later. The General hoped Markham had gotten the e-mail he'd sent from Schaap's BlackBerry; hoped he'd stop first at the taxidermy shop or perhaps the

Resident Agency before coming home. That was important, for the General's plan would only work if Markham got home after dark.

Of course, as with the tattoo parlor, the FBI would find nothing at the taxidermy shop. The General was always careful not to leave any fingerprints, but the idea of sending Markham on a wild-goose chase excited him. He was tempted to send him another article or a text message, but knew he could play his little game only for so long before the FBI agent caught on. Indeed, the General suspected the game might already be over when he heard the voice mail notification on the BlackBerry. After all, Markham would grow suspicious when he didn't hear from his partner in person.

He needed to be careful. There was no room for mistakes, and time was running short. The General had seen it all in the doorway.

Andrew J. Schaap had proved invaluable. The Prince was no longer angry with the General. He couldn't come right out and say so (as the General suspected, such communication took up too much of the doorway's power), but the General could tell from the Prince's visions that he had forgiven him. Of course, Edmund Lambert's mother was nowhere to be seen, but the Prince *did* show him Ereshkigal. She was most certainly part of the equation now. But exactly how she fit in, the General still wasn't sure—he could only see himself running with her across the smoking battlefields. However, in the part of his brain that he could still keep hidden from the Prince, the General felt confident that he would be able to save his mother in the end. He didn't know where she was—there was still so much about Hell that he didn't understand—but knew that Ereshkigal would help him. Plus, the fact that the Prince would actually expect him and Ereshkigal to be together filled him with hope. Perhaps they could conspire behind his back. Perhaps she knew where the Prince had taken his mother. Perhaps, if the General promised to restore her to her throne she could—

He was getting ahead of himself again. That kind of thinking needed to go on the back burner for now. The equation must take precedence, and there was still time to balance it. The Prince had shown him this in his visions. And if everything went according to plan, as of tomorrow more than half of the nine would be complete. After that, and once Ereshkigal had joined with him—the General would eventually be told what to do next.

After all, eventually had always been part of the equation.

First things first, the General said to himself, and he fished out a pair of binoculars from the glove compartment. Even though George Kiernan had messed things up for him by not canceling the show, he needed to take care of business here in Raleigh first.

He'd already telephoned Doug Jennings—told him his aunt had been in a car accident and that he wouldn't be able to make the photo call. Then he left Cindy a voice mail saying would call her once he got his aunt home from the hospital. He had only a short window before Markham would come looking for his partner along with his friends, so it was critical that he be alone for what the Prince had in store for him.

Besides, despite the scene he had laid out in Cox's apartment, the General knew it was only a matter of time before the police began questioning people. They would question everyone and would eventually get to Edmund Lambert. In that respect, the variable of eventually would not bode well for the equation.

True, even the Prince had no idea how long it would take before the police, and then the FBI, would start trying to connect Cox's disappearance to Vlad the Impaler. But this Sam Markham character knew the murders had nothing to do with Vlad the Impaler; and judging from the FBI's military profile for the killer, any interaction with the authorities was too risky for the former 187th Infantry Screaming Eagle. And that's what had the General worried.

"But the seal-tailed lion left the FBI a present back in Greenville," the General said, raising the binoculars to his eyes. "If they find it before I get to Markham, I'll have to consult the Prince again. Either way, we'll know exactly when the FBI figures out Andrew J. Schaap is missing."

The General fingered the focus knob and trained the binoculars on Sam Markham's front door. And in an instant he felt his worry drain away; for although there was still so much about the Prince's plan that had yet to be revealed to him, one thing was certain:

Sam Markham was now part of the equation, too.

Chapter 75

Markham arrived at the Resident Agency to find Andy Schaap's office empty. He flicked on the light and sat at his desk—stared grimly at the scattered papers before him and picked up a stack with a yellow Post-it note on top.

First batch just came in, the note read. Markham stuck the Post-it to Schaap's computer screen. It was a fax from the Marines—a list of Iraq War veterans from units that fit Dr. Underhill's insignia profile, and who had undergone psychiatric counseling before, during, and after tours of duty beginning in April of 2003 through June of 2004.

Markham looked at the time and date stamp.

"Yesterday afternoon," he muttered.

He found two more faxes: another from the Marines and one from the Army. Both were stamped from earlier that morning and had been tucked underneath the first fax.

Markham ruffled absently through the other lists of servicemen that Schaap had strewn across his desk—faxes and printouts and PDFs from all the branches of the U.S. Armed Forces. There were some other lists, too, and Markham quickly deduced that Schaap's computer program had begun priori-

tizing the names according to various criteria. On one of the
lists, Markham discovered, Schaap had narrowed down
the names further by inputting birthdays that fell under the
astrological sign of Leo.

Still, there were a lot of names—hundreds of them.

"Oh, it's you," said a voice, and Markham looked up,
startled.

It was Big Joe the Sox Fan Connelly. He stood in the
doorway.

"Sorry, Sam," he said. "I thought you were Schaap. Another batch of those medical records just came in. Air Force
is being a bit of a bitch, though."

He handed Markham the fax.

"You know where Schaap is?" Markham asked.

"I haven't seen him since before noon yesterday. Said
we'd start checking the lists against each other when you got
back."

"You know if he checked out the taxidermy shop?"

"Taxidermy shop?"

"Schaap sent me an article this morning about the theft of
a lion head over in Durham. Happened in November of last
year. He didn't tell you about it?"

"I haven't seen him today. Something you want my team
to look into?"

"No, no, I plan on heading out there tomorrow."

"Tech will have the Google Earth setup ready for us tomorrow morning," Big Joe said. "Schaap's already begun
narrowing down his lists by probability of location. Wants to
divvy up some addresses and have our boots on the ground
by noon."

Markham nodded.

"I'm gonna jet now if you don't need anything. Kid's got
a soccer game."

Markham gave him a thumbs-up, and Joe left. He sat
there for a moment staring at the yellow Post-it on Schaap's

screen. He returned the note to its proper place, then went into his office and turned on his computer—signed into Sentinel and saw that Schaap had not updated anything since Friday.

Markham sat back in his chair and closed his eyes—hundreds of names, unreadable, but scrolling upward, white on black like credits at the end of a movie.

"What are you up to, Andy Schaap?" he whispered.

Chapter 76

Bradley Cox felt as if his head were about to spin off his neck—the deafening pump of the Clone Six song over and over again, the flash of the strobe light threatening to drive him insane.

He was naked and strapped to a dentist's chair in the man's cellar—the cold, the writing all over his body, the newspaper articles taped to the wall. And his nose still hurt from where the man rammed him with the rag. However, along with his feelings of encroaching madness, Bradley Cox's senses were sharp. And, despite the swelling, his nose still worked fine; could smell the chemicals and taste the bitterness in the back of his throat. He could also smell Pine-Sol and something else—something faint, but foul and rotting underneath it all. He found that focusing on the smells helped him keep it together. He would need to have his wits about him when the motherfucker in the ski mask returned.

"How could you think? How could you think?
Tell me how could you think, I'd let you get away?"

Despite the ski mask and the bloody tattoo on his chest, Bradley Cox knew who'd come for him—knew it as soon as he woke up and the son of a bitch asked: "Will you know him when he comes for you?"

Cox had recognized that slow Southern drawl at once—but somehow, amid his growing terror, he was able to heed the advice of a voice inside his head. *Stay calm, Bradley,* it whispered. *As long as he thinks you can't identify him to the police you still have a chance.*

Cox had pleaded to be let go—repeated over and over that he had no idea what the man in the ski mask was talking about—but the dude had kept asking:

"Will you *know* him when he *comes* for you?"

"Yes," Cox had said finally, exhausted. "Whoever you want me to know I'll know, okay? Just let me go!"

"And do you accept your mission?"

"What the fuck are you—"

"Do you *accept* your *mission*?"

"I don't know what the fuck you're talking about!"

"The nine to three," the man had said, pointing to the large numbers on either side of the chamber's doorway. "The three to one. Do you see them?"

"Yes," Cox had whimpered, "but I—"

"You are the nine, I am the three. You are the three and I am the one. Your destiny is written all around you, in the stars. The equation is in everything and always was. It is why you must accept. Do you understand?"

"I'm not accepting shit, you sick motherfucker!"

The man in the ski mask had deflated for a moment, seemed to sigh, and quickly left.

A minute later he returned with the razor blade.

Bradley Cox gritted his teeth as the searing pain in his chest reminded him what the man in the ski mask had done. The man in the ski mask—a.k.a Edmund Lambert, a.k.a

Vlad the Impaler. The fucking symbols he'd written all over his body, just like the ones on the Internet—*it had to be him!*

However, through all his hours of screaming—even through his ordeal with the razor blade—Bradley Cox had not let on that he knew the identity of his captor. A childhood spent watching countless episodes of *America's Most Wanted* and *Unsolved Mysteries* with his father had taught him that.

As long as Lambert doesn't know I'm on to him, he kept repeating to himself, *I still have a chance.*

But Cox hadn't seen Edmund Lambert for hours, and sensed that he was gone now not just from the cellar, but from the house above it, too. About twenty versions of the song ago, he heard an alarm go off briefly upstairs. Shortly afterwards, he saw a figure standing in the darkened hallway. He wasn't exactly sure when the figure disappeared, but in the transition between the eighties version and the Clone Six cover he heard the alarm again and a door slamming. Everything upstairs had been quiet in the transitions since then. And thank God there were no more sounds of hammering and power tools coming from the other room; no more flashes of yellow light and little breezes coming from the darkened hallway, either.

Bradley Cox had read all about Vlad and his victims on the Internet, and knew damn well what Edmund Lambert had in store from him when he returned. And there was no doubt that Edmund Lambert would return—the blood, the stinging pain in his chest where the Impaler had carved him up made that abundantly clear.

That had been another lifetime ago, it seemed, and the pain in his chest was nothing compared to the pain in his left wrist where the leather strap bore into it. But Bradley Cox had himself to blame for that. He'd been twisting and pulling on it for hours now; and as he gave his wrist another strong tug, the young man felt his thumb pop out of its socket.

He howled in agony, but paused only briefly to catch his breath before he began pulling again, twisting and squirming as the wounds on his chest cracked open. He could feel the blood trickling down to his naked groin, but rather than cry out, Bradley Cox began to laugh.

"How could you think? How could you think?
Tell me how could think I'd let you get away?"

Perhaps he was going insane; perhaps his senses weren't as sharp as he'd thought they were. But through all the pain, he could swear the strap around his wrist suddenly felt looser.

Chapter 77

It was almost eight o'clock when the black SUV pulled into a spot in front of Sam Markham's apartment building. The General recognized it as the same make and model as Andrew J. Schaap's, but only when it came to a complete stop and the driver emerged was he sure it belonged to Sam Markham.

The General recognized him immediately—thought he looked shorter in person than in his picture, and felt a surge of excitement at the thought of what he and the Prince had in store for him.

In this Sam Markham they had found the ultimate soldier. Someone who feared the Prince as much as those who had worshipped him in the old days. Someone who understood the inevitability of the Prince's return almost as much as the General himself. And surely this Markham was a gift of destiny; surely his delivery to the Prince via the randomness of the FBI agent's lists was no accident. It was almost too good to be true; and the thought of the power the Prince would draw from this man's service made his doorway tingle beneath the bandages.

Yes, the wound between the 9 and the 3 was already heal-ing up nicely.

The General followed Markham with his binoculars until he disappeared into the apartment building. It had grown darker, but the General would wait a while longer. He low-ered the binoculars and gazed down at Andrew J. Schaap's BlackBerry. At that moment, his own cell phone began ring-ing on the seat beside him. He picked it up and read the name on the screen: Cindy Smith.

The General answered as Edmund Lambert. "Hi, Cindy."

"Hi, Edmund. How's your aunt doing?"

"Fine. Still a bit shaken up, but she's sleeping now. My uncle is here, too, so I'll be taking off shortly."

"That's good news."

"Yes, it is. Any word on Bradley?"

"No," Cindy said. "No one's heard from him all day. Looks like he just bolted after last night's show—car is gone and everything. I hope he's okay."

"I hope so, too," Edmund said. "Did the show and the photo call go well?"

"Yes, but it was weird playing opposite George Kiernan. The show ended up being pretty good, actually. We even got a standing ovation, but the whole thing seems like a dream. Everything, I mean—the show, me and you, what happened the other night. You think we can talk about it?"

"Of course. How about I give you call when I get settled back at the house?"

"That'd be awesome, yeah."

"But it might be late, okay? I still have some things I need to do."

"Okay. Talk to you later."

"Yes, you will. Good-bye, Cindy."

Edmund picked up the BlackBerry and held it up next to

his cell phone—stroked each of them with his thumbs and smiled. He was the General again.

"Sam Markham has no idea his partner is even missing," he said. "If he did, Ereshkigal would have told us."

Chapter 78

Markham sat at his kitchen table with the lists spread out before him like a big flower. He'd grown frustrated with the sheer number of suspects—knew that Schaap had to be working from a more specific list—and had just picked up his BlackBerry to call him when the theme from *Rocky* sounded off in his hand. He looked at his watch—*9:12 p.m.*—and felt a wave of relief when he saw the name on the BlackBerry's screen.

Schaap.

"Finally," Markham answered. "Where the hell are you?"

"Watching you from the sky, Agent Markham," said the voice on the other end.

Markham froze, his stomach dropping into his shoes.

"Schaap?" he said weakly, but the man on the other end only laughed and said:

"His body is the doorway."

The voice was deep and thick with a Southern drawl, and even as Markham's mind began to spin with "Dark in the

Day" and the thousand reasons as to why this couldn't be happening, all at once he knew that Andy Schaap had stumbled onto the Impaler.

"Who is this?" Markham asked, wincing at the futility of his question.

"I am the three," said the man on the other end, "but you are the nine. Will you know him when he comes for you, Agent Markham?"

Markham felt his words stick in his throat—managed to squeak out, "What have you done with Schaap?"—but the man on the other end only laughed.

"His *body* is the *doorway*," he said, his inflection like a child's. Markham felt suddenly as if he would vomit. He swallowed hard, was about to speak, when the voice in his ear said: "But there's still time, Agent Markham. If you hurry, if you truly understand the equation, you'll be allowed to touch the doorway, too."

"What have you done to Schaap?!" Markham screamed, but got only the blinking call timer for an answer.

And then he was moving.

He ran into the bedroom and grabbed his gun—punched a number on his BlackBerry and put on his Windbreaker.

"This is Markham," he shouted. He was back in the kitchen now, gathering up the lists. "Andy Schaap is in trouble. Get the tech unit to put a trace on his vehicle. Get them on his cell signal, too, and get the plate number into the local systems ASAP. I'm on my way back to the RA now."

Markham hung up and slipped the paperwork into his briefcase.

He was out the door in a streak; dashed down the front steps and reached his TrailBlazer in a matter of seconds— when out of nowhere he felt a searing pain shoot across the back of his skull.

He watched his BlackBerry and his briefcase fall from his fingers in slow motion; saw himself stumbling sideways as the cars and the streetlights and the shadows swirled about him and grew blurry.

But Sam Markham stayed on his feet long enough to see the man in the ski mask stuff the smelly rag in his face.

"Textbook," he heard Alan Gates say somewhere far away. Then everything went black.

Chapter 79

By ten o'clock that evening, the two blocks of Lewis Street between Third and Fifth had been cordoned off. The residents were ordered to evacuate, and the parking lot across the street from Bradley Cox's apartment building was completely surrounded by marked and unmarked vehicles.

A SWAT team leader gave the signal, and he and two other officers, weapons drawn, cautiously approached the black TrailBlazer in tactical formation. They looked first into the rear window, then into the front seat. And after a tense thirty seconds, the officer on the driver's side called out, "Clear!"

A collective sigh of relief was heard as the members of the SWAT team lowered their weapons.

Looking on from across the street, just a few feet from Bradley Cox's front door, an FBI agent from the Greenville Resident Agency said to his partner, "Call it in to Raleigh."

The other agent began dialing as the SWAT team leader tried the door handle. It was locked. Another signal, and a local police officer with a Slim Jim rushed up to the Trail-Blazer and slipped it down into the driver's side door.

"The car's clear," said the FBI agent into his BlackBerry. "But there's still no sign of Special Agent Schaap."

The FBI agent listened to the tech specialist on the other end. Something about Schaap's BlackBerry being off the grid; something about it taking time to get the tower records.

Then he saw the TrailBlazer's door open.

Even from where he was standing he could hear the series of loud clicks across the street. The tech specialist had gone on to say something about Sam Markham being unreachable, too—when suddenly the explosion sent the FBI agent's BlackBerry flying from his hand.

Chapter 80

Cindy was just stepping out of the shower when she felt the tiles rumble beneath her feet. *A thunderstorm's coming,* she thought, and dismissed the distant boom at once.

Fifteen minutes later she was in her pajamas, lying on her bed with her biology book, when her mother knocked on her door.

"Yeah?"

"You need to see this," her mother said, entering. She was dressed in her nurse's scrubs—graveyard shift this weekend, Cindy suddenly remembered.

"You're going to be late," Cindy said, and was about to complain that she needed to study, when the look on her mother's face changed her tune at once.

"What is it, Mom?" she asked, but her mother had already clicked on the TV atop her dresser—immediately changed the channel from VH1 to a local station and sat beside Cindy on the bed.

"This happened near the Theatre building," she said. "Over on Lewis Street."

Cindy listened in shock as the reporter, a pretty woman

with blond hair, recounted what the press knew thus far: something about a missing FBI vehicle, a parking lot, and an explosion; unconfirmed reports of at least four people dead, more people injured, shattered windows, a nearby resident said *this*, a nearby resident said *that*—

"Bradley Cox lives on that street," Cindy said suddenly.

"The boy playing Macbeth?"

"Uh-huh."

"You don't think this has anything to do with him not showing up today, do you?"

"I don't know," Cindy said.

"I need to get moving, honey," her mother said, rising. "I'm late, and if what they're saying is true, they're going to need me in the emergency room. Promise me you won't go down there, will you?"

"I promise."

"I love you," said her mother, kissing her forehead.

"Love you, too," Cindy replied absently, eyes glued to the TV. She didn't hear her mother leave; had no idea how long she'd been sitting there watching the news report, when her cell phone startled her from her trance.

She reached for it, saw that the call was from Amy Pratt, and let it roll over into voice mail—waited patiently for the ding, then listened to Amy's message. Typical Amy blabbering and nothing more to add than what she'd already learned from TV.

"Edmund," Cindy muttered. "I wonder if Edmund knows."

She dialed his number—let it ring and ring—and felt her stomach sink when the call went into voice mail. She left him a message—sent him a text, too—and began pacing her room, faster and faster as the minutes ticked away with no reply.

She had to get out of there; couldn't bear the idea of being alone and wanted nothing more than to watch the news with Edmund Lambert by her side. Something was wrong. The explosion of the FBI vehicle on Bradley Cox's street, the young actor's disappearance—it was all connected. Cindy could feel it.

"Fuck this," she said, and changed out of her pajamas into a pair of jeans and a Harriot T-shirt. She was downstairs and ready to go in less than a minute—grabbed her keys from the kitchen table, her denim jacket from the den, and dashed outside to her car.

Once inside, Cindy accidentally dropped her keys, cursed herself for being such a klutz, and ran her hand back and forth between the seat and the shift column. She reached under the driver's seat and found them—inserted the Pontiac's key into the ignition—but the car refused to turn over.

"Come on, Daddy's piece of shit!" she cried, turning the key and pumping the gas until finally the old Sunfire's engine sputtered to life. She didn't wait for it to warm up, just threw the shift into reverse and backed down the driveway.

As she drove out of her neighborhood and headed for the highway, Cindy felt not the slightest bit guilty about breaking her promise to her mother.

After all, she'd only promised not to go down to the scene of the explosion.

She'd said nothing about going to Edmund Lambert's.

Chapter 81

The General had just pulled Sam Markham from the Mustang's trunk and hoisted him over his shoulder when he felt his cell phone buzzing in his back pocket. He'd already destroyed the FBI agents' BlackBerrys and tossed them along with Markham's briefcase in a Dumpster on his way back to Wilson. They wouldn't be able to trace anything to him now—at least not until his work in the farmhouse was finished.

The General let the call buzz into voice mail. Other than the alarm company, only two people had his cell phone number now. And since he couldn't imagine why Doug Jennings would be calling him at this hour, he knew the call had to be from Ereshkigal.

The General closed the trunk and carried Markham from the horse barn—chained the doors from the outside with one hand, then reached into his pocket. He was about to check his message when the incoming text told him everything he needed to know.

Something's happened, it read. On the news now, an explosion near Bradley's apt. Please call me back asap. I'm worried and need 2 talk. Cindy

The General smiled.

The FBI had found Andrew J. Schaap's TrailBlazer and the little improvised explosive device that the General had rigged for them—courtesy of the 101st Airborne and almost ten months in Tal Afar learning from Iraqi insurgents. Even if the bomb hadn't gone off, its discovery would have made the news anyway. But how fitting, he thought, that Ereshkigal should be the one to notify him. After all, hadn't the Prince told him that Ereshkigal was part of the equation now?

Ereshkigal will help us, his mother had said, too—but the General could not preoccupy himself with that part of the equation now. He mustn't let on to the Prince that his mother was still the center of it all, mustn't even think it. He had to keep up appearances; had to put all his energy into serving the Prince. The answer as to how he would save his mother would come to him eventually—just as the real reason for the IEDs had come to him eventually, too.

The General had actually built the IEDs the previous fall: a pair of small but powerful hydrogen peroxide–based bombs similar to the ones used in the London terror attacks of 2005. The General wasn't sure why the Prince had originally wanted him to build the bombs after learning of the terror attacks, and had since stored them in the old horse barn. Back then, the General still had to decipher the Prince's messages without the doorway and the lion's head—from the newspaper and Internet articles and his research in the Harriot library. And until this business with Markham and the FBI, the General had planned on detonating the bombs with his home security system—after the Prince had returned, of course; a little surprise for the authorities once he had no more need of the farmhouse.

But then Andrew J. Schaap entered into the equation, and the General understood almost immediately why the Prince had him prepare the IEDs so far in advance. The Prince most certainly must have foreseen something like this occurring. Yes, the General thought, the Prince never ceased to amaze and terrify him with his power. And more than ever now, the General understood that he must never underestimate or second-guess the Prince again.

It hadn't taken the General long to rewire the homemade detonators to the TrailBlazer's battery and then rig them to be triggered by the SUV's electric locking mechanism. There had been no need to hide the bombs, either, and the General just left them in a pair of black duffel bags on the floor behind the front seats. The TrailBlazer's black interior and tinted windows would camouflage them nicely. Pretty amateurish by today's standards, he thought—a tape-and-bubblegum hack job at which most Iraqi insurgents would probably thumb their noses.

But now all that didn't matter; and, now that the General had Sam Markham, the little warning he'd given himself was moot. He didn't have to worry about the authorities surprising him and spoiling his plans just yet. The explosion, the disappearances of Schaap and Markham and Cox should keep the FBI busy long enough for the General to finish his business at the farmhouse. After that, the Prince would tell him where to go and what to do next to complete the nine.

The General returned his cell phone to his back pocket and made his way toward the house. He would call Ereshki-gal later—after he had consulted with the Prince.

And, of course, after he had finished with Sam Markham.

Chapter 82

What are you going to do if he isn't home? asked the voice in her head. *Are you just going to sit in his driveway and wait for him like the desperate stalker you are?*

"Shut up," Cindy said. But another voice—a voice that sounded a lot like Amy Pratt's—replied, *Maybe I will.*

The real question, said the first voice, *is what are you going to do if your handsome soldier is home?*

Cindy had no answer.

OCD stalker, chimed both voices in unison, and Cindy pumped up the volume on the radio. It was a Led Zeppelin song. Cindy couldn't remember its name. *All their titles have nothing to do with the lyrics,* she thought, and began racking her brain for the answer. She became irritated when she couldn't find it, but was nonetheless thankful that the voices in her head were finally silent.

Cindy took the back roads and turned onto Route 264 just outside town. She already knew the way to Edmund Lambert's house—had unconsciously memorized the directions from all the time she spent staring down at his property on

Google Earth. If she hurried, she figured she could make it in about half an hour.

But what would she do once she got there? And what was it about this Edmund Lambert that made her act so crazy; made her drive out, uninvited, to his house in the middle of nowhere so late at night?

Again, Cindy had no answer. Only a scene from an imaginary movie: a modern-day *Gone with the Wind* in which she saw herself rushing down a flight of stairs into Edmund Lambert's arms—spinning kisses and rustling petticoats, then mad, passionate lovemaking on an Oriental rug as the music swelled around them.

The Led Zeppelin song fit perfectly.

Led Zeppelin? asked Amy Pratt in her head. *Scarlett O'Hara and Rhett Butler doing it to Led Zeppelin?*

Impulsively, Cindy changed the station—old school hip-hop, Naughty By Nature's "OPP."

Cindy let out a laugh and pumped the volume louder. It had to be fate, she thought—Bradley Cox, the explosion, Scarlett O'Hara all at once a distant memory of a role she once played back in Greenville.

"You down with *OCD*?" Cindy sang. *"Yeah, you know me!"*

Oh yeah, Cindy Smith was *beyond* obsessed.

Chapter 83

The General laid Markham on the kitchen table, pulled back his eyelids, and studied his pupils. Still unconscious—*Will be for a while*, he thought—but best to bind his hands and feet and leave him in the workroom while he attended to Cox.

True, the young man hadn't been in the chair as long as the other soldiers, but the General hoped he would understand and be ready to accept his mission nonetheless. If not, the General would have to *make* him understand. Unlike the others, there wasn't enough time now to indulge his limited intellect.

The General smiled as the song transitioned beneath his feet, and set his handgun on the kitchen counter next to the pair of Glocks he'd taken from the FBI agents. Then he tied Markham's hands and feet together with the length of clothesline he'd set on the table before leaving.

Be a good boy and carry that rope for me, okay?

C'est mieux d'oublier. . . .

Everything was going according to the Prince's new plan; and when Markham was secure, the General washed his hands and splashed his face with cold water. He could feel the wound on his chest had split open again; could see that it had bled through the gauze and was beginning to spot his light-blue button-down shirt. There would be more blood, yes, but still he would have to change into his priestly robes. The ceremony of things demanded it.

The General toweled off his face and crossed to the cellar door—a heavy, steel door with recessed hinges and two dead bolts that he had installed himself. He unlocked them, the music instantly louder as he opened the door—but something was off; something about the light on the stairs was—

And then the naked man was coming for him.

Bradley Cox, smeared with sweat and blood, rushed up the cellar stairs shrieking like a cat—his left hand outstretched before him, his right holding a small ax high above his head. The General backed away at once—didn't have time to wonder how Cox escaped and found the ax in the workroom—and moved his head just in time to avoid the downward strike. But the blade caught him on his right pectoral muscle—sliced through his shirt, the gauze, and took out a nice chunk of the tattooed 9 underneath.

The General let out a grunt but kept moving—ducked a sideward swipe to his head and then brought his fist up hard on Cox's jaw. The young man cried out and staggered backwards—tried to swing the ax again—but the General caught his arm and hyperextended it at the elbow. A loud snap echoed through the kitchen, and Bradley Cox dropped the ax, howling in pain. The General grabbed him by the face and slammed him against the wall.

"I'm gonna kill you, Lambert!" Cox cried, slumping hysterically to the floor—but before he could recover, the General picked up the ax and swung it down hard. Cox raised his left hand just in time, and the General caught him on the forearm with the wooden handle. Another snap as the bones shattered, and the General brought down the ax again, this time on the young man's right shoulder—chopped through his trapezius and split his collarbone like it was a stick of kindling wood.

Bradley Cox's screams shook the entire house, both his arms useless now as he flailed about on the floor—but the General did not pause. He pulled out the ax and tossed it onto the kitchen table, the blood from the young man's wound spraying his jeans as he picked him up by the hair and threw him headfirst down the cellar stairs.

Bradley Cox was barely conscious when the General reached him—but conscious enough, the General thought, to understand what was coming next.

"You will know him when he comes for you," the General said as he dragged him down the darkened hallway. "You are part of the nine, and there is no turning back from your mission now."

Chapter 84

Music—that song, "Dark in the Day"—and screaming.
No. Not real. Something from a dream. Can't see the pic-
tures. Only silence now and big gaps of black behind me.
Time. Moving forward. I have returned, but it's raining. . . .

Markham's eyes fluttered open to a haze of yellow light.
He was on his side; felt something hard beneath his right
shoulder, and could hear the sound of running water.

Crappy hotel mattresses, he thought. *Someone in the*
shower—Michelle?

He licked his lips and swallowed hard. His throat was
parched and his mouth tasted like chemicals. He was about
to reach for the glass of water on the nightstand, but in the
next moment the pain kicked in at the base of his skull. He
couldn't touch it; couldn't move his arm—his wrists for
some reason felt glued together.

Groggily, he turned his head, and the yellow haze blurred
into movement—into what looked like an arm and pair of
buttocks pulsing out at him from the shadows.

What the hell is going on?

Then in a rush his vision cleared—his heart pounding instantly at his ribs as everything came back to him. The call from Schaap, the voice on the other end, the blow on the back of his head when he foolishly rushed out to his car.

He remembered it all.

Schaap, Markham thought. *Where the hell is Schaap?*

More body parts from the shadows. Yes, there, in the far corner of the room about fifteen feet away, Markham could make out a man's muscular back; could see the water reflected on his flesh in the dim yellowy light.

The Impaler, Markham said to himself. *The Impaler tricked me—*

Suddenly, the man in the corner threw his head back and turned. Markham's heart leaped into his throat as his eyes blinked shut. Surely he'd been caught, he thought—but the water continued to run and the sounds remained the same. He cracked open his left eye. In the shadows, he could see only a small portion of the man's profile, the rest of his face obscured by his arm. He held a garden hose above his head, the water washing over him and down his chest. There was a large tattoo on that chest. Markham could see it clearly— what appeared to be two elongated rectangles, standing upright and side by side, one decorated with the number *9*, the other with the number *3*.

"His body is the doorway," the Impaler had said on the phone.

The tattoo—a pair of doors! Nine stars in Leo, three in Leo Minor—

"I am the three, but you are the nine."

His body is the doorway!

"Will you know him when he comes for you?"

Schaap! Markham cried out in his mind—but then the doorway on the man's chest seemed to ooze something black—a thick line of goo between the *9* and the *3* that disappeared under the water, only to return again when the man hosed off his head. Markham could see a smaller gash through the top of the 9, too.

He's wounded, he thought. *Bleeding badly.*

The Impaler turned his back again.

Daring to move only his eyes, Markham scanned what little he could. Yes, he had to be in the Impaler's workshop. The tools, the unfinished two-by-fours propped against the wall. And he was elevated—*Tied down on some kind of workbench*—but still dressed. That was good. That meant the Impaler hadn't started on him yet. That meant—

Then Markham saw the chains. He followed them from the pulley that dangled above the Impaler's head, up through the ceiling beams to a winch on the wall next to the slop sink. The sound of the water traveling down the drain seemed suddenly amplified, and Markham understood all at once what the chains were for—felt his stomach flip when he imagined Andy Schaap dangling upside down, his blood draining into the floor. He'd seen it before—the Morales case, pictures of what the drug cartels did to their enemies—but that might not have happened. Schaap might still be alive. There was nothing in the autopsy reports about the Impaler bleeding out his victims—

I've got to find Schaap!

Markham told himself to stay calm; if the Impaler knew he was awake he was a dead man. And as if reading his mind, the Impaler shut off the water and began to turn toward him. Markham closed his eyes—could hear movement, the Impaler toweling himself off, he assumed—then silence, followed by what sounded like masking tape being peeled and snipped from a roll.

His wound, Markham said to himself. *He must be bandaging his wound.*

More movement now—the Impaler dressing—and despite his terror Markham had to fight the urge to steal a look at the man's face. Oh yes, he wanted to get a good look at that face so, so badly!

Markham felt a cool breeze rush past, and after a moment heard a clanging sound coming from another part of the cellar. He cracked open his eyes and quickly scanned his body. He was tied up, but not down to anything; he could roll over onto his back if he wished. Yes, he had to be in the Impaler's cellar—the cement walls, the trickling sound of the blood and water running down the floor drain.

But what to do, what to do?!!

Footsteps approached again and Markham shut his eyes—another cool breeze and the sense of movement behind him. His mind spun furiously; he was starting to panic, felt as if at any second he would open his eyes and try to bolt—when all of a sudden he felt the Impaler's arms slipping underneath his torso.

Markham's muscles tensed. He thought surely the Impaler had to have felt them tense, too—but a moment later he was being lifted off the workbench.

I'm to be next, he thought. *Whatever the Impaler did to the others before he skewered them he intends to do to me. I've got to make a break for it!*

No! cried the voice in his head. *Stay calm! The Impaler kept the others alive for days. He will undress you to write on you—will most likely untie you, too. The window will be short, but you can surprise him if you—*

Out of nowhere came a loud buzzing noise, like an old alarm clock, echoing throughout the cellar. Markham flinched, but at the exact same time the Impaler flinched, too. That's what saved him, he realized, and the two of them froze together.

Nothing—only the Impaler listening, breathing—and then Markham felt himself being lowered back down onto the workbench.

Movement again, behind him, and after a brief silence

Markham thought he heard talking coming from another part of the cellar. He cracked open his eyes and cocked his ear, straining to hear.

Another loud buzz, this one longer, and Markham flinched again.

"No!" a voice cried. *"The nine is not complete!"* A brief pause, then, *"No, please, the doorway is not healed! You must not come through!"*

Something else, inaudible, and Markham's mind began to race with what to do next. *He's hearing voices,* he said to himself. *Paranoid delusions, borderline schizophrenic—the god Nergal behind the doorway on his chest! The temple at Kutha, the doorway to Hell!*

Then came the sound of an animal growling, passing close, and quickly trailing off into footsteps—distant, hollow, bounding up a flight of stairs. The slam of a heavy door, then silence.

Markham didn't waste any time. He sat up, wincing at the pain in the back of his head, and glanced around the room. As he suspected, he'd been lying on a large workbench; saw racks upon racks of more tools on the wall behind him— saws, chisels, all kinds of cutting instruments—but using them would be slow work with his hands tied together. Across the room, he spied another workbench covered with bottles and jugs and twisted tubes—distillery equipment, it looked like—as well as piles of books and an old phonograph with a stack of old records on top of it.

Then Markham spotted something on the other end of the workbench: a large mechanical grinding wheel caked with blood. Impulsively, he made toward it—didn't pause to ponder where the blood came from—and jumped off the workbench. His feet were all pins and needles—he felt as if his ankles would buckle at any moment—but he steadied himself and reached the front of machine. He found the switch, but couldn't feel it with his fingers—numb and unresponsive, wouldn't have been able to grasp any of the smaller tools even if he had time. Markham had a fleeting premonition that the grinder was not going to work, followed by another that it would make too much noise if it did.

"Fuck it," he whispered, and flicked the switch with the back of his hand.

The lights dimmed in the power drain, but the soft whirring was music to Sam Markham's ears. He carefully laid his wrists across the spinning bristles and the rope began to shred. He hoped he'd be able to feel the wheel against his skin when it broke through. He was certain he could get his hands free, but what good would they be if he couldn't use them when the Impaler returned?

Chapter 85

Cindy waited—stood listening on the porch for an entire minute—then rang the doorbell again. Her trip had taken her a half hour longer than she expected; she'd missed the driveway in the dark and drove fifteen minutes out of her way before turning around. Her fault—stupid mistake—but now she was sure she had the right house. She recognized Edmund's old pickup and saw a light in the upstairs window when she pulled up the driveway.

He has to be home, she thought. The inside door was open a crack, and Cindy pressed her nose against the screen. *Maybe he didn't hear the doorbell.*

How could he not *hear it?* asked the voice in her head. *Such a strange sound, too. Like a buzzer on a game show or something.*

Then she heard what sounded like a door slamming somewhere inside, and Cindy waited a moment longer.

"Edmund?" she called out, knocking. "It's Cindy."

Nothing. She took a deep breath, opened the screen door, and entered.

"Edmund?" she called again, her voice coming back to

her in echoes as she closed the inside door behind her. The house was dark—the top of the stairs ahead of her, the rooms to her right and left, pitch black. But Cindy could see a dim light emanating from a room farther down the hall—at the rear of the house, just beyond the large staircase. *Must be the kitchen*, she thought.

"Edmund?" she said, heading toward the light. She got about halfway down the hall when suddenly a figure stepped out of the lighted doorway and into the shadows.

Cindy gasped, startled. "Edmund, is that you?"

A heavy silence—the figure just standing there, head jutting forward, shoulders hunched. Cindy could barely see him, but could tell it was a man. He stood looking at her sideways, his face completely obscured beneath the silhouette of his massive frame.

"Edmund isn't here," the man said finally, his voice deep and guttural. "And neither is the General."

"I'm sorry," Cindy said, confused. "I'm a friend of his— Edmund's, I mean—from school. Do you know when he'll be back?"

A burst of laughter—harsh and terrifying in its suddenness—and instinctively Cindy began to back away, her hand feeling along the wall.

"C'est mieux d'oublier," the man said, and Cindy's fingers found the light switch. Impulsively she flicked it, and the hallway sprang to life.

She took in everything in less than a second: the yellowed wallpaper, peeling in spots; the handful of bright cream squares along the stairs where pictures once hung; the thick trail of what looked like red paint stretching out from the man's feet and running up the staircase. And then there was the man himself. He looked like Edmund Lambert—his build, his jeans, his blue button-down shirt—but at the same time he looked like a completely different person. *Edmund's brother?* Cindy thought for a split second. His hair was wet, matted and messy; and his face was twisted in a maniacal expression that had to be—

A joke. Yes, a voice in the back of Cindy's head told her this had to be some kind of joke. Of course it was Edmund she was looking at, and in one moment she felt relief, in the next, terror when she saw the pistol in his right hand.

"What have you done?" she whispered absently—but her legs were moving again, backing her away toward the door.

"Ereshkigal," Edmund said, stepping forward and baring his teeth.

Cindy's eyes darted from the pistol to the trail of blood on the stairway then back to Edmund's face. *His eyes,* she thought—those eyes that had once licked her own—*No,* she realized with horror, *those eyes aren't the same!*

Edmund laughed again—a laugh that sounded to Cindy more like a growl.

"Ereshkigal will help us," he said, tucking the pistol into the small of his back. He was coming toward her now, and Cindy could feel her heart pounding in her chest; could feel the fear there welling up from her stomach.

"But where is the boy's mama now?" he asked, taking off his shirt to reveal a bloody white bandage on his chest. "Where *is* she?"

Edmund tore off the bandage and tossed it on the floor. Cindy froze when she saw the tattoo and the fresh blood running from his wounds to his stomach.

"Oh my God," she whispered.

"That's right," Edmund said. "Your god has returned."

And then he flew at her.

Cindy screamed and made a dash for the door—her legs weak, heavy like cement as her fingers closed around the knob. She got the inside door open a crack, but Edmund was close behind and slammed the door shut. Then he grabbed her by the shoulders and threw her down—backwards across the floor, sliding, until she came to a stop in the sticky trail of blood.

Cindy screamed again and scrambled to her feet—tried to run toward the back of the house—but Edmund Lambert caught her by the collar of her denim jacket.

"Please don't!" Cindy cried, the tears beginning to flow as she struggled against his grip. But Edmund Lambert only roared and gnashed his teeth—wrapped his arms around her in a bear hug, and dragged her kicking and screaming up the stairs.

Chapter 86

Markham staggered out of the workroom and into the darkened hallway—hit the opposite wall and almost fell over. Stumbling backwards, he leaned on the doorjamb for support, his wrists and ankles throbbing painfully.

He could tell he was in a narrow passageway, but could see only the brick wall in front of him. The light from the workroom was messing with his vision; his eyes needed time to adjust to the dark—

Suddenly he heard a scream—*a woman's scream!*—and heavy footsteps thundering above his head. He spun around, disoriented—could not feel the hammer in his left hand; could hardly maintain his grip as he tried to shake the blood back into the fingers of his other hand.

Another scream, and Markham steadied himself against the brick wall. Stepping forward into the darkness, he spied a dim light coming from another doorway farther down the passageway. He started toward it, groping along the wall. He could feel the texture of the bricks now. That was good; the blood was flowing back. His courage was flowing back, too, and he could feel his mind clearing, his senses sharpening—until he reached the lighted doorway.

Markham gasped and instinctively raised the hammer. A figure across the room, seated in a pool of light—a man with a lion's head!

The article Schaap sent me, he thought, and as if on cue he spied the thick platinum wedding band on the figure's right hand—could see his partner bouncing it on the conference table back at the Resident Agency.

"Schaap!" Markham cried, rushing across the room. He grabbed the lion's head by its mane, yanked it upwards, expecting to see his partner's face—but there was nothing underneath but the golden shelf on which it rested; a shelf with a carved panel identical to the tattoo he'd seen on the Impaler's chest.

His body is the doorway, he heard the Impaler say, and Markham stepped back in numb horror—the lion's head falling to the floor, his eyes glued to the temple doors at Kutha. His partner was sitting beneath them with his head cut off.

That's what the chains were for, he said to himself, his mind reeling. *The son of a bitch gutted and beheaded him—beheaded others, too. Their bodies are the doorway through which he speaks to the lion god in Hell!*

Markham's chest grew heavy with sorrow and with rage, but he continued to back away—out of the room and into the hallway, where he hit his shoulder against another doorjamb. Turning, impulsively he reached inside—pins and needles shooting through his fingers as he found the light switch.

The scene in this room made the one across the hall look like a Disney movie—the dentist's chair, the newspaper articles on the walls, the blood *everywhere*—dear God, it was worse than he could have ever imagined!

This is where they are sacrificed! Markham thought, and

the sight of the leg brackets at the bottom of the chair sent a wave of nausea through his stomach. He could hear them screaming: the Impaler's victims—Donovan, Canning—but Andy Schaap was with them, too. Yes, the blood on the chair was still fresh; appeared wet and glistening in the light from the single overhead bulb. Had the Impaler murdered his partner while Markham was unconscious?

For the briefest of moments the thought of it threatened to drive him insane, when suddenly he heard more screaming and thumping above his head—farther away now, from another part of the house. Markham spun around—registered the large 9:3 and 3:1 taped to either side of the doorway—and quickly made his way to the opposite end of the passageway. He found the cellar stairs; found the light switch there, too, and flicked it—his stomach sinking when he saw the heavy steel door staring down at him.

Then he saw the trail of blood leading up to it.

But Sam Markham did not pause. And without thinking he rushed up the stairs, his hammer poised to strike even as he assured himself that he would have to go back to the workroom for something bigger to break down the door.

Chapter 87

Cindy cried for help again and again as Edmund carried her down the hallway—her screams echoing in the emptiness as he kicked open a door and threw her down on the bed. The room was dark, but a shaft of light cut across the bed from somewhere to her right—the outline of a doorway and the wall of another hallway beyond.

Without thinking she scrambled toward it—then *thwack!*— a hard backhand across her cheekbone sent her flying onto the bed, the room at once turning from black to bright orange pain.

"Edmund, please," Cindy cried, holding her face. "Don't do this!"

Edmund passed through the shaft of light and disappeared back into the shadows—a belt unbuckling and the sound of it hitting the floor. Cindy screamed, but in a flash Edmund was on top of her, his breath hot and foul on her mouth as she struggled against his nakedness. He was incredibly strong, and with one hand he pinned her wrists above her head while the other tore at the zipper of her jeans. She could hardly breathe.

"No," she managed to squeak out, and Edmund stopped.

"Not here," he whispered. "Not on Mama's bed."

He left her, and Cindy gasped for air—had little time to move before she felt the cold barrel of his gun under her jaw. She was being lifted off the mattress, was being pushed toward the light.

"Carry that rope for me," Edmund growled. Then the light, the hallway—not a hallway, Cindy realized, but a long and narrow closet with stairs at the end—rushed past her in a blur. In her terror, she seemed to arrive at the top of the stairs in a single bound. But what she saw there sent her spinning, made her legs feel like electric spaghetti.

It was Bradley Cox.

I HAVE RETURNED! George Kiernan cried out from the theater in her mind, and Cindy felt as if she would vomit. But there was no time to vomit—not even time to scream—for Edmund scooped her up and hurled her across the room.

She landed on the floor in a crack of crushing pain. Her elbow, her left arm had to be broken—but she could not cry out, her mouth twitching like a fish out of water as her lungs went into spasm.

Edmund came for her again, set down his gun on the floor, and stood over her roaring loudly. It was the sheer terror of that roar that finally brought her wind back; but before Cindy could scream, Edmund Lambert was upon her, tearing off her blouse.

"Edmund, *please*," she whimpered, trying to rake her nails across his cheek. She felt no pain now, could even move both her arms, but Edmund Lambert was too quick and too strong for her—only snarled and grabbed her by the wrists and pinned her hands behind her head as he buried his face between her breasts.

Then she felt his teeth sink into her flesh.

Cindy thought for the briefest of moments that she had been teleported outside her body—watched the scene below as if from the attic ceiling, and thought it strange when she heard the girl on the floor howl like a coyote. But then came the pain, and in a lightning strike of unimaginable agony she was back inside her body and staring up at the twisted visage of her attacker.

He was chewing.

Dear God! she cried out in her mind, the blood running warm across her chest. *He's going to eat me alive!*

"My body is the doorway," Edmund said. And then he swallowed.

Cindy's muscles went rigid and the room began to spin. And amid a swirling kaleidoscope of pain, she could hear a young woman begging God to make him stop.

But as Edmund Lambert sank his teeth again and again into her flesh, a voice that sounded a lot like her father's told her that God was busy elsewhere.

Chapter 88

The taste of the goddess's flesh was indescribably delectable—sent shock waves throughout his entire body—and brought with it the chorus of the god's return.

C'est mieux d'oublier! C'est mieux d'oublier!

The General saw it all so clearly now. There was no need for the lion's head. The Prince had made that clear when he came through the doorway—a flash of revelation that was for the General both momentary and endless.

And now the Prince had transported them both back in time. No, the General understood—*outside* time. They were still in the attic, yes, but also in the Underworld palace of Ereshkigal, their surroundings both familiar and strange—the stone pillars, the high vaulted ceilings, the lush fabrics that adorned the goddess's bed chamber. And there on the other side of the room was the bathtub in which the goddess had let the Prince glimpse her nakedness for the first time.

The General could feel the eyes of the dead, the eyes of the other gods on his back. But his mother was there, too—hanging by her neck from the rafters, watching him. And there was the little boy looking up at her, smiling with understanding as the lines of the impaled stretched out along the road as far as he could see. There was no fear now. Only the end of the road; only the temple at Kutha and the hordes of worshippers calling his name; the battlefields and the souls of the impaled rising in the smoke to join with him in the stars.

C'est mieux d'oublier! C'est mieux d'oublier!

The twinkling stars—so many of them now that the sky looked silver—swirled around them and penetrated their flesh. The General could feel them inside and out; and suddenly he understood that the stars were not twinkling—they were *trembling* with fear!

I have returned! the entire universe seemed to cry, and all at once it was laid out before him; everything one in the same now amid the unimaginable bliss of total understanding—time, place, even his body did not exist for him anymore. Everything had been given up for the Prince; the scales had fallen from his eyes and the Prince had rewarded him with the vision of the gods. Soon his flesh would fall away, too. Soon, the doorway would be open for him, and he would join with his mother in spirit—a sense of joining that he did not understand until now.

"C'est mieux d'oublier," he heard her say, and the General understood that the Prince had been the true path all along. Ereshkigal was the enemy. Ereshkigal had tried to trick them. And the Prince had brought her to the attic, to the threshold of the doorway to devour her into his spirit just as he had devoured Edmund Lambert and his mother; just as he most certainly would devour the General. The nine and the three, the return, the dots connected to make a new equation—an equation that the General could not have possibly understood until now.

"My body is the doorway," said the General, said the Prince.

And then he bit into her again.

Chapter 89

Markham closed his fingers around the cold steel knob and pushed. The door cracked open. The Impaler, in his haste, had forgotten to lock it. *Thank God!*

He stepped cautiously from the cellar into a pool of blood. There was blood everywhere—on the walls; footprints and a thick smear tracking away from the cellar door as if someone had been dragged across the kitchen floor. *Not Schaap,* he thought. *No, this mess leads to someone else!*

He took another step, wincing as his shoes peeled from the linoleum—then he heard a dull *thwump* from above his head. He stopped and listened, then saw the handguns on the kitchen counter: FBI issue, .40-caliber Glock 22s. His own and Andy Schaap's.

Markham traded his hammer for the guns, checked the ammo, and followed the blood trail from the kitchen into the hallway. Now he could hear whimpering and squealing coming from the second floor. He mounted the staircase—when suddenly a deafening roar sent a shiver through his veins.

"Please, God, no!" the woman screamed, and Markham flew up the stairs like a ghost—kept his ears trained on the

cacophony of crying and growling and roaring and quickly negotiated his way through the darkened upstairs hallway.

He ended up in one of the bedrooms; saw light coming from the closet and went for it. He stood there for a moment, panting in the doorway as he gazed down the long, narrow passage to the door at the far end—open, light streaming downwards, and more stairs. They were in the attic.

Markham swallowed hard—could hear muffled sobs and grunting and then the word *"Ereshkigal"* spoken in that low, growling voice.

Ereshkigal, he thought. *The Nergal myth—the rape of the goddess in the Underworld!*

In the next moment he was bounding up the stairs with his pistols thrust out before him like an outlaw. The old boards creaked noisily beneath his feet, but what greeted him in the attic froze him dead in his tracks.

It was a young man—naked, bloody, and impaled on a stake that had been driven into the attic floor. There was a large, gaping hole in the ceiling, and the young man's neck had been broken—his head tied back so that his lifeless eyes stared toward the stars. On his chest, in streaks of blood still shiny, the words I HAVE RETURNED had been carved into his flesh.

Markham, his veins running cold, digested the entirety of the scene almost at once—but it was still enough time for the Impaler to react.

Another scream, and at the far end of the attic, on the other side of the impaled young man, Markham saw movement—a blur of bloody-sweaty muscles that glistened in the light from the single overhead bulb.

The Impaler growled and gnashed his teeth.

Then he fired.

The first shot burst through the dead man's side—missed Markham's head by inches, and buried itself in the wall behind him. Markham dropped to his stomach and slid backwards down the stairs—returned fire blindly as two more bullets whizzed past him. The Impaler kept firing—three more shots and the woman began screaming hysterically. Then the sound of movement—creaking and something falling—and Markham peeked his head over the top step.

A ladder lay on the attic floor.

The Impaler was gone.

Markham sprang to his feet—could hear footsteps above his head as he covered himself with his pistols. He skirted around the impaled young man, around the hole in the roof, and headed for the girl. She was on the floor, naked and sobbing and curled up in the fetal position near a stack of trunks—her face, her arms and legs, almost her entire body a glistening crimson.

Markham, his eyes darting back and forth from the hole in the ceiling, was about to speak, when two more shots from the Impaler rained down on him. He dove to the floor, knocked over an old dressing dummy and covered the young woman. More bullets buried themselves in the dummy's heavy torso, while others popped and splintered the exposed wood beams on the wall behind him.

A brief silence, and then Markham heard the Impaler scrambling across the roof. He fired both pistols, sending a trail of bullets through the attic ceiling in the direction of the footsteps—then a loud thump at the other end of the house.

Markham paused, wondering for a microsecond how many bullets he had left. Fully loaded, his Glocks held sixteen rounds apiece. If the Impaler was using his M9 Beretta—well, Sam Markham couldn't remember how many rounds that model held.

"Please, help me," the young woman whimpered.

"Are you wounded?" Markham asked her. "Are you shot?"

"It was Edmund Lambert," she sobbed. "It was Edmund. . . ."

Markham took off his jacket and covered her. She had

bite marks on her neck and shoulders; large patches of flesh missing from her breasts, too. She was bleeding badly, but he could tell for the time being she was going to be okay. She would *have* to be.

"What's your name?" Markham asked.

"Cindy Smith."

"Sam Markham, FBI," he said, checking his pistols. "Hold my jacket against your chest to slow the bleeding. You're going to be fine."

"It was Edmund Lambert! He killed Bradley—"

"I need you to find a phone, Cindy Smith," Markham said, tucking the pistols into the small of his back. "Call 911. Wait until I'm gone, then—"

"Don't leave me!" the girl cried, reaching for his leg—but Markham ignored her and replaced the ladder.

"I need you to be strong," he said. "Call 911—the kitchen. I saw a phone in the kitchen downstairs. You understand me?"

"No—he'll come back for me!"

Markham stepped onto the ladder. "All right, stay put," he shouted as he climbed. "You'll be safe here. I won't let anything happen to you. I promise."

"Don't leave me!"

But Markham was already at the top of the ladder. He poked his gun out of the hole and stepped up onto the roof as the girl went on screaming beneath him.

He was in the middle of nowhere; didn't know which way to turn—the silvery farmland stretching out for what seemed like miles in every direction—when suddenly he heard the sound of a car starting behind him.

Markham scrambled over the roof peak and headed to the other side of the house—jumped onto the porch overhang just as the headlights of the Impaler's pickup began backing away from him down the driveway.

Markham leaped from the porch roof and fired after the

truck—broke a headlight on the first shot, then heard the windshield shatter and the *hiss-pop* of the radiator bursting as he emptied one of the pistols. He let it fall in the dirt and began firing with the other.

He's going to get away, he thought—when unexpectedly the truck spun out and plowed backwards into one of the old tobacco sheds.

The weathered boards crumbled down and bounced off the hood as the truck came to a stop—its one remaining headlight cutting through the swirling dust like a laser beam. Markham ran for it, his stomach in his throat, as the old Ford's engine whined painfully, its tires spinning in the dirt.

He fired one last time—heard a loud crack—and then everything cut off into a long, menacing hiss.

Markham slowed as he drew closer to the shed; took cover behind some remaining wall planks and checked his pistol.

The clip was empty. Only one bullet left in the chamber.

He pointed his gun at the driver's side door and shouted, "FBI! Come out with your hands up!" His heart was pounding. He was a dead man if the Impaler called his bluff and decided to shoot it out with him. But there was nothing, no sound at all except for the hissy sputtering of the F-150's radiator.

Markham approached the driver's side door, leveled his gun, and quickly peered inside. The pickup's interior light was on, and he could see blood on the front seat—but the passenger door was open, the Impaler nowhere in sight.

Markham dropped his head and ducked behind the truck bed for cover. Silence—only the crickets, his breathing and the faint hissing of the truck's radiator dying out—when suddenly, he heard what sounded like boards cracking inside the shed.

He's trying to break out the back, Markham thought. He craned his neck—peered over the truck bed into the darkness—and saw the outline of the missing boards against the moonlight. No sign of the Impaler.

He squatted back down—closed his eyes and breathed deeply. "Come out with your hands up!" he shouted, frightened and feeling foolish. "There's nowhere for you to run now, Edmund Lambert!"

You sure that's his name? a voice taunted in his head. *Edmund Lambert. You sure that's what the girl said?*

Another board—*Crack!*—then a scraping sound.

Markham swallowed hard, and then he was moving, covering himself as he circled around to the rear of the tobacco shed.

Crack!

Markham stopped, listening.

Silence again, only his breathing.

He sidled along the wall—thought he heard a thumping from around the corner—and stopped short at the rear of the shed. He could see the field stretching out in the distance beyond the trees; could hear nothing now but his heart throbbing in his ears. The Impaler was on the other side of the wall—he was sure of it—and in a burst of adrenaline, he wheeled around the corner and dropped to his knees.

Nothing.

Markham rose to his feet, saw where the Impaler had broken through the rear of the shed, and moved away from the wall. There was an old oak tree only a few yards away. The Impaler might be behind it—but he hadn't heard any footsteps in the dry grass.

And then Markham understood.

He turned just in time to see the Impaler jumping from the low roof of the overhang. Instinctively he raised his gun, but the Impaler came down on him hard, his forearm slamming into Markham's face as the gun went off.

Then they fell together to the ground.

Chapter 90

Now he is Edmund Lambert again, a boy on the road holding hands between the General and the Prince. He knows they are there but makes no attempt to look at them; understands that he is too small to see their faces, and keeps his eyes fixed on the light in the distance as they escort him past the lines of the impaled.

But the boy's steps are their steps. Giant steps. And before the boy can wonder at it he has reached the temple doors at Kutha.

The Prince and the General leave him. The boy feels their hands slip away.

Now he is alone. Now there is only his mother, standing with her arms outstretched high above him at the top of the stairs—a silhouette in the temple doorway with the light of a billion stars behind her.

"Be a good boy and carry that rope for me," she says.

"It's not my fault," the boy replies. "I only did what they told me."

"C'est mieux d'oublier," another voice echoes from

somewhere, and his mother beckons him, disappearing slowly into the light.

Now the boy is climbing the stairs—black stairs, like rows of forgotten pictures in a yearbook—when all at once, it seems, he is standing in the doorway.

But the boy hesitates, unsure if he should enter. He hears the other voice again—a man's voice that reminds him of his own—but cannot make out what it's saying. Two words, only two words—but the voice is behind him now, far away in the void at the bottom of the stairs.

It doesn't matter, the boy thinks.

And then he steps forward into an attic full of stars.

Chapter 91

Markham was sure he'd lost consciousness; was vaguely aware of a loud explosion in front of his face—but then the pain, in a burst of bloodred stars, shot across his nose and sent him flying backwards. Something happened next— blurry movement and a loud buzzing as the sky threatened to iris into black—and then the taste of blood in his throat brought him back, started him coughing.

He rolled onto his stomach, shook the cobwebs from his skull, and spat into the grass. The buzzing in his ears was replaced by ringing, and something whispered of a blink forward in time—how long a blink, he wasn't sure. One part of his brain told him his nose was broken, while another part registered his gun lying a few feet away. Instinctively he crawled toward it, his hand reaching for the warm barrel when suddenly, underneath the ringing, he thought he heard the footsteps crunching in the grass.

And talking? Did I just hear someone talking?

Markham turned and saw the Impaler staggering out into the field beyond the old oak tree. He grabbed his gun and rose on all fours. A wave of pain at the bridge of his nose sent him reeling, but he found his feet and stumbled toward the tree—took cover and peered around it to discover the Impaler had slowed. He could see him clearly now in the open field—naked, about thirty yards away, his muscular flesh a milky gray in the moonlight. He was unarmed.

Markham whirled from around the tree, his empty gun trained on the man's back. "Stop or I'll shoot!" he shouted, but the Impaler seemed to ignore him—staggered a few more steps and then sank to his knees.

Markham lowered his gun and watched in fascination as the man in the field began clawing upwards at the open air. He struggled to stand; and when he did, he lifted his left foot and dropped it quickly. He repeated the motion with his right and then his left again, stepping in place over and over as if he were trying to climb an invisible staircase. Then all at once he stopped, stood motionless, and fell face-first into the grass.

Markham rushed to his side and turned him over, pulling back immediately when he saw the blood gushing from the hole under the young man's right eye. He was handsome, Markham thought, suddenly detached; younger than he expected, too—but his breathing was shallow, and his lips moved as if trying to speak.

"It's over," Markham whispered. But it was clear the Impaler didn't hear him, didn't see him either; for the young man seemed to gaze past him and up toward the sky.

"Come back," he managed to say at last. "Come back."

Epilogue

"Would you like some?" Gates asked, raising the pot of coffee.

"No, thank you," Markham said. "I don't touch it anymore." He stood with his hands in his pockets, staring up at the large bulletin board: dozens of photocopies of newspaper articles taken from the Impaler's cellar.

Gates nodded and replaced the pot on the burner. "Meant to tell you yesterday that the nose looks good," he said. "But I have to admit I liked it better before the swelling went down. Gave you a sort of street cred."

Markham smiled thinly, and Gates sat down—slipped out one of Claude Lambert's notebooks from the pile on his desk and leaned back in his chair.

"Lambert," he said, opening the notebook. "Family history in North Carolina goes back to the late nineteenth century. Before that, the line hailed from Louisiana. Looks like they were run out of New Orleans in the decade following the Civil War. We found records of an absinthe house established on Bourbon Street around the same time. Seems to be a connection there, some kind of falling-out between business partners, but we'll never know for sure. The notebooks speak of an absinthe recipe in the Lambert family dating back generations. The old man was simply building on tradition."

Markham fingered a newspaper article.

"Claude Lambert was an interpreter in World War II. Did you know that?" Markham nodded. "He was stationed in France for some time after the Allies took Normandy. Guess he kept up the tradition of speaking French, too. We interviewed his son in prison. Said his father only spoke French when he was down in the cellar cooking up his experiments. Claims he never really understood what was going on down there. Odd part of it is I believe him."

Markham said nothing, only scanned the bulletin board.

Gates closed the notebook and set it back on the pile. The business with Schaap, the names from the cemetery—Markham couldn't understand how he missed it. True, Gates thought, given the size of the cemetery, without the military connection it would've been like shooting blind from the white pages—thousands upon thousands of names, over one hundred Lamberts listed in the city of Raleigh alone. Add on how the gravestone marked Lyons had confused them—no, Schaap stumbling onto the Impaler was literally a one-in-a-thousand shot. They would've found him eventually, but Schaap shouldn't have gone it alone. That was reckless, unacceptable, and stupid. But still, Gates knew his supervisory special agent felt somewhat responsible.

"How's the girl doing?" Markham asked.

"I talked to her mother today," Gates said. "Says she's doing better but still wakes up in the middle of the night screaming. That'll soon pass, I expect. Or at least it'll become more manageable."

"Part of the equation."

"What's that?"

"General equals E plus Nergal," Markham said absently, tracing his finger over an article. "The equation the Impaler spoke of on the phone—the nine and the three—all this must be a part of it, too. Gene Ralston equals Stone Nergal."

"The obituary, you mean? The one we found on the cellar wall?"

"Yes. Looks like Ralston committed suicide just after Lambert returned from Iraq. Lambert wrote out these anagrams on the obituary and in one of the notebooks. You can tell by the way he crossed out his letters in the notebook that he was trying to solve a problem. Looks like he found part of the solution in Gene Ralston's name. Stone Nergal. Christ, what are the chances of that? Even a sane person would have a hard time denying some sort of cosmic connection."

"What about the word 'general' itself? You think that was in play before or after he made the connection to Nergal?"

"Not sure. His excessive narcissism, his military aspirations, perhaps paralleling his delusions of being a second in command to the Prince. E plus Nergal equals General. His real identity, part of the equation."

"Other parts are here," Gates said, patting the pile of notebooks. "Claude Lambert's formulas, the experiments with his own children, the hybrid absinthe production, and the drug supplies from Ralston. The abuse had been going on for years, but seems to have stopped once Edmund reached puberty. And from what we can gather from Claude Lambert's notes, Edmund never had any idea. At least not while his grandfather was alive."

"Not consciously, no, but I suspect he knew something was there. Like the death of his mother. A problem, an equation that needed to be solved. The word 'general' and the first seven letters of Gene Ralston's name—a connection of which his subconscious might have been aware."

"The old man made his notes in coded French. Even with the help of French Intelligence it took us a while to figure it all out. Hard to believe that Edmund Lambert could've deciphered anything in here. His grandfather was quite frank about what he let his buddy Ralston do. Basically pimped out his own children and grandchildren all in the name of science. Some paranoid, insane scheme about a mind-control drug that he and Ralston would sell to the government."

Markham was silent.

"However," Gates continued, opening a file on his desk, "Claude Lambert seems to have been far from insane. A textbook sociopath, yes, but there's something almost Nazi-esque in his writings—the meticulous documentation and his twisted rationale for the continued abuse he let Ralston inflict upon his family. He even talks about the suicide of his daughter as if it were simply a failed experiment." Gates flipped through his file and read, "'Have to be more careful with the boy's prompt,' the old man says in his notes. 'His mother took hers too literally. I didn't think she'd remember, but at least we know the prompt worked.' You ever hear of anything like this, Sam?"

"*C'est mieux d'oublier*," Markham muttered, removing a newspaper article.

"What?"

"This clipping," Markham said. "This one about the theft of the lion's head from the taxidermy shop in Durham. It's quite different from the other articles that were found on the cellar wall. The only one on which he wrote *c'est mieux d'oublier*."

"He wrote that phrase in one of his grandfather's notebooks, too. Translates as 'It's better to forget.' "

"Claude Lambert refers to a prompt in his notes but doesn't say what it is specifically. I'm willing to bet we found it."

"Then perhaps Lambert had some kind of suppressed

memory of the sexual abuse by Ralston. Perhaps the identification with the god Nergal, the anagrams and whatnot, were simply the young man's way of negotiating in his mind something that was too terrible to for him to remember; something that he might've been *incapable* of remembering because of the drugs, but that his subconscious nonetheless knew was there."

Markham nodded and stared down at the article.

"It would make sense," Gates said, leaning back in his chair. "If the psychoactive suggestion is something rare, something only the person in control knows, then there's no risk of anyone else saying it. But to give a child that kind of drug repeatedly . . ."

"Hard to imagine the long-term effects on the brain. Then again, with Edmund Lambert, we don't have to imagine. Delusions, hallucinations, some form of paranoid schizophrenia, perhaps. Classic symptoms."

"Appears as though he thought the god Nergal was communicating with him everywhere. Everything had the potential to be a message, including that song and the play he was working on at Harriot. I saw the trap he designed for *Macbeth*—exactly the same design as his tattoo."

"Everything connected. All part of the equation that proved he was Nergal's chosen one."

"Mix in a family history of mental illness and . . . . well, life sure served this kid quite a cocktail."

"And the bottle?" Markham asked. "The one they found with the notebooks under the floorboards labeled 'medicine'?"

"Trace Evidence Unit found residue of the absinthe hybrid, but says the bottle hadn't been opened in years. And we know Edmund Lambert never used drugs on any of his victims."

"A souvenir, I'm willing to bet, that Lambert kept after the old man passed away. Part of the equation that needed solving. The letters on the bottle and in the anagrams. Lambert wrote them the same—dash-dash-dash."

"Our labs corroborate Claude Lambert's notes," Gates said. "To a certain extent, that is. Everything is still being tested, but the preliminary report says that, with the right dosage, the old man's absinthe-opium hybrid could possibly have an effect similar to Sodium Pentothal."

"Truth serum?"

"Yes, but specifically with regard to how it's administered to patients suffering from extreme psychological disorders. Has an almost hypnotic effect on them and opens their minds up to suggestion."

Markham frowned and returned the article to the bulletin board—thrust his hands in his pockets and stared up at the scraps of paper. He appeared to Gates as if he were looking past them, through the wall and into the next room.

"Claude Lambert was married twice, you know," Gates said. "The first time briefly, to a woman he brought back from France after the war. No children, but records indicate she died under suspicious circumstances. Alcohol poisoning was ultimately listed as the cause of death."

"I'm willing to bet alcohol was only part of the formula," Markham said. "A formula that the old man didn't get right until he remarried and had children. And grandchildren, for that matter."

"Edmund Lambert's mother committed suicide when he was only five years old, but it was the boy who found her. She had a lot of problems as a child, James Lambert told us—cutting, self-abuse, and whatnot—but by all accounts she was a great mother until one day she just snapped. She hanged herself in the attic."

"A lot of violence in that family," Markham said.

"James Lambert said he only met his nephew a handful of times; said he didn't regret killing the kid's father and would do it all over again if given the chance. He also added that his father and Rally never laid a hand on him when he was a child."

"The old man's notes tell a different story."

"Edmund Lambert's contacts at Harriot, his fellow soldiers from the 101st are a dead end, too. All of them saying he seemed like a nice enough guy, but kept to himself mostly. Dedicated and loyal are two words that keep popping up."

"Loyal's a good way of putting it," Markham said. "I'm willing to bet the same thing could be said about James Lambert. Loyal to his old man even now."

"The Smith girl is our best shot, Sam, but we'll never really know what made Edmund Lambert tick; how those drugs affected his mind, or to what extent some kind of underlying mental illness played a part. Most disturbing was his psychological profile from the Army. Nothing to indicate there was anything wrong with him. If we assume that it was Edmund Lambert who either found the ancient seal or played a part in its induction into the black market, maybe that was the final tick of the clock that set him off—the message for which he'd been waiting all along."

Markham shrugged, and a heavy silence fell over the office as he stared up at the board.

"The superposition principle," Gates said finally. "It's eating away at you isn't it? Still so many questions now that the Impaler's dead. You never got entirely in his wake. Can't see the messages, the equations from his point of view. Not all of them, anyway."

"No. Not all of them."

"But you saw enough to catch him, and that's what matters."

"Is it?"

"As far as we can tell, Edmund Lambert had been killing since late December, early January. Twelve victims in four months, including the two drifters we found buried behind the barn—the ones you said he used as his doorways. Andy Schaap, Cox, and the four he got with the car bomb were only icing on the cake for him."

Markham was silent.

"I know how it looks," Gates continued. "You flying in from Quantico and catching the Impaler in just over a week—"

"I didn't catch anybody," Markham said, turning. "It was Schaap who found Lambert, and Lambert found me. I got lucky the Smith girl showed up when she did. I've been getting lucky a lot lately. Lambert, Briggs—most of all, I'm lucky people don't start seeing me for the fraud I really am."

"Trust me," Gates said, rising. "I understand how difficult it is to wrap your mind around the reasons why Schaap bit it and you didn't. The same goes for the Cindy Smith factor. You saw what Lambert did to her. It was only a matter of time before he tore her to shreds. You saved that girl's life, Sam, no matter how much you try to deny it because she saved yours."

Markham narrowed his eyes at him.

"That's right," Gates said. "Schaap found Lambert and Lambert found you, but the fact that Schaap is dead doesn't give you the right to feel sorry for yourself because you're not. Nor does it make you any more of a fraud than it makes Schaap unlucky."

Markham studied him. His boss was staring up at the clock above the door.

"You're a good man, Sam," Alan Gates said distantly. "You deserve to live. I suggest you remember that in the days ahead. To think otherwise will only drive you insane."

Later that evening, Markham placed the thank-you card from Marla Rodriguez on his bureau—*"I jumped for joy!"* it read; a smiling, cartooned frog leaping from a lily pad.

He'd kept his promise—returned her computer to her family and bought the little girl her own laptop. He also showed her how to password-protect her startup so her brother Diego couldn't use it. Marla had really appreciated that, and kissed him on the cheek and told him she loved him. Markham told her he loved her, too.

He missed her terribly; had felt closer to her in that one moment than he had to anyone in the last ten years. And as he stared from the card to the plaque above his bedroom door, the FBI agent felt suddenly like he couldn't breathe.

Abandon all hope, ye who enter here.

A flash of Edmund Lambert's tattoo—of his bloody chest and the temple doors at Kutha, the doorway to Hell.

Markham reached up and pulled the plaque from the wall—tossed it into the closet, put on his Windbreaker, and dashed outside.

The fresh air felt good, and he breathed it greedily as he walked down to the pond. He could hear the ducks rustling in the thickets and wondered if he was disturbing them. He didn't care to look up at the stars just yet; preferred instead to gaze out over the water to the lights that dotted the opposite shore. Lights from town houses just like his own; lights from lives that couldn't be more different.

He thought of Andy Schaap and the life he left behind; he thought of his people at Quantico, of their lives and the distance from him that had already settled in their eyes. But he felt nothing for them. Like the lives across the water, like the stars above his head, they were all so far away from him.

Markham saw a light go out in one of the windows and immediately thought of Edmund Lambert—of the look in his eyes when he spoke to the stars and breathed his final breath. To whom did the Impaler speak—*His grandfather? Eugene Ralston? His mother? The god Nergal?*—well, that was anybody's guess now.

Then again, Markham thought, *what's the use in guessing?*

He sighed and gave in—gazed up at the stars and began searching for the constellation Leo. Despite the crescent moon he could not find it—*too much light, too close to civilization to see the stars clearly from out here*—and suddenly Sam Markham felt painfully alone.

He sat down in the grass by the thicket; could hear the ducks shifting and gurgling in the darkness and was thankful for their company. But it was not enough.

He lay back on his elbows, closed his eyes, and tried to imagine the beach—tried to imagine the stars as they had looked on that night a thousand years ago when he and Michelle had made love for the first time. But in his mind he always ended up on the beach alone—no Michelle, no Cassiopeia—nothing but sand and waves and stars. And those stars looked different tonight, too. For tonight, and for many more nights to come, the sky that was his mind had room for only the nine and the three.

"Come back," he whispered.

To whom Sam Markham spoke, well, that was anybody's guess now, too.

ACKNOWLEDGMENTS

I would like to thank my editor, John Scognamiglio at Kensington Publishing Corp., and my agent, William Reis at John Hawkins & Associates, for their assistance in developing *The Impaler.* Also, my sincerest thanks to all the great people at Kensington who try their hardest to make me look good (not an easy task), including Arthur Maisel, Lou Malcangi, my publicist Frank Anthony Polito, and Meryl Earl and Colleen Martin, both of whom have done a terrific job promoting my books abroad.

For their advice and counsel, I am especially beholden to Milo Dowling, retired FBI agent; Reid Parker, technical director here at ECU; Chris Christman, hunter extraordinaire; Yesenia Ayala, for her Spanish expertise; and Marylaura Papalas, for her lightning-fast French translations.

To the members of my family who slugged through *The Impaler* in its various drafts, I owe you all much love and gratitude: my wife, Angela; my father, Anthony; my mother, Linda Ise; my brother, Michael; my uncle, Raymond Funari; and my grandmother, Lois Ise. The same goes for my friends and colleagues: Robert Caprio, Jill Matarelli-Carlson, Jeffery Phipps, Steven Petrarca, Jessica Purdy, Vance Daniel, and Adam Roth.

And finally, even though he spilled tea all over my original manuscript, a hearty "thank-you" goes out to Michael Combs for never letting me off the hook. I owe you one, my friend.